SPY FOR THE
QUEEN OF SCOTS

———✳———

THERESA BRESLIN

CORGI BOOKS

SPY FOR THE QUEEN OF SCOTS
A CORGI BOOK 978 0 552 56075 7

First published in Great Britain by Doubleday,
an imprint of Random House Children's Publishers UK
A Random House Group Company

Doubleday edition published 2012
This edition published 2013

1 3 5 7 9 10 8 6 4 2

Text copyright © Theresa Breslin, 2012

The Random House Group Limited supports the Forest Stewardship Council® (FSC®),
the leading international forest-certification organisation. Our books carrying the FSC
label are printed on FSC®-certified paper. FSC is the only forest-certification scheme
supported by the leading environmental organisations, including Greenpeace. Our paper
procurement policy can be found at www.randomhouse.co.uk/environment

Set in Adobe Garamond by
Falcon Oast Graphic Art Ltd.

Corgi Books are published by Random House Children's Publishers UK,
61–63 Uxbridge Road, London W5 5SA

www.**randomhousechildrens**.co.uk
www.**totallyrandombooks**.co.uk
www.**randomhouse**.co.uk

Addresses for companies within The Random House Group Limited can be found at:
www.randomhouse.co.uk/offices.htm

THE RANDOM HOUSE GROUP Limited Reg. No. 954009

A CIP catalogue record for this book is available from the British Library.

Printed and bound in Great Britain by CPI Group (UK) Ltd, Croydon, CR0 4YY

PRAISE FOR
SPY FOR THE QUEEN OF SCOTS

'A gripping historical thriller from the brilliant Breslin'
The Bookseller

'Full of passion, intrigue and deceit at the court of Queen Mary'
Sunday Express

'Fans of historical fiction will enjoy this carefully-crafted and exciting
story, which offers up a thoughtful and intriguing portrait of the young
Mary Queen of Scots'
Booktrust

'An intriguing, historical thriller which takes in 3 countries, 30 years
of history and an interesting cast of characters. A great historical thriller
from Breslin which cements her place as one of the best contemporary
writers for young adults'
LoveLiterature

'A wonderfully enthralling and page-turning read which fans of
Philippa Gregory, Alison Weir and Victoria Lamb will lap up'
WeLoveThisBook.com

'A thrilling tale, full of midnight escapes and daring rescues'
Historical Novel Society

'Nicely paced… Breslin paints a vivid picture…
Recommended to all fans of historical fiction. Enjoy'
Jill Murphy, *The Bookbag*

This is TB's book

Historical Note

Mary, Queen of Scots, lived in one of the most turbulent periods of European history, and in a time when royal marriages were arranged for political reasons.

Scotland and England had been in constant conflict for centuries. In the hope of bringing peace, Margaret Tudor – sister to Henry VIII of England – was married to the Scottish king. But her son, King James V of Scotland, then married a French noblewoman from the family of Guise, making an alliance between Scotland and France. They had one daughter, Mary, but James V – who died when Mary was only a few days old – also left behind illegitimate children, the eldest of which was Lord James Stuart*.

Mary was crowned Queen of Scotland whilst still only a baby. Henry VIII wanted the child given to him to be wed to his son. The Scots, unwilling for England to control Scotland, sent Mary to France, to grow up and marry the heir to the French throne.

France, under King Henri and his wife Catherine de' Medici, was firmly Catholic. Scotland was a Catholic country too, but it was becoming increasingly Protestant, and the Scots lords feared that France would aim to rule Scotland through Catholic Mary. Meanwhile, in England, the country became Catholic under Queen Mary Tudor – but on her death, it would pass to her half-sister, the Protestant

Elizabeth, daughter of Henry VIII and Anne Boleyn.

Some English nobles, however, believed Elizabeth to be illegitimate. Thus, to them, the rightful heir to the English throne would be Mary, Queen of Scots, and in this time of spies and intrigue Mary's very existence would therefore always be a threat to Elizabeth . . .

*'Stewart' was the original spelling of the Scottish family name until Mary, Queen of Scots adopted the 'Stuart' version. For clarity, 'Stuart' is used throughout this book.

SCOTTISH ROYAL SUCCESSION

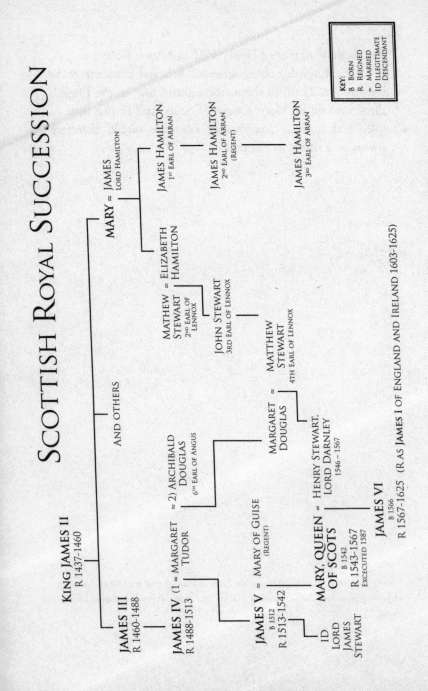

KEY:
B   BORN
R   REIGNED
≈   MARRIED
ID   ILLEGITIMATE
     DESCENDANT

KING JAMES II
R 1437-1460

JAMES III
R 1460-1488

AND OTHERS

MARY ≈ JAMES
        LORD HAMILTON

JAMES HAMILTON
1ST EARL OF ARRAN

JAMES IV (1 ≈ MARGARET TUDOR)
R 1488-1513

≈ 2) ARCHIBALD DOUGLAS
6TH EARL OF ANGUS

MATHEW ≈ ELIZABETH HAMILTON
STEWART
2ND EARL OF LENNOX

JAMES HAMILTON
2ND EARL OF ARRAN
(REGENT)

JOHN STEWART
3RD EARL OF LENNOX

JAMES HAMILTON
3RD EARL OF ARRAN

MARGARET ≈ MATTHEW STEWART
DOUGLAS   4TH EARL OF LENNOX

JAMES V ≈ MARY OF GUISE
B 1512   (REGENT)
R 1513-1542

MARY, QUEEN ≈ HENRY STEWART,
OF SCOTS   LORD DARNLEY
B 1542   1546 – 1567
R 1543-1567
EXECUTED 1587

ID
LORD
JAMES
STEWART

JAMES VI
B 1566
R 1567-1625   (R AS JAMES I OF ENGLAND AND IRELAND 1603-1625)

ENGLISH ROYAL SUCCESSION

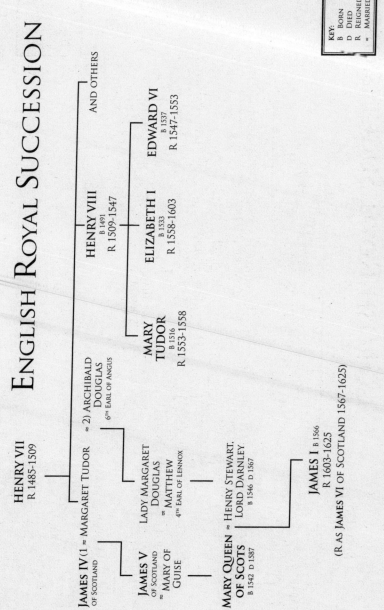

HENRY VII
R 1485-1509

JAMES IV (1 ≈ MARGARET TUDOR   ≈ 2) ARCHIBALD
OF SCOTLAND   DOUGLAS
                                                         6TH EARL OF ANGUS

JAMES V   LADY MARGARET
OF SCOTLAND   DOUGLAS
≈ MARY OF   ≈ MATTHEW
GUISE   4TH EARL OF LENNOX

MARY QUEEN ≈ HENRY STEWART,
OF SCOTS   LORD DARNLEY
B 1542 D 1587   B 1546 D 1567

                   JAMES I B 1566
                   R 1603-1625
                   (R AS JAMES VI OF SCOTLAND 1567-1625)

HENRY VIII
B 1491
R 1509-1547   AND OTHERS

MARY   EDWARD VI
TUDOR   B 1537
B 1516   R 1547-1553
R 1553-1558

ELIZABETH I
B 1533
R 1558-1603

KEY:
B   BORN
D   DIED
R   REIGNED
≈   MARRIED

Prologue

'They are ready for you, my lady.'

'But I am not yet ready for them,' Mary Stuart, Queen of Scots, replied abruptly, looking up from her writing desk in a disdainful manner. Then she recovered herself and spoke more kindly to the man standing at the door of her chamber. 'I need a few extra minutes to prepare. Would you grant me that courtesy?'

'Highness.' Thomas Andrews, High Sherriff of Northampton, bent his head and backed from the room. 'I will await you in the corridor.'

Mary Stuart laid down her pen. 'I have written all I can write.' She stood up. 'Now, I must think what to wear.'

She smiled as her ladies glanced at each other. 'It will be noted in history,' she told them gently, 'what I wore, and how I conducted myself at the time of my death.'

At this they let out a moan of grief. Mary regarded them seriously. 'When the moment comes, be mindful of your own dignity. For myself, I will die as I lived, as a woman and a queen.'

She pointed to a clothes chest in the corner of the room. 'I intend to put on the crimson petticoat Ginette left to me.'

As one of her ladies fetched the garment, Mary's

composure faltered and she gave a small sob. 'I wish Jenny were here,' she said. 'If only Ginette, my sweet loyal Jenny, were here, it would be so much easier to bear.'

And the Queen of Scots gathered the petticoat in her hands and crushed it against her breast. 'Red!' she cried. 'Red for the blood that has been spilled, and red for the blood that will soon flow from my severed head.'

PART ONE

MARIE
QUEEN OF FRANCE

France, 1558
(29 years earlier)

Chapter 1

The Castle of Blois, spring 1558

Clothes were always important to Mary Stuart.

She liked to wear pretty things and was well aware of the effect her appearance had on others. And I, her closest companion, had learned from her example.

Therefore, on one particular morning when we were staying at the Castle of Blois in the spring of 1558, I deliberately chose to put on my new red dress. I knew that the blazing crimson colour emphasized my fair skin and enhanced my blue eyes and blonde hair. On my feet I'd put matching beribboned shoes with soft leather soles that made no sound as I ran through the huge royal residence of the King and Queen of France.

We were all running – Francis, the Dauphin, eldest son of the king, and heir to the throne of France, his younger sister, the Princess Elisabeth, myself, and other noble ladies, friends and attendants – each of us thrilled to take part in one of the exciting games that Mary Stuart devised for us to play.

Anyone who took the time to know this young woman, future bride of the Dauphin Francis, would, like us, have followed her to the ends of the earth. Her beauty dazzled those who met her. Slender and tall for her fifteen years, Mary had a fine long neck and a perfect oval face with a creamy white complexion. Her eyes were large, their amber colour highlighted by her wealth of luxuriant red-gold hair. But it was her conversation – intelligence pierced with shining wit – her humour, her graciousness, and her innate goodness that caused people to linger in her company. One couldn't help but love her. Both King Henri of France and his son, Francis, adored her. His wife, the Italian-born Catherine de' Medici, was less enchanted with her prospective daughter-in-law, for the queen was besotted with her own children; she had the highest ambitions for them, and felt it should be she who had absolute command over their lives.

But Mary ruled the children's household and we did as she bade us, and no one frowned at the disturbance made by our games. She was so charming that servants and courtiers alike smiled and moved out of our way when we went rushing from the summerhouse in the garden up the magnificent tower staircase and along the corridors of the castle.

The boys' shoes clattered on the marble steps and wooden floors. The girls' slippers made less noise, but their shrieks of laughter echoed loudly from the walls. As her noble kinswoman and dearest friend, I'd felt it to be my duty to stay beside Mary – although I knew she'd be with Francis for they'd been inseparable since childhood. He was a year younger than us and was never in good health but she'd not leave him to trail alone in the rear. As I hesitated, Mary urged me on, and so I deliberately raced away to get ahead of the rest.

In fast pursuit after us came the young Scots nobleman, Sir Duncan Alexander of Knoydart. Mary had elected him Chief Huntsman in our game of Hide and Chase, and he'd given us no more than a fifty-second count to find a hiding place within the castle. We sped into the upper hall. Now everyone was quieter, whispering and giggling as they concealed themselves behind chairs and chests and tapestries. They were hoping that the Huntsman, Duncan, would pass through the room without spotting them. Then they would snatch the opportunity to escape back to the garden summer-house. All were anxious not to be found.

All except me.

I wanted to be caught – for I fancied myself in love with this Sir Duncan Alexander, a handsome, dark-haired young man who'd only recently arrived to join the Scottish nobles attending Mary Stuart.

'Yet another Scot whom we must prevent from influencing our future queen,' I'd heard one of the French noblemen grumble, when Duncan was announced at court.

Being only fifteen, I wasn't much interested in politics or court intrigue and had no notion of how these things might affect me. At this point I didn't care that there was tension between Scottish and French courtiers. My life consisted of lessons, with instruction in cultural pursuits such as embroidery and music, and many pastimes – hunting, pageants, parties and receptions where there was a chance to meet young men. It was at one of these latter occasions that I met Sir Duncan Alexander when he was presented to the Queen of Scots. He reacted as men often did when meeting Mary Stuart for the first time: eyes opening wider, taking in both her beauty and her height as he approached us. But I am quite tall too – almost equal to Mary, who is taller than most women – so he'd no need to bend his head to see my face when introduced to me.

'Lady Ginette,' he said, boldly meeting my eyes. 'I like to

meet a person whose expression I can see without having to stoop and get a crick in my neck.'

Mary clapped her hands. 'Well, that is indeed pleasant to hear,' she told him. 'Women like myself and Jenny, who are above ordinary stature, have difficulty in finding a suitable male with whom we may have a conversation when dancing.'

'I'll remember that when I'm choosing a partner for your wedding ball, majesty.' The look on Duncan Alexander's face had changed to one of cool appraisal.

'I think you will find that there are many men waiting to take Jenny's hand to lead her onto the floor. Not only is she very attractive in appearance and manner, her father is the Comte de Hautepré, one of the noblest families in France; he holds a high command in the French army stationed in Scotland. Her mother was the daughter of the Italian ambassador at my father's court in Scotland and, until her untimely death some years ago, a good friend to my own mother.'

I was glad that Mary had replied on my behalf to let this slightly arrogant young man know my lineage – and that I didn't lack suitors.

'That I will also bear in mind,' he replied slowly, continuing to study me.

As he could gaze at me, so I could at him, and I didn't lower my eyes as a more demure lady might have done. I was still half smiling at his initial reaction to meeting Mary Stuart.

'You are amused?' he asked me as she turned to greet yet another ambassador.

'The Queen of Scots is very beautiful,' I said. 'It's no wonder that men are overcome when first seeing her.'

'The queen?' Duncan seemed startled. 'You think that I ' He broke off and glanced at Mary. His face cleared of its superior expression and the look he gave me was honest and open. 'With no disrespect to our queen, I assure you that I'm not the type of person to be "overcome" by superficial aspects, Jenny.'

His voice was low and sincere when he said my name, the familiar pet name 'Jenny' that friends and family used. My heart contracted and my breath caught in my throat. I think that was the moment when I fell in love with him.

So, when I heard this morning that Duncan Alexander would once again be in our company, I knew exactly what dress I'd wear – my new full-skirted crimson satin with slashed sleeves edged in black lace. I brushed my hair until it shone, and Marie Seton, one of the four Maries – the maids of honour who'd come to France as children with Mary Stuart – arranged it in curls held up with long pins decorated with beads of jet. Around my throat a single strand of matching jet glittered in the sunlight. I saw Duncan glance at me when I appeared in the garden. Ignoring him, I chatted amiably to one of his fellow countrymen and laughed at his remarks which, in truth, weren't as funny as I pretended.

And then Mary Stuart murmured to me, 'Sir Duncan Alexander has not taken his eyes from you these last ten minutes.'

He'd noticed my dress – as I'd planned he would!

After a while Mary, with mischief in mind, announced her game and gave Duncan his instructions. When he hesitated she said quickly, 'It is a royal decree.'

'In that case I can only obey.' A determined glint came

into his eye. 'I should warn you that I am a skilled hunter and am merciless with my victims.'

The boys laughed. The girls squealed in mock fright. A shiver went through me.

Mary took Dauphin Francis by the hand, saying loud enough that Duncan might hear her, 'I will accompany my best friend, Francis, who will protect me, but you must go on your own, Jenny, and fend for yourself.' She added in a whisper, 'Run fast and far, Jenny. That way you will be alone with the good-looking Scotsman when he catches you.'

Now I could hear Duncan's booted feet in the corridor. I slipped from the castle hall, but not so fast that he wouldn't spy a glimpse of bright red satin. I heard him discover the others, and the wild hullabaloo as they tried to outwit and outpace him to reach the safety of the garden summerhouse. But the rules of the game meant that he had to find all the players. He must come and seek for me.

Courtiers were converging at the far end of the corridor, but I didn't intend to go back the way I'd come and let him catch me so easily. Guards and servants had gone to attend to these people so I ventured further and tiptoed through a half-open door into an antechamber.

Behind me, a noise!

My throat closed in excitement.

I wanted to be found and seized by Duncan. I'd resolved to search for a quiet place in the hope that, having captured me, he might steal a kiss.

I slipped into a smaller inner room.

Blois was not a castle I was familiar with and this was somewhere I'd never been before. The room was panelled, the walls covered with different woods sculpted in the Italian style with motifs of candelabra. The curtains were drawn and one lamp burned on the mantelshelf. It wasn't richly furnished: beside the fire stood a simple chair and desk. Despite the lack of gilded hangings I knew that I was somewhere I shouldn't be: I sensed an aura of privilege, authority and power. Above the fireplace I saw initials painted out in gold.

Was that a C intertwined with an H?

Catherine and Henri. The monogram of the king and queen.

And on the desk and the chair back, a single C.

I turned to leave.

Footsteps behind me.

The hunter was at my heels!

Swiftly I went to the window. It looked down into a service yard. I slid behind the heavy curtain drapes.

A man's voice in the outer chamber.

Duncan was almost in the room! Would he merely grip my hands to capture me and lead me to the summerhouse, as Mary had decreed? This would be the proper way to play the game, and I should submit and meekly follow him. But perhaps – perhaps, as we were alone, he might put his arms around me. I could make a show of trying to struggle free. I trembled in pleasurable anticipation.

Footsteps approached across the wooden floor.

Silence.

My heart dipped. He might not think to peep behind the curtain. Should I let out a squeak of pretend fear to alert him to my presence? I was just about to do so when the voice spoke again, very quietly. 'In here?'

It was not Duncan.

'Yes. Now shut the door. We must be private.'

Two people. Neither of them my playmates from the game.

One voice, the man's, I didn't know, but the other – the one that had given the order – I did recognize, and my heart began to beat in alarm.

It was the Queen of France, Catherine de' Medici!

Chapter 2

Fear flooded through my body.

The significance of the single royal initial on the desk and chair was suddenly obvious. I had strayed into the private study of the Queen of France!

No more than the thickness of the curtains separated me from being discovered. Catherine de' Medici was fiercely protective of her status and punished those who didn't respect it. I'd intruded into her personal room without express permission! I could be whipped. Maybe banished in disgrace.

I should let her know of my presence in her study. I should . . . But I could not move.

'You expressed an interest' – Queen Catherine spoke slowly and deliberately to the other person in the room – 'in some of the . . . medicines that I keep for special use.'

She was speaking Italian but I could understand that language, for my mother had spoken it to me when I was a child.

'Majesty,' the man replied humbly; although he too spoke Italian, he was not a native speaker. 'I thought it was you who summoned me to—'

'I have a substance' – the queen didn't let him finish – 'to show you. In Florence it was a sure method to get rid of' – she hesitated and emphasized the next word – '*vermin*.

It leaves little trace of its presence within the body; merely some mottling on the neck that's likely to be confused with measles. I am talking here of animals . . .' Then she paused, as if in afterthought, 'However I expect it would have the same result on humans.'

In the gap between the curtains I could see into the room. They were standing in front of the panelling at the fireplace. The queen lifted the hem of her skirt and, using her foot, pressed down upon a certain floorboard. There was a click, and the door of a secret cupboard within the panelling opened.

Catherine de' Medici took out a flat box and raised the lid. 'Let me bring it nearer to the light that you may see more clearly.'

They were so close now that I could hear them breathing!

'There,' she said as she held the box next to the lamp. 'It resembles sugar crystals and is sweet, but with an aroma and taste similar to mint. A liberal amount is needed, else the . . . creature will only sicken and may recover. Although,' she mused, as if to herself, 'sometimes the use of continuous small doses is more effective, for if a person is frequently indisposed, then they are less able to meddle . . .' She tailed off.

'I could sweeten the dessert of any unwelcome visitor,' the man laughed.

'Quite what you do with it, sir,' Queen Catherine said coldly, 'is your own business.'

'Of course, majesty. I beg your pardon.'

'It is true' – the queen's voice was loaded with what sounded like artificial regret –'that there are guests at my court who do mightily outstay their welcome. They are often in the company of my future daughter-in-law, whose welfare it is my duty to mind, and their conversations, as reported to me, are somewhat critical of our state. I have noted Mary Stuart's half-brother, her *illegitimate* half-brother, Lord James Stuart – the eldest of many such brothers her kingly father managed to sire before his death . . . he may be kinsman of yours?' Between the first sentence and the last her tone had become nasty and suspicious.

'No!' The man reacted in terror. 'Countryman, yes, but only of my Scottish grandmother. The Stuarts are no true kin to me. And I do not share their ways of thinking.'

'That is indeed reassuring.' Queen Catherine mellowed in approval. 'For one wonders if the influence of a man like Lord James Stuart over a young and vulnerable girl is quite benign. Mary's own mother will rule Scotland very well as regent until Mary comes of age and I see no good reason why Lord James Stuart should interfere in royal business. But now, to the matter in hand.' She snapped down the lid of the box and handed it to him. 'I allow you to have this substance only because I have heard that you are a person who wishes to develop skills as an apothecary.'

'Yes, indeed, indeed I do.'

'Therefore, to that end' – the queen took a roll of parchment from a drawer in the desk –'I now gift to you a house with some land adjacent to the Palace of Fontainebleau where you may grow herbs and other plants for the benefit of mankind.' She paused. 'I will, naturally, be very interested in your work, in hearing of whatever new and interesting preparations you concoct . . . that might be useful to me.'

'Majesty, I thank you. Most humbly and gratefully. I am very conscious of the honour you bestow and your generosity to me. I will be your obedient servant for life. This I swear.' The man hesitated. And then, stuttering, he spoke once more. 'M-majesty . . . I would serve you in any way I am able.' Again he stumbled over his words. '*Any – anything* I might do to please you . . . anything at all. If you but give me the command.'

'There are commands,' Queen Catherine spoke carefully, 'that a monarch is not able to give.'

'Ah.' The man's reply was barely audible.

'I will arrange a role for you as a visiting apothecary at court. A person who can come and go at will. We will rarely be together but a good servant knows the unspoken wish of their master and does not hesitate to carry it out.'

'Yes,' he replied. 'I think I understand.'

'You are dismissed.' The queen waved him away. The man slipped both parchment and box inside his tunic and withdrew.

For what seemed like an age I stood there quaking.

I could hear nothing. Perhaps if the queen had departed it might be safe for me also to go? I put my eye to the gap. Catherine was leaning her forehead against the mantelpiece, gazing into the dead ashes in the grate. She roused herself and murmured, 'As a mother and a queen, is it wrong to try to safeguard one's children?' She heaved a great sigh. 'I protect them for France . . . and I protect France for them.'

There was a tap on the door to the outer room.

'Majesty,' a courtier announced when she bade him enter, 'the king awaits your presence as he would walk with you in the gardens.'

Catherine's voice was pleased as she answered him. 'Inform his majesty I will be with him at once.'

For several minutes after the queen left the room I stayed behind the curtains. I was petrified of moving but knew that I couldn't remain in hiding for ever. I gathered my courage and made ready to leave. Before doing so, I glanced down into the yard below.

He was there! The man who'd been in the room with Queen Catherine. There must be a private staircase leading from her apartments to the service yard so that messengers could come and go at her bidding without the rest of the court being aware of their presence.

His horse was being brought by a groom who held his stirrup as the man took the reins. Just before mounting he raised his head and glanced up in my direction.

I leaped back from the window, but I knew that I was too late. He had seen me!

Chapter 3

Wrenching the curtains apart, I ran out of the queen's study.

I fled through the next larger room and into the upper corridor. At one end the cluster of courtiers had been joined by a group of nobles, and Catherine de' Medici was among them. Their backs were to me. I spun round and began to hasten in the opposite direction.

What had happened in that small study? What had I witnessed?

During my early years in the distant northern kingdom of Scotland, I'd heard of the infamous Queen of France, Catherine de' Medici. Credited with bringing recipes for perfumes from her own country of Italy to France – to the extent that the French were becoming known for their skill in blending fragrances – she'd also acquired a reputation in another art: that of mixing substances to make poison. And, it was said, being devious, had rid herself of many enemies by this method. My mother, who was herself Italian, smiled when these stories were repeated at the Scottish court.

'The French don't like the Italians,' she'd told me. 'There is always discord between countries whose borders meet, like here with Scotland and England. But also, the French prize royalty very highly and Catherine de' Medici is not of the blood royal so the French nobles spread gossip and ill rumour about her. She's a daughter of the Medici family of Florence

who are bankers to the world, and King Henri was contracted to marry Catherine mainly for her dowry and the
loans that could be secured from her family to finance French
wars. Catherine was very young when she arrived in France.
She fell hopelessly in love with her new husband, Henri. But
he doesn't care for her in that way and has, in fact, a long-
standing liaison with a Duchess, Diane de Poitiers, who is
established in the court as all but his wife.' My mother's face
became thoughtful and she murmured to herself, 'I suppose
to live like that for so many years, constantly humiliated
because your husband openly favours another, could drive a
woman to desperate measures.'

How I wished that my wise mother were alive and that I
could run to her as I used to when I was troubled and lay my
head on her lap and pour out all my fears and worries. But
she died when I was nine, and my father, being on active
duty as an army commander in Scotland, thought it best that
I return to France to be looked after as a ward of the court.
Mary Stuart, in kindness to me, for our mothers had been
close, drew me into her circle of companions. And, as we
were of the same age, during the last six years I had been her
playmate and was now her bosom friend. So now, out of
loyalty and love, I must calm myself so that no upset over this
morning's events reached her.

I forced myself to walk more slowly and tried to clear my
mind and think sensibly as my mother would have advised.
The rumours about Queen Catherine were lies. The man in
her room, whoever he was, was an apprentice apothecary. She
was mentoring him. I knew that she sponsored the sciences
and had discussions with like-minded people. That was it.
He was an apothecary who had found favour with the queen.

The snippets of conversation I'd heard were meaningless. I shouldn't be afraid. Not for Mary Stuart, nor for those around her. My imagination was conjuring something from nothing.

Nothing.

There was no danger to anyone within the court, no plots, or intrigue. What I had seen meant nothing.

Nothing, I told myself. *Nothing. Nothing. Nothing.*

Arms grabbed me from behind. I screamed in panic.

'I have you!'

I struggled frantically, but to no avail: I was held fast in a firm grip. A giddy swoon engulfed me. Blood thundered in my head.

'You must pay a penalty!'

It was Duncan Alexander. He wound his arms around my waist and, in a voice of teasing menace, spoke into my ear: 'What suitable forfeit should I ask of you?'

'Horrid man!' I cried out. I swivelled round, slapping his face, and pushed him away. 'Stupid, horrid man!'

He sprang back from me in shock, putting his hand to his cheek, where I had drawn blood with my nails. 'I only meant . . .' he stammered. 'I thought you wanted . . .'

I didn't know whether I was going to faint or have a fit of hysterics. Instead I burst into tears and ran off.

The calls and laughter of the other young men and girls came to me from a distance. I needed to get away. Beyond the hall were the servants' stairs. I stumbled down them and ran towards the stable yard behind the castle. I would go and be with the horses, for I always found their presence soothing.

There was a lane beside the grooms' quarters. If I took that less direct route then, for a minute or two, I would be out of sight of both castle and stables. It would give me time to recover. I stopped and leaned against the wall. My whole being was shaking. I tried to collect myself and went on.

Someone stepped from a doorway ahead of me. The figure of a man. The same man who had been in the queen's apartment. The man to whom she'd given the strange sugar crystals.

'Oh!' I coughed nervously. 'I am going to the stables.'

I dipped my head and made to walk past. He moved to block my progress.

'Sir?' I looked up, feigning surprise.

He surveyed me. 'What is your name?' he demanded.

'Lady Ginette.' My voice cracked as I said it.

'Lady Ginette,' he repeated. 'I will not forget that name . . . Ginette.' He pronounced it in a most unpleasant manner.

'Sir,' I said, searching my mind as to how I might make him believe I hadn't been in Catherine de' Medici's rooms until after he'd left. 'I – I was playing a game, and when I saw the queen join her courtiers in the corridor, I ran into her study by mistake. I fear I lost my way.'

'It is not good for a maid to lose her way,' the man said. He took my chin in his fingers and held it firmly. 'Not good at all.'

He was very close to me. I felt my eyes drawn to his tunic, to the place where he'd hidden the box the queen had given him.

He followed my gaze. 'Ah,' he said. His free hand slid to his belt, and the next moment the point of a dagger was under my chin. 'Such a pretty dress you wear, Ginette. Red. A colour that shines brightly. A colour that flashes from a window nook. Red,' he repeated. 'A *very* distinctive colour

. . . like blood.' He loomed over me. 'Blood that might flow from a scarred face . . .'

I whimpered in dread.

'. . . or gush from a cut throat.'

He was going to kill me!

'There you are!' a light voice exclaimed.

The man released his grip on my chin and slid his dagger up his sleeve as Mary Stuart came down the lane towards us.

'Monsieur, the Count of Cluny, you have found my best companion!' she addressed the man.

Immediately he stood back and made a formal bow to Mary. 'Your grace,' he said. 'Anything to be of service to the future Queen of France.'

'Come along, Jenny,' Mary said. 'Everyone awaits you. They believe you to be hiding inside, but I thought: Jenny loves horses so much that she might go to the stables. It was my idea. And I was right!' She gave an exclamation of delight.

I almost fell into her arms as she reached out to take my hand.

'Sir Duncan Alexander has gone into the most tremendous sulk. He refuses to be the huntsman any more, Jenny. I told him that he would lose the game if he didn't capture everyone, but he professed not to care. He said he'd found all the others and he wouldn't search for you.' She took my hand and drew me to her. 'But I'm surprised Duncan didn't see you leaving the castle, for you stand out so vividly in that dress.'

Mary chatted on, unconscious of the tension in her audience. 'Red suits you, Jenny.' She gave the Count of Cluny one of her lovely smiles. 'Don't you think?'

'Oh, I agree,' the count purred in reply. 'I do *so* agree. Red is a most . . . *noteworthy* colour.'

'We bid you adieu, sir,' Mary said. She turned to go ahead of me, and so she didn't hear what I heard. The sentence the Count of Cluny uttered next came in a sibilant whisper, following me as I hurried after her, the words coiling round my brain.

'Yet,' he hissed, 'one should be careful. For red can signify blood . . . and death.'

Chapter 4

Thus, a few weeks later, at the beginning of April, when Mary mentioned that I might wear red for her Betrothal Ball in Paris, I refused.

'But it's a colour that accentuates your looks, Jenny,' she said.

I shook my head. As soon as I was able, after the game of Hide and Chase in the Castle of Blois, I'd given away my beautiful crimson dress. Wearing red had brought me no luck in my hoped-for friendship with Duncan Alexander and had put my life in danger. I was convinced that if I ever wore red again, then disaster would befall me.

We were in the long sewing rooms in the attics of the Louvre Palace, and Mary, the four Maries and I were viewing bolts of cloth and opening packages containing embroidered stockings, scented gloves, exquisite lace and gold tissue. To satisfy the needs of the royal household for the forthcoming nuptials a vast amount of material had been ordered from all over Europe and beyond. Eastern silks via the Venetian trade routes, taffeta from Spain, English linens and fringed scarves from Savoy were laid out ready for inspection by the bride.

'I have been practising some new hairstyles,' said Marie Seton, examining an elaborate *perruque*, 'and I intend to have your queenly headdress dripping with every ornament possible!'

'Indeed,' Marie Livingston agreed. 'Arms, fingers, ears, neck festooned with jewellery.'

'There's a surfeit to choose from,' I remarked, for Mary owned a vast collection of jewels, with unique pieces like her golden belt studded with rubies, large enamelled buttons worked as flower heads and beaded with tiny diamonds as dewdrops, and a parure of pearls, dark as damsons, that was the envy of every queen in Europe.

'Francis has sent me so very many tokens of his devotion,' added Mary: 'rings and necklaces, brooches, earrings . . .'

'Your husband-to-be does idolize you, which is not always the case in an arranged marriage,' said Marie Fleming, who was less reserved with her suitors and therefore more experienced in matters of the heart than the rest of us.

'And I love him too,' replied Mary.

I glanced at our queen as she went along the tables picking through the items on display. Although she was deeply attached to Francis, I wondered if her love for him matched the thunder of emotion that vibrated through me when I thought of Duncan.

'For the wedding at Notre Dame the bride's outfit should be the most glamorous of anyone present,' declared Marie Beaton. She unravelled a skein of thick gold thread and held it up so it caught the light from the window. 'You must shine like the noonday sun.'

Mary fingered a rich cloth of deeply piled white velvet. 'I am at a loss to know what to choose. What do you think, Jenny?' she asked. 'Jenny?' she repeated when I didn't answer.

I shrugged. In truth I wasn't particularly interested in our appearances for her coming betrothal and wedding to Dauphin Francis. My heart was aching because Duncan

Alexander had become aloof with me. He took pains to avoid any group I was in, and, when we were forced to be in each other's company, strained to even be polite. The events of the day when I'd scratched him were such that my mind was clouded with mistrust and fear and I didn't know how to explain why I had behaved so rudely.

Also I was more concerned about Mary's safety than what she might choose to wear for the occasion. The conversation I'd overheard while hiding behind the curtain at Blois seemed to indicate that Catherine de' Medici saw Lord James Stuart as a nuisance to be dealt with. And I'd noticed that as the wedding drew nearer, instead of warming to her daughter-in-law, Catherine was becoming increasingly irritated by her popularity. Francis wasn't the only one of Catherine's children who cared deeply for Mary Stuart; he had half a dozen younger siblings who'd joined us in Paris to attend the forthcoming celebrations. They pleaded to be allowed to take part in our games and accompany us on walks and out riding. Mary was generous with her time. She enjoyed the company of Francis's sisters, Elisabeth and Claude, who were closest to him in age, and told stories to the younger royal children at bedtime. Charles, the second son of the king and queen, began to refer to her as his 'angel'. He suffered from nightmares and would call for Mary when he awoke screaming in the dark. She would break off supper and sit by his bed, stroking his head and singing to him to help him fall asleep again.

And then, on the night of the Betrothal Ball, my agitation increased when I heard that the Count of Cluny had returned to the court. When his name was announced to the king and queen, Catherine behaved as if she'd never seen him before! Once again I felt the alarm I'd experienced at Blois. If the Queen of France had a poisonous scheme in mind that this man was here to carry out, was Mary her target?

During the last weeks I'd become more observant and sensed intrigue and double-dealing within the tortuous negotiations of Mary's marriage contract. The rulers of Europe grabbed wealth and power in any way they could – through wars and intermarrying – and in this, France and England were in deadly competition with each other. I thought of the land of my childhood; the northern country of deep glens and wild mountains that I'd grown to love and considered a homeland as much as France. In all these machinations, what would happen to Scotland? I wondered.

At the Betrothal Ball in the great hall of the Louvre I wore a dress of yellow silk. Marie Seton arranged my hair like Mary's, in a style of soft ringlets, unbound and lying on my shoulders. Because of my recent experience I'd no wish to draw attention to myself and kept my jewellery very plain – pink pearls entwined in a circlet of gold wire on the crown of my head and a similar necklace around my throat.

Mary had designed complementing outfits of silver and gold for herself and Francis. 'You are the sun and I the moon,' she told him, taking both his hands in hers before they entered the ballroom together. 'I reflect the light that the future King of France shines upon me through his presence.'

Francis was enthralled when Mary spoke like this to him. Her gift for poetic utterances in his praise was a pleasant respite from the harsh, critical comments he often received from his mother.

They shimmered under a thousand candles as they paraded onto the polished floor. But the weight of Francis's clothes seemed to tire him, and after the royal couple had led off the first set he begged to be excused. I was beside Mary when King Henri himself came to escort her back onto the dance floor. I moved away but the king said, 'This is your companion Ginette who attends you?'

'I call her Jenny, sire,' Mary replied.

'And are you hoping to be betrothed soon too, Jenny?'

I blushed.

'Ah!' said the king, laughing. 'I see I may have touched a sensitive point. Your father is one of my best commanders. I sent him to Scotland to help our good friends there in the fight against the English, and there he found love and married your mother. Why should his daughter not come to France and find an equally good match at my court? Like you, my child' – he drew Mary Stuart to his side –'who came to France for romantic reasons, yes?'

Despite being only fifteen Mary was the height of the French king, and she gazed at him directly and said, 'Not only have I found love, but also respect and kindness and happiness – and am blessed with a new family.' Caught up in her emotions, she cast herself upon his neck and embraced him.

As she did so, I saw Queen Catherine flash a look of malevolence at her – a younger, prettier woman wrapping her arms around the neck of her husband.

'Marie! Marie!' Using the French form of her name, King Henri put his hands on Mary's waist. He lifted her and placed her away from him. 'You must not be so impetuous,' he chided her. 'It doesn't do for a person of royal blood to show their feelings so openly.'

'But I do love you very much,' she protested, still smiling and in no way chastened by his admonishment. 'You are the papa I never had. My royal father, King James of Scotland, died soon after I was born. I have never known a father's guiding hand, and of all the men in the world, you are the one I would most like to be my father.'

Although he scolded her, it was obvious that King Henri was pleased. 'You may call me "Papa",' he instructed her.

'Papa!' she cried, and kissed him on both cheeks.

'So you are now first of my children.'

He took Mary by the arm. Such was her charm that his own children didn't mind that they had acquired a new sibling, a possible rival for their father's affections who took precedence over them. But a mother doesn't welcome a cuckoo in her nest. Maybe the king only meant that Mary was first because she was older in years than his royal children. No matter – a mother does not want the father of her children to declare in front of all France that someone else has supplanted one of hers to come first with their father.

Catherine de' Medici's face was suffused with anger. Her eyes protruded slightly and she clenched her hands and ground her teeth together. Her figure was stout and she lacked conventional beauty, but she was an intelligent woman and knew that any outburst would serve her ill. She managed a sickly smile as her husband led the lissom Mary onto the dance floor, where the Master of the King's Music awaited his command.

I was never sure if what happened next was contrived by Mary for she could surprise one by suddenly seizing an opportunity and acting, not always sensibly but with good intentions. I saw her lips move. The king nodded and then announced: 'A partner for Jenny! The king calls for a partner for Mary's companion, Ginette de Hautepré!'

I bent my head.

'Let us have a good Scotsman to escort a lovely French maiden! You, sir!' He waved his hand as though he had only just caught sight of a young man standing by a pillar.

I glanced over to see who'd been chosen. And my heart stopped still.

The king had summoned Duncan Alexander.

'Your name?'

'Sir Duncan Alexander of Knoydart,' Duncan replied, steadily enough. Was there displeasure in his tone?

'Good Sir Duncan, pray oblige the King of France and escort the Lady Ginette, daughter of a Frenchman who protects our favoured kinsmen of Scotland from the dastardly English.'

It was an order that could not be refused.

Duncan Alexander stood before me. He made a formal bow and then held out his hand for me to take.

I placed my fingers lightly in his. By sheer force of will I prevented them trembling. His hand was cool and his grip firm. I stole a look at his face. There was a slight flush of annoyance and his lips were set.

'I apologize if this inconveniences you, sir,' I said.

'One must do as the King of France wishes. After all, if we disobey, perhaps his majesty will recall the brave, noble and infinitely superior French army now billeted in my homeland and leave us helpless Scots as prey to our enemies.'

'I think the king meant well by his remark,' I said, surprised by his resentment.

'Perhaps he did,' Duncan replied.

His eyes roved around the hall. I followed his gaze. The Scots lords were in a cluster, gesticulating and talking animatedly together.

'There are those who might be of the opinion that, saving the king's presence, such sentiments could be seen as implying, or' – he paused – 'even assuming that Scotland now lies under the rule of France.'

There was truth in what he said, but I felt I had to speak up. 'My father, who is a captain in the French army in Scotland, believes he is there to help keep the kingdom safe from invasion by England. Mary is the legitimate and anointed Queen of Scots, and such a small country needs an ally against an aggressive neighbour.'

'Indeed?' Duncan's tone suggested that he was not convinced.

I chose my next words carefully. 'It's true,' I conceded, 'that an intention, even an action, perhaps of one individual against another, can be grievously misinterpreted.'

Duncan Alexander raised one hand to finger the spot on his cheek where I had scratched him. 'Is that so?'

I longed to reach out and touch his face and explain to him what had taken place that day. Impossible to do it here before the court, where hundreds of eyes were upon us. Anyway, I had no evidence of any wrongdoing, and if there was something sinister involved, it might put Duncan in danger if I told him what I'd heard and seen. In all my years at court meeting young men, Duncan was the only one who'd aroused any depth of feeling within me. Oh, I flirted and carried on light-hearted conversations as every girl did but always resisted whenever the man wanted to become more serious. When Mary and I discussed love or listened to the romantic ballads and music she was so fond of, she agreed with my decision not to give myself to anyone merely for position or power. It would have to be love, true love, I said, before I'd wed. In this I was supported by my father, who assured me in a recent letter that he'd not barter me away without my consent:

> When I have finished with this last commission King Henri has given me to support Scotland in her time of need, you and I can spend time together on our estates. We can talk then of what path you might follow in your adulthood, whether it be to continue at court or to share your life's journey with another. But I would rather you wed for the reason I did, for you have no need to marry to secure a title or wealth.

As my father had found true love with his life partner, my mother, so, he wished, should I. For myself, I was devoted to Mary Stuart and felt my life was complete being her confidante and companion – until a certain Scottish noble-man had appeared and sent my emotions whirling.

The music began and Duncan placed his hand very firmly under my arm. 'If one believes that one has been mis-judged, then one should make that clear to the person one has offended,' he said.

'It may be that this is not possible.'

He must have taken this to mean that we'd had no opportunity to speak to each other alone. 'Personal conver-sations can be difficult to arrange in a crowded court.' He glanced at his countrymen. 'Scottish society is based on family clans, and I suppose we do congregate sometimes to the exclusion of others.'

I was glad he'd mentioned this. 'Yes,' I said, 'the Scots lords always group together. They don't mix, and many have made no effort to learn the language of the country of their closest ally.'

He tilted his head and a glimmer of a smile showed on his face. We had been conducting our conversation in Scots, but when next he spoke to me it was in perfect French.

'I had no idea that French was your preferred method of communication,' he said.

'Not always,' I replied to him in Latin.

'Well then,' he said, also in Latin. 'You must let me know, Lady Ginette, which language you like best.'

'Touché, Sir Duncan,' I countered.

'I am not fencing with you,' he said.

The dance ended before I had a chance to judge if we were fully reconciled. Certainly his face was not as chilly and remote as it had been when we'd met over these last weeks.

The king led Mary to her seat, which had been placed near to his. Both his attendants and hers applauded as they returned. But there was one in his retinue who was not so content with the situation: the dumpy woman who herself had been forced for many years to take second place in her husband's affections and feared that her own children might follow suit.

Queen Catherine's eyes also surveyed Duncan and me. We were identified as being friends of Mary Stuart. Was it my fancy or did she now include us in her baleful glances? If

Mary was friendly towards Duncan, did that mean that the anger of the Medici might fall on him too?

I'd thought that by not speaking of what had happened in the queen's private study I'd save him from harm. Save us both.

But nothing could save any of us from the coming storm.

Chapter 5

'Isn't it wonderful that King Henri allows me to call him "Papa"? I am so glad to be considered his true daughter.'

It was about a week after the Betrothal Ball and some ten days before her marriage, and Mary was hosting a reception for the Scottish wedding guests.

No one responded to her remark. Negotiations of the terms of the marriage settlement between Scotland and France had been difficult. The Scots lords, led by Mary's half-brother, Lord James Stuart, suspected that the French wanted to rule Scotland through her.

'It is indeed a great honour,' I commented quickly. Marie Seton exchanged a glance with me. She and the other Maries were young ladies from the noble families of Scotland; they had always been close to Mary Stuart and very mindful of her welfare. Marie Seton was the quietest, and often a quiet person is more perceptive than a noisy one. I guessed that she, like me, was concerned that for Mary to be King Henri's favourite child was not altogether a good thing.

'I have always felt the want of a father,' Mary prattled on. 'I never saw my own, although I'm sure he would have honoured me had he lived.'

'I'm not so sure,' remarked Sir Malcolm Cowrie, one of the Scots lords, 'for when your father found out on his deathbed that his wife had given birth to a female child, it hastened his end. He knew he needed a boy heir to grow to manhood and take control of Scotland – I've heard that he said: *It cam wi' a lass. It'll gang wi' a lass* . . . he was talking about the Stuart inheritance,' he added, in case anyone present did not fully grasp his meaning. 'It was a girl who brought the crown to the Stuart family when the daughter of King Robert the Bruce, his only heir, married into that family, and now you, a girl, look set to lose it to—' He broke off as he realized he might have gone too far.

For a moment Mary's face crumpled in distress. Then she reacted in a manner I'd never seen before. She drew herself up to her full height. 'You, sir,' she declared in a steely tone, 'are presumptuous.'

There was a sudden silence in the room. I saw Lord James Stuart's eyes narrow as he looked at his half-sister, who was usually pleasant and accommodating in his company. This more regal and commanding side of Mary was new to him.

She pointed at Sir Malcolm Cowrie and her hand did not waver. 'Sir Malcolm Cowrie, you will leave and not appear in my presence again until I summon you.'

'I . . .' he began to protest. 'Madam, your grace, I do beg you—'

She held up her hand, palm out. 'Enough! You are dismissed.' Then she swivelled round, and linking her arm with mine, began a conversation on trifling matters.

I risked a glance over my shoulder. What would happen at this first assertion of her authority over these difficult men?

Malcolm Cowrie turned to appeal to Lord James Stuart as one or two others came to support him. My eyes sought out Duncan Alexander, and as I did so, something registered in my mind. Since the Betrothal Ball we'd talked about religion and politics on occasion, but he never attached himself to one specific group. The Protestant lords generally kept apart from the Catholics, Lord James Stuart, a Protestant, had his own coterie. Duncan moved between them, yet remained separate from any specific faction. In any gathering he positioned himself so that he could see without necessarily being seen. Now he had an intent, watchful expression on his face. Lord James put his hand on the hilt of his sword and strode past Sir Malcolm Cowrie and his friends, making it clear that he wanted nothing to do with anyone who was in disagreement with his half-sister. Sir Malcolm was surprised by the snub, as if Mary's competence to rule had already been the subject of speculation. He excused himself at once and made to depart. I noted that his erstwhile supporters had deserted him and he left the room alone.

Before a wedding a bride should be filled with happy anticipation, but this scene had caused a great gloom to settle over Mary. The four Maries and I, along with the rest of her ladies, did our best to cheer her up. Every day shoals of personal gifts arrived from nobles in Scotland and France: fine coifs and collars, and pairs of sleeves heavy with luminous embroidery and precious jewels. Many of these donors were unknown to her and we would speculate as to what favour they might seek in return when Mary became Queen of France. The more simple presents of monogrammed handkerchiefs and lace-edged pillowcases from her mother's sister, Renée, were the ones Mary valued most. This devout lady was the abbess of a convent in Rheims, and Mary had spent much of her childhood in her company.

But none of these gifts lightened Mary's mood. She was constantly worried that the wedding might be forestalled by the Scots lords, who were arguing amongst themselves.

'We are in thrall to the French as once we were to the English army,' complained one.

'Not so,' said another. 'This alliance with the French will make us stronger. They'll protect our ports that we may trade directly with Europe without our ships being harried by the English fleet. The Scottish merchants are grateful to have French forces present.'

However, I knew from my father that the French were not welcome everywhere. He had written to tell me this:

We are Catholics in a country where some powerful lords and clan chiefs have decided to be Protestant. These Scottish lords look at the riches of the Catholic Church and would have them for themselves. Several have banded together to call themselves the 'Lords of the Congregation'. They are supported in their aims by a Protestant preacher called John Knox, who presently lives in Switzerland but is in constant communication with Scotland. Knox urges true Protestants to resist the Catholic Church and all its adherents. With his encouragement they challenge the author- ity of the queen regent of Scotland, Mary of Guise, and look to the leading Protestants in England for support.

Scotland looking to England for support! I could hardly credit this. Down through the centuries it was the English who'd destroyed Scottish crops and towns, stealing cattle, burning abbeys and castles, and killing thousands of Scots in the process. Mary's father had refused to join with King Henry the Eighth of England in his break with the Pope and disbanding the monasteries, and it had been Henry's army that had brought ruin to him. Now that Henry was dead and his Catholic daughter by his first wife was on the throne, surely this meant a better relationship between Scotland and England?

John Knox has called the English queen a 'cursed Jezebel' [my father's letter went on], *and, in truth, Queen Mary's rigorous persecution of those she regards as heretics does her cause and the Catholic faith little good. Her health is precarious and ambitious men are now congregating around her half-sister Elizabeth, who, although she gives the appearance of obedience to the old religion, is known to favour Protestantism. Please take care, my darling daughter, in what you say and to whom you speak. Try to avoid being enmeshed in intrigue. These are volatile times.*

'Do you think I was too harsh with him?' Mary asked me after the reception was over.

'Who?' I asked, knowing full well who she meant but trying to give myself time to think of a suitable reply.

'Sir Malcolm Cowrie.' Then she giggled. 'Did you see his face? So smug and superior when commenting on the value of a woman, and then so stunned and cast down when a woman speaks back to him. I do believe he must be a follower of the Scots preacher John Knox, of whom we hear so much and whose opinion of women as rulers is so very low.'

'A number of your Scots lords are in sympathy with Knox in his views on the right of people to choose a different form of worship,' I replied. I was thinking of one Scots lord, Sir Duncan Alexander, who had given me cause to think more on the subject.

'Yes, but my Aunt Renée, who is capable of efficiently running her own convent, tells me that John Knox also preaches that women are unfit to govern because they are intellectually and emotionally inferior to men. When my mother had to take over the ruling of Scotland Preacher Knox declared that having a woman rule a kingdom was as ridiculous as putting a saddle on the back of a cow!'

'My father writes to me that John Knox exerts a very dangerous influence throughout Scotland,' I told Mary.

'I've heard that too,' she agreed, 'but I've been informed that his main influence lies in his ability to turn the minds of his audience by personal appearance and a powerful gift of oratory. Fortunately for myself and Scotland,' she quipped, 'he does not reside there.'

We weren't aware that John Knox had already received an invitation from certain Scots lords to return to Scotland.

Talk of these insults to Scotland's queen regent affected Mary's mood even more. The position of Mary of Guise in Scotland was so insecure that she couldn't travel to France, and Mary was missing her mother, as any bride would in the days leading up to her wedding. Always prone to phases of melancholy, supposedly inherited from her father, she retired to her rooms. In an effort to console her, I suggested that she read through some of her mother's letters.

With the box containing the letters between us, we sat together in a window nook of the Palace of the Louvre. Elaborate preparations were under way for Mary's wedding. The marriage of the Dauphin was to be a magnificent occasion, the first wedding of such grandeur Paris had hosted for many years. We watched the workers below us in the courtyard erecting tiers of seating for a jousting tournament.

'Ah,' Mary sighed. 'If only my mother could be here to share this with me.'

The lack of a mother was something I knew well, and Mary, always sensitive to the feelings of others, went on, 'I appreciate your sadness too, Jenny.' She stretched out her hand to me.

Tears came to my eyes. 'Sometimes I just want her here to hold and hug,' I said. We sobbed and clasped each other in our arms. 'And sometimes for her opinions,' I added, thinking of my quandary over the scene I'd witnessed in Queen Catherine's study at Blois.

'That too,' said Mary. 'Wise counsel is what I need; someone to let me know what's really best for Scotland. Always it seems that those about me are there for self-advancement. The marriage settlements have been so protracted, and—' She stopped, and placing her knuckles against her temples, squeezed them together with great force.

I looked at her. Was she going to have one of the fainting fits that she'd developed in her teenage years? I put my hands over hers and drew them away. 'The formal discussions are done now,' I said reassuringly, 'and although there may be disagreements as to the practicalities, the Scots lords did finally agree terms.'

'Not all of them.' Mary glanced over her shoulder and whispered, 'Can you keep a secret, Jenny?'

'What?' I asked. 'What kind of secret?'

'A very important one. You must swear not to speak of this to any other person.'

I hesitated. Was this the kind of involvement my father had warned me against in his letters?

'Please.' Mary's face was anguished. 'Who else can I trust, if not you?'

Reluctantly I nodded. 'I swear I will tell no one.'

'My lords haven't seen all the papers I signed as part of my marriage contract.' Mary spoke very quietly. 'I put my name to a special agreement that if I die childless before Francis, then the Scottish throne and any claim I may have on the English throne will pass to France.'

'But that is not acceptable!' I stared at her. 'The stated terms are that, although Francis and you are king and queen of Scotland, if you die, the Scottish throne passes to the nearest Scottish heir, the head of the Hamilton Stuarts. What was in the mind of Lord James Stuart that he agreed to that?'

'Lord James Stuart doesn't know about it.'

Such was my distress that I cried out and stood up, the letters spilling from my lap onto the floor.

'Hush! Hush!' Mary pulled me back down.

'This cannot be,' I said fiercely, thinking that those Scots lords, Sir Duncan among them, were right to be worried. 'You signed an official state paper without the advice of your chief adviser, your brother?'

'My *half*-brother . . .' Mary said deliberately. 'My half-brother,' she repeated. 'Remember, Jenny, that Lord James Stuart is illegitimate.'

'I'm aware of this,' I said. It was an accepted fact of life that a king could conduct himself in this manner with women other than his wife and that the resulting children would be given rank – though never succeed to the throne. Lord James Stuart was one of many half-brothers and one half-sister who were the result of Mary's father's liaisons with various women. 'But Lord James is the most prominent of these, has a great deal of power, and has always been supportive of you.'

'When I do as he wishes,' Mary said. 'But he neither wishes nor likes me to think for myself. He pressures me constantly to embrace the Reformed faith, and you know that I would be bereft to leave the Catholic Church.'

I nodded. Since her early years Mary's faith had been a constant in her life. She attended mass and received Holy Communion every day, and found prayer and meditation a source of comfort and strength.

'The actions of many people in this matter are based on political expediency rather than religious belief.' To my surprise I'd quoted almost exactly the words Duncan Alexander had said to me in one of our exchanges. Perhaps we were more in accord with each other than I'd thought.

'Indeed, I sense that Lord James has his own agenda,' said Mary. 'His motives are not solely for the good of Scotland; he seeks personal gain.'

'In that he would be no different from any of the other Scots lords – or, indeed, French nobles.' I laughed as I gathered up the fallen letters and sat down beside her.

At this she smiled, and then went on seriously, 'I hope history doesn't judge me too harshly. I have prayed hard for God's guidance in this matter. I also took the private advice of my mother; she lives with the squabbling Scots lords, who frequently swap loyalties for their personal advantage. She writes to me that Scotland relies on French troops to keep the English army at bay and so, as the child of a royal house, I am prepared to do what is expected of me. I have enough knowledge of politics to understand that if I didn't sign the agreement, then, much as King Henri loves me, he would find another, more profitable bride for his son, and Scotland would be abandoned – to be torn apart by selfish warring nobles, easy prey for any invader. I must protect the people and hold the land for my heirs, so I did what I thought best for the crown and for the realm.'

After relieving herself of the burden of this terrible secret by sharing it with me, Mary's mood lifted. 'In any case,' she declared brightly, 'it won't come to pass. I intend to have many children, and both Francis and I will live long and happily together.'

Chapter 6

Mary chose to wear white on her wedding day.

It was a startling decision, for it was the custom of king's brides to come to church dressed in cloth of gold or royal purple.

'King Henri wants to astound both his subjects and the foreign ambassadors; he wants it to be recorded in history as a day to remember,' said Mary. 'So I will play my part to make that happen.'

Her height and bearing and striking looks alone would do that. But as I saw her walk before me, clad in purest white with a full queenly train of immense length, spangled with diamonds, and a golden coronet sitting atop her auburn hair, I knew she was unforgettable.

Her dazzling dress and jewels brought gasps of amazement from the Parisians thronging the streets. They'd already watched the bridegroom and his attendants make their way to Notre Dame, with Francis, a year Mary's junior, and smaller and thinner, looking slight and pale in his majestic robes. But it was Mary they'd turned out to see; the young bride, reputed to be the most beautiful woman in Europe, who would one day be queen of all France.

A roar of approval greeted her appearance: '*La Reine Blanche!*'

The words ran like a river alongside us as they cried out

for the White Queen. Like a bird taking flight, my spirits soared on this wave of acclamation.

'*La Reine Blanche! La Reine Blanche!*'

At that moment I felt her to be *my* queen, yet I did not mind sharing her with these others. Mary had given them something unique to reward their hours of waiting in cramped conditions. I smiled and waved at the well-wishers. Now they'd have a story to tell their children and grandchildren. They'd be able to say that they were there, on the streets of Paris, and that they saw her, the White Queen, as she walked past. And they'd boast about it – this seamstress, or friar, goose girl, or butcher's boy: *I tell you it as truth, may the Lord listen to my words and judge me if I lie, I was standing not more than four feet away when the procession halted, and Mary Stuart looked directly at me!* Below the banners and the flags, amid the singing and shouting, through the tumult and clatter, the world stilled for that second when Mary Stuart stopped to smile at them alone.

With an unerring instinct for spectacle and impact and her innate talent for personal connection, Mary paced slowly through the streets of Paris on the arm of King Henri. Now and then she paused to acknowledge the people, so that those who'd been there since yesterday morning vying for a good position and were now crushed against the barriers felt part of this great occasion. To the sound of tambour and trumpet we arrived before the massive main doors of the cathedral. Fabulous sapphires and rubies studded the crown on Mary's head, while the one enormous brilliant diamond pendant round her neck flashed in the spring sunlight. The crowds pressed forward. Her stature made it possible for many to catch a glimpse of her splendour as she mounted the steps of the arched stage erected outside Notre Dame. Here, below the bell towers of the cathedral, elevated so that prince and peasant might bear witness, the wedding was conducted by the Archbishop of Rouen. The spectators went wild with delight and continued to applaud and cheer as the ceremony began.

'Who would warrant that there would be such a reaction to a girl in a pretty dress.' Sir Duncan Alexander was standing beside me.

'A woman's worth is more than being a girl in a pretty dress,' I responded.

'Yes,' he replied after a moment, 'indeed it is.' Then he glanced at my own dress of sparkling silver laced over a stomacher criss-crossed with translucent pearls, his eyes travelling up to my hair, braided and entwined with matching seed pearls stitched on silver thread. His gaze came back to my face and he tilted his head and said, 'Not to deny the truth of your remark, yet beauty doth touch a man's heart.'

Now I was confused. I believed him to be enchanted with Mary Stuart, but had Duncan Alexander just paid *me* a compliment? He'd been looking at me, not Mary, when uttering the words 'beauty' and 'heart'. With him standing so close enough during the proceedings, my mind was a jumble of conflicting emotions.

As commander of the army, Mary's uncle, the Duke of Guise, had a major role in organizing events. He promenaded up and down, ensuring that everyone was in their correct place and not obstructing the view of the populace – in the process ensuring that he himself was noticed. As he made an elegant salute to a section of the crowd who called out his name, I saw Catherine de' Medici scowl. Then she looked at the bride, the daughter-in-law who, from this day, would exert greater influence over her son. For a moment the scowl remained on her face before being replaced by a frozen smile.

Mary Stuart stood erect and dignified. Francis gazed up adoringly at her as they made their marriage vows. King Henri took one of his own rings and gave it to his son to place on his bride's finger. A great hurrah went up. And with it came a sense of optimism. It was done. The French throne secured, with a healthy bride to bear children, Scotland protected, and the Guise family gloating that, through Mary, they were now one of the supreme power brokers in France.

When the nuptial mass, held within the cathedral itself, was finished, we came out into the spring sunshine and a riotous welcome. The royal family and their friends were carried in litters to the wedding reception.

The streets were even more crowded than before, with people packed together, eagerly awaiting the expected largesse. Sweetmeats and coin, ribbons and fancy goods, souvenirs and favours of every kind were distributed as our procession wound its way among them. Rapturous applause accompanied us.

Marie Seton peered ahead, where we could see Francis and Mary waving and smiling from their litter. 'It's heartening to hear common folk shout out their love and approval for our queen,' she commented.

'Ha!' said Sir Duncan, who was riding beside us. 'I suspect that the volume of their cheers corresponds to the amount of largesse being thrown out.'

'Oh, tush!' I said, annoyed with him for spoiling the mood when, not one second previously, I'd been thinking how handsome he looked: long legs in black boots and hose, topped by mauve breeches and tunic with a gold collar beneath his chin. 'Can a dour Scot like yourself not enjoy the day as it is?'

'Perhaps it's because at home in Scotland our folk live in such circumstances that—' Sir Duncan looked down at my upturned face and broke off. Our eyes met and our gaze locked. He looked away first. Then, turning back to lean into our carriage, he gathered up some coin from the basket at our feet and flung it directly at a fat friar standing near us.

The Maries and I were overcome by laughter as this supposedly mendicant monk charged forward, elbowing children out of his way to grab as much as he could.

'Long live Mary Stuart!' the friar bellowed. He held up fists full of pennies. 'Long live Marie, Queen of France!'

Duncan grinned at me and gestured with his hand, as if to say, *I prove my point.*

And I, happy that we were again on speaking terms, smiled back at him.

After hours of feasting and dancing, jesters, jugglers and musical interludes, then yet more dancing and feasting, King Henri rose from the table, clapped his hand together and announced the bedding of the bride.

Beneath the heavy damask tablecloth Mary reached for my hand. I squeezed her fingers in response and looked around for the four Maries. As the afternoon and evening progressed, nobles and courtiers had come and gone, occupying different places at the tables, and now I saw that Maries

Fleming and Beaton, reckoned to be the most vivacious two, were sitting in a corner with some male admirers around them, while Maries Seton and Livingston were closer to me. Marie Seton saw me glance about and at once signalled to the others, for we'd decided in advance to protect Mary as much as possible from any unseemly behaviour that might erupt at this stage.

No one knew what capers the king's attendants, nobles, friends and relatives would get up to. Neither Mary nor I had drunk much wine but some of the guests were wildly intoxicated. These included several of the Scots lords, who nominally had the duty of conducting their queen from the wedding reception to the royal bedchamber. Francis's male friends and relatives hustled him away, no doubt to pour alcohol down his throat and tell him questionable stories while he waited for word that his bride was ready for him. Mary knelt to receive a sapphire necklace from Queen Catherine as a gift to welcome her into the family. In return she pledged that she would be an obedient wife and a loyal member of the king's household. Catherine de' Medici gave her daughter-in-law a perfunctory kiss on the cheek and wished her goodnight. Then Mary's two uncles, the Duke of Guise and his brother, the Cardinal of Lorraine, attended the king, who came to escort her. Behind them were some other nobles, both Scots and French. The Maries and I wedged ourselves between these groups and, holding fast together, kept Mary some distance from their jostling and ribald remarks.

'Poor Francis.' Mary was trembling as we undressed her from her bridal gown into her night attire. 'He has no true confidants as I have. This will be so much worse for him.'

'He has taken part in frolics like this himself,' Marie Seton soothed our queen as she loosed her hair ornaments and pins, 'and will know what to expect.'

I exchanged a look with her. We knew that Francis was not the kind of lad who enjoyed rumbustious games.

'Let us prepare you as quickly as possible,' I said to Mary. 'The sooner we send for Francis, the sooner his ordeal will be over, for they will not tarry to bring him to you.'

She made a face at the prospect of having to accept her husband from the drunken youths who comprised the bridegroom's supporters.

'As your Guise uncles came with you, so Lord James Stuart went with Francis,' I told her. 'Your half-brother is firmly Protestant in his beliefs and his Church professes temperance. I'm sure he'll not have taken in too much wine and will moderate their worst excesses.'

'Who would have thought it?' said Marie Seton, who was almost as deeply devout in our Catholic religion as Mary herself. 'We have found an advantage to us in the Reformed faith.'

With our reassurance and quips we managed to make Mary smile as we eased the sumptuous nightgown over her slim body. Creamy satin ribbons looped into bows set with tiny diamonds made a collar for her throat. Pin-tucked stitching decorated the sleeves and bodice, with froths of delicate lace cascading from neck to hem.

Mary looked at herself in the mirror. She reached up and brought long curls of auburn hair forward to frame her face.

'You are very beautiful,' I told her. 'I will write to my father tonight and tell him how beautiful you look.'

'I wish it was me,' sighed Marie Fleming, who'd given her

heart away more times than the number of years she'd lived in this world. 'I'd love to have a gallant who loved me as much as I loved him.'

I thought of Sir Duncan. I decided not to let him suspect my feelings for him. Not until I was sure he felt the same about me.

Next we helped Mary don her long dressing robe of burgundy velvet. It was a heavier garment, part quilted, with extended shoulder pieces, but sleeveless and fastened loosely at the front with a thick silken cord. Then we led her from the dressing room into the anteroom of the bedchamber where the king, duke and cardinal awaited her.

King Henri looked at her approvingly. 'Yes,' he nodded, 'I have chosen well. My eldest son is the first Dauphin to be married in Paris for two hundred years and you are a worthy bride for him.'

'Thank you, Papa,' Mary whispered with a little sob.

I was not surprised to see a tear shine in the king's eye. He was demonstrative in his love for his children and visited the nursery more often than their mother.

One by one the Maries kissed Mary goodnight and she presented each of them with a gold brooch in the shape of a fleur-de-lis as a token of her wedding day.

As she gave me mine, I knelt before her to say farewell. 'Adieu, sweet maid Marie,' I said. 'I will greet you in the morning as a woman and a married wife.'

Mary drew me to my feet. She began to quiver, tremors running over her body as she twisted the gold tassels on the cord of her robe between her fingers.

'You will fray the belt of your dressing robe sent from Florence by the Medici family,' I chided her with mock severity, and then, seeing that she was genuinely frightened, added, 'It's not as if this is some coldly arranged marriage where you've never met the groom before your wedding day No harm will come to you tonight,' I assured her. 'Francis is your best friend.'

Mary blinked in agreement, those wide amber eyes filling with tears. 'And you, Jenny,' she said. 'You are too.'

The door crashed open and Francis, half undressed, was practically flung through.

Mary shrieked. Francis, face blotched and smeared with ladies' rouge, was almost weeping. With banging drum and bawdy songs, his rowdy companions made to follow him inside. The Duke of Guise nudged his brother and laughed loudly.

But King Henri was less amused. 'Enough,' he ordered. He wasn't an unkind man and probably realized that if this went on much longer then Francis would have some kind of seizure.

The groom's party retreated from the doorway.

'The king remains,' Mary whispered to me, 'and with him my two uncles.'

'You know how this is,' I said. 'As representatives for each of you, they should conduct you to your marital bed.'

'Oh, who would have a royal crown and suffer such indignity,' Mary moaned.

I glanced at Francis. As always, he was relying on Mary to be strong for both of them. Unless she rallied, they'd be over-come with nervous hysteria. But I had to go. Already King Henri had glanced in my direction. I made to take my leave, stooping to kiss Francis's hand.

'Stay, stay,' he urged me, more at ease in my company

than that of the others present. 'There is no need for you to rush away.' He was very immature for his fourteen years and sick with worry at the prospect that he might be forced to perform the duties of a bridegroom with witnesses present.

Mary was in no better state, unable to be the support that she often was to him in situations where he felt over-whelmed.

I went closer, and said in very low tones. 'You might say you are so consumed with love for each other that you wish to be left alone in your bedchamber. Perhaps they may wait in the anteroom and come to wake you in the morning. Mary,' I spoke directly to her, 'appeal to the king. He loves you so, he'll not deny you this.'

Mary embraced me closely and I took the chance to murmur in her ear, 'No matter what passes between you and Francis tonight, you are aware of what you must tell the king and your uncles tomorrow?'

Her breathing was rapid and I wanted to forestall any swooning on her part. I took her face in my hands and made her meet my gaze. 'You understand?'

She gave a brief nod of her head, and then turned and went quickly to King Henri. Wiping tears from her eyes, she spoke as I'd suggested: 'My liege lord, whose heart overflows with affection for your children and generously includes me as the same, and further, as one who appreciates great love, know that your son and I adore each other and beg you to allow us to be alone to express this love. I implore you.'

What man could refuse her anything? She stood, hair tumbled down, in her night robe and gown, a vision of vulnerable loveliness.

King Henri harrumphed and made protest, but Mary

told me later that she'd deliberately mentioned his own experience of love in the hope that he might think of Diane de Poitiers and be glad of a reason to excuse himself.

Mary had played her part well. King Henri drew his son aside and spoke to him quietly. Then he led them both to the bedroom door, ushered them inside and closed it. Relieved of his duty, he'd no intention of waiting around all night to ensure that his son properly bedded his new wife – not while Diane de Poitiers awaited him in some other part of the palace. He bade the Guise brothers to guard the 'children', told them he'd return in the morning, and departed. Banned from actually entering the bedchamber, the pair settled themselves to spend the night in the anteroom. Rather grumpily they called for dice cups, a gaming table and more wine to be brought.

Immediately after the king left, I slipped away. The royal corridor was heavily guarded, but the side corridor and short stairway to my room were empty. Far away, the sound of music indicated that there were those who'd not yet tired of dancing. But I was physically and emotionally spent and wanted only to rest. Head half bent I hurried up the stairs and almost collided with a late-night reveller.

'Ah, girl' – the man lurched towards me – 'you are looking for some midnight sport?'

'No, sir,' I said firmly, and made to walk on.

'I think you are. You are saying no as a tease to me.'

'I have no wish to tease you, sir,' I said, 'or indeed annoy you in any way. But I am very sure that my answer is no.'

He took me by the shoulders and pulled me to him, his grip surprisingly firm for one inebriated. 'Let me persuade you to say yes.'

Now I was concerned. With so much noise going on elsewhere no one would hear my cries for help. I recognized the beginnings of panic in my head, and tried to quell them.

'The lady has made her intentions clear, I think.'

Sir Duncan Alexander appeared beside me and placed his arm between myself and the drunken lord.

'I have encountered such rebuffs before,' the man said, winking at him, 'but they are easily overcome.'

'You seem to be having difficulty understanding the lady's meaning, but there will be no such difficulty understanding mine.' And saying this, Sir Duncan swung the man round and booted him soundly on the backside. Then he pushed him forward and sent him sprawling down the stairs. I gripped the banister and looked out over the stairwell. The man got up and limped away, cursing.

I turned to Duncan. 'I thank you,' I said.

My heart was fluttering, as much now for being close to him as for my frightening experience.

He looked me up and down. 'You are unharmed?'

I gave a quick nod of my head. I was beginning to react to the fright and thought that if I spoke, I might cry.

'Best go inside your room now,' he said gently, 'and lock the door.'

Again I nodded.

We gazed at each other. My reluctance to speak had become something else. We stood as if transfixed by a spell that both of us were afraid to break.

Duncan broke the silence. 'I'll bid you goodnight.' He lifted my fingers to his lips and kissed them.

I went into my room and shut the door behind me. I

pressed my ear against the panelling and stayed there until I heard his footsteps fade. Then I lay down, spread my fingers beside my cheek on the pillow and put my mouth to the place where he'd kissed them.

Chapter 7

Many days of festivities followed. Banquet after banquet, each more lavish than the last: musical tableaux, masques and balls; and a stupendous entertainment with silver-sailed ships that floated over the ballroom floor with King Henri and bridegroom Francis as captains.

With the formal part over and the duties of the wedding night fulfilled to the king's satisfaction, Mary and Francis were able to enjoy the celebrations.

She'd reported to me, giggling, that on their wedding night she and Francis had romped on their bed like two naughty children, hiding behind the bedcurtains, making tunnels among the blankets, and throwing cushions and pillows at each other until eventually, worn out, they'd fallen asleep cuddled together. The duke and the cardinal, finding them like this in the morning, with Mary's nightgown ribbons all undone and the bedclothes rumpled, had declared the marriage consummated.

One evening they excused themselves from dinner. Mary professed to be suffering from an attack of dizziness and said she and Francis would eat alone. In reality, Francis was irked by the tedium of meals spent listening to important ambassadors and trade delegates whose names he could never remember. Mary was indulging him by feigning illness so that he could spend the time setting out a wooden model castle he'd been given, complete with miniature cannon and soldiers. Although both King Henri and Queen Catherine wanted them to be present, on show to their favoured guests, the newlyweds were excused; the idea that Mary might already be pregnant could not be dismissed.

Mary laughed when she heard this and shook her head. She cupped her hands and whispered in my ear, 'Francis is not quite ready to be a father, and I will not force him yet to do his duty by me.'

So now, at the request of Catherine de' Medici, a diversion of a different sort was to take place at dinner. Her love of astrology and mystical interpretations was renowned, and she employed a Florentine astrologer by the name of Cosimo Ruggieri, whom she frequently consulted. This evening she called him to her side and bade him announce a special guest who would perform before the king. It was the prophet known as Michel de Nostradamus.

I was, as now often seemed to be the case, seated near Sir Duncan Alexander. At first I thought this accidental, but having noticed his movements during the incident with Sir Malcolm Cowrie, I now believed that Duncan took care as to where he placed himself in a room. And after his remarks to me and the looks we'd exchanged on Mary's wedding day I hoped that he was next to me because of personal attraction.

He groaned when Nostradamus's name was called. 'Merciful Heaven! Save us from the proclamations of this fraudulent trickster.'

'From one who has stated to me that Heaven may not in fact exist,' I said, 'that is a strange request.'

'No matter what faith one does or does not have, surely,

Jenny, you give no credit to the belief that the planets rule our lives?'

'Do you say then that the phases of the moon have no impact upon the earth? Perhaps you might care to explain the movement of the tides at sea. And further' – I gave him no chance to interrupt –'it is documented in scientific books that a full moon can influence moods in animals and humans.'

'I applaud your reading of scientific journals,' he said.

I do think he meant that, for his voice had a note of surprise.

'But,' he went on, 'that's not what this fellow is about. Nostradamus claims he can, by divinations and visions, see future events.'

'He should wager on the jousting tournaments and win a fortune.'

'Exactly so!' said Sir Duncan. 'But he does not. These four-line verses he writes, his famous quatrains, are invariably obscure, with a threat of impending doom. He scares the wits of the gullible, like our most esteemed Queen of France.'

I glanced around. We were speaking Scots, but even so it wasn't wise to be talking of Catherine de' Medici in such a manner.

The Florentine, Cosimo Ruggieri, ushered in an older man, tall, full-bearded and wearing a wide-shouldered long black coat with winged sleeves.

'Oh!' I breathed. His clothes flowed around him as he walked, and his shadow, like a dark angel, menaced the room.

Observing my reaction, Sir Duncan leaned closer as

though to reassure me. 'The soothsayer dresses dramatically to impress us,' he said as Nostradamus strode to stand before King Henri.

'Remind this person,' the king instructed a courtier, 'that in the days of a wedding we want happy thoughts.'

The courtier went away and came back looking nervous as he relayed his message. 'The man, Nostradamus, says that with the king's permission he will depart at no charge for his journey or his time, but if he remains, there is no guarantee that what he might say will please anyone. He cannot change the visions he has and must speak as they direct him.'

The king clicked his teeth in annoyance. Queen Catherine laid her hand on his arm. 'Sire, you promised me this,' she reminded him.

'Very well' – the king waved his hand – 'let the performance begin.'

In the manner of most news meant to be kept secret at the royal court, everyone already knew that the great prophet and alchemist Nostradamus was due to appear. People crowded into the dining hall, some of them driven by curiosity or scepticism – or perhaps a belief, or a need to believe, in the man who was a doctor as well as a seer. They sought cures for illnesses and afflictions – or the recipe for an elixir of eternal youth, of high value in a society where appearance mattered very much.

'I tell you plainly, sir,' King Henri said to Nostradamus, 'that I rate science over magic.'

Nostradamus bowed and replied, 'As I do, sire. And yet there are liars and naysayers who would deny a king's God-given power to lay his hands on those afflicted by scrofula and so effect a cure.'

'Clever words,' Sir Duncan Alexander said as murmurs of agreement echoed around the hall.

The gift of curing scrofula, an inflammation of the neck glands, was one that kings were supposed to have been blessed with. On a royal progress Henri would occasionally stop when someone by the roadside reached out and cried in supplication, 'Seigneur, if you could but touch me, then I would be made well again.'

'Proceed,' King Henri directed Nostradamus. 'It will amuse us for a while this evening.'

'Sire, with respect, I do not perform like a jester or juggler for the sport and pleasure of an audience. My predictions are based on visions.'

'Then tell us a prediction that might warrant our attention.' The king yawned.

'Concerning the throne,' Queen Catherine suggested at once. She glanced at Mary Stuart. 'I would hear of the royal succession.'

'Madam, wife,' the king spoke quietly to her, 'have a care as to what you ask for.'

'Husband . . .' Catherine said meekly. She chewed on her lip in vexation but bowed her head. 'Perhaps the prophet could be allowed to speak about our male children?' she wheedled.

The king nodded at Nostradamus.

'France will have a great king,' said Nostradamus quietly. 'Henri, by name.'

'You see?' the king grumbled. 'This is what I mean. Anyone of my courtiers could do this.' He beckoned to a young servant. 'Come here, boy. Give me a prophecy.'

'What?' Overcome by fear, the boy fell to his knees.

Everyone laughed.

'Go now,' the king ordered him. 'Stand in the centre of the room and foretell my future and that of my sons.'

The boy scuttled into the middle of the hall. 'The King of France is a mighty king,' he squeaked, 'and will reign for many days over many people, and so will his sons. Long live the king!'

'Excellent.' King Henri threw a coin to the boy, who scooped it up and ran out.

Throughout this charade, face impassive, Nostradamus stood without moving. Then he spoke: 'I will make a prediction. A vision comes to me. The vision of the one subject that people do not want to hear.'

'A death,' someone in the hall whispered. 'He is preparing to foretell a death.'

'Death! Death! Death!' Nostradamus intoned. 'Three deaths!' He threw back his head and stared at the ceiling. 'Royal and brave to meet their end.'

'Do you speak of those present here tonight?' Catherine de' Medici craned her neck towards him.

'Death comes to all. Our life ends. The sparrow in the tree, the mighty lion in his den. The lion who will fight and not be gainsaid. Death cannot be turned aside.' Nostradamus's head sank upon his chest and he hunched down to crumple onto the floor like a heap of old sacks. 'It cannot, *cannot* be stayed. Not for one minute, not for one second. I see only what I see. The truth, the terrible truth.'

Without realizing what I was doing, I gripped the arm of Duncan Alexander as the prophet got to his feet once more. Candles flickered to elongate his shadow so that it appeared enormous. Nostradamus raised his hands high and his cape fell in folds from his arms like the two wings of a monstrous mythical beast. In a thunderous voice he proclaimed:

'*The lion in his cage!*
The rise of the poison!
The fall of the axe!'

He beat his breast with his fist. 'Combat should not take place. The lion's cage will be ruptured. I cannot prevent it. I predict yet I am ignored. Why should I expect to be heard when even royal pleas are not heeded? Like Christ upon the Cross, days of agony endured. Death not deflected.'

Silence swept over the gathering like dark clouds across the sun. Even Diane de Poitiers, usually outwardly un-emotional, shifted uncomfortably in her seat.

'I would have him be more precise on this,' King Henri said, almost wearily. 'Why do these foretellings have to be so mysterious? Can they not be couched so that any common man, far less a king, can understand?'

'There is a veil of shadows upon our world,' Catherine de' Medici explained. 'Even the greatest prophet cannot perfectly discern what the future holds.'

'Speak exactly what you see!' the king commanded Nostradamus.

'Nay, nay. I cannot. For my tongue cleaves to the roof of my mouth and I am unable to utter more. Yet I have written of that which all men fear, be they king, courtier or kitchen maid.'

There was a hush within the hall. If the king chose to take this amiss, Nostradamus could be executed. In an instant his life could be forfeit.

'I have written what I have written.' Nostradamus moaned and pulled at his beard. His shoulders twisted this way and that and he struggled as if to slide out from under a great weight. Then the fit seemed to pass from him and he became calm again.

'Majesties.' He bent low before the king and queen. 'Forgive an old man if he has been intemperate. I am weary of the burden that these visions place upon me. I will make a prophecy, yes. I will tell you of something I have seen. Your children will be proclaimed kings of France, and kings of other countries too. This I do know.'

'Very good.' Far from being annoyed, King Henri was bored. He ordered a sum of money to be given to Nostradamus. As this was being done he took the chance to murmur to Diane de Poitiers, 'I would have been as well to pay the servant boy this money, for that is the very thing he foretold in faster time and with less theatre.'

'And Mary Stuart . . .' One of the Scots lords spoke up. 'She is now also considered a child of the king. What of Mary Stuart? What great things can we expect from such a blessed and fortunate marriage?'

'I have already spoken on this.' The soothsayer closed his eyes.

The man shrugged and raised his goblet to his lips. But my heart leaped; I loosened my grasp on Sir Duncan and leaned forward. What part of Nostradamus's prediction applied to Mary?

'And yet I sense you had even more to say.' Queen Catherine, realizing that the performance would soon be over, wanted as much information as possible.

'I speak of what I see . . .' Nostradamus paused and then words – disjointed phrases – jerked from his mouth as though he had no control over them: 'Henri. A great king.

Not now, but years from now. Henri, King of France, will be a great king. Honoured through the ages. One of the greatest kings of France.'

Nostradamus suddenly bowed and left the room – a breach of etiquette as he had not been dismissed.

'There! We have it!' King Henri cried out loudly in exasperated amusement. 'I am a great king now, and many years from now.'

'That is not what Nostradamus said,' his wife whispered. 'No, that is not what the prophet said at all.'

But the onlookers had drifted away, and those at dinner had returned to their food and gossip. Only Duncan and I were silent with our thoughts. King Henri was restless and obviously desired to spend time with Diane de Poitiers. He smiled at her, and she acknowledged him with a wave of her hand. He glanced at the queen, hesitating to insult her quite so openly, but she knew her place, and said, 'If your grace so pleases . . .' She beckoned to her ladies. 'I am tired and would be excused.'

With relief King Henri rose and escorted his wife from the table. Someone else had engaged Duncan in conversation, and on an impulse I rose up and followed Queen Catherine's entourage. As we reached the door, I heard Diane de Poitiers laugh. The queen faltered and I saw her clench her hands so tightly that the nails might draw blood as they dug into her palms. It wasn't true that she was at peace with the arrangement allowing her husband to consort openly with his mistress.

'I have need of only one attendant to walk with me to my apartments,' she dismissed her ladies. Speaking to Ruggieri, she said, 'Bring a lighted taper – you will accompany me. I want some explanation of tonight's revelations.'

I too wanted to know more about what had been said. When the Scots lord had enquired as to Mary's future, Nostradamus said that he'd already spoken of Mary Stuart – but which part of his prophecies referred to her? I stepped into the corridor. The queen and her astrologer were not walking in the direction of her apartments. They were going towards the tower where her observatory was situated.

Nostradamus had foretold three deaths, *royal and brave to meet their end.*

I took that to mean that the prophet had a vision of three royal deaths. Was one of them Mary's? He'd also spoken of poison. I thought of the Count de Cluny's meeting in Catherine's private study when poison was mentioned. She didn't like her son's deep attachment to Mary, especially with her daughter-in-law so closely allied to the Guise family, whose power she feared. Would she go so far as to poison her? Was this what Nostradamus had seen?

The rise of the poison.

No one else seemed to sense that Mary might be in danger. It was up to me to find out what I could. And so I made my decision then – to become a spy for Mary, Queen of Scots.

Chapter 8

Not daring to follow too closely, I delayed until Queen Catherine and her astrologer reached the foot of the tower and disappeared into the stairwell. I debated the best thing to do. I desperately wanted to know if there was a real threat to Mary, not only out of personal love and regard for her welfare, but because I really believed that she was crucial to the greater good of Scotland and France. I'd not noticed the Count of Cluny among the guests tonight, but I knew that he had leave to come and go as he pleased and could be skulking anywhere. But I didn't expect to be caught. Queen Catherine had a hearty appetite and, having borne the king nine children, walked with a cumbersome gait. If she turned to come back downstairs, I could surely escape unseen.

I waited until I thought they had ascended a flight or two, then entered the tower and began to mount the staircase. Ruggieri must have lit the wall sconces with his taper and they flared above my head, making my shadow and my heart leap as I climbed. Frequently I had to pause to listen, for there were rooms off the landings and I needed to make sure they'd not gone into one of those. I was practically at the top before I heard the queen speaking to Ruggieri:

'The proclamations of the soothsayer have disturbed me. There was much left unsaid.'

'Perhaps, majesty, it would be appropriate to question him further?' Ruggieri replied.

'That would be useless. I've dealt with Nostradamus before. His visions, when they come, are in broken pieces. They exhaust him completely. It can be weeks before he recovers so there is no point in pursuing him just now.'

The queen and her astrologer had reached the top of the tower, an open space with a glass roof and a balcony where one could observe the night sky. I peeked round the corner. Ruggieri was lighting an oil lamp on a table spread with star charts and signs of the zodiac.

'I will do what I can, your grace, but it's hard for me to interpret the visions of another.'

'Is that so?' Queen Catherine said testily. 'Then maybe you could let the spirit move you to acquire some of your own?'

'I do have a way of seeing into the future . . .' Ruggieri hesitated and then went on, 'Allow me to make some preparations, and while I do so, please take something to refresh yourself. There is wine and some sweetmeats here.' He offered her a plate.

Catherine de' Medici had a fondness for cakes and biscuits. She helped herself to several of the dainties, pushing them rapidly into her mouth one after the other and washing them down with gulps of wine.

Meanwhile Ruggieri lit an incense burner and then blew out the lamp. 'This requires the rays of celestial light.' With a flourish he flung aside the curtain of an alcove to reveal a long mirror.

Catherine took a pace towards it.

'Have a care!' Ruggieri cried out. 'There are forces at work here that neither you nor I understand.'

She nodded and retreated at once while the astrologer lifted the incense burner and removed the lid. The heavy scent of frankincense and myrrh filled the room. Charcoal smouldered, the red glow bouncing off the mirror, sending out myriad images. My own nerves were jangling, but curiosity drove me on. I crept closer. This was no ordinary flat looking-glass but one whose surface had been constructed in an unusual way, with different facets and angles. Reflections seemed to double and redouble. I caught a flicker of movement and realized it might be me. I shrank in against the wall.

When I ventured another look, Ruggieri had gone behind the mirror and tilted it towards the glass roof. 'Tell me what you wish to know and the light of the heavens will reveal all it can.'

'I would know the fate of my sons.' The queen's voice was hoarse.

'Then summon up the power of your deepest affection, for a mother's love is stronger than the ties that bind us to this mortal realm.'

'Yes!' she said. 'I agree! The love a mother bears her children is the most powerful bond in Heaven and earth.'

'Speak their names and they must obey your command to appear.'

The moon shone brightly, making the queen's face pale as a waxen model.

'Louis . . .' she whispered. This was her fourth child, a son who'd died less than a year after his birth. 'Louis, my dearest dead boy.'

A most disturbing thing then happened. Echoing clearly through the tower came the sound of a baby's cry.

'*Santa Madre di Dio!*' The queen staggered as if to fall. She grasped the edge of the table and held on as if her life depended on it. I put my fist to my mouth to stifle my own exclamation.

The mirror trembled. Ruggieri spoke confidently. 'Indeed, Louis is with the Mother of God. The little one plays at the foot of the Virgin's throne in Heaven.'

A heartbreaking sob wrenched from Catherine's lips and she asked, 'Can you show me that scene?'

'Watch the mirror!' Ruggieri was strong and commanding. 'The spirits of your living sons await your summons. Name them now and discern their presence!'

'Francis.' The queen called for her first born.

Was it my fancy that her tone was neutral when she spoke? According to the Maries Catherine was disappointed in Francis's frailty and resented Mary's apparent good health because it made her son look even weaker.

'Charles.' Again the queen's voice was unemotional as she named her second son.

'Edouard Henri . . .' Her tone softened as she mentioned her favourite.

'They appear!' Ruggieri chanted. 'Through the swirls of time they strive to answer their mother's call!

'And Hercule,' she added.

I went forward as far as I dared. The heavy smoke of the incense all but obscured the glass. There were shapes, but quite what they were I did not know.

'There,' Ruggieri said in satisfaction. 'All is well. Each son doth have a crown upon his head. Your heirs are called upon to rule in many lands.'

'You are sure?' Queen Catherine asked anxiously. 'You *did* see that?'

'Distinctly,' he said, replacing the curtain over the alcove while the queen sank into a chair.

'Yet one more thing,' She drank more wine. 'Nostradamus mentioned a prophecy he has written.'

Ruggieri sighed. 'Nostradamus has written numerous things, almanacs, books, journals.'

'I am referring to his quatrains, the four-line verses that contain his most famous predictions.'

Ruggieri went to a shelf and selected a book.

'Find me the one that refers to my husband, the king.'

'Ah yes,' He hesitated. 'I was so overcome by the force of Nostradamus's presence that the essentials escaped me. Perhaps your grace could remind me of the words?'

'It was quite specific,' she stated. 'More than once Nostradamus mentioned a lion. Don't you see? It is the symbol the king wears on his breastplate.'

'But that was in connection with a foretelling of doom,' Ruggieri said cautiously.

'This I know!' Catherine snapped.

'I believed that to mean another person,' Ruggieri told her, trying to allay her fears. 'Nothing to do with his majesty. Indeed, he proclaimed that King Henri was a great king now, and would be a great king for many years.'

'Do you take me for a fool?' The queen was angry now. 'That is *not* what Nostradamus said. He proclaimed Henri to be a great king; *a* Henri would be a great king *many years from now*. It is not the same as saying that the present King Henri will reign for years to come. It is not the same thing at all.'

There was silence in the room.

I could sense Ruggieri's dilemma. He did not want to further anger the queen, yet he had to respond. I too was now on tenterhooks, poised for flight should she decide to cut short this session and leave in a temper.

Catherine passed her hand over her brow. 'Nostradamus does not deal in platitudes. Don't you see that the one thing a monarch needs is the truth? With a proper prediction then I can arm myself to protect my husband and children.'

I felt myself relaxing at the pathetic note in her voice. The queen was merely a small fat woman who adored her husband so much that, while he was consorting and amusing himself with his mistress, she was desperately seeking a way to avert any catastrophe that might befall him.

Ruggieri pointed to a page of text. 'Nostradamus refers there to the court being in a troubled state because of a one-eyed king.'

'There is a quatrain . . .' Catherine de' Medici insisted. 'I know there is.'

He riffled through the books. 'Here is one,' he said slowly, 'in Nostradamus's first collection of quatrains, that refers to a lion . . . two lions, the young and the old.'

'Read it to me!'

> '*The young lion shall overcome the old,*
> *On martial field in single combat.*
> *In a golden cage, his eye will be put out.*
> *Two into one, then to die a cruel death.*'

'That is it! And more than once has Nostradamus seen this vision of the king, the lion, brought down. O cruel death! It is he. I know it!' The queen sobbed and pulled at her hair. 'The king will die. My husband is doomed. Henri will die a cruel death!'

'Madam, be still, I beg you.' The astrologer tried to calm her. 'Some water . . .'

There was the gurgle of water being poured from a jug, and the lower sound of a woman weeping piteously.

'Sometimes' – Ruggieri was choosing his words with care – 'that which we think we see in the future does not always come to pass.'

He was in a difficult situation. If he denied the strength of Nostradamus's predictions, then he placed his own on a shaky foundation.

'And there can be different interpretations—' He stopped.

Although upset, Queen Catherine was beginning to recover herself. 'I am glad to be prepared. I appreciate that the visions can be warnings and I will take them as such and be on my guard.'

'The queen is always wise in her interpretation and understanding,' said Ruggieri, 'but these séances can be draining. May I respectfully suggest that you take some rest?'

Now I must flee! I tiptoed away and started down the staircase. Above me, the queen and Ruggieri prepared to descend. I lifted my skirts and ran.

And then I heard a noise. I stopped in alarm. The noise wasn't coming from the top, but from the entrance to the tower. Someone was approaching from the ground floor.

Great God! I was in extreme danger, trapped between the queen coming down and an unknown presence hurrying up. For a second my thoughts froze; then I recalled a chamber on the landing I'd just passed. I darted back up, pulled open the door of a dingy turret room, tiptoed inside and drew the door behind me. The grate of a boot heel on the stairs!

Then complete silence. The person outside was listening at the door – as I'd done earlier to check if there was anyone inside. I held my breath. A rustle of clothes as whoever it was moved quietly on and up. It had to be someone known to the queen, who knew the way to her private tower and was allowed to meet her and speak to her alone late at night.

I must get away. As soon as the person had passed, I slipped down the stairs and into the corridor. Dinner had ended and the passageway was now bustling with people making assignations, preparing to retire, or heading for different salons to game or drink or gossip.

I mingled with a knot of Scots courtiers, managing to dally long enough to see who came out of the tower.

Three people.

First the queen, Catherine de' Medici.

Next her astrologer, Cosimo Ruggieri.

A delay. Then the last person. Emerging into the corridor, his cloak pulled up to make himself less conspicuous, a man melted away into the crowd. But not so fast that I couldn't identify this person who'd passed me on the stairs to go and consult privately with Queen Catherine de' Medici.

The Scots Lord of Knoydart, Sir Duncan Alexander.

Chapter 9

Festering amidst the continued wedding celebrations was a mood of religious and civil unrest which those at court contrived to ignore.

Northern France, especially Paris, was mainly loyal to the Guise family, who were fervent Catholics. If some Huguenot heads were knocked together and ended up in the Seine, there were few city magistrates prepared to act on any complaint made.

However, a chance encounter meant that I could not remain oblivious to the changes within French society. Most mornings I went riding with my servant, Maurice, and a groom. Our route was always carefully chosen to be safe and as private as possible – we used the nearest royal park to wherever the court was assembled – but I had already noticed posters attached to buildings and trees along our way. On this particular day, when we'd stopped to let the horses rest after a gallop, I heard the pleasant sound of voices lifted in song to praise God.

'Maurice, who are these people who are singing hymns so early in the morning?' I asked my servant.

His eyes opened wide, but he did not answer, no doubt thinking that I was angry at the disturbance. We trotted on and the singers' words became clearer. And I realized they were singing in French.

'Oh!' I said.

Maurice exchanged a look with the groom that told me more than any wordy explanation. If the words were not in Latin, then it must be a group belonging to some branch of the Reformed faith and it was unlawful for them to gather in public. Suddenly, above the singing, I heard another noise. Hoofbeats behind us. A larger party of nobles from the palace were out for a morning ride – escorted by armed soldiers.

And now both Maurice and the groom looked truly fearful. Scarcely thinking what I was doing, I wheeled my horse round and galloped back the road. Waving my hand in the air, I called out, 'A tree has fallen across the path ahead! Best go by another way!'

The nobles readily followed my suggestion and we headed off down a different forest track.

The incident was never spoken of, but subsequently, on occasion, Protestant tracts and leaflets appeared in places where I could not help but find them. In this way I became educated in the current thinking of the Reformers. When they spoke of the excesses of the established Church, their grievances seemed just. I was less sure of their interpretation of Biblical texts. With respect to politics I relied on my father's letters to give a truer picture of what was happening in the world outside the court:

In England Mary Tudor's measures to promote Catholicism are pitiless [my father wrote to me from Edinburgh in the summer], *and the bonfires claim Protestant martyrs. Within predominantly Catholic Scotland the Reformers, encouraged by John Knox, are now in open defiance of the queen regent. The situation here deteriorates from week to week. Religious fervour*

*is used to mask political aims, and ordinary people are
manipulated by those seeking wealth and high office. Our
French soldiers haven't been paid and are no longer viewed as
protectors but as invaders. My commission will soon be at an
end, and although I am loath to leave my men in these straits, I
will be glad to return to the peace of our estates in Hautepré.
Perhaps you might ask to be excused from court and meet me
there?*

The thought of joining my father in the south of France
did appeal to me. I recalled many happy childhood holidays
with my parents in between my father's tours of duty. But I
was glad that his commission was not yet done: I couldn't
abandon Mary at this time. She required my presence, for her
new bridegroom, Francis, spent more time out hunting than
in the company of his wife.

'Francis is still a boy,' Mary told me, 'while I' – she
blushed – 'I am ready to be a woman.'

Others also thought it time she became a woman – not
only as a wife but as a mother. However, the weeks passed
and there was no indication of any pregnancy.

'I am content to wait for motherhood,' she said, 'for
Francis is happy as we are.'

'He's more a child than a husband,' was Marie Fleming's
comment.

'Perhaps you, who think you know so much about the
ways of men, cannot appreciate that this can be a satisfactory
relationship,' retorted Marie Seton.

We all stared at this outburst. It was at odds with Marie
Seton's quiet nature to be so vocal. But then, she was older
than us and had turned down offers of marriage, so utterly

devoted was she to Mary and determined to remain by her side.

'I meant no offence!' Marie Fleming cried, and went at once to hug her, for although we bickered as young women do, it was never with malice, nor did we ever hold a grudge for long.

'I confess that I cosset Francis,' said Mary. 'His mother never did, and mine has been absent in my life, so we recompense each other in that way. Perhaps I indulge him too much.'

'There are far fewer official receptions to attend,' I pointed out, 'now that most of the Scots lords have gone home.'

This was an additional reason why I preferred to stay close to Mary. Her personal guard was depleted and the court was at Fontainebleau for the autumn; on several occasions I'd glimpsed the Count of Cluny here.

I tucked my father's latest letter into a fold of my dress as I saw Mary coming from the garden, escorted by the Scots who'd remained with her. Duncan Alexander was among them, and on seeing him, I acknowledged to myself that he was the reason I wanted to be here and not at Hautepré. My heart was pulling me towards this man with a strength that outweighed any other family ties.

'Ah, Jenny,' Mary called, 'I do insist that you come to supper with us. I want to play a challenging game of cards, and you and Sir Duncan are both worthy opponents!'

His eyes met mine and he raised an eyebrow. 'Are we opponents?' he asked me lightly.

'Leave off teasing!' Mary tugged at his sleeve. 'You know I didn't mean that you opposed each other.'

'I understood that, your grace,' he replied silkily. 'I was making a jest.'

Since the episode in the tower, I'd tried to find out more about Duncan Alexander. Whenever I considered the events of that night, my thoughts ran in circles. I couldn't fathom his purpose for being there. He was a man who didn't speak of his family or background, and, upon making enquiries, I discovered that no one knew much of his lineage or allegiances. Knoydart was a remote part of Scotland left to him by an uncle who'd neither wife nor children of his own. Some years ago Duncan arrived in Edinburgh to legalize his inheritance, part of which consisted of a position at court as one of the monarch's advisers on formal occasions. Nobles who held a court office like this could interpret it as no more than expressing an opinion on the most suitable dress for a ball. How Duncan viewed his duties I really did not know.

I went to my room to change for supper and chose to return by a shorter route that went past the serving pantries. Someone was walking ahead of me and, although he was quite far away, I recognized the Count of Cluny.

I stopped at once. It was inevitable that I would meet him again at Fontainebleau. After all, this was where Catherine de' Medici had awarded him land and a house in which to practise his apothecary skills. Hoping to avoid him while I was alone I waited until he disappeared down a corridor, and then walked slowly in the direction of Mary's supper room. As I passed the pantry, I noticed that the curtain was partly open and glanced inside. Boards of sweetmeats were laid out. There were over a dozen varieties: cherries dipped in syrup, raisin cakes, dainty marzipan shapes and pastries sprinkled with sugar dust.

Sugar . . .

The scene in Queen Catherine's study was before me. I

could hear her voice speaking of the poison she kept hidden in the secret compartment: *It resembles sugar crystals and is sweet, but with an aroma and taste similar to mint . . .*

I gazed at the trays, a cold sweat breaking out upon me. If I made an alarm I would have to say why I suspected the food had been poisoned. The Count of Cluny was under Queen Catherine's protection so I couldn't risk it being discovered how I knew. If I did nothing, then these would be served and Mary might eat one. I recalled Catherine telling the count that small doses of the poison could make someone constantly unwell and therefore easy to control. This could be the queen's way of reducing Mary's hold over Francis and reasserting her own. What could I do?

I picked up a pastry that I knew was one of Mary's favourite kinds, hesitated, then opened my mouth and popped it in. No minty flavour. That was the solution! I would taste a sample of each one. If there was any trace of mint then I would throw that sort away. I ate another and another. There was nothing amiss with them. They tasted of marzipan and sugar and plum and orange, as they should.

But now I did not feel well – not because they were poisoned, but because I'd eaten so much rich fare that I was about to be sick. I moaned and clutched my throat.

There was a sound behind me. The curtain opened to reveal Duncan Alexander standing there. Moving swiftly, he emptied a bowl of dainties onto the floor and put it under my chin. He looked at the food trays and then at me in a most peculiar way. 'I don't how your waist stays so trim if you consume so many pastries and sugared foods.'

Diplomatically he diverted his eyes as I spat the contents

of my mouth and some of my stomach into the bowl. Then he handed me a napkin.

'I thank you,' I said shakily.

'The Queen of Scots sent me to find you to see if some indisposition had delayed you. What should I tell her?'

'I – I was hungry,' I stammered.

'It ill becomes a lady not to control her appetite,' he observed.

The pain in my stomach was easing, and shame and sickness were replaced with annoyance at his condescending tone. 'And yet a man may drink and wench as much as he pleases and no comment is made!' I retorted. 'If you'll excuse me' – I almost pushed him aside – 'I should go.'

'Perhaps you need some assistance?' He was grinning in amusement.

'I do not need your help,' I said, and attempted to sweep out of the room in a dignified manner but spoiled the effect by tripping. I heard him laugh out loud; he was still laughing behind me when I entered Mary's apartments.

'We are waiting for you to begin our game of cards. Where have you been, Jenny?' she asked.

'I – I . . .' I could not think what to reply. I can make pleasantries as well as anyone but outright lies do not form easily on my tongue.

Behind me Duncan interrupted, 'I beg your pardon, majesty. It is my fault. I delayed your lady Ginette in conversation.'

We took our places and I waited for him to make some flippant remark, but he said nothing of my disgrace. Perhaps he was more kindly than I thought.

Our card game continued until Mary declared herself

weary and said she wished to see Francis before she retired for the night. She was on the point of rising from her chair when there was a commotion in the doorway. A messenger, out of breath and dishevelled, begged to be admitted with news that must be relayed directly to Mary Stuart. He was speaking urgently to the guard who'd brought him to the door: 'I was told to ride hard to Fontainebleau and make sure that I speak personally to Mary, Queen of Scots.'

'Who gave you these instructions?'

'Lord James Stuart, before he collapsed.'

'My brother is unwell?' Mary stood up.

The messenger came past the guard and dropped on one knee before her. 'Disaster has befallen your Scots lords on their journey home. All have taken seriously ill. One is already dead and more were dying as I left.'

Chapter 10

'James! My brother! James! James!' Mary's voice pitched into hysteria. Half swooning, she swayed and her knees buckled.

Duncan Alexander caught her as she fell. I was at her other side and we bore her to a couch. Attendants ran for cloths and vinegar water. Her complexion was bleached of colour, her fingers tinged blue. I rubbed her hands between my own to stimulate the circulation. Mary's eyelashes fluttered and she moaned, 'Is he dead – my brother and my friend?'

'Hush, hush,' I soothed her. 'We will try to find out.' I turned to ask Duncan Alexander to question the messenger, but he'd disappeared.

Marie Livingston offered to go and find Francis, but the French court was a close-knit community, and courtiers were already running between the royal apartments with the news.

'Lord James has a strong constitution,' I assured Mary. 'Whatever this sickness is, he's sure to survive. He'll send another message soon.' I said this with more conviction than I felt, for if all the Scots lords were ill, then so might be their servants and grooms.

The Maries and I took turns to sit by Mary's bed through the long night. Francis had no great affection for Lord James Stuart. He'd complained to Mary of her brother's behaviour on his wedding night, when, instead of protecting him from the worst excesses of his rowdy companions, he had plastered rouge and face paint on the Dauphin's face. Yet, out of sympathy for Mary, Francis curled up in a chair in the corner of her chamber and fell asleep with his mouth hanging open, drooling like a little boy. He would have remained there, but for the fact that his mother heard of it and ordered his personal manservant to lift him, still asleep, and take him to his own rooms. Although they sent messages of commiseration, neither she nor the king came to offer support.

Duncan Alexander did not reappear until past midnight. He knocked softly on the outer door, and when Marie Seton saw who it was, she brought me from Mary's bedchamber to speak to him.

'How fares the queen?' he asked.

'How would you expect?' I answered, angry and disappointed that he'd forsaken us in the midst of the frenzy. 'Where were you when we needed you?' I demanded.

'I left her in the best hands possible,' Duncan replied with equal vehemence. 'Yours!' he added, in case there was any doubt.

'But your presence was required here!'

'No it wasn't. What was required was for me to find more of the Scots Guard to double the ones on duty outside these apartments. Don't you realize the potential danger of a situation like this?'

'Yes, I do!' By now I was shaking with relief at seeing him. 'The chambermaids and lackeys have been coming and going with wild tales of murder and massacre. We thought we might be attacked.' I didn't want to admit that I'd also wanted him here so I'd know he was safe.

Duncan looked at me more closely. 'I appreciate that you

are under stress, Jenny, but there was no time to explain. I had to find out if any other messengers came into Fontainebleau tonight in addition to the one from Lord James.'

'And did they?' I asked, my calm returning.

'Yes, several . . .' he said slowly. 'And they were reporting to a variety of different people.'

'Oh.' I sat down upon a nearby stool. 'I forgot – there is a web of spies and counterspies all around this court.' I looked up at him. His face was unshaven, his eyes red-rimmed.

'It has taken all my skill and contacts to try to piece together what is happening. I've dispatched a courier of my own but won't know any details until he reports in,' he went on.

We sat together, not speaking, until dawn, when Duncan's messenger returned. They spoke in the corridor. When Duncan came back into the room, his face was grim.

'Four are dead. Lord James is not one of them.'

'Praise God for that at least! What cause?' I asked.

'The flux,' Duncan said deliberately. 'A doctor has stated that they died of the flux.'

'Poison,' I declared.

Duncan looked over his shoulder. 'Do not say such things.'

'But it's true.'

'All the more reason not to say it. The official story is the flux.'

'They were poisoned for certain. I know it.' Then I realized that I'd said too much, and turned away.

Duncan grabbed my wrist. 'What makes you think of poison?'

'Oh, I don't know.' I tried to sound offhand, but my pulse had quickened.

His fingers tightened their grip. 'Whom do you suspect? What do you know?'

'Nothing.'

'Under different circumstances I might have accepted that. But yesterday evening I caught you gorging yourself in the pantry and then spitting out pieces of food . . . as if you were testing them for poison.'

'You are hurting me,' I said, twisting my wrist out of his grasp. There was a red weal where his fingers had gripped me.

Duncan frowned and said, 'I do not mean to hurt you, Jenny. Whatever happens, please believe that. There is no harm intended to you.'

'The queen is awake and calling for you, Jenny.' Marie Beaton had come into the room.

'Ask if Duncan Alexander may be admitted,' I asked her. 'Say that he has some news that she would like to hear.'

Mary wept tears of happiness when she heard that Lord James was recovered. She sent everyone else away and then asked Duncan, 'Which Scots lord died first?'

'Crawford, Lord of Drumore.'

'Ahh!' Mary gasped.

'Lord Drumore was quite old,' said Duncan, 'his body worn out, less able to withstand the flux.'

'The flux?' Mary looked at him searchingly. 'You really think it was the flux?'

'A doctor diagnosed it.'

'Yes, but . . .'

We waited. There was something troubling her.

'Lord Drumore was one of my mother's closest confidants.'

'I know,' said Duncan.

A tear escaped Mary's eye and trickled down her cheek. 'I had made him a confidant of mine too. I know that letters can be read by others, so I thought, as I had something important and secret to tell my mother, that I might entrust it to him to deliver by word of mouth.'

'An important secret?' Duncan repeated.

My heart wobbled. There could be only one important secret that Mary had told this lord – the private papers she'd agreed to sign in addition to the public terms of her marriage contract.

'As you know,' she said, gazing at Duncan, 'my mother told me the names of the few – the very few – people at her court whom I might trust to personally convey secret messages between us. Lord Drumore was one.'

'You think that perhaps he may have been killed because of this?' Duncan asked.

Mary nodded, tears spilling down her face now.

Duncan let out a long breath. 'I do not know what this secret might be' – he held up his hand – 'nor do I wish to know. But this I will say, either Lord Drumore died to keep your secret, or he died because he believed he must tell your secret for the good of Scotland, and was prevented from doing so. Or' – Duncan knelt down by Mary's bed and looked directly into her eyes – 'Lord Drumore died because he caught the flux. No matter the cause, he died as a true Scot, and we should honour him for that.'

King Henri and Queen Catherine weren't overly concerned

with the fate of a few Scots lords. It was an inconvenience, in that it affected the mood of their son's wife and might delay her conceiving a child. But Catherine de' Medici considered there were far too many Scots nobles in France – and besides, soon after that another event was to have a fundamental effect on the future of both France and Scotland.

Chapter 11

We were with the king under the trees in the Long Walk behind the palace when the Spanish ambassador came scurrying towards us.

Queen Catherine gave him a peevish look. Occasions when she and King Henri could spend time surrounded by their family were rare and she resented any interruption. 'Sire, do please send that man away,' she pleaded, 'and let us enjoy our walk.'

King Henri patted her hand, which was nestling in the crook of her arm. 'Alas, I cannot. I fear he brings the news that all Europe awaits.'

We strolled on as the king withdrew to speak to the ambassador.

'Do you think Queen Mary of England has died?' Mary asked.

It wasn't so out of order that a Spaniard would bring us a message from England. The ailing Queen Mary Tudor was the daughter of a Spanish princess, Catherine of Aragon, and was married to King Philip of Spain.

'I confess I do not know' – Dauphin Francis yawned – 'nor do I much care.'

'You *should* care,' Catherine reprimanded him. 'Whoever takes the throne of England after her will have a great impact on France. And, my son,' she added, ignoring

Mary altogether, 'your father believes it should be you.'

Mary bit her lip at this slight to her own position. As granddaughter of the sister of Henry the Eighth, she could claim to be Queen Mary Tudor's nearest relative, but she did not contradict her mother-in-law. I looked from one to the other. Mary had told me that she didn't want the encumbrance of another volatile country; nor did she bear any ill will towards the princess Elizabeth, who, whether one believed her to be illegitimate or not, was a cousin of her blood. Queen Catherine's views were harder to discern. Long years of suffering the public presence of Diane de Poitiers had resulted in her becoming adept at hiding her true feelings. But recently I'd made time to dally with the ladies who attended her and gossiped about their mistress more freely than the Maries would about Mary, and so I knew that Catherine's overriding concern was the state of the treasury. She reckoned the new territory not worth the price it would cost in armaments and soldiers. Maintaining a court like ours was expensive, and Queen Catherine liked to spend money on extravagant spectacles and unusual artefacts and animals with which to impress visitors.

But Francis was bored and wandered off in the direction of the animal enclosures where exotic species were kept. Mary followed, trying in vain to coax him to return. When she came back without him, she was rewarded for her efforts by a look of disapproval from her mother-in-law.

'If Queen Catherine cannot make Francis take an interest in state affairs, how does she expect that I might?' Mary whispered to me.

'Queen Mary Tudor is dead,' the king announced as he rejoined us. 'May God greet her as one of His own for the work she has wrought for Him here on earth.'

'Amen,' said Queen Catherine in a noncommittal way, for on this she differed in opinion from her husband. She preferred appeasement and discourse rather than brute force when dealing with members of the Reformed faith.

'Amen,' we all repeated and blessed ourselves.

'And the succession?' Catherine prompted the king.

'As always, the English nobles are wrangling amongst themselves, but it will fall to the Boleyn brat, Elizabeth – who is, I am told, ready to declare herself, and her country, Protestant.'

'It is no surprise,' said the queen. 'That is the stamp of the coterie who wooed her favours these many years.'

The king lowered his voice. 'It means that Philip of Spain is in want of a wife. He has a son by his first marriage but the boy's health is not good. Therefore Philip is bound to seek a young bride to secure his dynasty.' He looked to where his eldest daughter, Elisabeth, was playing on the grass.

Catherine de' Medici nodded slowly. 'Uniting France with Spain makes a strong alliance for us against the English.'

Listening to this conversation, I was suddenly and frighteningly conscious of the great shift the world had taken. My reading of the Reformers' pamphlets and my rising awareness of politics meant that I could foresee the potential changes a new ruler of England might make upon the rest of the world.

Mary too grasped its import for her. 'England becoming Protestant puts Scotland and my mother in danger,' she said.

Queen Catherine looked askance at Mary for interrupting her own discussion with the king. But Henri, who made more recognition than his wife did of Mary's status as the crowned Queen of Scotland, acknowledged her by saying:

'When the English ambassador, Throckmorton, comes to me with the official news, I'll receive him in private and express my concerns. He will, of course, reassure me that all will be well. I will insist on certain points. He will undertake to communicate these to his new queen. I will . . .' The king flapped his hand in the air. 'And so on, and so on . . .' A crafty expression came over his face. 'Only after the coronation has taken place will I declare my outrage.'

'I understand,' said Queen Catherine. 'If you protested loudly now, then we'd attract any number of requests for you to provide money and arms to support a coup.'

King Henri nodded. 'Best to wait and see how things fall out. Elizabeth may not last long, or, if she does, some ambitious lord will wed her and beget a child upon her. Thereafter it would be him, not her, we'd deal with.' He mused for a moment and then said, 'Perhaps we might engineer who that lucky lord could be.'

'Husband,' Catherine said in the tone she used when she wished to broach a subject on which her husband might disagree, 'is it any worth to us to incorporate these islands within our realm?'

'Whoever controls the stretch of water between Europe and England can blockade the trade or troops of any other country wishing to pass through that channel. And there is wealth. Not so much in Scotland' – he glanced at Mary – 'but England has fertile pasture and cargoes coming from the New World. Yes, we will advance our claim through our son, and' – he pinched Mary's cheek – 'our much-loved adopted daughter.'

Mary looked bewildered. No amount of study of texts on

statehood could teach this level of guile. 'Sire . . .' She faltered. 'Papa . . .'

Queen Catherine looked with pride at her husband. 'Sire, you are a ruler most astute. In time France will govern all Europe.'

'But I—' Mary began again.

Catherine de' Medici waved her imperiously to silence.

The king was more benign. 'This is politics, my dear daughter,' he said kindly to Mary, 'which you may leave to your men-folk and elders to manage for you, hopefully for many years to come.' He turned to his wife. 'With regret I must go now. I should speedily compose a letter to King Philip lest anyone else moves before us. I will let you know if you need to prepare Elisabeth.' He kissed her hand – and I saw then that he did value his wife, not just for bearing him children to continue his line, but also for her efforts to understand and support his policies.

We strolled on in the direction Francis had taken, past the bear pit to the menagerie where the queen's pet monkeys were kept. Instantly recognizing her, her favourite swung across the spars of his cage towards us, jabbering in excitement.

'My pet!' Catherine's face dimpled in delight. She motioned for the cage door to be opened, whereupon the monkey leaped out into her arms. He put his tiny paws around her face and tried to kiss her, as she'd trained him to do.

'Clever thing,' she laughed. 'But I know you.' She wagged her finger in his face. 'You do this to please me, that I might give you a titbit.'

The animal keeper handed her some nuts, and seeing

this, the monkey clawed at the queen's fingers, scratching her enough to draw blood.

'Aiee!' She jerked away.

'Let me return him to his cage.' The flustered keeper made to grab the animal.

'No, no,' the queen said indulgently, wiping her bloody finger on a handkerchief given to her by an attendant. 'He is an animal and knows no better.' She waved away her ladies. 'I will take him with me on a solitary walk.'

With the monkey perched on her shoulder, the queen set off in a direction which, by discreet enquiry, I'd found out led to the Count of Cluny's house. Mary and the rest of the children were already on their way to meet Francis. What should I do? Catherine might be going to consult with her assassin. This was an opportunity . . . Yet I hesitated. If I was discovered spying, what excuse could I give? When the count spotted my red dress at the window in Blois, I told him that I'd not entered the study until after the queen had left. Unsure whether he was completely convinced, I later realized that it wasn't in the count's interests to let the queen know that their conversation might have been overheard. It would compromise his position and he'd lose valuable income. Also I believed that he thought he'd terrorized me into silence – even if I had heard anything. I recalled his dagger at my throat and I shivered. And yet, and yet . . . With political events changing so fast, I wanted to keep Mary, and indeed all of us, safe.

Keeping amongst the bushes and trees that lined the path, I followed the queen. Beyond the shrubbery she diverted onto a trail through a dense thicket to a long shed with a glass-panelled roof. She went inside. Like a persistent drum beat, part of my brain kept reminding of the danger I was in. But a greater impulse drove me on. Yes, I wished to protect Mary, but now, faced with the option to go further, I forced myself to acknowledge the most pressing reason I was here: I needed to know to what extent Duncan was involved with the Queen of France.

Cautiously I approached.

The murmur of voices. One demanding, the other obsequious.

The door was ajar. Carefully, carefully, I stepped over the lintel.

The Count of Cluny was speaking. 'I am working to perfect a quick-acting substance in the form of a pellet that dissolves instantly in liquid. It will be tasteless and cannot be detected in the body, yet is almost immediately fatal.'

'That is of interest . . .'

'And less violently painful,' he added.

Queen Catherine chuckled. 'That is of less concern, in most cases.'

'Ah, yes, majesty,' the count replied. 'These cases that you speak of . . .?'

There was a silence.

Awkwardly he continued, 'It is hard for me to know quite what action to take. Is it, as you've said before, to administer enough to keep the perso— the subject,' he quickly corrected himself, 'continuously unwell but alive, or should it be . . . a final act?'

The monkey began gibbering and the queen responded, making nonsense noises to him in return. Under cover of this I shifted my position, going right into the shed. I was now standing behind shelves with boxes stacked on top of each other, but I could see between them. The queen and the count were beside a table laden with scientific equipment and jars of potions and powders. The monkey had clambered up to perch on her shoulder.

Eventually the queen gave the count his answer: 'I will tell you when I seek a permanent solution.'

Again a silence, and then he spoke. 'And I should carry out this instruction even if the person is extremely close to you in kinship?'

'You see this monkey?' The queen gathered the animal to her breast, stroking his head and tickling his ear. 'You know how much I care for him.'

'Indeed, yes, he is frequently in your company.'

'You have witnessed the affection I bear him?'

'I have seen him sit at table with you and feed from your own plate.' The count looked mystified as to where this conversation was leading.

'But earlier today he scratched me.' The animal looked at the queen with bright eyes, head cocked to one side as if he sensed a change in her mood. 'Let me demonstrate to you how I deal with those who attack me.'

And Catherine de' Medici put her thumb on the windpipe of the monkey and, with a quick twist of her strong stubby fingers, she snapped the little creature's neck.

'Aaah!' I cried in horror and disgust.

It was fortunate that the queen's action also shocked the Count of Cluny. He let out an exclamation and his arm shot out, knocking over a pot, which shattered on the tiled floor.

In the confusion and noise, I fled.

Chapter 12

'The Princess Elizabeth cannot become Queen of England.'

It was February of the next year, 1559, and King Henri, having granted a public audience to Throckmorton, the English ambassador, made this statement in front of the whole court.

Throckmorton replied formally, 'With respect, majesty, she already has. Our new queen, Elizabeth, was crowned on the fifteenth of January.'

The king gave a dismissive gesture. 'It is not lawful. She is an illegitimate product of a union between England's previous king and a woman who was not his properly wedded wife.'

'In the eyes of England, Queen Elizabeth's mother, Anne Boleyn, was married to the king before their child was born.'

'That is impossible, for his first wife was still alive at the time.' King Henri shook his head. 'Think what might happen if kings did not respect their wives and allowed the children they sired elsewhere to inherit. There would be a thousand bastards fighting for the thrones of Europe.'

'Perhaps if a king truly respected his wife, then there would be no irregular offspring to upset the balance of power,' I said under my breath. To share someone I loved with another woman in this way would be unbearable.

'I suppose it is something that a queen must put up with,' Beside me Mary sighed, 'That's what my mother told me, and I know she had to, many times. But I don't think my husband, Francis, is capable of behaving in such a way . . .' She hesitated, as if about to say something else, but Throckmorton spoke again.

'Her majesty, Queen Elizabeth, has expressed a desire that France and England might seek a common good.'

King Henri regarded the ambassador for a long while before speaking and said finally, 'You may tell your upstart queen that I do not recognize her as such. The true claimant to the throne of England is my son's wife, Mary Stuart, whose grandmother was a sister of Elizabeth's father; she is therefore the nearest heir to King Henry the Eighth. And to that end the royal coat of arms of England will henceforth be included in that of my son, Dauphin Francis, and his wife.'

Throckmorton bowed his head.

'Pity him,' Duncan Alexander murmured, 'to have to convey those joyful tidings to his new English queen.'

Despite the shortness of her reign, tales of Elizabeth's fiery temper were already spreading.

'I've been told that she took a pair of scissors to a lady-in-waiting with whom she was displeased, and stabbed her in the back of her hand,' said Mary.

'Should we advise Throckmorton to keep both hands behind him when next he meets her?' asked Duncan.

We laughed, and then, looking at the forlorn expression on the face of the English ambassador, Mary said, 'Monsieur Throckmorton looks so downcast. As King Henri has concluded the official business, I will speak to him.'

She beckoned, and Throckmorton approached with a smile – another man who, despite his office, was under Mary's spell.

'I cannot help ease any of the words my adopted father has spoken,' Mary said gently, 'but perhaps we might talk of music for a while to relieve your stress.'

'You are so gracious,' he replied sincerely.

'Are you happy that our Queen Mary of Scots, your mentor and friend, is now proclaimed Queen of England?' Duncan Alexander fell into step beside me as I followed in Mary's train.

'A display of gamesmanship,' I said. 'Throckmorton will not send that message to England. King Henri has known of Queen Elizabeth's coronation for weeks and accepts the best he can hope for is that Elizabeth names Mary as her heir should she die childless. He agreed that Mary could wed his son so that, in time, France might rule England. He'll have her bear the English coat of arms, but he'll recognize Elizabeth as queen and conduct business with her, and indeed has probably already told the English ambassador this in private.'

'My lady Ginette!' Duncan halted in mock surprise. 'You have become a cynic?'

Witnessing how Catherine de' Medici, without mercy, dispatched her favourite pet, and knowing of King Henri's machinations to have his fourteen-year-old daughter, Elisabeth, become third wife to the King of Spain, many years her senior, had indeed made me more cynical. 'I have become wiser in the ways of the world,' I retorted.

'Is it because you are so much older now?'

Duncan knew my age, for he'd sent me a bouquet containing sixteen flowers for my birthday the previous month.

'You are being sarcastic at my expense, sir.'

'In no way,' he replied, but his eyes let me know that he was teasing.

'A girl is a woman at sixteen,' I said. 'Indeed, many are married by then.'

I wasn't being intentionally coy, but was gratified by the startled look on his face. 'Are you intending to be married?'

'I may be,' I said airily. 'Lots of suitors apply to our queen as to my availability.'

'Indeed' he replied, 'that may be one of them making such an enquiry at this very moment.'

The elderly Duke of Malpassant had stooped to kiss Mary's hand as she passed.

I refused to take his bait. 'What of yourself, Sir Duncan? Are there ladies in Scotland pining for your company?'

He laughed. 'Oh, my time is too much taken up with my official duties to be going courting.'

'And what exactly *are* your official duties?' I stopped and looked into his face.

'Ah . . .' Duncan glanced away. 'I do believe our queen requires my presence.'

And he was gone, giving me time to reflect that he had not answered my question. But this was frequently the way of it with him. He flitted in and out of the court and my life, sometimes away for weeks at a time. Mary never seemed to notice or comment on his absences. From his conversation I was sure that on occasion he'd been to Scotland, although my only trusted source of information on what was happening there was my father's letters.

In May my father wrote that John Knox was back in Scotland. With his preaching, and Queen Elizabeth encouraging the Protestant lords the strength of feeling against the French soldiers was increasing:

The English queen meddles in Scottish politics. As England provides shelter and support to the enemies of the queen regent of Scotland, it means they now have a safe refuge. Agents of Queen Elizabeth send swords and guns to the Border lords so that they are equipped to fight amongst themselves, and thus the best growing and grazing lands are constantly ravaged. The single exception is James Hepburn, Earl of Bothwell, who tries to keep the queen's rule in those lawless lands and has reaped English enmity by kidnapping their supply trains. The preacher John Knox now seeks the favour of Queen Elizabeth of England. No longer does he say a woman is an unnatural ruler – well, not to her, at any rate.

If only half the stories about the English queen were true, then it was wise of John Knox to ally himself with her. If he got in the way of Elizabeth, she'd snap him like a dry twig.

By June we were in Paris again to celebrate the wedding of King Henri's sister, and the betrothal of his daughter Elisabeth to the King of Spain. Elisabeth was younger than Mary and me, and had never met this older man but was ready to obey the wishes of her parents. It made me glad that I was not of royal blood for such a fate to befall me.

We'd had no rain for weeks and Dauphin Francis complained that the stifling heat of the city sapped his strength. On the day of the tournaments, unable to compete, he was carried on a litter to the Rue de St Antoine, where lists had been erected in the courtyard of the Tournelles Palace.

By chance the royal retinue arrived at the same time as that of the king's mistress, Diane de Poitiers. It was immediately obvious that Diane's seat was nearer the king than was the queen's. The two women regarded each other.

'You are well, madam?' Diane de Poitiers enquired.

I wasn't sure if the use of 'madam' rather than 'majesty' was an intended slight. Her demeanour was amiable but she couldn't be unaware that Catherine de' Medici, not being of true nobility, might take this as an insult.

'I am well enough,' the queen replied, giving the other woman no title at all, 'and glad that my eyesight is still youthful enough that I do not require proximity to an object to view it properly.'

This was a direct reference to Diane's age. She was years older than both the queen and the king, and had lately been seen using a magnifying glass when reading letters.

The barb went home. The queen was well pleased: she had bested her rival by hinting that Diane's special place was due to her failing eyesight.

But as Catherine walked on Diane smiled and spoke clearly to one of her attendants. 'Take this favour to the king' – she plucked the corsage from her wrist – 'and ask him to bear my colours in the tournament today.'

We took our seats in the grandstand. It was a sultry day with low cloud and a shimmering heat haze. As the king appeared a rumble of thunder sounded over the turrets of the Bastille prison. He wore the colours of his mistress, the white and black ribbons of Diane de Poitiers.

Catherine de' Medici clicked her fingers and a page ran off with a message for her husband. On receiving it, the king shook his head. When the page returned, she listened to the answer, cuffed the boy's ear, and sent him running back.

Mary gave Francis a questioning look.

'My mother had a vision of ill omen last night,' he told her. 'She sends a message to my father to ask him not to enter the lists.'

The king was about to mount his horse when the page approached him again. He brushed the boy aside roughly, sending him sprawling.

Courtiers were whispering behind their fingers and fans:

'Last night the king's wife dreamed she saw him lying in a pool of blood.'

'She has many dreams, our Queen of France. Too much dabbling in the occult, too much listening to the nonsense of soothsayers . . .'

I thought of Nostradamus.

King Henri sat in his saddle and waited while his squire selected a lance. The long rays of the evening sun reflected on his breastplate. His horse pawed the ground, the movement causing the light to dazzle on the emblem of the golden lion. It flashed, brilliant, like summer lightning and I flung up my hand to protect my sight. Too late. The intense glare had imprinted on my eyeballs the image of a lion. I squeezed my eyelids shut. Etched in red, the lion lingered before slowly fading to black. When I opened my eyes, around me, people were rubbing their own. I glanced at Catherine de' Medici. It was obvious that she'd had the same experience. From shielding her eyes her hands dropped into her lap, and then realization swept across her features. She let out a yelp of alarm and scrambled to her feet. Seeking the exit from the stand Catherine pushed courtiers out of the way. But when she reached the wooden staircase, her passage was barred by Duke Fernand, a cousin of the Duke of Guise, who was in the company of some other high-ranking nobles.

'Let me pass,' she demanded.

These men were slow to obey her command. They regarded her almost insolently, for they considered the blood that flowed in their veins more royal than hers. To them she was the daughter of common Italian merchants who'd clawed their way to prominence.

Catherine de' Medici almost stamped her foot in frustration. 'I know you think of me as a banker's daughter, but be mindful that the banker is the person who controls the money, and without money you are nothing!' she spat. 'Nothing!'

Duke Fernand wiped an imaginary speck of dust from the sleeve of his doublet and moved aside with calculated deliberation.

'History may not remember me,' Catherine hissed as she passed him, 'but your face is one I will not forget.'

'Now he has made an enemy for life,' a courtier commented.

'Perhaps for death,' muttered another.

Catherine's path to the king was clear, but already the squire was handing him his lance. She began to run. Ungainly in form and with sleeves flapping, she was a comic figure. Unkind remarks accompanied her progress and she stumbled and almost fell over.

'Hush!' Mary turned with a severe look to reprimand the ladies who were tittering in amusement.

Queen Catherine spoke quietly to her husband so we could not hear what she said, but his reply carried to us on the still air.

'Madam,' he said, not too unkindly, 'I ask you to desist. You are making an exhibition of yourself.'

She shook her head and continued to urge him not to fight.

'The lances are wooden' – the king showed her – 'made to break at the slightest impact.'

'It has been foretold . . .' Catherine's voice was louder now, more urgent. She took hold of the king's stirrup to stay him.

'Nay, wife.' The king was in no mood to debate further. 'You have made it that I cannot leave the field. Who would honour a king who ran away from combat at the behest of a woman and a necromancer?' He spurred his horse on, and it lumbered forward with his wife trotting pathetically behind.

She stopped, stretched out her arms and raised her tearful face to Diane de Poitiers who was seated in the stand above her. 'Speak to him,' she implored. 'As you do love the king, speak to him.'

A rapid buzz of interested chat ran among the onlookers. Fed a surfeit of tittle-tattle, they lapped up this exciting new gossip. The queen had appealed to the king's mistress for help! In public! Catherine de' Medici, acknowledging the love between Diane de Poitiers and the king, had let the court know that where she'd failed to persuade him, his mistress might succeed! The queen humiliating herself by owning that Diane had more influence over King Henri's actions than her!

Diane de Poitiers shrugged. It was graciously done and sympathetic, as if to say, *What can one do? We are mere women, and when a man's mind is set on a certain course then he can't be dissuaded.*

Mary said, 'At tournaments, men are like boys playing with toy soldiers—' She glanced at her husband. It was one of Francis's favourite pastimes: arranging his collections of soldiers, winning battles he'd never have the strength to fight in real life. Mary lifted his limp hand and kissed it. He smiled at her. His love for her was such that he'd never take offence at anything she said.

The elegantly coiffured Diane de Poitiers leaned back in her seat, but a worry line had appeared on her forehead. After my resolution to become a spy for Mary, I'd cultivated friendships with different ladies in the households of both Catherine and Diane. I'd discovered that Diane also consulted magicians and regularly had her horoscope cast. Her manner, which had previously been relaxed, enjoying the sight of King Henri decked out in her colours, now betrayed a thread of tension. He saluted her and then turned and made a conciliatory gesture to his wife. As if to mollify them both he pulled the visor of his helmet firmly down over his face.

'There,' Francis reassured Mary, 'my father is well protected – his face encased in a cage of metal.'

The lion in his cage! It was if Nostradamus were speaking in my ear.

I leaned forward. Duncan Alexander stood a few paces from me. He was scanning the crowds, methodically working his way along each section. As I watched, he gave a tiny shake of his head. I followed his gaze and saw a man in a short blue cloak acknowledge his signal.

Meanwhile Catherine de' Medici, retaking her seat, began mumbling to herself.

'The queen is praying,' Mary said.

But it wasn't a prayer. I recognized the words; the same phrases were echoing in my head. The words of Nostradamus:

The young lion shall overcome the old,
On martial field in single combat.
In a golden cage, his eye will be put out.
Two into one, then to die a cruel death.

For this joust the king was opposing Montgomery, the young captain of the Scots Guard. They advanced to their positions at either end of the lists. There was a quietness in the air, the hush before an expected din. The call to arms trumpeted out and they rode against each other. The horses' hooves kicked up clouds of dust from the dry sand spread across the street. The crowd cheered, but the two men passed each other without contact.

'Our king has been affected by his wife's untimely interruption.' Duke Fernand's voice, although low, was audible.

The queen gave him a venomous look.

The joust resumed. Coming together with a tremendous clash, the king jolted his opponent, causing him to drop his lance. The crowd roared and Captain Montgomery accepted defeat. However, the king would not agree to the submission as he had failed to unseat his opponent.

The Scot rode back to his station. His men were about him, conferring. One of them wore a short blue cloak. Captain Montgomery bent to listen to this man and then removed his helmet.

'Inform his majesty that I concede the joust. I will not ride a further time.'

Catherine de' Medici sighed with relief and Diane de Poitiers looked grateful.

But King Henri sent his personal attendant to Captain

Montgomery to say: 'His majesty does not accept your submission. He challenges you to joust again.'

The Scot returned a message: 'Beg his majesty to declare me a coward, for I would decline.'

Another messenger from King Henri, this time a nobleman: 'It is not possible for Captain Montgomery to decline. The king insists you must ride against him once more. It is a command. You cannot disobey.'

The exchange was relayed to the tiered ranks of onlookers. When she heard that the king would joust for a third time, his queen groaned and wrapped her arms around her stomach. Mounted and armed once again, with a wooden lance apiece, the two men trotted to either end of the lists and gathered themselves for the third encounter.

'No . . .' Catherine whispered. 'No. Please. Fate spins on the number three.'

The fanfare of the trumpet.

The fall of the flag.

The horses heaving and panting – the setting sun a red ball of fire.

'Henri! Henri! For France and King Henri!'

A thunder of hooves and a roar of noise. Nobles and commoners alike leap to their feet. The king's lance misses, but with a hideous *crack!* the lance of his rival, Captain Montgomery, strikes the plumed crest of the king's helmet.

And shatters.

A shout went up: 'A broken lance! King Henri breaks his rival's lance! Long live the king!'

Holding the jagged stump of his lance, Montgomery went on to the end of the lists. King Henri wavered in his saddle. Then he straightened up and everyone applauded.

But Catherine de' Medici had risen to her feet.

'The king!' she screamed. 'The king! Look to the king!'

What was amiss? What had she, the loyal wife, seen that no one else had noticed? Or was it just her belief in the prophecy that prompted her reaction?

King Henri's horse slowed to a walk and the reins fell slackly from his fingers.

'The king is hurt,' said one of the nobles.

'By a wooden lance?' another commented. 'King Henri can take many a blow like that without quitting the field.'

Then I heard Duncan Alexander say in a serious tone, 'There is a piece of wood sticking out of his visor.'

Catherine de' Medici had already left her place, and even the normally composed Diane de Poitiers stood up.

Mary clutched at my arm.

The king's head slumped on his chest, and he would have fallen from his horse had not his equerries caught him. They laid him on the ground and removed his helmet. A long splinter of wood protruded from his right eye. Blood poured from the wound, staining the sand red around the fallen king.

Chapter 13

King Henri was carried into the Palace of the Tournelles in agony.

Nobles and courtiers streamed after the procession, some silenced by shock, others shouting incoherent suggestions. But his wife, Catherine, displaying her worth as the king's consort, took charge. Issuing commands, she summoned the most experienced doctors to think how best to remove the piece of broken lance that had pierced his right eye and penetrated his brain.

I went into the king's bedchamber with Mary and Francis. In one corner, standing beside a table, were a group of doctors and a barber surgeon. They were studying a row of severed heads with splinters of wood protruding at various angles from their eye sockets. The surgeon was in the process of sawing off the top section of one head to reveal the brain inside.

Mary put her handkerchief to her mouth.

'Well?' Queen Catherine, who'd been pacing the floor, rounded on them. 'What are your conclusions? How are we to proceed?'

The doctors shuffled their feet, spread their hands and wouldn't meet her gaze.

'My husband, the king, has a piece of wood in his eye that must be removed, else he will not live!' The queen's voice was husky with pent-up emotion. 'You must find a safe method of doing this.'

'We have tried to simulate his majesty's condition'– the surgeon indicated the inside of the skull he was working on – 'but the situation requires extra study.'

The king's personal physician agreed. 'There is insufficient information as to where the damage has been done.'

'Further harm might be inflicted by trying to ease the splinter out,' said another doctor.

And here was the crux of the matter. If the king died in his present state, then it would be from wounds caused by someone else, the hapless Captain Montgomery. But if he died due to the doctors' ministrations, then they could be held responsible for killing him. It was clear even to those with no medical training that this was a hopeless case, but Catherine de' Medici was refusing to accept that her husband was doomed.

'You need more heads for experiment?' she demanded.

Immediately the doctors nodded in agreement – anything to put off the moment when they had to move the bloodied splinter within the king's head.

Catherine hurried to the door leading to the outer chamber and called for the constable in charge of the Bastille prison. 'More!' she addressed herself to this old man. 'We need more heads of executed prisoners to simulate the king's wound in order to find out how to save him.'

'I brought you the heads of all I have,' he replied.

'There must be others who are shortly awaiting execution.'

'There is one prisoner due to be executed tomorrow.'

'Do it today.'

The constable had lived a long time and served under Henri's father; he was not to be bullied. 'The prisoner is a high-ranking noble awaiting his wife, who is travelling to see him before he dies. She should arrive by nightfall with their new-born son. King Henri gave express permission that this visit was to be allowed.'

'Execute him *now*!' the queen shouted in his face. 'Bring me his head within the hour. And any other who is awaiting execution,' she added.

The constable stood his ground. 'Apart from this wretched man there are no prisoners in custody who have been sentenced to death.'

'Well then, choose one that has offended our person most and have him beheaded.'

'Begging your pardon, majesty . . .' The constable spoke slowly. 'I do not understand. Do you mean I should behead someone who has committed a minor offence?'

'I don't care what they have done!' the queen shrieked. 'They may have spat in the street or failed to fly a flag on a holy day.'

The constable folded his arms. For a second it seemed as though he might disobey the queen. Then he looked beyond her into the room where the king was propped on his pillows. His gaze encompassed Francis, the king-to-be, fidgeting and nervous at the bedside, and, almost visibly, the thought passed through his head: with Henri gone, the true power in France would rest with Catherine de' Medici.

'Bring me a death warrant and I will have the king sign it.' As the constable still hesitated, Catherine, her face contorted with rage, stabbed a finger at him. 'Tell whoever resists my order that I might decide to use them as model and stick a splinter through their eye deep into their brain without the benefit of first removing their head!'

As the constable left, another man entered the outer chamber. I retreated quickly as the queen went forward to greet the Count of Cluny.

'You have brought something to ease the king's suffering?'

'I have, majesty – a powerful opiate I prepared with my own hand. A teaspoonful will dull the pain.'

The queen took the leather bottle the count gave her and went to offer it to the king, holding it to his lips that he might swallow a few drops. 'I have something for you, beloved,' she comforted him. 'This will give you rest while your doctors find a way to help you.'

'I am beyond help,' the king groaned. 'Were I commoner or king there is nothing can be done. Such a trifling accident to end my time on this earth.'

'*Accident?*' Catherine choked on the word. 'Carelessness, I'd say, on the part of your opponent.'

'Blame not the Scot,' Henri whispered. 'Blame not good Captain Montgomery. Blame not the Scot.'

But, like a maddened lioness, the queen needed to vent her fury. Bidding the priest resume the communal prayers, she went to the window and beckoned the count to her. Using the drone of voices as cover, she said to him, 'I thank you for this healing potion and for any other service where you might give aid . . . for there are vermin within our palace. You hear what I say: *vermin.*'

'I hear you, majesty, as I have heard you in the past.'

She gave a curt nod. 'So deal with it as you did before.'

I too heard her and, remembering how the queen had

throttled her pet monkey, took the earliest opportunity to slip away to warn Captain Montgomery. In the corridor of the annexe that led to his quarters, I almost bumped into Duncan Alexander. He was standing in close conversation with the man in the short blue cloak I'd seen him signal to during the joust – the same man who'd persuaded Captain Montgomery to ask the king to be excused from jousting for a third time.

Duncan jumped back when he saw me. 'Jenny! You shouldn't be in this area of the palace.'

'Why are you here then?' I asked.

There was an awkward silence while the man in the blue cloak looked me over in an interested manner. He was shorter than me but well built, with reddish-brown hair, a short beard and moustache . . . and the boldest eyes I'd ever come across.

'Oh, I do like her spirit,' he drawled in the accent of the Scottish Borders. 'You might introduce me, Duncan, so that I can be ready should you ever tire of her company.'

I blushed at his familiarity. Duncan responded by giving him a rough shove. 'Get on with it, James. Lives depend upon your speed.'

'Who is that person?' I asked as the man swaggered off down the corridor.

'James Hepburn, Earl of Bothwell.'

The infamous Bothwell! A womanizer and argumentative warlord who prowled his Border lands fighting with anyone who got in his way.

'And before you say anything about him, Jenny, I am aware of Bothwell's reputation. What is less well known is that he's one of the most loyal men on earth and has pledged allegiance to the Scottish crown and Mary's mother.'

'You have sent him to warn Captain Montgomery to leave the court.' I said this as a fact rather than a question.

'The captain is best away from here' – Duncan took my arm to walk me to the royal apartments –'as we also should be.'

'What made you send word to tell him?' I wondered how Duncan knew the queen's intentions as he hadn't been in the room when she'd spoken to the Count of Cluny.

He laughed. 'A blind cat can see that Catherine de' Medici will hold everlasting hatred for the man responsible for the death of her husband, even though it was an accident. It's only fair that Captain Montgomery should be informed that the king will soon die, and that when he does she'll need someone to blame. Her ire will be all the greater to avoid acknowledging that perhaps she herself may have had a hand in it.'

'The queen!' I exclaimed. 'It is inconceivable that she wanted her husband dead.'

'She may have contributed to the accident by distracting his concentration with her dire warnings,' said Duncan. 'Also the king has suffered dizzy spells these last weeks and he might have ridden gently to finish off the day of celebration. But her behaviour at the lists goaded him into a full gallop to prove his courage. I had Bothwell speak to Captain Montgomery to advise him to stand down, but by that time it was too late.'

'So you don't believe in prophecy?'

'I seek a practical cause for everything.' Duncan appeared amused. 'I thought you studied scientific books?'

'Yes, but . . .' I recalled the divination session I'd

witnessed with the queen and her soothsayer, Ruggieri. 'I know those who have seen strange images in mirrors called up by prophets.'

'Ah, yes.' Duncan was smiling broadly now. 'The magic mirror trick.'

'Are you so sure it is trickery?'

'These so-called prophets work by suggesting strongly what you might want to hear and see. They induce a certain mood in their audience, sometimes using pungent scents or offering strong wine as refreshment.'

Queen Catherine had eaten food and drunk wine in the tower that night! By telling her what she *should* see, had Ruggieri induced her to imagine what he said was there? It could be so, given her emotional state, combined with the alcohol she'd drunk and the smoke from the incense clouding the room. Except . . .

'That does not explain the sound of the baby crying,' I said.

'What baby? Where?' Duncan regarded me curiously.

'In the queen's tower.' The words were out before my brain caught up with my mouth.

'Ah!' Duncan breathed. 'You *were* there that night. I thought I smelled your perfume when I was climbing the stairs.'

I recovered from my confusion. 'And so were you,' I accused him. 'You admit that you were consulting with Catherine de' Medici in secret?'

'I wasn't in the tower to conspire with the Medici woman.' He looked at me intently. 'Were you?'

'Me! You think that I might ally myself with her?'

'If not, then why were you there?'

'I – I was interested in the prophecies, for they mentioned Mary's name. Why were *you* there?'

'For the same reason,' he replied.

We stared at each other. And then suddenly there were footsteps in the corridor. The sound of soldiers' boots. A flash of alarm crossed Duncan's face. 'That's the escort party for Captain Montgomery. Pray Bothwell got to him in time.'

'We are trapped here,' I said in fear, 'and could be arrested on suspicion of helping him escape. There's no other reason we might be in this corridor at this time.'

'Oh, I can think of one.' Duncan grinned, then grasped me forcibly round the waist and, pulling me towards him, crushed my body against his in a tight embrace. One of the approaching soldiers whistled. I barely heard it, for Duncan's mouth was on mine, his lips half open, pressing down, and my body was betraying me by responding.

The soldiers marched past. We staggered apart, I in shock, not only at Duncan's wild advance but at my own reaction.

'Forgive me, Lady Ginette, for that gross intrusion, but I thought it the only way to avoid us being implicated.'

I had no chance to reply, for Duncan grabbed my hand in his and we ran away together, only slowing down when we'd returned to the main part of the palace.

'So' – he continued our conversation as though we'd never been interrupted – 'you heard a baby cry that night in the queen's tower?'

My heart was racing, and not just with the exertion of running, but I decided I could be as cool as he. 'Indeed I did. Ruggieri mentioned the queen's dead child and I distinctly heard a baby cry.'

'A bird outside the window?' Duncan suggested. 'A seagull can make a noise like that.'

'It was night. And anyway, it would be very coincidental for that to occur just when it was needed.'

'Perhaps Ruggieri himself made the sound, like a court jester who can throw his voice and make it appear to come from elsewhere.'

'Maybe,' I said, not wholly convinced. 'But it did sound like a baby crying.'

By this time we were at the king's apartments. Duncan touched my sleeve. 'Best we're not seen entering the chamber together. I'll take my leave of you here.'

And once again, like a will o' the wisp, he was gone.

One of Diane de Poitiers' ladies stood in the outer chamber. She'd been sent to beg that her mistress might have a moment with the king, at least to say farewell. Queen Catherine was leaving the king's bedroom to eat some of the food laid out on sideboards. The woman seized her chance and prostrated herself before her. 'My mistress begs to serve your grace in these difficult times in any way she can.'

Catherine de' Medici narrowed her eyes, inspecting this representative of her rival as a snake might its intended victim. Her tongue flickered. 'There is no service that I deem your mistress capable of performing for me, be it the lowliest task of a scullery maid. But tell her it would serve *her* well if she left my court.'

An hour or so later I took Mary away so that she might also have some supper and change her clothes. The Maries were waiting for us in our rooms with all the latest news.

'Diane de Poitiers is already gone from court,' Marie Seton told us, 'begging mercy for any wrong she may have done.'

'She's returned the jewels that King Henri gave her,' said Marie Livingston, who minded Mary's jewellery and had an interest in such matters.

'My mother has directed me to write Diane de Poitiers a merciful letter,' said Francis, who was resting on a couch, taking refuge with Mary in order to stay out of Catherine's way, 'but mention in it that she might still merit punishment for exerting malign influences over the king.'

'Your mother instructed you to do this?' said Mary in surprise.

'It will be to keep Diane biddable,' Marie Fleming suggested, 'and because the queen wants the Château of Chenonceau from her with as little trouble as possible.'

'It's the most beautiful château in all France,' said Marie Beaton.

'Although my mother grieves for my father, she revels in the fact that she now has power over her former rivals and enemies,' Francis explained.

'I do not question your mother's motives.' Mary went and knelt beside her husband. 'It is only that, my love, when you are crowned King of France, *no one* can tell you what to do.'

There was a silence as the listeners were sharply reminded that, despite her sweet nature, Mary Stuart had been crowned Queen of Scots in her infancy and schooled all her life in the absolute rights of an anointed monarch.

Catherine de' Medici strove in vain to save her husband.

More severed heads were maimed until the king himself, in a lucid moment, called for an end to further experiments.

'I have spoken with my doctors,' he told his wife when

she begged him to reconsider. 'There is sepsis in my brain. My feet and hands are swollen beyond recognition and I am losing my bodily functions of movement, sight and speech. Soon my mind will follow.'

He reached his hand out to her. 'Late did I come to loving thee,' he said, 'but know that I did, as best I could.'

At these words, which she'd waited a lifetime to hear, Catherine broke down completely.

'Now bring our children,' King Henri commanded. 'Let me look upon their sweet faces one last time.'

Mary carried the smallest infant in her arms as the king gave them all his last blessing and bade them not forget him. Then he called his eldest son to him separately to give words of advice and instruction on looking after the kingdom.

Francis left his father's bedchamber haggard with fright and apprehension. He ran to Mary, crying, 'Papa is dying. What shall I do?'

'We will pray.' She led him to the kneeler below the crucifix on the wall of her room. 'King Henri was a good king and God will welcome him into Heaven.'

'I have no anxiety over my father's fate.' Tears trickled from Francis's eyes. 'It is myself that I fear for. They will make me king and I won't know what to do.'

Mary put her arms around her husband's thin shoulders. 'With God's grace we will rule together, husband dear. Do not fret.'

Francis went to lie down, and so I knelt with Mary for a while at her prie-dieu. I joined her in praying for King Henri, for we held him in affection and honour. He had welcomed us into his household and family, and we were deeply sad that he would soon pass away. Mary's faith was strong, more complete than mine. She knew that I read the writings of the Reformers and had even looked at some of these herself, but she would never abandon the old religion.

'My faith fills me up,' was how she explained it to me, 'and satisfies all the needs of my heart and body, soul and spirit.'

She had recourse to her religion to see her through this crisis. In need of consolation at the loss of a surrogate father, she asked her uncle, the cardinal, to have masses said and then spent time in the convent at Rheims with her Aunt Renée.

King Henri finally died on the tenth of July 1559, and almost immediately a coterie of favour-seekers clustered around Mary. She wanted to believe that they shared her sadness, but knew that the underlying reason was that she was the wife of the future king. As soon as Francis was crowned, Mary would be queen of one of the leading countries in the world; she was fabulously wealthy, and able to bestow gifts and take revenge on anyone who'd slighted her.

The Maries discussed the situation endlessly. 'Our Mary will be Queen of France,' they said, 'and help rule the court and the country. As widow of the former king, Catherine de' Medici is now a Queen Dowager these matters are no longer her concern.'

Duncan Alexander smiled when he heard this. 'Plotting and power-wielding have too long been a part of the life of the Medici woman,' he said. 'She'll not give it up now.'

Chapter 14

In September the bells of the Cathedral of Rheims pealed out to announce a new king.

As it was scarce two months since the death of his father, Mary had advised her husband to wear a suit of burgundy velvet, while she'd adopted white for her royal mourning. Francis, who loved bright colours and ostentatious displays of wealth, often appeared ridiculous when bedecked with rings and earrings and clad in cloth of gold and heavy lace. Today, with Mary at his side, the young king looked regal. Catherine de' Medici, officially now the Queen Dowager, was in deepest black and bore a new personal insignia of a broken lance. But it was the banners of the new King and Queen of France that caused most comment, for amidst the French and Scottish emblems was the English coat of arms.

Duncan's face was grave. 'I thought that with King Henri dead they'd have had the good sense to drop that pretension. Imagine the fury of Elizabeth of England when she reads the report her ambassador is sure to send her.'

'Mary is strongly influenced by her Guise relatives,' I said. 'They try to convince Mary that the English throne is her birthright.'

'At this very moment Mary's mother is struggling to keep even the Scottish throne secure for her daughter. She has barely enough troops at her disposal to defend Edinburgh, and cannot contain the rebels as she would like. The preacher Knox whips up his Scottish congregations to civil disobedience while many of the Protestant lords seek money and armed men from England to help them overthrow her.'

I already knew some of this from my father's letters. Duncan must have his own private sources of news. But if he was friendly with James Hepburn, the Earl of Bothwell, then he would be able to travel swiftly to and from Scotland: in addition to being a Border lord, Bothwell was Admiral of the Scottish navy, with a choice of ships under his command.

'The Guises wish to rule the world,' Duncan went on. 'If left unchecked, they will bring ruin to this country and mine.'

But who was there to restrain them? At the moment neither Francis nor Mary were enjoying good health. Francis's strength seemed to have dissipated further. He was now racked with coughs and his skin erupted in boils. Mary, who desperately desired to have a child, was suffering from bouts of swooning in an attempt to convince herself that she might be pregnant. Letters from her mother had prompted her to ask for an increase in the supply of arms and soldiers to Scotland.

She was distressed by the response. 'They are refusing to do it, Jenny!' Mary was trembling when she told me. 'I am Queen of France and Francis is king, and they will not do as we have requested!' She gave a harsh laugh. 'The queen dowager said I could leave her to manage the affairs of state and suggested that I occupy myself by planning the festivities to celebrate Christmas. I went to my Guise uncles and told them that my mother, their sister, is surrounded by enemies, and they say there is nothing they can do. I explained that she needs more soldiers to arrest the preacher, Knox, and the rest of those involved in this uprising, but they will not order a fleet of ships to go to her aid!'

'Francis's sister has been welcomed in Spain by her new husband, King Philip,' I said. 'And while we are happy for her, it means that France has secured the friendship of a larger country and no longer needs Scotland as an ally against England.'

'Then what will become of my mother and my realm?' Mary cried.

I shook my head. 'I do not know,' I said.

My father had written to say that he'd had to sell some of his furniture to pay his soldiers' wages. By Christmas everyone knew the seriousness of the situation in Scotland. The Protestant lords declared that, because of her French sympathies and Catholic religion, Mary's mother was not fit to be regent. They deemed her views injurious to the wellbeing of Scotland; her place should be taken by the head of the Hamilton Stuarts, who, after Mary, was next in line to the Scottish throne.

It was now apparent that there was also a power struggle going on in France between the queen dowager and the Guises as to who was actually ruling. To curb the mounting civil unrest, Catherine favoured appeasement and tolerance of Protestant views, whereas the Guises wished the reformers exterminated. But these reformers were not merely religious zealots. Among their number were high-ranking nobles who wanted change, and they began to join forces.

Worry about her mother overcame Mary and she took to her bed. With Francis also ill with winter fever, the court moved to Blois, where it was thought the air was better, for them both to recover. And it was at Blois in the spring of the new year that a messenger arrived to say that the Scots lords had signed an agreement with Queen Elizabeth· English soldiers would be sent to Scotland to fight the French army and drive them out.

'My mother's health is breaking down under the strain.' Mary lay in her bed and wept. 'She suffers from palpitations of the heart. English troops have entered Scotland and she is in extreme danger.'

'As we are – if we remain here . . .'

I caught my breath. Duncan Alexander had appeared unannounced in the doorway of the queen's bedchamber. 'Sir!' I protested.

'Here are men's clothes, plain and dark, for yourself and the queen,' he told me brusquely. 'Put them on and prepare to leave at once.'

'Her grace cannot be moved,' I said.

'There are rebels gathering in every village,' he told me. 'If we stay here, we will be trapped in a castle we cannot defend.'

'How do you know this?' I folded my arms. 'I will do nothing until you explain yourself.'

Duncan grabbed my shoulders and shook me. 'I'm going to the stables to arrange transport,' he said tersely. 'If you are not in boots, hose and tunic by the time I return then I will strip that gown from you and dress you myself.' He strode out of the room.

I rang the calling bell, and the Maries hurried in to assist the queen. Fingers fumbling, I donned the clothes as Duncan had instructed, and was barely finished when he returned. We began to put together some of Mary's things.

'Take no luggage,' he said. 'Bring only what is essential.'

Marie Livingston dumped the cases containing Mary's most precious jewels on the bed and bundled them in the top sheet. 'I'm ready,' she announced.

'Good girl!' said Duncan, and I was pricked by a thorn of jealousy that he'd praised her and not me.

Quickly I emptied our personal papers into a carrying bag and tied it to my waist.

'My husband, the king . . .' Mary's voice shook but she was calm. 'I cannot leave without him.'

'Arrangements have been made for King Francis and his mother. We are travelling separately.'

Carriages stood in the courtyard. Duncan helped me and the queen into one and got in himself. It was then that I noticed he was fully armed. We jolted out of the gate and onto the road for Paris, Mary and I clinging to each other as we were tossed from side to side. After about ten minutes Duncan stuck his head out of the window and shouted for the coachman to halt. He had the door open and the steps down before the wheels stopped turning.

'Get out as fast as you can and run for the trees,' he told us. Then he threw a bag of coins to the driver. 'Carry on to Paris. Stop for no one.'

We crouched in the bushes by the side of the road as the coach thundered away. Duncan took two daggers from his belt and handed one to the queen and one to me, saying quietly, 'Slide that down inside your boot. Hopefully you'll not have need of it.'

Mary gave a tiny cry of fear.

'Hush, I implore you,' he whispered.

Keeping low, we followed him on a rough track through the woods until we came to the river. There was a barge moored to the bank, of the type used to transport goods. The bargeman sat gnawing on a piece of cheese. He must have heard us but didn't turn his head as we clambered aboard and crouched down among the barrels and boxes. When we were settled Duncan cupped his hands over his mouth and imitated a bird call. The man threw the remainder of his bread into the water and cast off, poling his craft out into midstream so that the current would carry it forward. In this way Mary and I came safely to the huge castle at Amboise on the Loire.

And there we lived through a nightmare of utter horror.

Chapter 15

At first the reports of an armed uprising appeared to be a false alarm.

After fleeing Blois, the court reassembled, secure behind the ramparts of the heavily fortified castle at Amboise, and an effort was made to try to continue as normal. It seemed that the greatest inconvenience was to our new king, Francis. As no one could safely venture outside the castle, he was prevented from hunting. But by now I was well acquainted with one of Catherine de' Medici's ladies and knew that she was extremely worried. Infiltrators had reported back to her that the most prominent leader of the reformers, a man called La Renaudie, had met with representatives of a number of noble families at a place called Hugues. Among these were some who might make claim upon the throne, and they had agreed to supply the dissenters with men and arms. The movement was now an armed rebellion which could escalate into war.

On a personal level I was seriously angry with Duncan Alexander. He'd spoken to me rudely, giving me orders as though I were his servant. Moreover, despite his apparent loyalty to Mary, there was no real indication of where his sympathies lay. From previous discussions with him I knew that he was a religious sceptic, but I'd taken that to include all religions. Was he with these reformers or not? That he himself was a spy, and perhaps even ran a network of agents, was very likely. He'd had advance warning that an attempt was to be made to capture the king and had arranged our route to freedom through local contacts. But Mary wouldn't entertain any criticism of him. When I asked her how she thought Sir Duncan Alexander was able to get us secretly to Amboise, she said, 'Does it matter how he did it, Jenny? We are safe now.'

The episode energized Mary. The enforced activity of our flight and the success of the escape galvanized her into attempting to become more involved in state affairs. In this way she hoped to help her mother and her native country. She insisted on attending an ambassadors' reception arranged by Catherine de' Medici, who wanted to show the world that rebel factions would not be allowed to interfere with the running of the court.

'At times I am overcome with stress about our situation here; but then I think of my mother in Scotland, who is holding out against the rebellion of her lords,' Mary told me.

For once I took strength from her to calm my own anxieties. My father's latest letter was a scribbled note to say that the French troops were besieged in the port of Leith, while Mary's mother was a few miles away, trapped in Edinburgh Castle.

'I know that God has set me upon this earth for a purpose,' said Mary. 'Thus I will endeavour to do His will. Now let us show that we are not intimidated by any threat to our person.'

She waved Duncan towards me. 'Join me in the morelia. They perform this dance in England, and anything they can do, we must excel at even more.'

Duncan bowed and held out his hand to take mine. But I wasn't reconciled with him. He'd not apologized for the way he'd spoken to me in Mary's bedchamber at Blois, and I was still unsure of his motives. If I was to protect Mary, then I should remain watchful and aloof, so I hesitated to offer him my hand.

Duncan tilted his head. 'Do not feel obliged to—'

I raised my voice and interrupted him: 'How can you say such rude things?'

His face flushed; he was clearly offended by this public reprimand. 'You would rather not dance with me?' he said, dropping his hand.

Now I felt my own face colour. I was aware of a growing silence around us. Would he walk away and humiliate me in return?

'I'd not impose upon your time, sir,' I said, very formally.

Without speaking further he escorted me to my place, then crossed the floor and touched the arm of the Countess of Vierzon Bourges. She laughed up into his face, her dark curls bobbing as he led her onto the floor.

A spasm of jealousy convulsed me like a physical blow. Well, I wouldn't watch. I made to go and then the Duke of Malpassant was at my side.

'By your leave,' he said, 'I wondered if we might exchange a few words, Lady Ginette.'

'I have a headache,' I said miserably, 'and beg to be excused.'

I went to my room, threw myself upon a couch and cried. I must have slept, for when I awoke it was almost dark. From the window I could see burning torches moving in the woods. The Duke of Guise had said that men were assembling there to mount an assault on the castle. I shivered and looked at the river. A heavily guarded barge was approaching the water gate. There were many soldiers on board and a group of riders with their horses. Couriers! Immediately I felt better. At last we might hear proper news from the outside world. We'd been cut off for days and I was due a letter from my father.

The ambassadors' reception must have finished by now, I thought, so I decided to go to Mary's apartments and let her know. I fixed my hair, washed my face and applied some powder to mask the blotches.

Missives from Scotland were always eagerly anticipated by Mary – not only for the treat of letters and gifts from her mother, but for the gossip provided by the messenger. The one who delivered these was a friend of Duncan Alexander and he greeted him as he arrived.

'There is also a parcel, marked personal, for the Lady Ginette,' he added.

Something in the man's tone made me uneasy as I took the parcel from him. The only person who wrote to me from Scotland was my father, and of late he'd only had time to scrawl brief notes. To be private I carried the bulky package into a corner of the room. The writing on the outside was not my father's. I broke the seal and a flurry of letters spilled out. As I knelt to gather them up, I saw the messenger speaking to Duncan Alexander and gesturing towards me.

The letters I held in my hand were my own – the ones I'd sent to my father over the years. And there was something else. A locket. My hands began to shake; I recognized the locket. It contained a likeness of my mother – she'd given it to my father on their wedding day. He never took it off.

Fear squeezed my heart. I unfolded a larger sheet of paper and began to read:

My Lady Ginette, it is with deepest sorrow that I write to inform you of the saddest of news. English cannon was brought to fire upon us here besieged in Leith and your father was tragically killed. Know that he died a hero's death, when—

'No! Oh no!' Crushing the letters and locket to my breast, I began to sob. 'Father – beloved Father . . .' This was not how it was meant to be. His commission was ended. 'Come home!' I cried out. 'You are to come home. Home to the quietness of our lands at Hautepré. And I will visit you there and we will walk in the woods together and pluck flowers and . . . and . . . and . . .'

I sank down amidst the spread skirts of my dress and wailed. Someone was kneeling beside me on the floor. Arms encircled me as I rocked myself this way and that, keening in grief. Minutes of wildness . . . of anger with my father for remaining in Scotland; self-pity at being left alone in the world; and an aching, aching, loss inside me. And then, as I came back to the present, I became aware that the person bearing it all with me was Sir Duncan Alexander.

Mary Stuart had sent everyone else away. Only he remained. He didn't try to cheer me with hollow words or encourage me to stand up and dry my eyes. He kept his arms around me as storms of weeping took hold, and waited a long time until at last they subsided. When I was ready, he helped me to my feet. Exhausted with spent emotion, I swayed, and he caught me and held me fast. And, yes, I clung to him.

Forgetting all my suspicions and doubts, I was lost in the moment. Speaking gentle nonsense words, he patted me on the shoulder and smoothed my back with his hand. He was there. I needed him.

But then . . . something more. He stroked my head, brushed his mouth on my hair. I raised up my face, wet with tears. He kissed my forehead, then bent to kiss my tears away. His eyes darkening, and a wellspring of passion is there. I felt the thudding response in my own brain and body. I gasped.

Duncan sprang away. Hands by his side, fists clenched. 'I beg your pardon,' he spoke formally. 'I apologize.'

'I accept your apology,' I said, my voice sounding strange to my own ears.

'I meant only to assist you. To be kind. I'd no intent to take advantage—'

'Of course,' I said quickly. 'I thank you for your kindness and accept what passed between us as only that.'

'Yes,' he said slowly. Was there disappointment in his eyes? 'Only that.'

'Are you recovered a little, Jenny?' Mary was at the doorway. Had she seen us embrace? She looked distressed.

'Majesty,' I said, 'I'm sorry if I caused you upset.'

'Jenny, Jenny . . .' She ran to me. 'If it helps in any way then I gladly share the burden of your sorrow. Come and take some warm wine with me and we can talk of the happy times you spent with your father so that your memories remain pleasant to you.'

When Duncan Alexander had departed, Mary linked her arm in mine and said, 'I hope you don't mind that I went away with my attendants. I thought it best that in your worst moments I left you with Sir Duncan, your friend, to comfort you.'

I knew now that Duncan Alexander could easily become my lover – but was he a true friend?

Chapter 16

I was awoken in the night by the clanging of bells. Amboise was under attack!

Gunfire sounded outside. Soldiers shouting, one louder than the rest, bawling orders. The roar of cannon – ours or theirs? If the rebels had heavy armament then this massive fortress might not be so impregnable. Another cannonade, and a cheer went up from the castle battery. Ours, then.

I wrapped myself in a coverlet and ran barefoot to the queen's room. Mary was awake, with the Maries fussing around her. She insisted on going to the king. The corridors of his suite were heaving with courtiers and our guard had to push their way through. Francis went to Mary as she came into his rooms and they embraced. Catherine de' Medici, who was already there, frowned at what she considered unseemly behaviour. I thought it touching – it revealed the deep affection between the king and queen.

'The rebels mean to capture me.' Francis gripped Mary fingers. His face had a ghastly pallor and he looked as though he might vomit.

'They would have to come past me first, my love.'

'You are so brave,' he said. 'Promise you'll not leave me alone.'

'Never,' Mary promised him. 'I will never leave you.'

Catherine de' Medici snapped her fingers to summon

more sentries for the royal apartments, then departed to confer with the Duke of Guise and the army commanders. Francis gazed piteously after his mother. She'd given him no word of reassurance or encouragement.

Mary pulled her dressing gown about her and, smiling, said, 'Husband, this will be a long night, and you should allow me to regain the money you took from me in our last game of chance.'

In a surreal atmosphere, while men outside fought and died to save their lives, the King and Queen of France sat on the bed and played cards together.

So as not to be a target, we'd extinguished all lights except for the single candle next to the bed. I stood in the shadows by the window and wondered why Duncan Alexander had not appeared to assist us as he'd done in the past. Was he with the soldiers on the ramparts, or out there, moving silently through the darkness? A swathe of the forest was on fire, flames leaping high, sending sparks skywards. Then an explosion! A red and yellow blaze of light – and, from far away through the night air, the screams of injured men.

'They must have hit a cache of gunpowder,' I said.

Mary joined me at the window. I glanced towards the bed. Propped on his pillows, Francis had fallen asleep. 'Poor lamb,' Mary murmured. 'He should have been born a second or third son. He is too frail to carry the role of kingship.'

'And what of you?' I asked. 'How are you able to bear the burden of being queen?'

Mary took my hand in hers and kissed it. 'With your help, Jenny.'

The wisdom of moving the court to the stronghold of

Amboise was borne out: there were no casualties within the castle.

For most of March the situation was unresolved. But the Duke of Guise, rather than wait for future attacks, evolved a new strategy. Detachments of troops were sent out into the surrounding countryside to round up anyone lurking there. The tipping point in our favour came when the body of La Renaudie was brought in, shot dead by one of the Guise men. The rest of the rebels had no time or proper organization to mass their forces. And so the struggle was played out in skirmishes resulting in the capture of bands of men – genuine dissenters, but also mercenaries and a scattering of foreign troops. The castle dungeons began to fill with dozens, and then hundreds and hundreds of prisoners.

'Kill them all.'

I was behind Mary's chair during the council of war when the Duke of Guise stood up to make this declaration. Another noble, a suspected Protestant sympathizer, objected, saying, 'Their leaders declare that they intended no harm to the king. They wish only to speak to him and place their grievances before him.'

'Then why not apply for an audience with the king?' the duke asked.

At this point Mary spoke: 'Perhaps it would not have been granted to them.'

He raised his hand dismissively, as if he'd no need to explain the situation to her. Mary rose to her feet. Even in soldier's dress the duke was smaller than her. She faced him, eyes hard with lingering resentment that he'd denied her request to send more troops to Scotland to help her mother. The duke dropped his hand to his side.

Catherine de' Medici, watching this, did not interfere. She too was unhappy with the power that the Guises now held in France, but was in no position to take it from them.

'Majesty,' the duke addressed Mary more respectfully, 'no monarch can allow armed insurrection. If a person approaches the king bearing arms, and refuses to lay them down when ordered, then that person is guilty of treason. The punishment for treason is death.' He looked at the queen dowager for confirmation.

Catherine hesitated. The truth was far more complicated than that: everyone who approached the king was first thoroughly vetted by the Guises, so few who disagreed with them in faith or politics obtained a hearing.

'The punishment for treason is death,' the duke repeated. He stared at Catherine de' Medici. 'Is that not so?'

Catherine looked around the table and then replied, 'That is so.'

And thus we were locked into witness to a spectacle of such dreadful brutality that, despite differences in faith or politics, or petty jealousies, the women of the household came together to weep and pray.

In an orgy of barbaric killing, over a thousand men were executed. Commoners were tied together, sewn into sacks and thrown into the Loire. Lesser gentry and soldiers were cruelly tortured and strung up from the balconies and battlements overlooking the town, that their mutilated bodies might be seen and a message sent throughout France. The fifty noblemen who'd taken part were lined up to be decapitated on the same day.

The Duke of Guise upon his horse and Catherine de'

Medici on a chair sat stolidly through the executions. The king and queen were also required to witness the beheading of traitors, but it wasn't long before Mary, swooning, had to be led away. The possibility that she might be pregnant couldn't be discounted, and emotional stress could endanger the life of a royal child. Catherine de' Medici refused to permit Francis or his younger brother, Charles, now ten years old, to leave the courtyard.

And through all of this, of Sir Duncan Alexander there was no sign.

When next I saw him it was summer and the court was at Fontainebleau, where the state councils were assembling to address the problems of religious dissent and an empty treasury.

Despite being a Catholic, Catherine de' Medici saw benefit in negotiating with the Protestant Elizabeth of England so that both countries could enjoy a period of peace and prosperity. King Francis had neither the wit nor the will to involve himself in these matters. Mary's attempts to conduce him to do so were continually foiled by him sneaking away to go hawking and hunting like a child truanting from lessons. With the king absent from important meetings, Mary was left ignorant as to what was happening.

On the afternoon of a state assembly which I knew Catherine de' Medici was attending, I took the chance to renew my acquaintance with one of her ladies, Louise d'Albret. I had originally sought her out as a source of information, but I found that I liked Louise for herself. She was thoughtful, and cared about her country and her mistress. While Mary rested, I sent Louise a note inviting her to walk along the terraces with me, and deliberately led her in the direction of the rooms where the meeting was being held.

'Tush!' I said as we found our way barred by sentries. 'These endless assemblies! Whatever do they find to talk about for so long?'

'They have to deal with religious dissent,' Louise said seriously. 'Otherwise every country in Europe will be at war.'

'But that's unachievable! How can anyone do that?' I prompted her.

'I believe Queen Catherine has an innovative solution.' She bent her head closer to mine and continued to chat as we wandered off in another direction.

And so it was through me that Mary first heard of the treaty that decided the fate of Scotland.

Days later, Catherine de' Medici requested to see her. Forewarned as to the nature of the visit Mary chose royal purple for her dress, with sleeves of gold brocade that fell to the floor. She also requested high-heeled shoes from her wardrobe and, on her instruction, Marie Livingston strung her black pearls on a cordelle which Marie Seton wove through her hair. Around her neck we placed the sapphire necklace Catherine had given her on her wedding day to signify that Mary was now one of the French royal family. Mary also ensured that Francis, along with a full complement of both their attendants, was present.

As she entered the room I saw Catherine's eyes mark the black pearls and then fasten on the sapphire necklace. Its significance was not lost on her – nor was Mary's height, which forced her to look up at her daughter-in-law.

'There is a need for the king and queen as monarchs of France and Scotland to sign this treaty,' Catherine began, motioning to one of her attendants to hand over a document.

Mary regarded the parchment but made no move to take it. 'What treaty would this be?' she asked.

'The Treaty of Edinburgh.'

Mary widened her eyes. 'There is a treaty with the name of my capital city in Scotland and I have no knowledge of it?'

Catherine tutted in impatience. 'You are aware that lengthy negotiations have been conducted. We must leave off draining our resources. Constant battles to contain civil unrest are expensive in money and men, and we cannot afford a foreign war. Our people need to concentrate on tending the land, growing crops and breeding livestock, else there will be insufficient food for us and they will be unable to pay their taxes.'

'I have heard something of the terms of this Treaty of Edinburgh,' Mary acknowledged. 'It states that French troops will withdraw from Scottish soil, Elizabeth will be recognized as Queen of England, and also that she may take Scotland under her protection, thereby giving England an ability to interfere in Scottish affairs.'

'France, England and Scotland have come to an agreement to unite against their enemies. We allow that Elizabeth is the true heir and has the right to sit on the English throne.'

'Do we indeed?' Mary said. 'I am Queen of Scotland and I have not been consulted. My mother's position as my regent in Scotland has been reduced to nothing, and I hear that some Scots lords have welcomed English troops to aid them in overthrowing her.'

Catherine de' Medici pointed once more to the document. 'These decisions are made with your best interests in mind.'

'It further states that my heirs may not bear the royal insignia, arms, or title of England,' added Mary, 'even though if Elizabeth died without issue they would be next in line to the English crown.'

'It was a condition imposed by Elizabeth of England.'

'I will not ratify a treaty that reduces my country to a puppet state and denies my inheritance.'

'The terms of the treaty have been agreed,' Catherine stated.

'Madam,' Mary retorted, '*I*, not you, am Queen of Scots and of France, and entitled to make decisions and take action without recourse to others.'

Catherine de' Medici went pale and then puce. Francis cringed away so that he was almost behind Mary's skirts. But Mary Stuart had been crowned queen as a babe in arms and treated as such from her nursery days. She looked down at the smaller woman.

'My husband and I will not ratify this treaty that denies any children we may have their true heritage. As I have admired your love for your children, good madam mother, I am surprised that you'd agree to such a thing that would disinherit any one of them and your future grandchildren.'

Had she merely insulted her person, then Catherine de' Medici might have borne it better, but Mary Stuart had censured her on the one thing that was dearest to her – the promotion of her children – and called into question her statecraft.

'It is a betrayal of everything my mother worked for in Scotland,' Mary went on. 'A betrayal of our history and heritage, our faith, our vow to our people and our country, and I will not sign it.'

Catherine de' Medici stared at Mary. Then she switched her gaze to Francis. She smiled. 'My son,' she spoke softly, 'you have the crown matrimonial of Scotland, given to you by your own wife. There are times when a king must make a decision.'

Mary's look challenged her mother-in-law. Placing her hand deliberately in that of her husband, she declared, '*We* will not sign.'

Catherine de' Medici's eyes bulged. The courtier holding the treaty closed his. With obvious effort Catherine controlled herself. 'So be it,' she said curtly, and left the room.

'There now' – Mary stroked Francis's cheek, speaking to him as a mother might a child – 'it's difficult for the queen dowager to realize that she no longer solely governs France, but see how she does begin to accept our authority as king and queen.'

Chapter 17

Of course, Catherine de' Medici didn't accept that any authority other than her own should rule France.

Mary could be naïve, but even she recognized that. And she'd enough sense to study the terms of the treaty and was ready with an excuse when the English ambassador requested an audience to broach the subject.

Throckmorton pressed her, but Mary would not be moved on the issue of her inheritance and that of any child she might have. 'I can accept my cousin as queen of her realm, as a respected sister and, hopefully, a friend,' she told him. 'But I need to discuss the issue of inheritance with the Scottish Privy Council before I sign the document.'

She parted with Throckmorton in good spirits. He, like many others, was a little in love with Mary Stuart. As he left, she turned to me and said, 'I wonder what Duncan Alexander would think of this?'

'Who knows,' I said carelessly. 'He's never at court long enough for us to gain a true opinion.'

'Sir Duncan has an estate to run in Scotland,' said Mary, 'and . . . other matters to attend to.'

'He never tells us when he is leaving or where he has been when he returns. Who can be bothered with a man like that?'

Mary was studying my face. 'I thought you were quite keen to be bothered by him,' she said with a smile.

I shrugged. I was loath to admit how much I longed for Duncan's company. I felt more secure when he was there, but also it would have comforted me to talk to him about my father. Mary had extended her sympathy to me at this time. 'Someday, when we are able to travel, you and I will visit your father's grave together, Jenny,' she told me. 'In the meantime I will have my aunt's nuns say novenas for him.'

After Amboise I'd worried for weeks when Duncan had failed to appear. Had he sided with the rebels and been captured? I dreamed of his distorted face hanging from a gibbet and imagined him in the queue of nobles waiting to be executed. I both loved and hated him for causing me such distress. Then Mary said that in one of her recent letters her mother had mentioned he was in Edinburgh. A chill entered my heart when I heard that. He was safe and hadn't let me know! He didn't care for me – he was merely using me as a plaything to alleviate the boredom at court. I was seventeen now and should be looking for a husband. I'd soon be too old. Several noblemen had indicated their interest in me, especially after my father died and I inherited his estate. I resolved to consider a prospective bridegroom and not dwell any longer on a foolish, childish love.

There were other matters to distract my thoughts. We were again at Fontainebleau, where the Count of Cluny lived. Although I never saw him at any function, I was extremely watchful of what was happening at court here, and of the food and drink the queen might take. In this respect I was supported by the Maries and her other attendants, for since the rebellion at Amboise those nearest to her guarded her even more attentively. Our concern was vindicated when a member of the Guise household, Duke Fernand, collapsed and died after dinner one night. No cause for his sudden demise could be found. There was no indication of anything wrong with him . . . apart from a mottled rash upon his neck.

Catherine de' Medici directed that his body be burned in case he'd died of Plague or some other infection that might be carried to the king. This was done swiftly; his cousin, the Duke of Guise, unable to protest as this summer the king's health was more fragile than ever. Disposing of the remains in this way meant that no further medical examination could be conducted. If anyone remembered that it was the same Duke Fernand who'd delayed Catherine reaching King Henri on the fateful day of his death, then they were wise enough not to mention it. But I was acutely aware that we were within striking distance of the poisons of the Count of Cluny.

The meetings and state councils moved on with little reference to the king and queen. Francis was conscious of the opinion people had of him and sought outlet in hunting. Both he and Mary were fearless in the chase. Mary could hardly complain about his recklessness in trying to prove himself a man, when she rode with equal daring. I too sought release from my problems and frustrations by going out riding very early each day.

I was standing by my horse one morning when I saw Mary's uncle, the Cardinal of Lorraine, flanked by his men at arms, come clattering into the stable yard, dismount hurriedly and make his way in the direction of the queen's apartments. Had something happened? Should I forgo my ride out this morning?

As I hesitated, another figure came running across the yard. My breath faltered. It was Duncan Alexander.

'Go to the palace immediately,' he called out to me as he approached.

'How are you here?' I asked in amazement.

'I got in late last night,' he said impatiently. 'Never mind that now. Listen to what I say.'

'I'm not a servant,' I answered him haughtily, 'that you may order me around.'

He came nearer and spoke urgently. 'This is something that you *must* do, Jenny. I insist upon it.'

'And if I choose not to obey your command?'

Duncan took my wrists firmly in his grasp. He pulled me roughly towards him so that his face was close to mine. His eyes were of darkest green and flecked with anger, and he looked as though he wanted to strike me. But then he did something that both surprised and disarmed me.

'I beg you . . .' He went down on one knee before me. 'The news that the Cardinal of Lorraine brings to our queen is tragic. Her mother died of heart failure in Edinburgh Castle some days ago. Mary will be distraught. She has need of a true friend by her side. I beg you, Jenny, go to her. At once.'

Chapter 18

'Mama! Mama!'

I heard Mary's cries from several hundred yards away as I came hurrying down the long corridor.

'Aieeeeeee! Mama! Mama!'

I increased my pace as she began to howl like a madwoman.

Directly behind me came Duncan, barely keeping up with me as I raced on, still wearing my riding boots and with my skirts hitched above my knees.

Mary's face, always pale, was white unto death. The cardinal, his red hat awry, was trying to restrain her as she hurled herself around the room in a hysterical fit.

'Get these people out of here!' It was my turn to give orders to Duncan Alexander, and to his credit he didn't hesitate in emptying the room of the gawping servants and courtiers who'd run in at the sound of Mary's screams.

The cardinal was no match for a demented woman and was losing his grip on her wrists as Mary flailed her arms about. With one hand now free, she tore off her headdress and grabbed a fistful of her own hair to wrench it from her head.

'Mary!' I shouted in her ear. 'Mary!' I grasped her shoulders and pulled her round, forcing her to meet my eyes. 'I'm here!' I said. 'I am here.'

With the Maries' help, I caught her arms and wrapped my own around her, holding her against me as securely as I could. I felt her frantic heart beating like the wings of a trapped wild bird. She fought me, but I rocked her as Duncan Alexander had done with me when I'd given way to grief at the death of my father.

'There, there,' I crooned in her ear. Reverting to Scots, I began to half chant a traditional children's lullaby:

'Bonnie bairn, dinna fret thee,
I'll na let ony harm beset ye.'

Over and over I said it, along with any other lullaby I could remember from the nursery. Eventually Mary let her head drop on my shoulder, crying less wildly.

Weeks later, with Mary still closeted in her apartments in deep mourning, another Scots lord rode up to Fontainebleau. He stood in the queen's outer chamber, gazing around, but not in the least overawed. I recognized him at once.

'The Earl of Bothwell wishes to speak to her majesty.'

'The queen is indisposed,' I said. 'Grief at her mother's death has left her prostrate.'

But this Borders lord was not to be put off. 'If the queen is to deal with what is happening at home in Scotland, then she has to be stronger than this.'

'A woman is a weaker vessel,' interposed the Cardinal of Lorraine, who was also waiting in the hope of seeing the queen. 'The female of the species is not built to suffer the calamities of fate and reign over a country.'

'Yet the Scottish Royal Stuart line was founded by a woman,' said Bothwell. 'And if I was a betting man I'd wager on the queen dowager, Catherine de' Medici, against your own family of Guise to gain supremacy in this country.'

'We try to maintain good relations,' Duncan Alexander said in exasperation after the cardinal had flounced away in a temper. 'You've undone years of hard work here, James, and not yet wiped the dust of the road from your boots.'

Bothwell was unperturbed. 'I would not be a lackey of the French. The Scots didn't fight the English for three hundred years to trade that yoke for another.'

Marie Seton came to the door and beckoned us into Mary's chamber.

'I warn you to be careful,' Duncan told Bothwell. 'The Guises have many armed soldiers in their pay.'

'If a man blocks my way then he must be prepared to step aside or fight for his right to remain there.' Bothwell laughed. 'Whereas a woman' – he gestured to where Mary was sitting, ready to receive him – 'would pay a rather different price.'

'And, my Lord of Bothwell,' said Mary, 'what might that be?'

'It would vary, depending on certain attributes.' Bothwell studied Mary's face and figure quite boldly, almost to the point of rudeness. He removed his plumed bonnet and bowed. 'Obviously a queen as beautiful as yourself is free to go where she pleases.'

Mary affected a disdainful air but there was a sparkle of interest in her eyes. Here was evidence of Bothwell's effect upon women. In this case I was grateful, for it was the most animated Mary had been since the news of her mother's death.

However, she was not to be disarmed so easily. 'What is

the business you wished to discuss with me, Lord Bothwell?' she enquired coolly.

'With your mother gone, there should be no dispute now as to who may or may not be regent of Scotland,' he said. 'You are queen, and a grown woman. As such you should rule. You must stand up on your own, draw upon your courage and queenly dignity and govern your Scottish kingdom before the warring nobles tear themselves and it asunder. Already they are forming factions to carve up the kingdom between them, with the Catholic Earl of Huntly preparing an army in the north for battle. I tell you now that I declare for Protestantism but do not hold with the deeds of Protestant reformers who despoil churches and loot abbeys.'

'What say the lords within the Governing Council convened after my mother died?'

'The Hamilton Stuarts with their half-mad heir, Arran, think they'll be head of it because they are your nearest legitimate kin. The Lennox Stuarts are contesting their claim, while the Earl of Argyll' – Bothwell laughed – 'sits facing backwards on his horse so that he can go in whatever direction he thinks is winning. But they will all be swept aside by the clique led by the Earl of Morton, that spawn of the villainous Douglas clan.'

'May I remind you, sir,' Mary said primly, 'that my half-brother, Lord James Stuart, is also of the Douglas family.'

'I have my suspicions of James Stuart the bast—' Bothwell checked himself as Duncan Alexander made a noise in his throat. 'Majesty,' he modified his tone, 'Lord James Stuart is close to the Protestant preacher, John Knox, whose oratory emboldens the people. Knox is violently against the Church of Rome. Already the Scottish Parliament has met to pass Acts outlawing Catholicism, rejecting the authority of the Pope, and making the saying of mass in a public place illegal.'

'But Acts of Parliament cannot become law until they have royal consent,' Mary protested.

'Nevertheless,' said Bothwell, 'this is what has happened.'

She put her hand to her heart. 'No wonder my mother gave up and died,' she said. 'For years she tried to find a middle way. She allowed Knox into the country and gave appointments to Protestant lords. Yet within weeks of her death they repay her by doing this.' She raised her face to him. 'And you, my Lord of Bothwell . . .' Mary asked him. 'As a professed Protestant, whose side are you on?'

In answer Bothwell knelt before her. 'Though you be Catholic, and remain Catholic, I declare for you as the true-born Queen of Scots.'

Chapter 19

There was no time for Mary to consider Bothwell's proposal that she should actively rule Scotland. And no way that she and Catherine de' Medici could continue to avoid each other's company.

As winter approached, the king's health began to disintegrate entirely. They nursed him together, his mother and his wife, consulted every possible doctor and tried the most bizarre remedies, but were unable to halt Francis's decline. By November both women were desolate as they were forced to come to terms with the truth. An infection that had first taken hold within the king's ear had spread into his brain.

It was heart-rending to watch the suffering of the boy who had never quite become a man, who had never wanted to be king and, if he hadn't, might have lived a happier and longer life. Francis clung to Mary's hand and she held fast to him with one of hers, while in the other she grasped a crucifix. I watched and prayed with them through the final wretched night at the beginning of December, when the royal doctor advised that the king should make his last confession. As we left the cardinal to prepare the holy oils, I heard the doctor say, 'Majesties, I am truly sorry, but there is nothing can stop the rise of the poison.'

Catherine de' Medici made a croaking sound. '*The rise of the poison!*' she repeated.

I was possibly the only one present who knew that she was quoting the prophecy of Nostradamus.

King Francis died that night.

The very next day Catherine de' Medici sent word that Mary must immediately return the crown jewels.

'She cannot mean this!' Marie Livingston, who looked after the queen's adornments and jewellery, was disgusted at the unfeeling speed of the request.

'It is unthinking,' I said as she unlocked the jewel cabinet.

'Kindness was never one of her attributes,' Marie Seton pointed out.

Marie Fleming was more vociferous, declaring Catherine to be 'cruel and heartless'.

Duncan Alexander was with us as Mary had charged him to take the items to Catherine de' Medici.

'Catherine de' Medici has coveted these for many years,' I said, putting the black pearls to one side, 'but she cannot have them. They are Mary's own.'

We debated over whether to include the sapphire necklace given to Mary by her mother-in-law on her wedding day.

'It was a gift of state,' I said, reluctantly putting it into the bag.

'Keep only what belongs personally to our queen,' Duncan advised, 'and I'll dispatch the rest at once. Don't forget how Catherine de' Medici deals with those who thwart her. It may take her years but she always exacts revenge.'

Marie Fleming nodded. 'Remember how swiftly she acted against Diane de Poitiers. Hardly was King Henri laid in his tomb before she confiscated the beautiful Château of Chenonceau and banished her from court for ever.'

'They say she has agents following Captain Montgomery of the Scots Guard,' Marie Beaton added, 'watching his every move in England, where he sought refuge after the accident that cost the king his life.'

'And Duke Fernand,' I broke in. 'I believe he was poisoned at Fontainebleau.'

Duncan looked at me curiously but waited until the others had left the room before saying anything more.

'Jenny,' he began, and my heart contracted at the way he spoke my name, 'I know that you wish to protect our queen, but be mindful of yourself over these next few months.'

'Why especially over the next months?' I asked him.

'Because I will not be in the vicinity of this court. After Christmastide I must go away for a while.'

'Why?' I asked in annoyance. 'Why do you come and go so often without any obvious reason? And leave before at times when we have need of you?'

'There are matters to be seen to . . . politics—'

'Oh, fie!' I interrupted him. 'Don't patronize me by thinking that you may say the word "politics" and there's an end to any explanation. Do you think, as the preacher Knox does, that a female cannot understand such matters?'

'Not at all. Catherine de' Medici and Elizabeth of England are mistresses of that science.'

'So is it just me then?' I demanded. 'Poor simple-minded Jenny whom you can fob off because of her limited intellect.'

'No!' Colour had risen in his cheeks, indicating that his indignation was genuine. 'That is not so. It's my concern for you that makes me share less with you than I might, believe me.'

He had picked up the bag containing the jewel cases and was already walking towards the door

'Make me believe you . . .' I whispered the words so softly that he could not possibly have heard me, and yet he stopped. I waited and so, I felt, did time itself.

Duncan turned and came back across the room to stand in front of me. Very gently he put his mouth close to mine. His breath was warm and intimate on my face. And then he brushed my lips with his.

I closed my eyes. When I opened them, I was alone.

The eighth of December heralded Mary's eighteenth birthday. We made paper decorations and Marie Seton dressed her hair with flowers, but Mary did not respond to our attempts to cheer her spirit.

'Has there been such a woeful queen?' she lamented. 'Within the space of two years I've lost the only papa I ever knew, my own sweet true mother whom I loved dearly, and now my husband, and a kingdom.' In anguish she asked us, 'What is to become of me?'

It wasn't long before we found out how Catherine de' Medici had decided to deal with her widowed daughter-in-law. Having failed to produce an heir, Mary was now an encumbrance and a possible focus for dissenters, and from January of the following year she was excluded from official court business and state affairs.

Mary sat within her black-draped room and stared out of the window, clutching a sodden handkerchief. 'I have sent word to Scotland to let them know what is happening with me,' she said.

It was I who greeted the messenger who returned with the

letter still in his hand. 'My lady . . .' He glanced around nervously.

'Come inside,' I said, closing the door behind him

'There are guards at the end of each corridor and at every exit and entry. No one is permitted to leave,' he told me.

'This letter bears the seal of the Queen of France!' I said. 'Who dares prevent you from carrying out your mission?'

'It is the orders of the queen dowager, Catherine de' Medici. She has set up guards on all roads. Every note must go through her offices.'

I put my hand to my mouth. Were we prisoners? I didn't want to worry Mary with this, but I needed to speak to someone. As I was prevented from communicating with Louise d'Albret, there was only one other person who might have information. I was embarrassed to seek out Duncan Alexander for I'd not seen him since he'd been in our apartments to collect the French crown jewels. He'd excused himself, saying that he was packing for a long journey.

We were polite with each other, but when I told him that Mary's messages were being openly intercepted, his face showed concern. 'I will try to find out what is happening.'

He returned that evening to tell me, 'Catherine de' Medici has called a meeting of the premier council of France, the Estates-General.'

'She has no authority to do this. Mary is Queen of France. It is for her to command what will happen.'

'I am not sure that it is now within Mary's right to do that,' Duncan said slowly, 'but, even if it were, would it be within her capability?'

His voice ended with a question and I thought of Mary,

like me, merely a girl, sitting by her window staring out into nothingness.

'This is a dangerous time,' Duncan continued. 'There are other contenders for the throne of France who could sweep this court away and dispose of everyone in it.'

I shuddered as I remembered the massacre at Amboise.

'Cunning is needed, and we might all benefit from the wily ways of the Medici woman.'

Duncan was correct. Catherine de' Medici acted adeptly to fill the vacuum of authority and power created by the death of Francis. She proclaimed her next son, Charles, the King of France.

'Charles is scarcely ten years old!' Mary said when we told her.

'Yes indeed,' said Duncan, 'but no one can deny the legitimacy of his claim. And Catherine has declared that she will rule through him as governor of the kingdom. Both the Guises and the leader of the French reformers, the Huguenots as they are now called, have promised their obedience. And France's new Queen Governor has issued a pardon to those not captured during the rebellion at Amboise.'

'She would change the religion of France?' Mary asked.

'No. But she says she believes that brutality does not dislodge belief and gentleness might work where harsh punishment has failed.'

'Perhaps she is only doing what is necessary so that the various powerful nobles will support her and her son until he is old enough to rule as king,' I said. 'Her overriding concern is that her children inherit the throne.'

'Is this compromise not a denial of one's beliefs?' Mary wondered.

'Perhaps, in itself, it is a worthy thing to do,' I said.

'Surely one's faith, above all, should rule one's life,' she replied. 'And yet, my mother sought a way to have both religions co-exist in Scotland.'

Duncan Alexander nodded. 'We should be able to follow a personal faith without imposing our beliefs on another.'

For the first time in many months Mary stood up straight and raised her head. 'Do you think that I might achieve this if I returned to Scotland to rule as queen?'

Chapter 20

In the spring of 1561 Mary was approached by a representative of the Catholic Earl of Huntly. He'd heard that she might return to Scotland and asked her to land in Aberdeen, where he'd meet her with his army. They could then march on the capital together.

With few advisers and even fewer people she completely trusted, Mary had to come to a decision on her own.

'I do not want to enter my kingdom at the head of an army,' she said to me, 'be it Catholic or Protestant. I see how my own family of Guise are disliked in France for their ruthless suppression of those who disagree with them. My former mother-in-law is engineering a more temperate solution for the religious problems in France. Perhaps I can follow her example.'

I agreed with Mary that taking Scotland by force was not a good idea but privately doubted whether she could ever be as devious as Catherine de' Medici.

Then Duncan returned to say that an envoy of Protestant Scots lords were on their way to consult with Mary. They were led by her half-brother, Lord James Stuart.

'Scotland is weary of wars,' Lord James addressed Mary. 'You are undisputedly the heir of our former king and recognized as such by those of differing beliefs.'

'Yet you did not recognize my mother as my appointed regent,' Mary replied caustically.

'It was a very difficult situation.' Lord James spread his hands. 'If the Protestant cause had remained officially unrecognized, the country would have descended into anarchy. I tried very hard to mediate between the two sides. When she was dying, her majesty summoned me to Edinburgh Castle and asked me to forgive her if she had done any wrong and begged me to protect the kingdom. I stayed with her to the end. Truly a brave and noble woman.' He bowed his head. 'God rest her soul.'

'Amen,' said Mary, and openly blessed herself.

Lord James controlled his irritation at this gesture but said, 'The Scots will not accept a Catholic ruler.'

'You tell me what others will not accept. I tell you that the presence of John Knox in my country is repellent to me. I've heard he mocked my mother's death and yet is now appointed minister of the cathedral church of St Giles in Edinburgh.'

'John Knox will not go away,' Lord James replied, 'nor will he remain silent. If he were executed, then he would become a martyr and you would lose the love of your subjects for ever.'

'Much as I dislike him, I do not desire his execution.'

'What other alternative is there?' Lord James Stuart said reasonably. 'Banishment? There are those who would support him in a coup to overthrow us.'

I drew in a breath. By using the word 'us', Lord James Stuart was subtly manoeuvring himself into Mary's favour.

'It would also be necessary for you to agree a Bill to go through parliament absolving all those engaged in the previous . . . unpleasantness,' he added.

'You want me to agree that those who rebelled against

my mother should go unpunished?' Mary asked him.

'For the good of Scotland it is something she herself would have done,' Lord James replied. 'And indeed similar to what Catherine de' Medici is doing at this moment in France.'

Duncan made a movement that indicated he wished to say something. Mary looked at him and inclined her head.

'Majesty, you may wish to keep those who disagree with you near at hand, so that you may hear what they are saying and watch what they are doing.'

Mary pondered this. It was a strategy employed by Catherine de' Medici in her recent rearrangement of the offices of government within France. But I shivered, remembering the fate of Duke Fernand, and the scene in the shed at Fontainebleau. The difference between Mary and her mother-in-law was that Catherine de' Medici would not hesitate to remove, by any means, someone who obstructed her.

'It may be that if you met John Knox you would be convinced by his arguments,' Lord James pressed her.

'I have no wish to meet him,' said Mary. 'I will not be swayed by anything he has to say against the faith of my forefathers.'

'I beg of you,' he pleaded, 'give it up. Convert to Protestantism.'

'Don't you understand?' Mary tried to explain. 'I cannot cast off my faith as I would a cloak that I'd no more use for. I find both solace and support in my religion.'

'To be Catholic is to be a puppet of the Pope in Rome.'

'My faith is more to me than politics, James.' Mary's voice became surprisingly firm. 'It is my life. I know there are men who would make me their puppet. They want me as a doll to be dressed up and brought out and made to play sweet music and say pleasant things. But I have a higher purpose in life, and when I meditate I reflect upon the will of God. I was scarce out of my mother's womb when I was crowned Queen of Scots and that, with my faith, is who and what I am.'

'Then have your religion,' James Stuart said suddenly. 'Return to Scotland and I'll guarantee that you may practise your faith, and I will help you keep a guiding hand on government.'

'Truly?' Mary said in astonishment.

'Yes. Truly.' He spoke gruffly, but seemingly with sincerity. 'It must be private worship, mind. No flaunting of icons and other trumpery.'

'Oh, I promise that I will be most discreet.' Mary blinked back tears of gratitude.

I was impressed with Lord James Stuart's change of heart and commented on it to Duncan Alexander afterwards.

'Lord James is so good that he would risk the wrath of the Protestant lords to support Mary in this.'

'You think so?'

'You do not?'

'I see a woman manipulated into accepting conditions to claim her rightful kingdom.'

'But there was no other way,' I protested. 'One must be practical. If the people do not wish a Catholic to be their queen . . .'

'This is not about the ordinary people. It's about lords and nobles seeking position and money.'

'Given the laws being passed in the Scottish parliament

to affirm the country as Protestant, it seems a reasonable compromise.'

'I suppose . . .' Duncan reluctantly conceded the point. 'But she'd be safer if she were his cousin.'

'Why so?'

'Then he could marry her. I do believe if he were not her half-brother that's what he'd do, for he is an ambitious man.'

'You think Mary is vulnerable?'

'Very. Why suddenly does he, a staunch Protestant and friend of John Knox, who loathes Catholicism, agree that Mary may hear mass privately and have a priest among her attendants to minister to her? It is because Lord James Stuart, being illegitimate, cannot contest the claims of the Hamilton Stuarts to be next in line to the throne. If they establish themselves as leaders of a governing council they will fill every government post with members of their own clan. To counteract this, Lord James hopes to rule the realm through Mary.'

'You do not trust him?'

'Who can one trust? In this situation, who can one trust?'

I had no answer for him, for as he went away I was thinking, *Who indeed? Who can one trust?* Could I even fully trust Duncan Alexander?

There was one last duty for Mary to perform before she left France. Her mother's coffined body, returned from Scotland, was to be interred within her Aunt Renée's convent of St Pierre in Rheims.

I spent the night before the funeral service keeping vigil there with Mary. In the morning a calm came over her and, although our farewells to her relatives and friends were tearful, Mary was resolved on where her duty lay.

'I feel my mother is with me,' she said as we prepared for our journey to Scotland. 'But what about you, Jenny? Are you happy to come to Scotland? If you would rather go and live on your family estate at Hautepré, you are free to do so.'

'The manager appointed by my father has run the estate honestly and efficiently for the last twenty years so I have no need to be there.'

'Yes, but it is your family home,' Mary replied. For a moment she looked sad. 'I do not have such a thing as a family home.' Then she brightened. 'But I do not begrudge you yours.'

It was one of the reasons I loved her so much. She had no jealousy within her and found pleasure in the happiness of others.

'*You* are my family!' I held out my arms to her and we hugged. 'I want to remain with you, and in Scotland I can visit my father's grave and see the places he saw during the last months of his life.' *And*, I thought to myself, *I will also be near Duncan, the one other person whom I love.*

On the road north, Duncan met us with worrying news.

'Once we are clear of the French coast the English may try to waylay our ships,' he said. 'I've heard they seek revenge, angered that Francis and Mary's arms were quartered with that of the English crown. They may try to capture the queen.'

'But Lord James Stuart assured Mary that he would approach England and secure a safe passage,' I said.

Duncan grimaced. 'I should have anticipated that our smooth-tongued James Stuart had already spoken to the English government.'

We waited in Calais while he went off in search of more information. He returned with a message from Throckmorton, the English ambassador, which said that Elizabeth was still considering the request for the ships to travel unhindered.

'It appears the English court was subjected to one of their queen's famous temper tantrums,' Duncan told us. 'When she received the letter asking for an assurance that Mary could travel safely home, Elizabeth shouted that if Mary of Scotland wanted to return to her own country, then she must sign the Treaty of Edinburgh and renounce all claim to the English throne.'

'I instructed my ambassador to reassure Elizabeth of my best intentions,' Mary protested. 'I wrote most particularly to say that it was the late King Henri of France who decided that I and his son be addressed as the queen and king of England. Now that he and my beloved Francis are dead, I do not use this title, nor do I wear the English coat of arms among my colours.'

'These facts were communicated to Queen Elizabeth and her advisers,' Duncan reassured her.

'In any case,' she went on, 'I cannot ratify such an important document until I reach Scotland and appoint a privy council of my own men to advise me on this matter.'

'Mary has made up her mind on this,' I told him when I spoke to him later. 'She thinks this treaty surrenders Scotland's independence as a nation and ruins the inheritance she holds in trust for those who will reign after her. She hopes, when in Scotland, to collect around her men who will be sympathetic to her way of thinking on this.'

Duncan shrugged. 'Lord James Stuart has probably

already decided the make-up of the privy council.'

'Can he do that?' I asked in surprise.

'Mary has no real knowledge of her lords, and Lord James will tell her only what he wishes her to know. She has to be very strong to resist his will, and wily as a fox to find out what that is. You must help her.' He made to go, then turned back and said, 'Although I fear for your safety, I am glad you are coming to Scotland, Jenny.'

My heart lifted with happiness. I searched his face, but I could see only worry there. It came to me then that to go with Mary was to place myself in danger. But instead of feeling gloomy at the prospect, my spirits were high with anticipation of this new adventure. Duncan's words were all I needed to convince me that I had made the right decision to make Scotland my home.

The English ambassador followed us to Calais to speak to Mary. It was obvious that he too was concerned on her behalf. He tried to persuade her to await the outcome of a further appeal that had been sent to the English queen.

However, in an impressive show of her queenship and bravery, Mary declared, 'My good Throckmorton, may I remind you that I am queen of an independent Scotland. I do not need the permission of another to sail upon the open sea. I am confident that our Scottish sailors can elude this famous Elizabethan fleet.'

'Oh, well spoken, your grace!'

I whirled round. Another man had entered the room. James Hepburn, Earl of Bothwell, wearing his insignia of Scottish Lord High Admiral of the Seas.

'Excuse my boldness in interrupting. I am sorry if I have

offended,' he said, sounding not at all sorry. 'But I do admire your grace's courage in being prepared to face down the aggression of the English navy.'

Throckmorton coughed. 'I am assured, informally of course, that we have no fleet in the North Sea. Just a few ships that patrol those waters to protect our coasts and merchant galleys from pirates.'

'*Pirates!*' Bothwell laughed out loud. 'The English claim that they must protect themselves from *pirates*! Elizabeth of England turns a blind eye to her own sailors who fly the black flag and harry the Spanish galleons bringing spices and silver from the New World. Why, English ships are the biggest pirates on the high seas!'

'My Lord Bothwell, I do believe you say this with a touch of admiration,' Mary commented shrewdly.

He tilted his head and had the audacity to wink at her.

She ignored this. 'It would appear,' Mary spoke equably but amusement trembled in her voice, 'that the best way to protect myself against these piratical sailors is to have a gallant buccaneer of my own.'

With a grand dramatic gesture Bothwell swept off his hat in a low bow to his queen. 'While I am Lord High Admiral of your fleet, no English ship will delay your passage home to Scotland.'

PART TWO

MARY
QUEEN OF SCOTS

Scotland 1561

Chapter 21

The Earl of Bothwell was true to his word.

Although we spotted English ships and they certainly saw us, none tried to delay us or interfere with our progress. We learned later that Elizabeth had grudgingly agreed not to impede Mary's journey from France to Scotland, the message sent to arrive after we'd sailed.

Once beyond the shelter of the Channel we headed up into the North Sea. This was a different sea from any other we had known. The waters were grey and cold and full of dangerous currents and treacherous sandbanks. As we ploughed northwards a strange fog enveloped the ships so that we couldn't make out the lanterns of our neighbours. The bells of the watch clanged, and shouts and hails were exchanged, but we soon lost contact with the other vessels bringing the livestock and household furniture.

Early on the morning of Tuesday 19 August we were roused to prepare for landing. On deck most of the courtiers began to shiver, begged to be excused, and retreated to their cabins. I stayed outside with Mary and one of her younger Guise uncles, the Duke of Aumale, who'd volunteered to be part of her escort to Scotland. Sir Duncan Alexander looked as if he might leave us too, but then changed his mind and, wrapping his cloak about him, stood apart. The white mist writhing around the masts made ghosts of us all.

'It is haar!' Mary exclaimed suddenly.

'I beg your pardon?' I said in surprise.

'I remember now.' She was laughing. 'It's the Scots word for sea fog.'

'In August?' the Duke of Aumale complained. 'Fog? In August? What kind of country are we in?'

'A very beautiful country, albeit more rugged and less warm than your own,' Duncan replied immediately. His voice was eerie, coming disembodied as it did.

'Stand forward, Sir Duncan,' Mary commanded. 'You lurk there in the shade like an assassin.'

She was joking, but her words had an instant effect on him and on her uncle. Duncan stepped forward at once, while the duke moved to one side.

If Mary noticed that her uncle had shifted in order to protect himself against possible harm, she gave no sign of it. My spirits plummeted. Here was a member of the French nobility, her close relative, who thought more of his own life than that of the woman he was supposed to guide and protect. If this was how she was treated by her own attendants, then what kind of reception could we expect from the Scots who hadn't seen her for many years?

'I am no assassin, your grace.' Duncan Alexander regarded the duke with contempt. 'I have been charged to guard you, and that is what I will do.'

Mary touched his arm. 'I do believe you,' she said softly.

He looked pleased and I had a fleeting pang of resentment at the power this woman had over men.

Her eyes met mine, and she smiled as if to reassure me

and then said, 'I do also believe that Jenny is feeling the cold and would benefit from the warmth of your cloak.'

Duncan began to untie the cords at his neck.

'I am perfectly well without it,' I protested, although my body was chilled with the fog seeping into my bones. 'I do not want it,' I reiterated firmly as he swung the cloak off his shoulders.

'Best to do as our queen commands,' he said, and draped it around me.

It was a cloak of fine wool, still warm from the heat of his body, and it smelled of him. The sudden sensual shock caused me to fall quiet. A host of emotions tumbled within me. I looked away and frowned. I didn't want to be beholden to Duncan Alexander. I'd resolved to control my feelings when I was near him, yet I enjoyed his attention. I risked a glance at him. He had gone to the rail of the ship and was peering ahead.

The wind freshened as we approached land. The fog thinned and the sea became visible with white caps on the waves. By this time the face of the Duke of Aumale was tinged with nausea, but as Mary remained on deck, so must he.

'I was five years old when I left these shores,' she told me. 'But it's my native land and I wondered if I might recall anything.'

Suddenly in the distance we saw several small craft – early morning fishermen hoping for a catch.

'Oh!' Mary put her hand to her nose. 'The smell!' she cried in delight. 'I recognize that distinctive smell from the curing huts! I do recall it. I must have travelled with Mama to a place the fishermen brought in their catches. Newhaven! There, I remember!' She was overjoyed to have rediscovered this personal memory of her life with her mother. 'The fish-wives made us welcome and had sewn a striped apron to fit me.' Mary closed her eyes and breathed deeply. The wind had coloured her normally pale complexion and she looked very beautiful with curls of copper escaping from her headdress. 'My mother's presence is very near.' She sighed and murmured, 'I do not see it with my eyes but I feel it within me.'

I sensed the bond between me and Mary growing ever stronger. Tears came into my eyes as I thought of my own mother and saw the land where I'd once lived with my parents. I did not care that some of my memories might be wish-dreams, there were disjointed scenes I could recall, as Mary was doing. The feel of the silk of my mother's dress between my chubby fingers; being cradled in her arms; the sound of her voice singing to me in Italian; the musky smell of the perfume she wore.

Although Mary hadn't seen her native land for thirteen years, and therefore her memories be more tenuous than mine, I did empathize with her mood. And so when the Queen of Scots clasped my hand and spoke, her words chimed with those in my own heart. 'I have come home, Jenny,' she said. 'I have come home.'

Chapter 22

But it was a raw, unwelcoming homecoming and, to begin with, no welcome at all. There was neither party of nobles, nor town burghers, nor officials, nor any attendants waiting to transport the queen to a royal residence.

'Perhaps it is some kind of test of my endurance,' Mary declared calmly as we waited on board while Duncan Alexander and others went ashore to announce her arrival. 'The Scots are reputed to be hardy folk, but my father's blood runs in my veins and I will prove myself their equal.'

When he returned Duncan's mouth was set in a tight line. 'Majesty, they did not expect you so soon and have made what arrangement they could muster at such short notice.' Approaching the jetty we saw a few tousled men-at-arms. 'This is your escort. You are to be conducted to the house of a local burgher, there to await the official party of nobles from the Palace of Holyrood at Edinburgh.'

'The queen is to walk?' I was surprised. I'd been about nine years old when I left Scotland and my childhood impressions were of a friendly, hospitable people.

Duncan inclined his head. 'It is not far and I have asked them to sweep the street ahead of you.'

The Maries made expressions of annoyance and dismay and the Duke of Aumale began to bluster in protest. It was then that Mary displayed her usual readiness to make the best of a bad situation.

'If there is no one here to announce my presence in a proper fashion, then we must do it ourselves,' she said.

She called the ship's captain and asked him to confer with the captain of the other galleon. Some minutes elapsed, and then the cannons of both ships fired a salvo out to sea. People came rushing out of doors. Seeing the two magnificent galleons, one painted white, one all red, flying the flags of France and Scotland, they realized what was happening in the harbour.

'There,' Mary said with some satisfaction. 'They are sure to have heard that cannonade in Edinburgh and know now that their queen has arrived in her realm.'

As we descended the gangplank my first thoughts were of my father. There were still signs of the bombardment where his French soldiers had made their last stand before surrendering to the combined forces of the rebel Scots and English armies. This was where he had died doing his duty for his country and my queen. I concentrated on the fact that his death was an honourable one and on my resolute belief that his soul had joined my mother's in Paradise.

On reaching the burgher's house, the four Maries complained loudly on Mary's behalf. I thought of France where, when the court moves from one place to the next, teams of servants are sent on a week or more ahead of time to prepare the castle or château. This Leith merchant's house was well appointed but it didn't compare to any mansion we'd visited in France. We were given an upper floor consisting of a dining chamber, a receiving room and a bedroom.

When the escort of nobles finally arrived to transport

Mary to the city it was a doleful sight The horses and trappings were of poor quality. Instead of a thoroughbred stallion or a bedecked and bejewelled palfrey for their queen to ride upon, they presented her with an old mare, a sad swaybacked piece of horseflesh.

'I thought it best, good sister,' Lord James Stuart said, 'that you have a mount that would give you no trouble to control.'

And yet he must have been aware that she was a fine horsewoman. He'd spent enough time in her company in France, and surely his spies had informed him of her skill in the hunt. Was it carelessness on his part or the beginning of his campaign to bring her down and make her easier for him to manage?

Mary's face registered her disappointment. She'd been eager to show her subjects a resplendent queen whom they might be proud to have as their monarch. These horses were not caparisoned like French horses, with decorated cloth to show rank and wealth. Some lacked bridles and one had no saddle.

Small knots of townsfolk stood around chatting and pointing. They watched as the luxurious goods being unloaded from the two galleons onto wagons – mirrors, bales of cloth, boxes of gold and silver plate, barrels of wine, and crates of crystal glasses packed with straw – brought the ordinary work of the port to a standstill. There was as yet no sighting of the other vessels, which meant that our hunting dogs and birds and, more importantly, our ponies and horses, their embossed leather saddles, silver bridles and rein hangings, were not available.

When we heard this news tears welled in Mary's eyes. 'This is not the way I had thought to make my triumphal entry into Scotland,' she whispered to me. 'It is important that the people who have first glimpse of me know me to be a queen.'

'We could wait here a while,' I suggested. 'Our other ships might arrive or better horses be summoned from Edinburgh.'

'No!' Duncan Alexander, who must have been listening very intently to hear our quiet conversation, was at my elbow. 'With respect, it's already afternoon. It wouldn't be wise to delay until evening to travel the road, and this place is not secure enough for her majesty to spend the night.'

Mary regarded him for a moment and then nodded. She called on Lord James Stuart and gave him a sunny smile. 'I will accept the horse that you have so generously offered to carry me to Edinburgh. I won't impose upon this good merchant any longer, and besides, I would rest tonight in one of my own royal residences.'

The queen and her ladies took the laird's own bedroom. The Maries fussed about, making sure that essential items from her wardrobe were brought from the ship that the queen might change, ready for her journey to the city. Still officially in mourning for the death of her husband Francis, Mary's gown and train was predominantly black, heavily embroidered with bead work and jet. But, to relieve the un-relenting darkness of her dress, she had chosen a stomacher decorated with pearls and diamonds to sit around her middle, and patterned hose and shoes shot through with silver. In matters of fashion and dress Mary was very sure of her own choices. She knew that with her height, slim figure and pale colouring, too much ornament might appear crass or vulgar. She was conscious that her stunning hair and eyes were her best features and paid attention to her coif and neck ruffs, settling on an ornate black and silver headdress with a long white veil edged with diamond thread. About her neck and breast gleamed the necklace of fat black pearls, while upon her fingers we placed rings of ruby, emerald, gold and silver. On her brow was a simple band of white pearls with wisps of her golden auburn hair being allowed to show. I looked at her and marvelled. She appeared womanly and vulnerable so that men might want to protect her, but aloof and dignified as a widow should be, yet her manner was composed and regal to command respect.

Her attendants were also obliged to wear public dress of sober mourning colours and I had donned a dove-grey dress with trims of white lace at my cuffs and neck. Beginning at my brow, my cap covered my hair, but as I surveyed myself in the mirror, on an impulse, I drew out some of my blonde curls to frame my face as Mary's did.

As we arranged a velvet-trimmed Florentine riding cloak around Mary's shoulders, an equerry came to say that Lord James Stuart, with a number of nobles and lairds, was ready to ride with her.

'Let them wait,' she said when she heard this. 'Their expectation will sharpen. They have come to see a queen and I will not disappoint them.'

But when it was time for her to depart and she started down the staircase, Mary's face paled and her body shook with nerves.

'Here . . .' Duncan Alexander, who had been waiting outside the door, proffered a leather bottle. 'This is usquebaugh, distilled here in Scotland, more potent that any you might taste in France.'

I knew of this drink. On occasion we had sipped it at the French court. Translated as 'Water of Life', and known in English as whisky, it was so fiery that the taste of any strange substance would, I realized, be disguised.

I stepped between them. 'Her majesty takes nothing to eat or drink except that given to her by her attendants.'

'What?' he exclaimed.

'I'll serve it in a glass,' I said, and, hurriedly fetching a goblet, poured out a large measure of the amber liquid. I took a gulp before handing it to Mary.

Duncan glared at me furiously. The Scots were noted for their pride and I had insulted him. The liquid burned like fire in my throat and then down into my stomach, sending a wave of heat through me.

'That will certainly warm your bones,' he observed.

I could feel the alcohol taking hold within me – not the slow languor of wine, but a more potent brew suited to this wild country that sent my senses whirling. I coughed.

'I'd advise you to give your mistress somewhat less than what you took for yourself,' Duncan said in a superior manner before going outside to organize the guard who would march beside us.

He held Mary's stirrup as she mounted the mare. Her Scottish lords and her family from the royal houses of France assembled around her. The bulk of the minor courtiers, maids and servants would have to walk, but the maids of honour and those of higher rank had been allocated places on wagons. On my way there I passed Sir Gavin of Strathtay. A few years older than me, he was one of the young Scots lairds who'd come from Scotland to meet Mary at Calais and escort her home, and had been very attentive to our needs during the sea journey. He was preparing to mount a farm horse that he'd bribed a local resident to loan him.

'If you wish to accompany your queen, you may ride with me,' he said.

I hesitated.

He was very attractive, with neatly combed brown hair and an open cheerful face. Smiling into my eyes he made a bow. 'It is entirely your choice. If you go in a wagon you'll trail far behind her.'

As I'd appointed myself to watch out for Mary, then I should really keep as close to her as possible. I glanced about me. Some other young gallants had also hired horses and were offering ladies a seat. I looked again at Sir Gavin and inclined my head.

He linked his fingers and clasped his hands so that I might put my foot there. This I did while gripping the horse's mane and he helped me up. Then he followed, leaning forward to gather his reins which meant that his arms were on each side of me.

Not far in front of us I saw Duncan Alexander. He swivelled round, eyes roving through the assembly. His gaze passed over me and then snapped back. For a moment he stared at me, snug between the arms of one of his fellow countrymen. He pursed his lips and then turned to face the front.

'You might want to take hold of my belt.' Sir Gavin's mouth was very close to my cheek.

The whisky was ringing in my ears and I was unsteady, but I was still rebellious enough to demand, 'Why?'

'Else you might fall off.' He laughed and, kicking the horse's flanks, we lumbered forward to join the queen's cavalcade.

Chapter 23

By the time we were on the road from Leith to Edinburgh, word had spread and people were flocking to see Mary. Some had obviously hurriedly changed into better clothes and scooped up their children, tidying their hair and wiping their faces in the hope of receiving a royal blessing or perhaps some more worldly reward. Others had left their labours in the fields and farms to view the spectacle. Soon each side of the roadway was lined with an assortment of folk gaping at their queen.

Mary's Scottish lords clustered close to her, almost as if they wished to block her from the people's view, and them from her. It seemed that this publicity wasn't really something they wanted. I think they'd hoped for an ignominious arrival – for the queen to come quietly into her country as if by stealth. The day was turning out to be more of a royal progress, and now I appreciated the queen's wisdom in taking time with her appearance. Mary sat tall and elegant in her saddle. The breeze whipped at her veil, exposing her face. She didn't replace it to shield herself from their gaze, but instead raised a hand in greeting and smiled and waved. I was so proud to be with her. Light sparkled on the silver of her headdress and stomacher as she cast her cloak back from her shoulders. Her jewels and rings flashed fire. She was the focus of all attention, a dazzling figure of authority and power.

As we climbed up the slope towards the city the sun came out, and what had begun in cold mist and gloom as a raggle-taggle of riders with a line of pack mules and wagons trailing behind became a pleasant slow ride on a warm summer's evening. We came to the crest of the hill, and there was the Scotland of moor and mountain and, before us, the jewel of the capital city of Edinburgh.

'Oh, this country is so beautiful!' Mary exclaimed, loud enough to carry beyond her immediate company. 'What glorious mountains! I had no idea the landscape would be so arresting.' She turned excitedly to her companions. 'What gorgeous colours! It is all quite breathtaking.'

She reined in her horse. At once a section of the onlookers surged forward to see their queen, only to be prevented by the men-at-arms on either side of us. Mary was unperturbed by any danger these people might present, and went on talking animatedly: 'If these are my subjects, then I am well pleased with them. Look at the handsome men and the pretty girls. See the comely women and their bonny, bonny bairns!' She smiled, and as she spoke confidently in Scots, the crowd cheered. 'Give some pennies to these mothers, some sweetmeats to their children.'

She beckoned to a senior courtier, who looked very uncomfortable, crushed with another on an ancient plough horse. 'Make sure one of the wagons is halted and that this is done.' She raised her hand and, breaking free of her entourage, spurred her horse to trot on ahead. Great hurrahs came from the onlookers; mothers lifted up their children to see her as she passed and prayed for blessings to shower down upon her. One man tossed his bonnet in the air and shouted out, 'Long live the daughter of James the Fifth, rightful heir to the throne of Scotland!'

Lord James Stuart flinched. It was clear that the fact of his illegitimate birth was, once again, being flung in his face.

Mary was impervious to any frowns or scowls from her Scots lords. And I was too. Buoyed up by the adulation our spirits lifted so that when we reached the outskirts of the city we were full of joy. Mary remarked upon the tranquillity of the waters of the loch, the unusual architecture of the spire of St Giles, the quaintness of the houses huddled together on either side of narrow lanes and wynds, and the elegance of the buildings with their crow-stepped gables ascending the hill to the heavily fortified castle squatting on its rock. The majesty of this castle dominated everything, its vast bulk louring over the city, the loch and the countryside beyond.

Then we saw the Palace of Holyrood. And I understood why Duncan had wanted us to travel there before darkness. Although situated outside the city walls, it stood secure and gated at the bottom of a long street leading directly up to the castle on the rock.

'Why, it's like a château of France! Don't you think, Jenny?' Mary called to me. 'Like Chenonceau?'

'Or Chinon,' I agreed. The design of turrets and pinnacles with interior courtyards was in the French style, and although the stone was different, it suited the city. The parkland and trees surrounding it made for a beautiful setting below the craggy outcrop known as the Chair of the legendary King Arthur.

And now my memories were real, swamping me with their vividness, evoking bitter-sweet recollections of my past times. I recalled my father sitting me in front of him on his horse, much as I was seated now, and cantering with my mother through Holyrood Park. I brushed tears from my eyes.

Gavin touched my hand. 'Are you well?' he asked solicitously.

'I left Scotland as a child. Being here again makes me think of my mother and father, now sadly dead.'

'Ah,' he murmured in sympathy. 'Lean on me a little and let me share your sorrow.'

I closed my eyes and relaxed against him and he drew his arms more tightly around me in support.

Inside, Holyrood Palace was distinctly less agreeable.

It was evident that, since the death of Mary's mother, Mary of Guise, no female hand had taken care of the fabric and furnishings. It was a shocking change from the splendour of my early upbringing. Then I had skipped up and down the imposing staircases and hidden behind beautiful tapestries and handsome furniture. Now the floor coverings needed cleaning, the canopies and wall hangings were dusty. It smelled stale, as though the windows hadn't been opened for months. The decoration was vastly different to the opulence we were used to in France. But Mary's mood was such that it refused to be dampened.

'There is elegance to this austerity,' she commented, pretending not to notice the state of disrepair, 'and a certain dignity in the design.' As we went through the main hall and into the royal apartments at the western end of the palace, she stopped to admire the carved scrolls and emblems.

There was a moment of deep sadness when we entered the bedchamber that had been her mother's. 'How lonely she must have been, with no husband or child for company,' said Mary. 'So far from home, so far from France.'

'But this was her home,' I reminded Mary gently. 'My mother told me that yours did love her adopted country. She stayed here after your father died when she could have retired to France. She remained in order to keep Scotland secure for you to inherit.'

'You are right, Jenny.' The queen smiled through the tears glistening in her eyes. 'And therefore I owe it to her to be the best ruler possible.'

It was evident then that some preparation had been made. A fire burned in the grate and the bedsheets were clean and smelled of lavender. Some wild flowers sat in a jug on the windowsill. Mary bent to smell the fresh scent. She tilted her head on one side and said, 'Summon the maid for this bed-chamber to my presence please.'

The maid was brought in. She could have been no more than thirteen years old and she was shaking with fear.

Mary indicated the jug of flowers at the window. 'Did you do this?' she asked the girl.

'I meant nae harm, ma'am – I mean, majesty, your honour,' the girl gabbled in such broad Scots, her teeth chattering with fear, that we could scarce make out what she was saying. 'I only pulled a few wild flooers fae the park – no noble ever walks there. I thocht it would be allowed.' And she prostrated herself, almost weeping in terror.

The queen went forward and touched her on the head and bade her rise up. 'I wanted to thank you for the work you have done in this room to make it so comfortable for my rest,' she spoke gently in Scots. 'I am not much older than you and very far from the home I have known since my childhood, and to see these flowers has cheered my heart enormously.'

The girl managed to raise her eyes to look upon the queen. 'Thy mither liked wild flooers.'

'Why, so she did!' Mary exclaimed. 'I had forgotten that. Is that the reason you chose these flowers for me?'

The girl nodded. 'Ye are like thy mither in looks. She was a bonny brave wumman.'

'I thank ye,' Mary replied. 'Perhaps another time we will speak more of my beloved mither. Meanwhile' – impulsively she pulled a small silver ring from her pinkie – 'accept this ring as a token of my favour.'

The girl's eyes grew wide with wonderment.

'What is your name,' the queen asked her.

'Rhanza,' she replied.

'Hold out your hand, Rhanza,' Mary instructed. And when the maid did so, she dropped the ring into it. 'This ring has my initial, the letter "M", as a monogram. When you wear it, I'd like you to pray that I am as good a queen as my mother was.'

Marie Fleming laughed as she closed the door behind the girl. 'Rhanza was hardly in the corridor before she was biting the ring to see if it really was silver.'

We took supper in the great hall. Present were the lords who had escorted us from Leith plus some other nobles and lairds. The food was plain but wholesome and there was plenty of it, as well as copious amounts of strong drink. I had a headache, the result of imbibing too much whisky, and so I sipped only light wine. Most of the rest of the company were not so moderate – apart from one man, William Maitland, who listened to everything that was said on a subject before passing comment himself.

It was still summer and the sun doesn't set in these northern lands until late. As the meal ended, in the gloaming of oncoming darkness Marie Beaton pointed to a window and cried, 'Fire! Look! Upon that hill! The city is on fire!'

We rushed to the window. For an awful moment I thought that some madman, his mind inflamed by John Knox, who objected to a Catholic woman ruling Scotland, had decided to burn the town with us in it. But then I saw what it really was.

'I think it's a bonfire,' I said in some relief. The flames leaped into the air, with sparks from the kindling sending a merry trail across the sky.

'Where is that?' Mary asked.

'Calton Hill,' answered one of the lords. 'We skirted past it on our way up from Leith.'

'It's the ordinary country folk who have done this then.' Mary's voice showed the depth of her pleasure.

'See! There's another bonfire!'

'And one here,' someone called from the other side of the room.

'There are several upon the hill of Arthur.'

'And look to the castle!'

We strained to see the short mile to the castle. The tiny chapel was illuminated by the glow of firelight. And then, all over the ramparts, bright red signals pierced the darkness. Even though the night wasn't cold the soldiers must have lit their braziers to join in the welcome for their queen.

Mary clasped her hands together. 'This is most heartening to me,' she rejoiced, 'and all the more so as it wasn't a planned celebration.'

From below us came a sound of music: fiddles, rebecs, pipes and a side drum beating time. And then a whole chorus of voices singing.

'I am being serenaded,' said Mary. She opened the window and stood, all unprotected, at the casement.

'Come away, sister,' Lord James Stuart advised her. 'You might catch cold standing there.'

'Good brother,' said Mary, 'I am very well.'

'Besides being unseemly, it's dangerous,' he said testily. 'What if some person of ill intent looses an arrow at you?'

'It would hardly reach the window,' Mary answered him. 'Although' – she laid her hand on his arm – 'I do thank you for your concern on my behalf.'

Her attempt to mollify him didn't work. He continued to tut and look with displeasure at the commotion below us and said that most likely they'd use bawdy language and show no respect to the queen.

Seeing Mary watching, the singers redoubled their efforts. More folk joined them and they began a round of traditional harvest songs and then a variety of verses, some from Maying time, romantic and flirty. Mary laughed at their merrymaking and ordered ale and quince cake to be sent to them. When that was done, they raised their flagons and toasted her, and she turned to Lord James, saying, 'Brother, this is the best welcome a homecoming monarch could ever have. It is unorchestrated and thus comes straight from the hearts of my people.'

I glanced at him, expecting him to be happy at this. But he was not pleased. Rather James Stuart frowned and bit on his thumb the way a child might when seeing another receive a toy they had especially wanted for themselves.

Chapter 24

The next few days were a frenzy of activity.

We'd yet to get hold of most of our household goods as our lost cargo ships had been forced by bad weather to dock at English ports and were impounded there under some pretext of tax problems. But we had plenty to do: rooms had to be allocated and the Wardrobe established for the multitude of clothes and accessories brought from France. These were supplemented by what remained of Mary's mother's belongings. As the tally for those didn't match the inventory lists for the late queen's goods, it was obvious that items had been pilfered. Some of the most expensive gowns and headdresses could not be found.

'Those that are missing are very special pieces that were sent from France,' I told her. 'I recall one, a birthday gift to your mama from your grandmother.'

The rest of Mary's ladies made sympathetic noises. It seemed such a low thing, to rob the dead, and we remarked on the character of someone who could do this. It was Mary herself who banished our despondency.

'I suppose we should take it as flattery,' she joked, 'that the goods that are gone are of French origin. We will speak no more of this and take it as a sign that the Scots admire French fashion and style.'

I thought it brave of her to dismiss what was both theft

and insult to her person so lightly. Even more so because she was weary with the constant round of meetings on matters of state with Lord James Stuart – and with others seeking appointment to a whole range of offices. Duncan's predictions were coming true. Mary's half-brother had already vetted applicants and many appointments went to those he nominated.

We were glad when Sunday arrived and we could enjoy a day of rest. The queen was keen to visit the private chapel in Holyrood where it had been agreed she could hear mass. In France she attended mass daily and had felt the lack of it over the last days. We made a procession with her chaplain and some of our, mainly French, attendants, and set out along the corridor. Mary looked forward to these times of quiet reflection and drew strength from the sacrament of Communion. Not everyone in her retinue was as devout as her, but they accompanied her as she read from her book of meditations. I was the last in line and was not immediately aware that, ahead of us, the entrance to the chapel was blocked by a group of men.

'No pope here!'

I craned to see what was going on. One of the men who'd attended dinner on our first evening, Lord Lindsay, had stepped forward to bar the queen's way.

Bewildered, Mary lifted her eyes from her book; then, recognizing the man who spoke, she replied in an even tone, 'Indeed, Lord Lindsay, you are correct. There is no pope here.'

'No mass!' He jostled one of his companions so that the man almost fell against the queen. 'Scotland is a Protestant country!' he shouted. 'There will be no mass, I say!'

Several things happened all at once. Those barring our way began to yell, 'No mass! No popery! Death to all priests!' One of the women screamed. And then two arms came firmly around my waist and I was lifted off my feet and placed in an alcove. I struggled free and whirled round, nails ready to claw at this person.

It was Sir Duncan Alexander.

'Hush! Hush!' He sidestepped my lunge at his face. 'I'd rather avoid another scratching from you. Remain here while I try to rescue the queen.'

He ran off down the corridor. I stared in surprise at his retreating back: running away didn't constitute a rescue. Immediately I went towards the chapel. I wasn't prepared to take orders from him, and anyway I'd no more leave Mary alone in these circumstances than I would abandon her in a forest full of wild beasts.

I pushed through to the front. The queen stood there, holding onto her prayer book as might a drowning sailor to a spar of wood.

Most of the men in front of the chapel door were dressed plainly, not unlike the French Protestants who'd adopted a distinctive dark attire, but these clothes were of rougher cloth. They were milling about, with Lord Lindsay leading the shouts of condemnation. Since arriving at Holyrood we had tried to tune our ears to the broad vowel sounds and strongly pronounced consonants, but it was hard to make out exactly what was being said. Mary turned to one of her Scots aides and asked in French, 'They are speaking so fast that I cannot follow. Help me with this.'

The aide replied, also in French, 'They protest that mass is to be celebrated here while the law of the land forbids it.'

'But I am going to mass in my own private chapel,' Mary said in Scots. 'This was agreed. No?'

'You are right to say "no", madam.' Lord Lindsay spoke to the queen even more insolently than before, talking as if to a slow-witted person or a doltish child. 'It was *not* agreed. Not by us, the people of Scotland. Nor by our parliament, which has passed a law against the saying of mass.'

'I was assured that I could attend mass privately.' Mary retained her dignity and her stance.

'Let us inform you on this,' Lord Lindsay broke in, staring directly at our chaplain. 'A priest may be executed for celebrating a mass in Scotland. What say you?' he addressed his supporters. 'Shall we spare the expense of a trial and do it now? Let's hang him, and then we will be assured there will definitely be no mass.'

Whether they really meant to lay hands on our poor chaplain, who was now shaking so badly he could hardly hold the ciborium containing the unconsecrated hosts, I do not know. He gazed at the queen in supplication. Mary Stuart was firm in her faith and had, on occasion, defied the fearsome Catherine de' Medici. So, despite her being only eighteen, I knew that she would try to defend her beliefs.

There were mutters and growls at Lindsay's suggestion, but not all of them in agreement. Obviously some were true Protestants who had come to join in the protest but baulked at murder.

Mary seized the moment to speak out: 'To administer such a sentence would go against your own rules.' Her gaze was steady as she looked at Lord Lindsay. 'You make Scots laws for Scotland. How will anyone else respect them if you do not do so yourself?'

Lord Lindsay began to reply: 'In Scotland the people have the sovereign right to—'

'Ah, yes,' Mary interrupted quickly She might not have understood all of what was being said, but she knew the general meaning and had picked up on the word 'sovereign'. 'I am the sovereign and you are my people,' she said. 'I will worship as my conscience dictates. And I guarantee you that you will too.'

But the protestors had moved to surround us, and more came from we knew not where. This situation was different from France where lesser courtiers were not permitted to approach the royal personage unless it was to make a special plea or present a gift.

'This is an outrage!' said the Duke of Aumale. Someone caught at his sleeve, and he cried out and pulled away.

I saw Mary's colour change and thought she might faint. Marie Seton and the rest went beside her to bear her up.

I stepped in front of the queen and, putting on an act of bravery, said, 'You must stand aside. All of you.'

Lindsay, who had suggested hanging our priest, pushed his face into mine. His teeth were black and broken and his breath was foul. He pointed at the image of a crucifix on the cover of my missal. 'That is idolatry,' he said, 'and is forbidden in the Bible. Graven images, statues, holy pictures – all popish frippery.'

'They are a means of concentrating the mind on devotion,' I replied.

He snatched a Bible from the one of the others and shook it under my nose. 'Listen to the true word of God.'

'I do,' I said, my voice beginning to waver. I couldn't believe that these men would refuse to defer to the royal presence.

Lord Lindsay raised the Bible above his head, and I thought he meant to strike me. My heart quailed. And then Duncan Alexander was at my side.

He pushed me behind him. 'I told you not to move from where you stood. I had you safe in the alcove.'

'I am protecting my queen. As you should be,' I retorted.

'You are not in France! Here the monarch has no army to call upon. I ran to bring Lord James Stuart here. He's the only one who can quiet this rabble.'

And suddenly Mary's half-brother, Lord James Stuart, appeared. His servant struck the shaft of a sword upon a shield while Lord James shouted angrily, 'Be quiet! Be quiet! Disperse at once! Do you hear me? This I will not tolerate!'

I!

Lord James had used the word 'I'! In the presence of the queen he had just stated that there was something *he* would not tolerate – as if he owned and governed the realm! I was dumbfounded, but no one else seemed to notice it. By now Mary was close to fainting and, helped by Duncan, she and her company took shelter in the chapel. And there we stayed long after mass was over until we were knew that the unruly crowd had gone.

That evening Mary enquired as to the names of the men who had tried to prevent us from entering the chapel. 'I recognized Lord Lindsay,' she said, 'but who were the others?'

Lord James claimed that everything had been so confused that he hadn't noticed exactly who they were. It was frankly not credible that he didn't know or have the means to find out their names. Surely he, who had contacts everywhere, must have heard rumours of a protest planned for Sunday morning? Had he waited until the mood became so ugly that only he could calm it? Was this so that Mary would be grateful to him as defender of her right to hear mass? Yet we knew he was a declared Protestant. Was he, as Duncan thought, manipulating both sides for his own ends?

William Maitland, whom Mary had asked to attend this meeting, opened his mouth as if about to say something and then changed his mind. But he and Lord James spoke with the queen at length – with the result that the very next day she issued a proclamation stating that she wanted an end to religious discord. Her view was that everyone should have the freedom to worship as their conscience dictated, and though she might differ in her own practice, she accepted Protestantism as the religion of Scotland.

'Hopefully this will appease the more militant Protestants,' Mary told me, 'and allow John Knox to preach a sermon of conciliation in St Giles.'

It occurred to me that Rhanza, the maidservant to whom Mary had gifted her ring, might attend St Giles and be willing to let me know what was being said. I decided to speak to her as soon as possible: she would be a useful recruit to help me in my role as spy for the queen.

Now that Mary had her royal cloth of state above her throne in Holyrood, it was time for her official entry into the city of Edinburgh. As if to make amends for the neglect of her first welcome, her nobles and courtiers organized a superb dinner at Edinburgh Castle, followed by a formal progress down through the city from the castle to Holyrood Palace.

French cooks were in place in the kitchens, and the meats served for dinner were accompanied by smooth sauces made from fine wine and herbs. One or two of those present made derogatory remarks about French cuisine. Again I wondered at the apparent lack of respect towards the monarch. Perhaps it was better that discontent was openly expressed than kept secret to fester. However, no one's appetite was diminished. I glanced around the tables. From where he sat, Sir Gavin of Strathtay nodded at me and I smiled in return. He'd asked to be my escort in the procession, and I'd accepted.

Since we'd arrived in Scotland Sir Duncan Alexander had not been near the queen's apartments. True, he'd arrived outside the royal chapel with Lord James Stuart in time to stop an ugly situation becoming worse. But was this planned to enhance their reputation and draw Mary closer to them? It was obvious what Lord James wanted. As a reward for his support Mary had already promised him an earldom to celebrate his forthcoming marriage. But Duncan Alexander's motives were much harder to ascertain.

After we had eaten, Mary insisted on spending a few minutes alone in silent contemplation in the tiny chapel of St Margaret, a former Queen of Scotland. When she came out, Mary seemed at peace with herself and there was a quiet resolution in her manner.

'I have prayed to this Scottish saint that her life might inspire my own,' she told us. 'She too came here in difficult circumstances and had to reign over a troubled, warring land. I will try to imitate her example of fortitude and patience.'

We looked down upon the city and, beyond it, in the distance, the waters of the River Forth and the North Sea. I wondered if it crossed Mary's mind that she might quit this country, sail back the way she'd come and live pleasantly in the sun on the lands she owned in France. At that point I hoped she would not, for I had a sudden overpowering presentiment that my own fate would be decided here in Scotland. If she entertained any thought of leaving, Mary did not share it with us. Instead she made her way down towards the main gate of the castle, where her lords were waiting to accompany their queen on her formal royal entry to the capital city of Scotland.

Chapter 25

Under a canopy of purple velvet and flanked by the highest nobles in the land, the Queen of Scots began her stately progress. As we took our places to walk behind her, I noted that Duncan Alexander was between me and the queen. With a deafening fanfare of trumpets we set off.

A huge mass of folk had come into the city to see and be part of the historic occasion. Just beyond the castle esplanade stood a cluster of young men, full-bearded, dressed in plaid, and carrying claymores. One raised his arm, and I saw Duncan start and grasp his sword hilt. But the man had only a kerchief in his hand. He waved it above his head and cried out,

'Welcome home, Mary, Queen of Scots!'

Mary looked directly at the lad, tilted her head and gave him a captivating smile. He blushed! Being on that side of the street, I was close enough to see this rough Highlander's cheeks actually redden like a young girl being paid her first compliment by a man. But far from being embarrassed, he crowed with glee and made some remark to his friends, who punched his arm and slapped him on the back to congratulate him – as though he'd been given a lady's favour in a tournament.

We paused on the crest of the High Street. Flags bearing the lion rampant of Scotland and the diagonal white cross of

St Andrew upon a blue background flew from public buildings. Tapestries and coloured hangings were draped over the sills of upper windows and the projecting galleries of houses, where burghers and merchants stood with their wives and children, all dressed in their best clothes. Wooden platforms had been built at intervals so that the nobles not taking part in the procession might have a better view, while a guard of honour on either side restrained the commoners. A troupe of actors dressed as Moors in splendid sparkling costumes stepped out in front of us, and a great roar went up as the waiting spectators realized that the queen was on her way.

We gasped as a waterfall of flower heads and petals tumbled from on high onto the street before us. Mary smiled up at the boys perched on the roof slates, who were emptying baskets crammed with roses, lavender, herbs and leaves. Reaching out, she caught a handful and threw the petals back at them. They whooped in delight and the queen joined in their laughter. The incident set the tone for the rest of the progress. Nervous tension slipped away from Mary, for she was now in a situation where she was supremely confident – making personal contact with other human beings. She was fully aware of the power of her looks and personality and used these to best advantage. In this relaxed, happy frame of mind, she began to work her magic.

Suddenly the drum beat and the music seemed louder and merrier. The mummers who capered in front of us were lighter of foot. The pungent smell of roasting meat from the taverns promised tastier meals. The cries of the vendors were light-hearted and witty. Children skipped along beside us, mimicking the mummers. Mary took some of the coins she had put in her purse and scattered them over their heads to draw them out of the way of the horses' hooves.

They cheered her for this gesture, and people pressed forward to get a better view. In addition to the gentry looking from their windows, the common folk had been given time off their work to watch the royal progress. The streets were dense with apprentice boys and maidservants, men in blue capes and bonnets, shopkeepers and washerwomen. Parents hoisted their children up onto their shoulders so that they might catch a glimpse of the queen. Little girls held out offerings of posies and Mary's ladies collected them as we passed by.

Wine flowed from the water spouts at each junction. Mary halted at Tron and Tolbooth to inspect each tableau or watch dancers and singers perform. Scenes depicting virtue and grace were acted out by young women dressed in flowing robes. I wondered how John Knox viewed these, and where he was amongst all the joyous celebration.

But his influence was soon felt. As we neared the Butter Market the scenes became biblical, and a group of children stood ready to present the queen with gifts of books. They seemed unsettled when doing this, and as I watched, they glanced anxiously at the dark-clad adults standing to one side. Among these I recognized the man who had tried to intimidate me outside the chapel in Holyrood. There was a look of grim satisfaction on the face of Lord Lindsay. The queen received the books graciously, glanced at them and lowered her head. Duncan Alexander hurried to her side and asked if she wished him to take them to one of her attendants for safekeeping.

Mary gave him a grateful look, and he handed the books to me, narrowing his eyes as he noticed Sir Gavin at my elbow.

Taking them, I saw why Mary was upset, for they were of the Protestant religion. A calculated insult – or perhaps a reminder to her that it was only through Knox's tolerance that she could ride unmolested in her own city. I looked up. Her head was turned to see my reaction. I flashed my eyes towards Lindsay and lifted my chin high. Mary followed my gaze and understood my message. She raised her head and sat proudly in her saddle, making her smile brighter, her largesse more bountiful.

At the end of the High Street we reached the Canongate, where several children stood to recite some verses. When they'd finished, one girl spoke up: 'Ye must walk in the ways of the true religion and cast off the false words of the Roman priests.'

'I will hold dear what is true to me,' Mary replied civilly, 'as you must hold fast to what is true for you.'

The child nudged the one beside her, who'd no doubt been primed to deliver a similar maxim to the queen. But Mary urged her horse on, and we saw the gateway to Holyrood and within a short time we were safely inside.

The queen was wearied with the day's events but she called Lord James and William Maitland to discuss the incidents. 'Preacher Knox arranged these events deliberately to rile me,' she began.

'If so, I'm sure he merely wanted a representation of the Reformed religion of our country,' Lord James said, trying to soothe her.

'I'm prepared to interpret the gift of books as such, although it might surprise you to know that I have already read the Book of Common Prayer and find much that is good within it. But when a chit of a child has the effrontery to lecture the queen in public on the error of her ways, then something must be done.'

'I'm sure no harm was intended. After all, you did say that everyone should be at liberty to express their own beliefs.'

'Good brother, Lord James,' Mary replied in irritation. 'I know that you seek to keep my life trouble-free, but I am aware that John Knox delivered a sermon against me decrying my private observance in the most vituperative terms.'

'You are?' he said.

'I am indeed,' she snapped. 'For every one person who brings me pleasant news there are half a dozen others to burden me with tales of woe and discord.'

'Perhaps John Knox has yet to come to the accommodation that your proclamation regarding religious freedom applies also to Catholics,' suggested William Maitland.

'Then it is time that he did,' said Mary. 'I can delay no longer. Summon Preacher John Knox to my presence.'

I was glad that she hadn't revealed the sources of her information regarding the utterances of John Knox. In addition to what Rhanza told me, my new acquaintance, Sir Gavin of Strathtay, repeated portions of his sermons to us, adding in caustic comments and jokes as he did so. John Knox had been incensed by Mary's insistence on attending mass despite his express wish that it and all priests be banned. On the Sunday after the incident at the chapel in Holyrood he'd delivered a sermon in St Giles, declaring the mass to be the most serious danger to Scotland in all history, and that he'd rather face an invading army of ten thousand men than allow it.

'John Knox told his congregation that if they accept the mass being said in Scotland, then God will desert the country,' Sir Gavin reported to us. 'The force of his rhetoric had them terrified. For all that he scorns masques and balls, he himself provides pure theatre. He is such a showman. I swear that more than half the folks who attend do so for the drama of his presentation.'

Gavin had taken to joining us for an hour on the afternoons when we worked at our embroidery. It was a favourite indoor pastime of Mary's, one of which John Knox would have approved – unlike the dancing and gaming that she also loved.

'He threatens hell fire to scare the wits out of his flock,' said Gavin, 'and then throws in a promise of redemption every now and then to keep them hopeful.'

'And also so that they will return,' Mary added shrewdly.

'I'm sure he deliberately doesn't trim his eyebrows so that his expression is more fearsome,' Gavin went on cattily. 'He dresses in a black winged overcoat, flings his hands in the air and juts out his chin with its horribly unkempt beard, glaring and shouting at folk to make them quake with fear.'

Gavin loved to personalize his attacks and, on occasion, Mary had to chide him for being uncharitable, but it was useful to have extra news in addition to that coming from the official channels of the queen's advisers.

Lord James was wary of calling Knox to Holyrood to meet the queen. 'He may overwhelm you. John Knox is a powerful orator.'

'And dangerous,' added William Maitland.

'I know that he is dangerous,' said Mary. 'He is in constant touch with John Calvin in Geneva, who has been an insidious enemy to Catholic countries for many years.'

The two men looked surprised that she received reports not given her by either of them.

'Calvin has infiltrated spies and agitators throughout the whole of France, some of whom have recently been arrested for causing trouble,' Mary continued.

'Have you heard that this is so?' William Maitland asked cautiously.

'Oh, letters come from France . . .' Mary waved her hand carelessly.

Lord James and William Maitland exchanged glances.

It might have been wiser for Mary not to draw attention to the fact that she had independent sources of information. Although she loved playing with codes and using symbols in her embroidery work, she wasn't skilled in real artifice. She hadn't the guile required to manage a network of spies. In this respect Elizabeth of England and Catherine de' Medici were far superior. Lord James immediately took steps to ensure that her personal mail, both incoming and outgoing, was filtered through him.

And I think that was why, when she realized her correspondence was being intercepted, Mary later decided to appoint as her letter writer someone she befriended and trusted. Thus she would come to depend greatly on the services of an Italian called David Rizzio, who first came to her attention as a musician but eventually became her private secretary – with disastrous consequences.

Chapter 26

In the first week of September John Knox came to Holyrood for his meeting with Mary.

The privy councillors were not present as Mary had decided to try to make it as informal as possible. She hoped to win Preacher Knox over with directness and an offer to work together for the benefit of the people and the country. I stood at the window, Lord James was by the fireplace, while Mary remained seated.

The outer rooms and corridors were crowded with the queen's French attendants, avid to see this man they'd heard so much about. I too was interested in meeting him and noted the accuracy of Sir Gavin's description as he strode into the queen's receiving chamber. John Knox had the mien of an evangelical prophet, with thick eyebrows, beard and hair, and stared at us unabashedly with bright blue eyes, his piercing gaze seeming to condemn our dress, which appeared gaudy compared to his sombre clothes. His manner radiated anger and suspicion, but perhaps with a glimmer of delight at the prospect of a fight with a foe he might easily vanquish.

But Mary was intelligent and resourceful and had prepared for this encounter. Together we'd discussed the Protestant pamphlets and read his infamous text, *First Blast of the Trumpet Against the Monstrous Regiment of Women*, in which he stated his belief that women were frail, feeble and foolish creatures.

'Sir,' she began, 'I strive to understand why you attacked my mother in the past and now myself as queen of this country. You say that it is not natural for a woman to rule, that it's a subversion of good order, equity and justice; yet it is by God's providence that I stand here as the natural and rightful heir of my father, King James of Scotland. Surely if God had wished it otherwise then He would have sent my father a son in place of me?'

John Knox examined the queen, casting his eyes over her, before replying. Mary had dressed modestly, in the most discreet of black dresses, with a plain headdress and no make-up. When he answered her, I sensed a tinge of disappointment at finding nothing to criticize in her appearance.

'Your father, the king, was sent sons,' Knox reminded her. 'Two boys who, by dint of who knows what carelessness, died prematurely.'

Mary's hands fluttered to her throat.

I was appalled. Was he blaming her mother of neglect – or worse – for Mary's two baby brothers dying in infancy? He must know that she had a deep affection for her mother and that such a statement would wound her.

With great patience Mary went on, 'Nevertheless, it has come to pass that I am anointed by God's grace Queen of Scotland and therefore govern I must. Do you say that you will not abide by my rule because I am a woman?'

Knox gritted his teeth and replied, 'I suppose as St Paul suffered life under the Emperor Nero I must thole it as best I can.'

'Yes,' said Mary, 'but not, as reported to me, without never-ending derisive remarks and criticism.'

'Perhaps you should attend my sermons,' Knox suggested, 'and listen yourself to what I say. I have a duty to speak out.'

'You have no duty in that respect,' said Mary. 'You are not a member of my council.'

'As a minister to my congregation, it would be wrong of me to keep silent.'

'But you go so far as to incite against me. What right have you to do that?'

'I speak only the truth.'

'The truth as you see it,' Mary answered smartly.

'By close study of the Bible, with prayer and advice, I interpret the word of God.'

'It is by God's grace that I am anointed Queen of Scots,' Mary repeated. 'One is not born into one's place here on earth by happenstance. And God has set me over my subjects and thus they should obey me. If you go against that, you go against the will of God.'

'A subject is not bound by the religion of their ruler,' argued Knox.

'Do you further say then it is lawful for subjects to act against their ruler?' Mary asked him.

'Children might act against their father if they thought their father intended to kill them, and so subjects should imprison a ruler who plans to kill the children of God.'

It was at this point Mary told us afterwards that despair seeped into her soul. John Knox was learned and able, with a wealth of knowledge of theology and experience in debate. She saw that no matter what she tried to argue, he would make a counter claim and attribute it to be right by Divine will.

I also saw that Knox was impervious to Mary's personal appeals to him. His face was unflinching, his stance unchanging since he entered the room. He seemed to absorb Mary's nervous energy into himself and clearly relished the chance to air his views, becoming swayed by the passion of his own rhetoric.

Mary lapsed into doleful silence. Seeing her despondency, Lord James approached and spoke quietly to her.

Eventually she said, 'In essence, what you are saying is that rather than my subjects doing as I say, it is for me to do as they order me.'

'Both princes and people must obey God's rules.'

'Aye, sir,' Mary retorted. '*Your* God in *your* kirk is what you mean. But I believe the kirk of Rome is the true kirk of God, as my conscience tells me.'

'Your conscience is that of an unschooled woman.'

'A woman I am,' said Mary. 'Unschooled I am not.'

'Unschooled in the manner of right judgement.'

'Who shall be judge?' Mary addressed her question to everyone present.

Lord James looked at John Knox as the dinner bell began to sound within the palace.

'I will pray for you,' Knox said as he took his leave.

He bowed his head but I, who ushered him out, was discouraged to hear him say to the friend awaiting him in the corridor: 'The woman has a proud mind, a crafty wit, and an indurate heart set against God and His truth.'

Duncan Alexander was one of those in the antechamber when I returned. He was watching my face and it looked for a moment as though he would speak to me. I would have liked to talk over John Knox's comments with him, but Sir Gavin came up to me and said, most kindly, 'I see that Mr Knox's lecturing has cast you down. Perhaps we can meet later and I will try to cheer your spirits?'

'Perhaps,' I replied absently.

Abruptly pulling on his gloves, Duncan left the room.

When Mary went with Lord James to report to the privy council on what had passed between her and John Knox, it was clear that the lords themselves thought that the preacher had gone too far.

There were murmurs of dissent and annoyance, with the Earl of Argyll saying, 'John Knox takes too much upon himself that he interferes in the social order. That should be no concern of his.'

I was by the door, where I usually stood during these conventions yet was able to hear and see very well. I was amused by the earl's remarks, for it was widely known that John Knox had lectured him and his wife, the Countess Jean, about their public arguments and separation.

'It may be that John Knox feels that the people should be heard,' William Maitland said carefully.

Mary stated equally carefully: 'I am a ruler placed in this position on earth by the Lord God Almighty. Let us have absolute clarity here. If, as John Knox says, his God is the true, all-powerful one, then it is *his* God who intended this to happen. Thus I, as anointed Queen of Scotland, brought up since childhood to be aware of my duties and taking advice from yourselves, the best of men' – she included them all in her gaze –'make rules to govern the realm. Yet if the ordinary people, untutored and with little learning, unable to read or write, deem these decisions to be unwise, then am I to regard them as not just my equal but my superior?'

Lord James looked to William Maitland, who raised his hands, palms up, and shook his head as if he had nothing to add.

Mary was trembling with suppressed rage and exhaustion. 'This man Knox preaches insurrection. Have a care, gentlemen, for if the day comes when the people sweep away my power, they will also do the same to yours.'

William Maitland was vexed by the outcome of the meeting between Mary and John Knox. He'd hoped that she might see reason in the Reformed faith and be guided towards Protestantism.

'My faith is imbued in me and I in it.' Mary spoke gently to him, for she had come to respect his advice and admire his diplomacy. 'If I do not hold true to my faith, who would believe me true to any other thing?'

'John Knox has unyielding dogmatic opinions, and his belief that his interpretation of the word of God is the only one leaves little room for manoeuvre,' William Maitland conceded.

'Yet the man is inconsistent in his obduracy,' Mary replied. 'He rants so much against women and called Mary Tudor a Jezebel, but when her sister Elizabeth ascended the English throne he took pains to write her a most obsequious letter to ingratiate himself with her.'

William Maitland lapsed into silence when he discovered that Mary knew of this. He was yet to learn that Throckmorton, the English ambassador to France, had a sympathy and secret admiration for Mary and had on occasion been indiscreet.

The meeting with Knox troubled Mary for months. His personality was a topic of discussion among her ladies as we sat one evening eating in the small supper room attached to her bedroom. I'd not mentioned the comment Knox had made to his friend as he left Mary. She was dejected enough by her lack of success with him.

'I did not think he would throw over his beliefs and embrace our faith,' said Mary, 'but I did think we might come to an accommodation within our disagreements. I can appreciate the writings of the Reformers.' She smiled at me. It was a secret between us that I had shown her Protestant pamphlets. 'But although they are insufficient for me,' she went on, 'I respect that this is not the case for others. I'd hoped John Knox might respond in kind.'

'It is nigh impossible for any woman to gain the respect of John Knox,' said Jean, Countess of Argyll. Since becoming estranged from her husband, the earl, she lived at court. She was one of King James's illegitimate children, and Mary kindly welcomed her older half-sister into our company. 'He urges me to avoid wrong-doing, which he declares to be the natural trait of females.'

'It is hard to believe that John Knox married and lived content with his wife until she died,' Mary commented.

'Many men do consider women their inferior,' I said. With sudden insight I saw that this was not the case with Duncan Alexander. When we'd debated serious issues of religion or science, he'd always listened to my views and responded with sound arguments.

'Yes,' Mary agreed. 'But often with men it is so they may

have the opportunity to act as our protectors in order to present themselves as dashing and strong. John Knox not only believes us to be inferior, he holds to the opinion that women are in some way evil.'

'The sin of Eve to tempt Adam besmirches all of us for ever after,' said Marie Seton.

'No one mentions that Adam should have been stronger willed,' I said crisply. 'If it's true that Man is supposed to be the head of women, more intelligent and stable, and put on earth to guide and govern them in all things, then surely the greater sin was that of Adam's, in that he did nothing to help a poor weak creature.'

'Some women do like to be dominated,' said Marie Beaton. 'I confess I like mastery in a man.'

Marie Livingston put in, 'I've heard that many women go to hear Preacher Knox speak and seek his advice, not only on Biblical interpretation but on personal matters.'

'Isn't that curious?' Mary mused. 'That he berates them and they accept this?'

'Is it because he gives them a place for their opinion, whereas before there were few opportunities for women to be heard and not much to talk about apart from domestic matters?' I asked. 'Surely it's a good thing that, as women, we can now enquire and debate upon religious matters.'

'Except,' Mary laughed, 'Preacher Knox permits no debate. It is his opinion and his alone that supersedes all others.'

'I fear that by his own hand he will be undone,' I said.

'How so?'

'One of the new Acts of parliament is to allow each child in Scotland to be educated – albeit only if they attend his kirk. When women learn to read and write they will think for themselves, and then, truly, there will rise up a "monstrous regiment" who will not be so obedient to him, or indeed to anyone.'

We laughed as we ate, but Mary now knew that this man would not go away or modify his manners. Knox had tasted the power of his own words and seen their effect, and nothing would silence him. With him using the pulpit as a platform for his opinions, Mary's rule in Scotland would always be turbulent.

But soon there were more pressing matters to worry about. Within a year, the north of Scotland, under the Earl of Huntly, had risen up in rebellion.

Chapter 27

Although Scotland lagged behind France in material wealth and opulence, I found the intrigue taking place equal to that of the French court. And the blood ties of the nobles with their links to royal lineage were, if anything, more convoluted.

Gavin had given up trying to explain the intricacies of the Scottish clan system to me: 'Suffice it to say that clan chiefs, lords and lairds have their own personal armies and rule their estates like kingdoms. Clan members owe loyalty to their chief first, before any monarch. To complicate matters, Mary's father, King James, had about a dozen children from all sorts of liaisons. Reaching adulthood, these children have ever greater ambitions. We have the Hamilton Stuarts warring with the Lennox Stuarts as to who has the closest royal bloodline. Lord James Stuart, as eldest natural son of our former king, is in fact the nearest, but being illegitimate he is barred from the succession. But as he is allied to the omnipotent Douglas family, with Morton at its head, he might claim supremacy over all.'

'That happens with every monarch,' I said. 'It was the same with the kings of France.'

'Yes, but the advantage France has over Scotland,' Gavin quipped, 'is that it is so much larger. A French king can dispatch an illegitimate son to an inaccessible spot in the

Pyrenees, award him a pension, and never expect to see him at court again. Scotland is o'er small to do that. Some of King James's offspring have ended up in Falkirk, scarce a half-day's gallop away.'

Falkirk may have been only a short ride away, but there were more remote, mountainous places in the kingdom. Mary was determined to tour as much of her country as she could, but journeys were difficult. There were wolves prowling the woods, and bad weather made roads impassable. Moreover, Protestants became bolder in their attacks on Catholic places of worship. A visit from the queen, who insisted on having her private mass, would often cause an outbreak of vandalism in a town, with statues smashed and abbeys and convents raided.

'They are as barbaric as the English army once was when they pillaged our country,' the queen's chaplain complained. 'Beautiful works of art are being wantonly destroyed.'

'We might hope for a better welcome in the north,' Mary said, for she was determined to see the Highlands.

During the summer of the following year a royal progress took place in the area of Aberdeen, near the home of the Catholic Earl of Huntly. Huntly, alarmed at the rise of Protestantism, decided to grasp an opportunity while the queen was visiting the north. The Earl of Morton and Lord James, who were travelling as our escorts, brought news that Huntly had armed his men. He was setting out to capture the queen and compel her to marry one of his sons, who had declared undying love for her. Mary's reaction was swift. Acting on the advice of Morton and Lord James, she sent for reinforcements.

Among those who answered her call was Lord Lindsay.

I was taken aback when Sir Gavin told me this.

'You've already met Lord Lindsay?' he asked me.

'Yes,' I replied, 'and have no wish to again.'

'He can be a bit of a boor,' Gavin said, 'but he has a stout heart nonetheless.'

'A bit of a boor!' I exclaimed. 'When we tried to attend mass on that first Sunday, Lord Lindsay barred the way of the queen and physically threatened me.'

'Oh! I didn't realize. He is no personal friend of mine,' Gavin said quickly. 'I hardly know the man. I was only repeating what I'd heard others say of him.'

'Best not to do that in future then,' I replied in chilly tones.

It was a unique unpleasantness between us. Afterwards I felt guilty, especially as Gavin had taken time to ride beside me on our journey north to point out interesting features of the countryside as we passed through his family estates. Contrite at having upset me, over the next days he plied me with little gifts to restore us to our former friendship. As Duncan Alexander seemed to have withdrawn from me, I welcomed his company.

Lord Lindsay arrived with his men and joined forces with the rest. We watched them assemble at Corrichie and then dressed Mary, as she'd commanded us, in the colours of Scotland. Wearing an iridescent blue velvet riding habit with white leather gloves and boots and a long white veil trailing from her silver headdress, she could never be mistaken for anyone but a queen. As she rode beyond their forward positions to face them, I followed with her page, Anthony Standen, who carried her personal banner. A loud hurrah! went up from the soldiers. Lord James and the other commanders came to meet her. They did not look best pleased at the presence of their queen. Lords Morton and Ruthven glowered at her; Lindsay gave me an evil grin.

Morton barely saluted before saying to Mary, 'Madam, retire to the rear and let us do our work.'

Before she could reply, Lord James said, 'More fitting that you remain in safety, dear sister.'

But the soldiers could see her and were stirring in expectation. 'The queen!' they shouted to each other. 'The queen! Today we fight before the queen!'

'I hear the battle cries,' said Mary. 'Were I a male heir you would not doubt that I could lead my army. I will prove to you that I have as much courage as any king.'

She snatched the standard from Anthony Standen and, holding it aloft, left us to canter up and down in front of the massed ranks of cannon, horse and infantry.

The roars of her delighted troops echoed off the mountains: 'For Mary! For Mary! For Mary, Queen of Scots!'

It was a heart-stopping moment. And then Mary turned and began to gallop furiously back towards us.

'Oh no!' I gasped as I realized that she'd no intention of halting.

'Great God!' Lord James swore. 'She means to lead the charge!'

A rider detached himself from the sidelines and raced to intercept her. His bonnet flew off and I saw that it was Duncan. But he was already too late. Mary would be past us before he caught up with her. Across the space I heard him shout my name:

'Jenny!'

Snapping out of my daze, I spurred my own horse to

intercept Mary's. Her mount spied me approaching and veered to the side, towards Duncan, who reached over and grabbed the reins. In seconds I was beside them and we ushered Mary away. When we reached our base she was afire with pleasure, for the men's shouts of praise still sounded in our ears.

The queen's army soundly defeated Huntly's men, with the result that the earl died of a seizure. His son was caught and executed. The Moray lands that bordered on Huntly were given to Lord James Stuart; with Huntly quelled he was now officially known as the Earl of Moray.

In the circumstances this seemed to me to be correct and fitting, but Duncan Alexander's analysis of the situation was different. He'd been appointed Mary's battle messenger and I was with her when he returned, unsmiling, with the news of Huntly's death.

Noticing his expression, Mary chided him: 'Won't you rejoice with me, Sir Duncan, that Huntly's power is broken?'

'I am glad that the queen's peace is no longer threatened,' Duncan replied, 'although whether your grace's life was in danger is a matter of conjecture.'

'Sir, may I remind you that the Earl of Huntly rose in rebellion against me! Are you declaring yourself in sympathy with his cause?' It was the first time I'd heard Mary rebuke him.

'I do have some sympathy with the earl, less so for his infatuated son.'

Mary rose to her feet, a red flush of annoyance spreading over her face. My heart began to beat wildly in fear for Duncan. 'Explain yourself, sir!' she commanded.

I willed Duncan to be silent, or to mollify her in some way, for although Mary had seen the sense in leaving the battlefield, she was still irked that he had curtailed her glorious moment. A lesser man might have done so, but this man, whom I thought I still loved, did not.

Duncan gazed at Mary and then spoke slowly. 'You decided to award your half-brother Lord James Stuart the Earldom of Moray before ever we set out for the north. I was told that you promised him these lands on the occasion of his wedding in February.'

I looked in surprise at Mary, who glanced away. It was a measure of how much Lord James had inveigled himself into her life that she'd keep this secret from her closest confidantes. I was gratified by Duncan's expression as he realized that I too had been kept in ignorance. And I saw why he was concerned by such manipulative power play. Moray bordered Huntly's estates, and in the past the Earl of Huntly had drawn tithe and arms rights from there and surrounding districts.

'By granting these to your half-brother, and other similar benefits to Morton and the rest, they grow in prestige, while Huntly's fiefdom is diminished and indeed now broken altogether,' Duncan continued.

'They are my lands, and I may do as I wish with them,' Mary stated, but her voice was less confident.

'Indeed, majesty,' he bowed his head, 'you may.'

'Fie, Sir Duncan,' Mary said, striving to lighten the exchange, 'I sense that there is more you wish to say on this matter.'

Duncan looked up. 'Only if you wish to hear it, majesty.'

Mary sighed. 'I do not know if I truly *wish* to hear it but a monarch seldom hears the truth, so it might be that I *should* listen to what you have to say.'

'There is a danger in a Scottish monarch awarding

already mighty lords extra lands and titles. It means that these lords have access to more men to recruit and arm against their ruler if they choose to do so. And further, although I do not practise the Catholic religion, with Huntly's domain shattered the balance of your kingdom is compromised.'

'I am determined to pursue a policy of religious tolerance, but I will think on what you have said.' To show that he was back in her favour, Mary held out her hand for Duncan to kiss as he departed.

I followed him to the door. 'It is something that I heard Catherine de' Medici say,' I said to him. 'That a monarch needs someone to tell them the truth.'

Duncan turned to face me and I noticed how tired he looked – greyed shadow under his eyes, stubble on his cheeks.

'Then Mary is fortunate that you will be beside her,' he said. He tilted his head and studied my face as though committing it to memory. 'Goodbye, Jenny.'

With a sudden sense of loss I closed the door behind him.

Mary's policies of appeasement seemed to be working. Lord James distanced himself from the extremism of Knox and with his and William Maitland's advice, the queen and her country struggled into a way of working during the next few years. Mary's wish for a personal conversation with Elizabeth of England to resolve the matter of the succession was thwarted when the Duke of Guise was assassinated as her uncle's murder provoked more violent religious dissension in France.

I was more than content not to have to prepare for what

would have been a fraught encounter between the two queens. It meant that we could relax and take more pleasure in life at court.

With threats to the queen's person not imminent, Duncan Alexander asked leave to go and visit his own estates. I now understood why he'd looked at me so intently and said goodbye. But he didn't contact me directly to tell me he'd be absent for a while. It was Mary who told me that he'd left the court.

'Jenny,' she squeezed my hand on seeing my reaction. 'You are sad that Sir Duncan is gone.'

I didn't wish to share my deepest private hurt with anyone, so I replied, 'I would have thought he might have let me know, that's all. No matter, Sir Gavin of Strathtay is an amusing companion.'

'And he is very attentive to you,' Mary said. 'I'd like you to know, Jenny, that you are free to marry if you so choose. I would not expect anyone who attended me to wait until I find another husband. I have told my Maries this too.'

'Aha!' I said, partly to change the topic of conversation, but also out of curiosity. 'I know that Marie Livingston hopes for a liaison with Master Sempill and Marie Beaton is also being wooed. Is there another romance in the offing?'

'That you may discover on Twelfth Night.' There was mischief in Mary's voice. 'I have spoken to the pastry cook, and it will be Marie Fleming who will find the bean in her breakfast honey cake. We will dress her in my clothes and jewellery to play the role of Queen of the Bean during the evening celebrations. Then we will watch and see who pays homage at her court.'

Marie Fleming wore the queen's coronet for Twelfth Night, along with a royal gown of green and gold. The rest of us prepared for the event with much giggling and rustling of taffeta, for we had decided that we would dress in the Spanish style, with tiers of lace, elaborate make-up and high combs of jet in our hair. Just as we were about to descend to the great hall, Mary brought me her black pearls and knotted them around my throat. 'There now, Jenny,' she said. 'You too are queen for the night.'

The hall was decked with greenery and smelled of pine and fir. In the light of the huge fire and the blazing chandeliers my eyes were alert to see what would happen. Gavin was included in our spying game, and it was he who first clapped his hands to signal that he knew Marie Fleming's would-be suitor. He whispered the name in my ear: 'William Maitland!'

'No!' I exclaimed out loud. 'It cannot be! He is so much older than she.'

'I tell you it is.' His face was alive at the opportunity for gossip. 'Look at him almost capering in front of her, a forty-year-old widower and she scarce twenty!'

'I think it is a sweet romance,' Mary said, tempering his remarks. Speaking behind her napkin, she went on, 'It is true, yet no one believes it. Kirkcaldy of Grange has declared that he as soon will be elected Pope than Maitland be accepted in his suit.'

'Mmm,' Gavin demurred. 'I would not be so sure that Master William will be rejected.'

'But Marie Fleming would have mentioned it to me!' Mary said. 'I'm sure she would have said.'

'Perhaps she does not know it herself,' he replied. 'I am

very observant of people – their faces sometimes belie the words that come from their mouths.'

'That is a fine attribute to have, Sir Gavin.'

He smiled at Mary's compliment. 'For another example,' he said, 'I know that Jenny misses the presence of Sir Duncan Alexander, yet she has such a gentle manner that I am hopeful she will say yes if I ask her to dance with me.' He held out his hand.

I placed my hand in Gavin's and we stepped out onto the dance floor. And at the end of the night he said very sincerely, 'I would like to be with you more often, Jenny, if I may. You are such agreeable company, and maybe I can help ease your loneliness.'

I was touched that he'd noticed I was lonely. Although I supported Mary at official meetings, increasingly she was closeted privately with Lord James Stuart. I agreed to his suggestion and Gavin was often by my side when we went hunting or hawking or attended masques and balls.

Mary was diligent in her duties of State but found time to enjoy herself. By dint of her personality and virtues, she established a small, tight-knit group of loyal friends and officials. An expert horsewoman, Mary adored riding through the wild countryside. The Huntly episode hadn't put her off, and as time went on she explored more of her kingdom.

'My father was known as the "Poor Man's King", for he travelled through his country in disguise so that he could mix with the common people. It is something I'd like to do, 'she told me.

And so, aided by Sir Gavin, I devised a scheme whereby we might escape the strictures of the court one day and go into the streets of Edinburgh.

In fanciful moments Mary talked of how it might be if she led a more rustic, straightforward life. She wasn't blind to the harshness of such an existence. But to be free of the constraints that bound her, to lose the heavy responsibility of state duties, must be a dream of every monarch. With Gavin as our protector and Anthony Standen, the queen's loyal page, in attendance, I saw no harm in us disguising ourselves as country lads to go to market. In this we were helped by Rhanza, who would do anything for her adored queen.

Rhanza had been born within the Palace of Holyrood itself, the result of a liaison between a kitchen maid and an unnamed courtier. The irony of her situation wasn't lost on Mary, who'd remarked to me, 'Poor child, if her mother had been better placed socially and caught the attention of my father, then I might be greeting Rhanza as my good half-sister.' She was, of course, referring to Jean, Countess of Argyll.

'I think Rhanza is content with her present lot in life,' I reassured her. Truly, the girl had a very happy disposition. She could be heard humming a merry tune as she worked and, whatever the season, always made sure fresh blooms were in the flower jug that sat on Mary's windowsill.

Sworn to secrecy, Rhanza was delighted to help with our plan and, early one morning, brought us ordinary clothes with hooded capes. We dressed in great excitement. I fetched the knife that Duncan Alexander had given me during our flight to Amboise from the drawer in my room. Rhanza led us by servants' stairs to the cellars and thence along an underground passageway to the abbey cemetery, and finally over a wall.

The city was stirring awake as we walked through the streets. Rubbish was piled in corners, and among these heaps of refuse we noticed children sleeping.

'Dear Mother of God,' said Mary. 'Jenny, we must find out why these children have no home to go to at night. Some of them are no more than babies.'

The Edinburgh we saw was not the one usually presented for the queen's inspection when on official business or visiting friends. Sewage ran in the gutters, and workers hurrying up and down the wynds and stairs looked lean and careworn. With Gavin's guidance we headed for the market and watched the stalls being set up and the farmers bringing in their produce. There was a buzz of commerce, but when we sat down in a quiet corner to break our fast, the talk was of the latest tax and the duties on goods to and from the Netherlands.

'Such a wealth of knowledge and insight I have garnered in a few hours,' Mary said. 'I understand why my father did this. There is more to be learned here in an hour than in a month's meetings with the privy council.'

We spent the remainder of the afternoon rambling on Arthur's Chair. From here we could look down on Holyrood. I could see the tower of the abbey church where Mary had kindly arranged to have my father's remains reinterred so that I could easily visit his grave. How insignificant it and the lofty turrets of the palace appeared when viewed from this height. Stretched out on our stomachs on the springy heather, we watched the soldiers and officials come and go like so many tiny manikins.

'Don't you wish, Jenny . . .' Mary paused, and there was a catch in her voice. 'Don't you wish that we didn't need to go back?' And beside me, lying on the grass, the Queen of Scots burst into tears.

'Yes,' I said truthfully. 'Yes, I do.' For sometimes I did indulge in wish-dreams where I was a girl with no encumbrances and Duncan Alexander had a less complicated role. I imagined him a wool merchant, or perhaps a court painter, and we would meet and declare our love, be married and live in harmony.

I gave Mary my handkerchief to dry her eyes. And then we rolled over onto our backs and made up names for the cloud shapes scudding above our heads, pretending these were countries we ruled where all the people were loyal and law-abiding.

It was dusk before we returned to the palace. At the agreed time Rhanza was waiting by the wall to help us over and take us back to the queen's apartments. The Maries had been instructed to say that Mary was indisposed and was spending the day in bed, with me in attendance. We slipped into the palace and up an internal stair to the queen's rooms without incident. Welcomed back with laughter and glee by the Maries, we fell into the small supper room and spent most of the night gossiping about our adventures.

But the secret got out. It didn't come from Sir Gavin or Rhanza or me – it was the queen herself who couldn't resist letting it be known what she'd done. Faced with the nobles' condescending attitude towards her, and frequently told that, having been brought up in France, she was ignorant of Scottish society, she announced that she'd made personal contact with her subjects.

'It wasn't just playacting that prompted me to go into the

streets in disguise,' she explained to her council. 'By doing that I can see what my people lack and how plain and simple are their needs.'

'The people have no sense of what they need,' said Lord James when he'd recovered from the shock of the queen wandering unprotected about the city and parkland. 'They only have wants, and sometimes, like children, these must be denied for their own good. That's why by divine providence we have anointed kings.'

'A queen,' Mary corrected him. She gave him a benign look to soften the impact of her words. 'Scotland is ruled by a queen.'

'More's the pity,' a mutter came from one of the nobles.

In France, had he dared utter such treason within earshot of Catherine de' Medici, this man would have been marked down and dealt with secretly.

Mary elected not to take offence. 'I am aware that we do have need of a king and I hope that I might bear the future King of Scotland. To this end I must seek a husband.'

William Maitland, who had visited England on diplomatic business, said, 'Queen Elizabeth of England has some views on this matter and may put forward the name of Robert Dudley, Earl of Leicester.'

'And why would Elizabeth feel moved to offer me one of her English nobles as a bridegroom?'

Maitland cleared his throat. 'I believe that her majesty, the Queen of England, may be thinking of who might reign after her. An alliance between the noble houses of both countries would produce a monarch to rule Scotland and England.'

An interested silence crept through the room. The problem of Elizabeth's successor was one that the English queen had vacillated upon for years. Mary had written many times to her cousin asking that the two countries come to some constitutional agreement on this, but Elizabeth always avoided any commitment. Now here was a tempting proposition for the Scots lords. If their queen or a child of their queen also ruled over their richer neighbour, there would be many benefits. In addition to the castles, mansion houses and vast estates owned by the English monarch, there was the prospect of untold wealth from the New World being ferried across the Atlantic in English ships. William Maitland looked expectantly at the queen.

Mary appeared to consider the suggestion and then replied, 'This man, Robert Dudley, is held high in Elizabeth's own personal affection. I know that the Queen of England has spies everywhere. I do not wish to bring one into my own bedchamber.'

That evening, when I left the queen's bedroom and went to my own rooms, someone was waiting there. It was Duncan Alexander and he was furious.

'Sir Duncan! I did not realize that you had returned to court—' I'd scarcely begun before he interrupted me.

'It's as well that I did! I have just learned that her majesty and yourself spent a day in the streets of Edinburgh in some ridiculous disguise!'

'That may be so,' I replied, 'although it is no business of yours.'

'I was charged to guard the queen. It is completely my business.'

'You have stated this before,' I said, 'that you have been charged to guard the queen, yet you have never said by whom.'

Duncan bit his lip. 'That I cannot say.'

'Why not?' I demanded. 'It is important to know what motivates you, for there is more than one way to interpret the word "guard".'

He looked taken aback by that, but then gestured impatiently. 'Don't change the subject. The matter in hand is that by recklessness you put the queen's life in danger.'

'We were not in danger. To protect us we had a loyal lad and Sir Gavin of Strathtay.'

'Gavin of Strathtay!' Duncan spluttered. 'That poltroon! He could no more protect a lady than he can dress himself unaided.'

'Sir Gavin was very effective, and anyway it is a royal prerogative to go among one's people. It was something the queen's father did often. He dressed as a commoner so that he could find out their true thoughts and needs.'

'He was a man!'

'And you think a woman is not as good as a man?'

'I think that a woman might not defend herself as well.'

'We could defend ourselves well enough,' I said. 'I carried a knife.'

'You carried a knife?' Duncan laughed. Seeing my annoyance at his attitude, and in order to provoke me further he cried in mock horror, 'Mercy! The girl has a knife!'

In anger then, I drew out the knife, stepped close to him and laid the blade against his cheek. 'Don't mock me, sir,' I said. 'I'm as capable of using this as any man.'

His eyes registered astonishment. I smiled in triumph and moved away. But before I'd time to take another breath he'd covered the distance between us and pinned my arms to my side with his own.

'*Never,*' he said fiercely, '*ever, do that* to me again.'

'There is no need,' I said with more lightness than I felt, for my heartbeat had increased at his touch. 'I have made my point.'

He didn't reply. Nor did he release me. I sensed his own heart beating close to mine.

'You may let me go free, sir,' I said.

'And if I do not wish to?' He turned me round and pulled me nearer to him.

And now I could feel the whole line of his body against mine. A passion was stirring within me: fascination mixed with fright. My voice trembled when I spoke. 'I meant you no harm.'

He looked intently into my face. Whereupon he released me and took a pace back. 'Nor I you, Jenny,' he said. 'Nor I you.'

Chapter 28

That night I could not sleep. In my mind I replayed our meeting, lingering on the moments when our two bodies were close. As dawn light edged through my bed curtains, I got up and went to the window.

I rested my head against the glass. I had tried to forget him, but I was still deeply attached to Duncan Alexander. The passage of years since we'd first met hadn't altered my feelings. I was woman enough now to know that he desired me. And I desired him. It flattered and thrilled me that he was attracted to me but I wanted more than that. I would never do as others did and engage in a meaningless liaison with a man.

I thought of Sir Gavin. He was such an amiable companion, making me laugh when the tedious business of life at court weighed us down. After some particularly vindictive sermons by John Knox on the subject of the queen's marriage prospects, he had Mary laughing out loud at his observations on Knox's own recent wedding, at almost fifty, to a sixteen-year-old girl. But his wit, often wickedly funny, was sometimes just wicked. Mary enjoyed his company although she didn't hesitate to upbraid him if she felt his personal comments were too sharp. He'd once casually enquired of the queen if she would be averse to me being married. I wasn't sure if that was just because, as marriage was in the offing for two of the Maries, our discussions had naturally turned to weddings – or whether there was another reason for his enquiry. Later she'd prompted me gently on my feelings for Sir Gavin and then mentioned Sir Duncan Alexander.

I diverted the conversation. My thoughts about Duncan were confused. Too much of his life was shrouded in mystery. With no specific duties at court, he came and went as he pleased. For his part he was polite when addressing me – an infuriating coolness, combined with an amused sarcasm. Except . . . last night when the mask had slipped. Neither of us had been aloof then. We'd teetered on the edge of a precipice with a ribbon of fire between us.

But it wasn't my eligibility to wed but Mary's that occupied everyone's attention. All Europe speculated on what partner might be suitable for the beautiful Queen of Scots and, to her annoyance, both John Knox and Elizabeth of England aired their opinions.

So it was in secret that Mary first began to explore the possibility of a liaison that would give Scotland a strong ally in Europe. And, as one of her emissaries, she chose Duncan Alexander.

Mary was walking with me in the palace garden when she told me this. 'Jenny, will you miss Sir Duncan when he is abroad?' she asked me.

I nodded, recalling how I'd missed his company when he'd gone off to see to his estates.

'I sense that you might love him, yet you are reticent with him.'

'I do not know whether I can truly love him or not,' I replied.

'Perhaps there is a time, Jenny, when one should listen to one's heart.'

I couldn't tell Mary that the reason I was reticent was because I mistrusted Duncan on her behalf.

'He carries important papers for me,' she went on.

'To France?' I enquired.

'Not France, no. He goes into Spain.'

'Spain?'

'Yes, marriage with the King of Spain's son has been mooted once more. Obviously this must be kept quiet for now.'

Spain! Even I understood how furious this would make Elizabeth of England. Using the pretext of religion, she had smashed Scotland's alliance with France so that this trouble-some country on her northern border now had no powerful ally to come to its aid in any quarrel it might have with England. If the Queen of Scots married a Spanish heir, then France would be replaced with an even more dangerous threat to England.

'These papers require the utmost discretion, therefore I send someone whom I know to be discreet.'

If Mary trusted Duncan, why then did I hesitate? Because the queen wasn't always a good judge of character, I told myself. Her tender heart made her inclined to believe that those with ill intent towards her could be won over with charm and soft words. Duncan was no oily-tongued flatterer, yet in France he'd slid between the diverse factions of the Scots lords and was doing the same here in Scotland.

His departure was no secret. It was given out that he was going to the Low Countries to settle matters of tax duties in order to promote trade. This would be believed as it was a genuine concern of Mary's. Ever since our foray into Edinburgh she'd sought ways to assist commerce so that the poverty of her people might be alleviated. He came to bid us farewell, and I'm sure it was Mary who engineered that he and I had a few moments alone together.

'I wish you a safe journey, sir,' I said. I was plucking at my handkerchief with my fingers.

His tone was light. *He doesn't care that we will not see each other for many months*, I thought.

'I brought you a farewell gift.' He handed me a tissue-wrapped parcel.

My eyes met his, but in their depths I could not fathom his mood. I tore open the paper.

'You always complain of the cold, Jenny. I thought it might keep you warm while I am away.'

It was an underskirt. Expensive. Made of heavy satin. Coloured deepest red.

I recoiled as if struck by a snake. My mouth slack with horror, I held it away from me.

'My gift is not welcome, I see,' Duncan said. 'And, I fear, neither am I.'

I could say nothing. I was reliving the awful scene in the Castle of Blois and its aftermath, when the Count of Cluny had threatened me with death. The red underskirt slid from my hands to the floor.

Duncan turned on his heel and left the room.

It was over a year before I saw Duncan Alexander again, but hardly a day passed when he wasn't in my thoughts. Messengers came and went, but there was no letter for me and I sent none to him. By rejecting his gift in such a way, I'd offended him. But it would be foolish to write to explain my apparent revulsion and mention my suspicions about the Count of Cluny. Mary and her retinue knew that our mail was frequently read by others.

Letters came from all over Europe. A lot of the queen's work consisted in replying to foreign dignitaries. Most of these missives went via her appointed secretary, the Italian, David Rizzio, who now managed her correspondence. He spent hours in her company as she dictated letters, and she enjoyed working out new ciphers with him for the ones that were sent in code.

Mary was an expert linguist. In addition to Scots and English, she could read and write in Latin, French, Italian and Greek. So could David Rizzio, whose first position within our court was as a singing musician. To many he seemed an odd choice to find favour with Mary. Short in stature, with stooped, rounded shoulders, he was usually passed over as unattractive. But Rizzio was clever, with a quirky sense of humour that men thought annoying but Mary found refreshing. More and more often, when her spirits were low or she'd had a trying day with her advisers, or when someone brought word that John Knox had launched another attack on her from his pulpit, she would invite Rizzio and a few other intimates to her supper room, where they'd pass the evening listening to music and playing dice or cards.

By the summer of 1564 we knew what Duncan's letters had been hinting at for months. The King of Spain finally and publicly declared his son would not marry the Queen of Scots.

John Knox was one of those who delighted in this news, as he'd been preaching against any union with another

Catholic country. The Scots lords who'd privately supported Mary's plans were disappointed – they'd anticipated more titles and wealth – and Mary herself was depressed.

'I thought to do the best for Scotland,' she complained. 'I feel as though I am still a child, to be sold as property. I am a woman with a woman's needs . . . and fears. The same fear of marriage that I believe Elizabeth has.'

I didn't understand this remark. Mary had been married to Francis and had been intimate enough with him to hope for a child. Although she guarded her virtue, she was in no way prudish, and Elizabeth of England was thought to have lovers – one of them the man named Lord Robert Dudley.

'Oh,' Mary laughed as she realized what I was thinking. 'It's not physical intimacy that we both fear, it is the prospect of losing control. Any man who marries us will expect to be given the crown matrimonial. He will demand to be made king in his own right, with all that entails. Then he may convene parliament, ratify laws, declare war, award honours to his friends, spend the purse on anything he sees fit. As women, we become brood mares, to stay in the background and produce children – sons as heirs, and girls to be bartered with princes and nobles for power and money. If we die, as women frequently do in childbirth, our husband's family will move in and secure every high position. If he later remarries, then the children of his new wife may take precedent, and our name and royal personage would disappear. My royal English cousin and I know this only too well. This is why neither of us rush to wed, and why we are so cautious when it comes to matters of inheritance. Elizabeth will not be cowed by the great lords who surround her and I do respect her for it.'

'Marriages arranged for reasons of state can involve personal feelings,' said Marie Fleming. 'Catherine de' Medici was sent as a child to marry King Henri but fell in love with him.'

'Only to find that he preferred his mistress,' Marie Beaton was quick to point out.

'As a child, you were betrothed to Dauphin Francis and were quite content to marry him,' said Marie Seton.

'Yes, but I knew Francis well and we had a great affection and respect for each other.'

'But had you not loved Francis, the marriage would still have taken place,' I said.

Mary groaned and held her head. 'When I say my night prayers, I will ask the Blessed Mother of God and my own dear mother, who I am sure is also in Heaven, to send me an acceptable suitor. One who is well connected but also attractive to me.'

'And rich,' added Marie Livingston.

'I like a man to have wisdom,' said Marie Fleming.

I glanced at her. Prior to meeting William Maitland, I would have guessed that she prized good looks above other attributes.

'Kindly,' I suggested, for I thought my queen needed a man who would care for her.

'Strong,' Marie Seton.

Rizzio strummed his lute and began to sing:

> *Rich or wise, kind or strong,*
> *Who can my true love be?*
> *I have waited for my gallant o'er long,*
> *And weary he'll ne'er find me.'*

He stopped, tilted his head at the queen, and smiled.

'Tall,' Mary said. 'I'd like him to be long of limb.'

Chapter 29

After Christmas I remained in Edinburgh suffering from a heavy cold while the queen and her court went travelling in Fife.

In the middle of January Mary wrote to me with birthday greetings and telling me to come to her as soon as I was well. A most attractive young man was on his way from England and had asked for an audience with her, she said. He was in fact a cousin of hers, for they shared a grandmother – the English Tudor princess, sister of Henry VII, who had married twice. Also, he was connected on his father's side to the royal Stuart line via the Lennox family.

> *He does not attend religious duties, although his mother is an ardent Catholic, and as such Elizabeth is not too enamoured of her. But my sisterly cousin the Queen of England has given this man a title and allowed him leave to visit Scotland so that he might meet me. I've heard he is most charming. His name is Henry, Lord Darnley.*

It was early February before I was fit to travel to Fife. I left Edinburgh with a groom and a few armed men to take me to the estuary crossing where someone would be waiting to conduct me to the queen at Wemyss Castle.

My escort was waiting by the quay. Mary had sent her recently returned emissary, Duncan Alexander.

Ah, now! My fingers tightened on my reins as I brought my horse to a halt. I quickly signalled to my groom, for I did not want to be dependent upon Duncan to help me dismount.

'My Lady Ginette,' Duncan said formally, 'I am commanded by the queen to convey you to her presence.'

I didn't blame him for his manner. It was my fault that we'd parted so badly. And now it was upon me to say something.

'Once again,' I said, 'I believe that my behaviour to you when last we met requires explanation.'

He affected a puzzled air. 'I do not recall . . . ?'

'I was rude to you when you gave me a gift and I would like to explain—'

'Oh, that,' he said lightly. 'I have not thought about it at all.'

This made me sadder than if he'd still been angry with me. He was tanned from his time abroad, but thinner. Had the failure of Mary's attempt at a Spanish marriage disappointed him?

Duncan rang the bell for the ferryman. We had only gone a few yards in our journey across the estuary when the sky darkened, yet the sun was still present.

'Look!' Duncan touched my arm.

I raised my head in the direction he indicated and saw a swiftly moving dense cloud of animated shadows approaching from the south. Suddenly there was a noise like the rustle of a thousand silken petticoats at a fabulous ball. Swinging and soaring above us, borne on the evening air, we heard the chittering of wild fowl as birds in their thousands came sweeping in.

'Oh!' I gasped in wonder.

Duncan too was gazing skyward. 'At my home in Knoydart,' he said, 'there is a similar sight worth seeing in spring and late autumn. It is a stopping place for the wild geese as they travel their migration routes.'

All about us the birds came in to land on the river banks as the sun set.

'It is quite wonderful,' I breathed. Fiery red rays of light were slanting through the mountains. It was as though some untutored painter had released his palette upon the sky, as if God himself had dispersed a rainbow among the snow-crowned hilltops.

'More beautiful than the stained glass of any grand cathedral,' Duncan murmured.

It was cold on the water and I shivered. He unhooked his cloak and offered it to me. I gave a proud little shake of the head. He pretended not to see this and wrapped the garment around my shoulders. I pulled up the hood and turned my face towards the castle, which we could see in the distance. He stood beside me and fleetingly I thought of his arms around me.

'Your mistress has not spoken of any future marriage plans?' he asked.

Ah! He was being friendly to elicit information from me. I decided not to tell him of Mary's letter.

'Why should she speak of her marriage plans to anyone?' I countered.

'She is the queen. Her marriage is an affair of state and therefore not her sole business but that of her people.'

'Too many people,' I retorted. 'Has she to consult with every crowned head of Europe and wait for their permission before she may select a husband?'

'If that's what it takes to preserve peace in her realm, then, yes, she must, Jenny,' he replied.

'It is England which interferes most in this matter and pretends to give helpful advice, but I think the English queen doesn't want her married at all,' I said. 'She is afraid that Mary would be fertile while she is barren.'

'Hush!' he said anxiously. 'You may speak treason.'

'I am in my own country. I cannot speak treason here!'

'Would it were so simple,' he sighed. 'It isn't merely womanly jealousy that makes Elizabeth fear a Scottish child.'

'Then why is she so against any wedding talk where Mary is concerned?'

'Because there are those who might use such a marriage and any child thereof to take the English throne' – Duncan put his mouth close to my ear – '*while Elizabeth is still upon it.*'

I turned my head to look at him, and my face was level with his. His eyes were the dense colour of fine emeralds, with the white around them very clear after a day spent outside. They were serious, a change from his usual mocking expression.

Despite his nearness and my rush of emotion, I found my mood matching his own. 'Then no suitor of Mary's will meet with Elizabeth's approval,' I whispered in return.

'Lord Dudley was proposed by Elizabeth.'

'Dudley was Elizabeth's lover!' I exclaimed. 'You cannot expect Mary to accept her cousin's cast-offs.'

'Shh.' He glanced at the ferryman. 'Well then, another

high-placed nobleman of Elizabeth's court. An alliance with England would make us stronger.'

'Stronger against whom?'

'Against France or Spain or the Emperor in Austria, or whichever larger state seeks to gobble a smaller one.'

'Don't you think that England too would eat Scotland up?'

'There would be a more equitable balance of power.'

'Not in matters of religion. Elizabeth has banished Catholics and executes priests.'

'I'd not like to keep score on that contest,' Duncan said drily.

'Mary has striven hard to ensure that no type of religious practice is deemed a crime. In all the time that her mother ruled, only one Protestant was burned.'

'Mary's mother chose the wrong man, for the one she burned was Knox's friend and mentor and he has never forgotten that. His sworn mission is to exterminate every vestige of Catholicism here.'

'Mary wants to see Scotland as a country where both faiths might thrive alongside each other,' I said.

But Duncan had the final word as our journey ended: 'You might as well say that a lion and a tiger can be caged together with no harm coming to either.'

Chapter 30

Lord James Stuart's face did not match his finery at the reception given by the Laird of Wemyss on the seventeenth of February for his English visitors. He glowered at the mention of Lord Darnley's name.

'Darnley is sent here by his parents for a purpose – that they may restate their assertion that their branch of the Stuart family, the Lennox Stuarts, is closest in line to the throne. His mother, Lady Margaret Douglas, is the most conniving woman in Scotland.'

Mary laughed. 'Every noble in Scotland connives in one way or another. And anyway, Lord Darnley's parents took up residence in England for many years after some trouble at the Scottish court about their royal claims, did they not?'

'Indeed, the Lennox Stuarts courted favour with Elizabeth. That in itself should let you know that they'll use any means to advance their ambitions.'

I thought that exceptional effrontery coming from a man whose own mother carried the name of Douglas and who himself had sought English help on more than one occasion to gain his own ends.

'My cousin Elizabeth has asked me to graciously receive Lord Darnley and forgive his family any wrongdoing,' said Mary.

'God's blood!' Lord James swore. 'Whatever plan is being hatched is more devious than I thought.'

But Mary didn't hear the remark. She'd been rearranging her skirts, then looked up as a young man of about eighteen approached. And it was as if a new planet had appeared in the sky. Lord Henry Darnley was exceptionally tall, beautifully dressed in the latest fashion, with a high collar of diamond-pointed lace that enhanced his mane of blond hair.

Mary drew in her breath. 'Why! He is even taller than I.'

'Ah,' Marie Fleming murmured in approval, 'he is made large!' adding under her breath, 'In all parts, one hopes.'

It seems such a trivial thing – that a man's height would make an immediate positive impression. But all her life Mary had had to bend her neck to hold a conversation. Mostly when she danced with a man his head was positioned under her chin or lower. She'd learned to make light of it, claiming that she could tell the history of the hair of every man at court, which pomade he used and who would be bald in a twelvemonth.

There was no such problem with this young man. His head was above everyone else in the room. Henry Darnley had a softly handsome face and long limbs, and his manners were like his appearance, elegant and gracious. His suit of silvered brocade, trimmed with white velvet ribbons, indicated a person of sophisticated tastes, a man who appreciated fine wine and gourmet food.

Within minutes of being introduced to the queen, he had charmed her. With courtly reverence for her person and majesty, he addressed her by saying, 'Lord Henry Darnley asks if it would be permissible for him to dance.'

'Do you mean with myself, Lord Darnley?' Mary asked.

He lowered his eyes, drawing attention to the length of his lashes, and said, 'I would not have presumed to ask such a favour. I only wished that I might join in your merry-making and celebrate with you.' He paused and then added, 'However, if your grace would like to help me in the steps of the morelia, then I would be greatly honoured.'

Mary was enchanted. Apart from his obvious physical attractions, this young man was displaying the kind of court-liness she'd been used to in France and which was in short supply since she'd arrived in Scotland. She loved to dance, and Lord Darnley displayed a fine leg in his silken hose and moved with assured skill.

Marie Livingston nudged me as they took the floor. 'They make a striking couple.'

I had to agree. Mary still wore mainly dark colours – tonight it was a gown of deepest blue. Beside her, Darnley, in lighter tones of silver and white, shone like a star in the night sky.

When the dance was over they wandered towards a window. The queen's laughter drifted over to her attendants, and we smiled at each other to see her so happy. But Lord James Stuart wasn't smiling. He crossed the room and, on some pretext, drew Mary aside. He prevailed upon her to meet an important dignitary, and then another and another, but ever she was glancing round to catch sight of Lord Darnley. For his part, he stood where she had left him, gazing after her like a moonstruck boy.

'He's waiting by the window in the hope that the queen will come back,' I said to Marie Fleming.

'He's by the window so that he can admire himself in the glass.' Duncan Alexander had taken her place behind me.

'Your words are unkind,' I reproached him.

'But true, nevertheless,' he said. 'Look at him. Preening and stroking his hair.'

I was annoyed with him for souring the romantic scene – even more so because, since he'd pointed it out, I now saw that Henry Darnley was indeed studying his own reflection in the windowpane. 'Are you jealous that the queen is attracted to a man?' I asked him. 'Is she not allowed the pleasure of an agreeable romance?'

'Not with that fop,' Duncan said crossly.

'I would dance again.' Mary rejoined us and beckoned to Lord Darnley, who came hurrying across the room.

They danced another two dances and then supper was served. By the end of the evening, if the queen was not totally smitten with Lord Darnley, most of the other ladies were. His charm was considerable and he could talk extensively and knowledgeably about music, literature and art. When we had eaten he begged the queen for one more dance before she retired for the night.

Mary whispered to me, 'I like a man who stands above me. It is delightful to have a companion I can look up to.' She raised her voice. 'Sir Duncan, you must partner Jenny. Let us show how gracefully we can do these steps so it can be seen that dancing is not wicked, as that grim preaching minister Knox would have us believe, but a way of using the bodies the good God gave us to display our talents.'

Duncan took my hand. I barely let my fingers touch his. When I was in the company of this man my emotions always ran contrary to what my head thought sensible.

But no one was watching us. Every eye in the room was on Mary Stuart and Henry Darnley as they dipped and swayed in the movements of the dance. Mary's colour was high and she looked more relaxed than she'd been for years. The appearance of this young man had roused her spirits in a way that no other Scottish lord had done.

'You will excuse me?' As soon as the dance was finished Duncan bowed and left the room.

'Where is Sir Duncan off to in such a rush?' Marie Fleming asked me. 'Have you arranged to meet him later?'

'Definitely not!' I said.

'Oh, don't be such a prude, Jenny. I was only teasing.'

'It's no concern of mine if he has a secret assignation,' I said airily.

'Of whom are we speaking?' Marie Seton had come in from the garden.

'Sir Duncan Alexander,' said Marie Fleming. 'You know, the man that Jenny has absolutely no interest in whatsoever, and doesn't care whether he has arranged a tryst with another lady.'

'Don't worry, Jenny.' Marie Seton hugged me. 'Sir Duncan is not with a lady. I saw him in the gardens. He had stopped to speak with Sir Gavin of Strathtay.'

'And why is my name being mentioned?' Gavin had appeared beside us. 'Not that I mind it being on your lips,' he added, looking directly at me.

'You were chatting with Duncan Alexander,' said Marie Seton, 'recently returned from Europe. I wondered if he was in good health.'

I gave her a grateful glance. She was always the most considerate and loyal of the Maries and I knew she was protecting me with her remark.

'I scarce exchanged a word with him . . .' He paused, and

then said, 'Sir Duncan was hurrying off to talk to one of the men attached to Lord Darnley's party – I believe it was the Count of Cluny.'

My throat constricted with fear when I heard that name, but I tried to steady my breathing. It was unlikely that the Count had followed me to Scotland to pursue me personally after a lapse of so many years. His presence must have something to do with Mary; with her attempts to find a husband. A cold suspicion seeped into my mind. Catherine de' Medici also feared the might of Spain and would have heard of the negotiations between Scotland and Spain. No matter that the proposal had been dropped: she considered her daughter-in-law troublesome and a possible focal point for those who would rebel against the rule of the queen governor. The Count of Cluny was here and speaking to Duncan. I would have to be mindful of Mary's safety.

But within a month or so it was not Mary's health that was causing concern. It was Lord Henry Darnley who fell ill.

Chapter 31

Mary was distraught. 'What ails him? He was well when last we spoke.'

It was Lord James Stuart who'd brought her the news, announcing unsympathetically that Lord Darnley was in bed with the ague. The court was at Stirling Castle, and Mary gave orders for an infusion to be made of herbs from the gardens there; so that she could bring it to him herself.

'Don't go so near that you might catch whatever ailment he has,' said her half-brother. 'My Lord Darnley has developed a nasty rash about his face and neck.'

I wondered what sickness it could be that started with the ague and then developed into a rash. The fact that the Count of Cluny had been in Scotland brought thoughts of poison to my mind.

'I'll take him a message from your grace,' I offered. It would mean I could get closer to Darnley and see and hear for myself any gossip or careless talk.

Mary wrote some lines and folded the paper within one of her monogrammed handkerchiefs. She doused it with scent and gave it to me. At Lord Darnley's apartments I was asked to wait alone in an anteroom as his attendants were helping him to the privy. The door was ajar. I might not have such a chance again, I thought. I slipped inside his bed-chamber and began to look around.

I scarce knew what I was searching for. What evidence would there be to show that his illness was caused by an agent of Elizabeth of England or Catherine de' Medici? From Lord James's description of the mottling on Darnley's face, it sounded similar to Duke Fernand's when he'd died at Fontainebleau.

'Jenny?'

I jumped in fright. Duncan Alexander stood at the door.

'What are you doing?' he asked.

Agitated at being caught out by him scattered my wits. 'You should know!' I burst out.

'I?' He seemed genuinely puzzled. 'What would I know?'

'If anyone had interfered with—' I stopped as caution reasserted itself.

'If anyone had done what?' Duncan asked, coming forward.

I shook my head. I wasn't going to tell him that he'd been seen conferring with the Count of Cluny and why I distrusted that man.

Suddenly we heard Darnley's servants carrying him back from the privy. We both retreated, first into the antechamber and then to the passageway, but there were footsteps echoing along the corridor.

'Go that way,' Duncan indicated the servants' stairway opposite.

I ran down the spiral stairs, past the food trays, dishes and goblets piled in the alcove where the water ran from the sluice system. At the foot of the stairs I stopped. The dishes! The evidence could be in Lord Darnley's food! Some of his uneaten dinner remained on his plate. If there were traces of mint-flavoured crystals, then I would have evidence that the Count of Cluny had tried to poison him.

I retraced my steps. But then a noise! I skipped down a few steps out of sight and hid round the corner. Someone on the top corridor had stopped at the sluice. I risked a peep.

It was Duncan Alexander!

As I watched, he picked up a napkin to wipe the dishes. He was cleaning off any evidence! Folding the napkin he put it inside his tunic. Half turning, he caught sight of me, gave a cry of alarm and then demanded angrily, 'Why are you there?'

'Sir, I ask you the same question,' I replied.

'I said for you to return to your rooms.'

'Sir, you are a minor laird and have no authority over me,' I retorted.

'And you are the daughter of a deceased army captain from a country for which the Scots bear no love, and an Italian mother – another race which, in the person of Master David Rizzio, is becoming even more unpopular within this court!'

I reeled back under his onslaught. 'At least I am loyal to the queen. She has need of people like me, for there are less and less of us with each passing day. So I will do as I think fit to protect her.'

Duncan came down the steps towards me. 'Do you not realize that treachery surrounds her? You should be more cautious in your actions. Have you no awareness of the deadly danger that you place yourself in?'

There was the sound of footsteps above our heads. Duncan looked up. I did not need to be told twice: before his gaze had returned to me, I had fled.

It was never established quite what illness Henry Darnley

had contracted, but the more notice the queen gave him, the longer he lingered in convalescing. His manner with her remained docile and pleasing, but as she became increasingly indulgent, his graciousness to others evaporated. His arrogance and petulance antagonized servants, courtiers and almost every notable lord in the land. Mary had no sense of the depth of disapproval aroused by her increasing closeness to Darnley. It was the most joyous time for the queen. She was happier than I'd ever seen her. All the natural affection in her nature she lavished on Darnley. She prepared nourishing drinks for him with her own hand. She brought him presents, read to him and sang songs to soothe him to sleep at night. And he, who was spoiled and petted by his mother, wallowed in this kind of adoration.

Mary, who'd pined for her own mother during child-hood, now took it upon herself to give this young man the affection she felt she'd missed. She rose early to see how he'd passed the night, and dallied in his room until after midnight so that she was sure he'd fallen asleep. She wrote poems and devised short plays and amusements that would not tire him. I was reminded of her care of the children of the French royal family. Had she, instead of ruling a kingdom, been a noble lady with a handful of children and a loving husband, then she could not have been more content.

Darnley responded to this treatment with an accom-modating, pliant manner when Mary was there. But then, when one is the centre of attention, with every wish granted immediately, who would not be charming?

As he regained his strength, he began to dress stylishly again and take a more active part in court entertainments. His soft features and pale blond locks stood out amidst the darker looks of the Scots nobles, his manners more akin to those of the French court where Mary had been raised, and he was skilled in gaming, which she loved. They spent evenings together in his rooms, playing and laughing together.

One night, Mary, caught up in a game, wagered a ring with a tourmaline stone that she wore upon her finger. It wasn't of huge worth, its value more sentimental than monetary. The cards fell wrong for her, she lost the game, and the ring was forfeit.

'Misfortune,' she whispered in distress. She hadn't really meant to promise the tourmaline ring in payment, but she would not go back on her word. She started to tug it from her finger.

'Nay,' said Lord Darnley, 'stay your hand.' And he took a valuable ring from his own finger, worth twice as much as Mary's, and offered it to her, saying, 'Use this to pay your debt, for I'll not have you looking so bereft.'

Their fingers entwined as he handed her his ring.

From that moment Mary was besotted. Against the advice of her councillors and in the face of stern warnings from Queen Elizabeth, she resolved to wed Henry Darnley.

'I don't understand,' she wailed, crushing the latest letter from England in her fist. As the number of complaints mounted, she'd summoned Duncan and me to her rooms for a conference. 'Elizabeth sends Lord Darnley to me with a recommendation that I restore his father's lands, confiscated by my father on account of some family transgression, yet when I do this and become enamoured of him, she writes to reprimand me!'

'Perhaps she is jealous,' I said, 'that you have found love and she has not.'

'Perhaps it's not such a trivial reason,' Duncan Alexander commented. 'Elizabeth might have allowed Lord Darnley to leave her court so that his family of Lennox Stuarts would cause acrimony as rival claimants of the Hamilton Stuarts to the Scottish throne.'

Mary put her head in her hands. 'I cannot thole this serpentine deceit.' She raised a tearful face to me. 'Where is my clear path through all of this?'

I shook my head. I could scarcely speak. Duncan Alexander had just dismissed love as trivial. How had I ever become so attached to this man?

On Mary's instructions, I went to summon David Rizzio so that she might compose a letter in reply.

Duncan Alexander hurried after me. 'Have my words in some way offended you?' he asked.

'You think love trivial,' I said tightly, not slowing my pace.

'I do not. But, as I have said before, love cannot be the prime reason that a ruler weds.'

Still feeling humiliated, I knocked briskly on Rizzio's door.

'Jenny . . .' Duncan Alexander said this so softly that I barely heard it. But as the Italian opened his door, my sense of humiliation was so strong that, on entering the room, I indicated to Rizzio that he should shut the door at once behind me.

Although Darnley did not attend mass, John Knox and certain Protestant lords objected vociferously to the queen's marriage on the grounds of his mother's adherence to the Catholic religion. Foremost among these was Mary's half-brother, Lord James Stuart, who was in truth, I thought, more concerned that his position as Mary's chief adviser would be usurped by the Lennox Stuarts and that Darnley would connive to secure his estates. And as this thought came upon me, I realized that there was wisdom in Duncan Alexander's words regarding a monarch's duty in selecting a partner. Lord James and others banded together to declare that they would not accept a marriage between the queen and Lord Darnley. There was talk of them arming their clansmen.

Those in the queen's intimate circle considered this a gross betrayal. It was a grievous blow to Mary, and at court she railed against them, Lord James in particular. 'I see these lords now for what they are,' she said. 'Power and wealth is their chief aim in life. Personal advancement is what governs their actions. With my wedded husband at my side, my half-brother James knows that he will no longer be the prime influence in my life. But I will proclaim Lord James Stuart outlawed and make Lord Darnley King of Scotland.'

There was a silence, and then Darnley's father, the Earl of Lennox, called out, 'God save his grace! King Henry of Scotland!'

Sir Gavin of Strathtay and others applauded, and then Mary's secretary, David Rizzio, who always tried to win favours from anyone above him in rank, followed suit. The queen's ladies, myself included, said nothing. Instinctively I looked for Duncan Alexander. The spot where he'd stood a moment earlier was empty.

The queen and Lord Darnley married on 29 July 1565. Mary went to her wedding dressed in black to show that she was still a widow and to send a message to her people that her marriage was a serious business and did not require huge ceremony. But after the service was over she formally cast aside her widow's garb, saying to me, 'Jenny, you who knew me before and since my widowhood, please help relieve me of my mourning clothes.'

As I removed the jewelled pin that secured her black hood, Mary tossed her head as if to shake all death and gloom away. Her hair came down, the pleated tresses uncoiling around her face, large curls of red gold spilling down onto her shoulders.

'I am happy, so happy.' She held out her hands to her attendants, pleading, 'I beg of you, be happy with me. Be happy with me.'

Chapter 32

Sir Gavin reported to us that John Knox had commented acidly on the amount of feasting that took place at the wedding. 'Three John Knox diatribes have I suffered on this subject in St Giles kirk,' he joked in mock complaint to me, 'out of duty to report this man's words to my queen.'

'I think not to worry her with the details,' I suggested. 'Suffice it to say that Preacher Knox is less than pleased.'

Mary heard of Knox's reaction from a variety of sources, but for once she was unconcerned for anyone other than her beloved husband.

Her gifts to him included titles and jewellery and his own apartments below hers, with a private staircase in the turret connecting them to her rooms. She named him king consort, but this needed the approval of parliament, which wasn't due to meet until next March. Lord Darnley, or King Henry, as he liked to be called, was unhappy about that – as he was unhappy about a great many other things. Part of his problem was that he had no grasp of the machinations of statehood and the function of the privy council and parliament. He didn't appreciate that his wife couldn't automatically grant him anything he demanded. Mary gave him land but he wanted more. I entered her royal apartments one morning to see a map of Scotland spread out on the table, with Darnley poring over it.

'Whose land is this?' he asked, indicating territory belonging to Lord James Stuart.

'It belongs to my brother, James,' Mary replied reluctantly.

'Why does he still own it when he has said that he will not countenance our marriage?'

'I am hoping that Lord James, who is my half-brother and your good brother now too, will realize that he cannot stand against the crown. We may yet come to a peaceable solution.'

'And this, and this,' Darnley jabbed his finger at the map, 'does he also own?'

'Those too,' Mary agreed. 'They are fiefdoms inherited by dint of James having Stuart blood.'

'*I* have Stuart blood,' Darnley said, 'and, being of legitimate birth a greater birthright than he.' He pointed to the Moray area. 'In what manner was the affluence of this estate wrested from the Earl of Huntly and given to *my good brother*?' He emphasized the last three words with heavy sarcasm.

'For loyalty.' Mary spoke quietly, but her colour was high. 'A wise monarch rewards loyalty.'

'An unwise monarch gives away too much,' Darnley replied. 'Lord James Stuart has a plenitude of land and I'm minded to take a piece of it from him.'

A deep revulsion for this man's foolhardiness rose up in me. Lord James Stuart had worked hard to gain his present position and wielded too much power to bend his head to a petulant teenage boy. Did Darnley not even have the wit to be silent about his intentions rather than bray them aloud? Already some spy would be running to inform Lord James of what he planned. And this might be enough to prompt him to direct action.

The speed with which they moved surprised us all.

The following evening Duncan Alexander came to Mary's supper room, where she was sitting with Darnley, to say that Lord James had formed an army with the Earl of Argyll and others, including the Hamilton Stuarts who did not want to be superseded by the Lennox Stuarts. Their aim was to rescue the queen and depose their new king.

Darnley's eyes became round with astonishment. 'This Lord James cannot do!'

'He aims to try,' Duncan retorted.

'Treachery!' Mary cried, rising to her feet. 'Treachery and base treason! Bring me armour! I'll ride to fight him myself!' She launched a tirade against her brother that he should reward her generosity to him in such a way. Her anger was so great that Darnley stood back and it was left to me to calm her.

'I am resolute, Jenny,' she told me. 'I will not be ousted by that ingrate, be there five or fifty-five lords against me.'

'There will be many lords who will not join in this revolt,' I said. 'And the ordinary people will see this pretend "rescue" for what it is – a grab for power.'

At Mary's first council-of-war there appeared among the lords loyal to her one James Hepburn, Earl of Bothwell. He strode in, clad in Borders battledress with a broadsword in his hand. One of the guards pointed out that he was not permitted to carry an unsheathed weapon in the queen's presence.

Bothwell shoved his face into that of the soldier. 'And are you prepared to stop me?' he enquired cheerfully.

The guard stood back and Bothwell entered, saying, 'I heard that your grace is seeking arms for your personal use.'

Duncan Alexander gave a shake of his head and rolled his eyes as Bothwell knelt before Mary.

'I present you with a broadsword I had forged especially for you,' the earl told her.

Mary touched Bothwell on the head and bade him rise, while Darnley stared suspiciously at him.

'Your experience in soldiering will stand us in good stead, my Lord Bothwell,' said Mary, accepting his gift.

Bothwell grinned. Standing up he struck his chest aggressively with his fist. The sound grated on his mailed leather jacket. 'Anyone who survives in my wild Border lands is a worthy soldier.'

'I think perhaps you outrank all others in this sphere,' said Mary. 'I have decided to appoint you lieutenant general of our army.'

At this announcement Darnley looked as though he might have a fit. 'I will not agree to this! I want my father, as head of the Lennox Stuarts, to have the chief commission.'

Mary paled as her husband contradicted her. All their other disagreements had been over petty things, like his name appearing after hers on state documents. This was their first major row and it was conducted in public.

'I honour your father,' Mary said, staring at him. 'But I *will* have Bothwell to lead the army.'

I moved closer to her as, incandescent with rage, Darnley began to argue with his queen. 'I, as king, must lead out our army. I've had a new suit specially made for the purpose.'

David Rizzio sniggered.

Darnley whipped round. 'Hold thy tongue, weasel,' he said, 'else I might cut it out.'

Mary's eyes beseeched the onlookers for support.

Duncan Alexander spoke quietly. 'I do believe the queen seeks to protect your grace. Let James Hepburn, the Earl of Bothwell, ride at the head of the troops rather than put yourself in danger.'

'I am equal to any in swordsmanship,' declared Darnley.

As Bothwell reached for his own sword Duncan leaped forward to restrain him. One of the lords present openly laughed and remarked to a friend, 'Yon laddie would mince up and down with a rapier in one hand and a lace handkerchief in the other while Bothwell's good broadsword cleaved him in two.'

Hearing this, Darnley stormed out of the room in pique.

'Every time I am in trouble, my Lord Bothwell comes to my aid,' Mary murmured. She was resting in her apartments after the council meeting.

'He is loyal,' I said in neutral tones.

'You are silent, Sir Duncan,' said Mary, 'which I have found to indicate that you may have reservations about what I am saying.'

'Bothwell is loyal enough,' Duncan replied. 'But he did ask you to pardon the Huntly children for their father's rebellion and grant the earl's second son, George, the right to inherit the title.'

'That I did gladly, if only to teach Lord James a lesson.'

'It is because Bothwell wants to marry George's sister, the daughter of the former earl, for the family can pay him a rich dowry.'

'I will consent to the marriage. Lord Bothwell deserves rewards. He keeps the lawless Border lands safe to benefit Scotland.'

'That he does,' Duncan agreed. 'And he is my friend . . . of sorts, but reckless with it. It does no harm to remember that what Bothwell does is for Bothwell's benefit. Unless, of course,' he allowed himself a smile, 'there is the prospect of a battle. In which case James Hepburn will fight with anyone.'

Mary herself led the troops to Stirling, and I was never more proud of her. She sat on her horse with a breastplate of silver steel in place of a sequinned stomacher, a pistol in her belt and Bothwell's broadsword in her hand. She'd relented so that Lord Darnley rode beside her, and he was well pleased with himself in his special suit of gilded armour. The queen was closely guarded by Bothwell's men, and to Duncan Alexander's annoyance I was not far behind in her train.

Marie Seton told me that she'd heard Sir Duncan say to the queen that it wasn't seemly for any of her ladies to be part of the active army. To which Mary had replied that if it was seemly for her, then it was seemly for any other lady. On the march I had no occasion to speak to Duncan, yet as we travelled he seemed to be always in my sight.

When we discovered that Lord James Stuart had moved west to Glasgow, Mary insisted we follow at once. The sight of their queen on the high roads, dressed for battle and prepared to defend her throne, caused more and more men to rally to her standard.

'The fox has run again for cover,' Bothwell gloated as the forward lookouts came back to tell us that Lord James had fled before we reached the city. 'We will find his trail and hunt him down.'

'Yes, but where?' Duncan asked.

'To Edinburgh.' Mary had opened a note she'd just received. 'Lord James thought the city would welcome him, but my faithful Lord Erskine has turned the cannon of the castle upon him! John Knox may fulminate from the pulpit, but the citizens and many of the Protestant lords will welcome their queen.'

'It is time to offer blandishments to his supporters,' Duncan advised her. 'Promise free pardons to Argyll and the Hamilton Stuarts with their lands restored, and they'll leave off their revolt.'

In triumph we went back to Holyrood Palace where Sir Gavin of Strathtay had elected to remain and garrison with his men. With what followers he had left Lord James was heading for the Borders, whereupon Mary, accompanied by Bothwell and his men, rode after him and chased the remainder of the rebels clear into England.

The people did love her for it. Scotland had a queen who was not only the most beautiful in Europe but as daring and brave as any king. They didn't believe Lord James's excuse for his rebellion – that he wanted to keep the kingdom Protestant. They saw his actions as one of the former king's illegitimate sons trying to steal the throne from the rightful heir.

And there was evidence to show that Mary had no intention of trying to reconvert Scotland to Catholicism. She'd given grants to Protestant churches, kirk ministers were now salaried – so much so that the pope in Rome wrote to chastise her for it.

Mary returned to Edinburgh elated, and with the hope of establishing a compassionate government which would bring the rowing nobles together to heal the wounds of division. But although she had circumvented a national rebellion the battles within her own household went on. Encouraged by his parents Darnley demanded that she give him the crown matrimonial – which meant that if she died, he and any future heirs he might have would inherit the throne. The ambitions of the Lennox Stuarts were an open secret within the court. Gavin tried to sound out our opinions, but Mary, showing loyalty to her husband, forbade any gossip on the subject. Unfortunately Lord Darnley was less discreet and made others aware of his displeasure.

One morning I came upon them arguing. I'd entered Mary's bedchamber, where Marie Seton was tidying the queen's clothes. She waved her hand in the direction of the adjoining supper room, saying, 'Her majesty has gone to sit and read her letters.'

The door was ajar and I went in, not realizing that Lord Darnley had come up from his apartments via the private staircase.

'The kingship of Scotland is my right!' he cried, scowling at Mary in fury. 'By my own lineage there is royal blood in my veins.'

'I do acknowledge you as king,' Mary replied in the tired voice of one who has gone through the same argument several times. 'Your head is on coin of the realm. You are titled King Henry.'

'I command you to award me the crown matrimonial. It is your duty as a wife to obey me.'

'May I remind you what "royal" duty entails?' Mary held up the paper she was holding. 'This is an ambassador's letter requiring reading, discussion and appropriate action. Do you do your duty as a king and attend to any such matters?'

I backed out of the room and into the bedchamber. 'He has taken to haranguing her of a morning,' Marie Seton whispered. 'That is' – she made a face – 'the mornings he is able to rouse himself at a reasonable hour.'

'No wonder she is weary,' I whispered back, for we'd both commented on how tired Mary was of late.

As her partnership with her husband became more strained, Mary's councillors fluctuated between supporting her and Darnley. With Lord James banished in England and a good deal of William Maitland's time occupied in romancing Marie Fleming, it was David Rizzio who increasingly attended to the queen's correspondence. He vied with Sir Gavin in putting forward his opinions and sought favours from the queen, wearing expensive clothes from the royal wardrobe and borrowing small pieces of jewellery for special occasions – which he then failed to return. When the keeper of the wardrobe approached one of Mary's attendants for advice on how to deal with this, a message was relayed to him saying that Master David Rizzio was to be accommodated without prejudice in whatever he wished.

But more important, in my view, was the influence Rizzio had on the queen's private business. I'd heard him discuss with the ambassador from Ferrara the contents of a letter that the queen had received from her Guise relatives. They knew of Darnley's bad behaviour and suggested that if he became too troublesome, then the marriage might be annulled. They referred to the fact that the papal dispensation for them, as cousins, to marry, had arrived *after* the wedding ceremony. Rizzio gave a crafty grin. 'This would make her majesty eligible to marry again.'

For him to talk so freely was both foolish and highly dangerous. I began to watch Master David Rizzio more closely.

He was indeed charming, as are many of those ill-favoured in appearance – as if God gave them grace and wit to compensate for their lack of looks. He was also musical, and Mary loved music. Often in the evening he played and sang to her. By day he began to encroach on William Maitland's duties, commandeering more of Mary's secretarial work.

Darnley complained of this to her. 'Why do you spend so much time with your private secretary, Master Rizzio?' he asked.

'I have a wearisome amount of work to do, my love. If you wish, you may read through the papers of state and give me your opinion.'

'I had planned to go hawking this morning and I fail to see why you can't accompany me,' he said moodily. 'It appears that you prefer to be with Master Rizzio and the lords of council. They call upon you and you do as they wish.'

Mary went to her husband and, taking his hand, murmured, 'There is only one person in all this land, one man on earth, who may command my body as he does my heart.'

Lord Darnley allowed himself to be placated and went off to the stables.

But, as on many similar occasions over the last months, a furrow had appeared on Mary's forehead. And although Lord Darnley had been coaxed into a pleasant frame of mind and the queen responded with smile of her own, today the worry line between Mary's brows did not quite smooth out. It marked a new departure, for they had now begun to row frequently in public; I did not doubt that there were many more rows in private.

'A shorter honeymoon than most, then,' commented one of the nobles.

Mary put her hand to her temple, something I'd seen her doing often recently, as if her headdress was constricting. Marie Seton had noticed this too, and let out the stitching on the caps the queen kept for daily use.

'I could have Rhanza bring an infusion of camomile,' I suggested, 'and you might leave off working for twenty minutes.'

'Yes,' said Mary, adding, 'And let us be alone together for that time.'

Due to her marriage and pressure of work it was seldom now that Mary and I talked privately. We went into her supper room and sat side by side on a bench like sisters.

'Jenny,' Mary said, 'I do believe I am with child.'

'Oh! Oh!' I hugged her tightly and then released her. 'I'm sorry. I did not mean to crush you. A baby . . . Oh, it's wonderful! A marvellous, marvellous happening!'

'Is it?' Her eyes were sad and she was very close to weeping.

'Why would it not be?' I was genuinely puzzled. 'The country and the crown need heirs, and you adore children. Since we came to Scotland your heart has ached for the company of Francis's younger brothers and sisters.'

'That's true.' Mary nodded. 'I am cheered by your words, Jenny.' She leaned her head on my shoulder.

'Are you are anxious about the practicalities of the birth?' I asked, seeking a reason for her melancholy.

'There is that,' she agreed, 'but also . . .'

I waited.

Mary sighed. 'I fear my husband may not welcome this news.'

Chapter 33

To begin with, like the rest of the court and the country, Lord Darnley was pleased. He was puffed up by the messages of congratulation – but then it must have struck him that the arrival of his child would take him one step further from the throne. He pressed Mary ever harder to award him the crown matrimonial.

Marie Seton and I often heard him mentioning the subject, alternating between ordering and begging her to comply with his wishes.

'My husband is young and too inexperienced for such responsibility, Jenny,' Mary confided in me. 'I believe his parents have raised his expectations so that he now believes it is his right to rule this country, with me as a subservient wife.'

'The Lennox Stuarts have high ambitions,' I said.

'And a host of relatives,' Mary added. 'His mother is kin to the Douglas family who seize what they desire by any means open to them.'

I thought it wiser not to remind her that, by dint of his mother having married a Douglas after he was born, Lord James Stuart was also linked to the clan.

Mary was anxious as to where Lord Darnley's increasing discontent might lead him. She didn't want him becoming embroiled with the warmongering Douglas side of his family. Even Gavin, who made mocking comments on every topic, had nothing to say against anyone associated with the name Douglas. They were unforgiving enemies and inspired terror in both foe and friend.

But there was one person within the Palace of Holyrood whose fealty to the queen I guessed would outweigh fear. I let Rhanza know of my concerns and she brought me word of movements within the household. Thus I knew that the most prominent Douglas, the Earl of Morton, with Lords Ruthven and Lindsay, was forming an alliance with Lord Darnley and his companions.

'Morton, Lindsay and Ruthven are three of the most detestable men I know,' Mary said in despair when I told her this. 'How can my husband keep company with them? I fear I have been a poor judge of character when choosing whom to wed. But Lord Darnley was so kind and affectionate that I fell in love with him.' She smiled sadly at me. 'You are wise, Jenny, to be cautious before giving your heart away.'

But my heart *was* given away. It had happened the moment I'd met Sir Duncan Alexander. The difference between Mary and myself was that I had chosen to keep my feelings secret.

Mary summoned him to discuss the situation – along with Sir Gavin, who had moved higher in her affection since he'd held Holyrood Palace against Lord James in the recent conflict.

'These lords have no care for my husband's welfare and will encourage him in his waywardness in order to make him their creature,' she told them.

'At the risk of becoming unpopular,' Gavin hesitated, 'may I mention your half-brother?'

'I have decreed Lord James outlaw and cannot pardon him until he makes his peace with me,' said Mary.

'This might be the way he can make amends,' said Gavin. 'Lord James Stuart is the one person who is strong enough to contain these men.'

'Or join with them in insurrection,' Duncan interposed, giving Gavin a look of pure dislike. 'Perhaps Lord James is already aware of what is happening in Scotland and even has a hand in it?'

'Are you in communication with him that you know this?' Gavin enquired with sarcasm.

Duncan put his hand on the hilt of his sword and stepped forward to confront him. 'What I do know, sir, is that when parliament meets in March, an Act will be passed to seize the lands of Lord James Stuart. And I have sense enough to see that he might take steps to prevent that happening.'

'I need a practical solution for this impending crisis,' Mary said sharply. 'If Darnley's family try to take the throne of Scotland, then I believe there'd be civil war and anarchy. I need to secretly prepare for such an eventuality.'

'The lords of the Isles and the Highlands would rouse their clans to defend you,' said Duncan.

'And James Hepburn, Earl of Bothwell, has never wavered in his support for the crown,' she added.

'I will make it my business to be about the streets of Edinburgh that Lord Darnley frequents and try to mind him as best I can,' said Duncan.

'Thank you.' Mary grasped his hands in hers. 'You have taken on a most difficult task.'

'And how will the queen be defended here in the palace?' I asked.

'I trust Erskine, the captain of the guard,' Mary said.

'I will also be here to—' Gavin began.

'Let us summon Bothwell and Huntly,' Duncan interrupted him.

'They are both Protestants,' said Gavin waspishly, 'Bothwell of long standing, and the new young Earl of Huntly does not follow his father's religion.'

'I've never tried to impose my faith on others,' Mary said testily. She turned to Duncan. 'Yes, send word to the Borders. I'd feel safer with the Earl of Bothwell at my side.'

Gavin raised his eyebrows and then said, 'Perhaps I would serve you better, majesty, by going to my lands to raise arms for you.'

Mary extended her hand for him to kiss. 'God speed, Sir Gavin. Now, away, both of you, and I will stall the demands of my husband to give him the crown matrimonial by feigning sickness.'

In truth, this was not difficult to do, for Mary was quite unwell in her pregnancy and suffered bouts of dizziness and nausea. Lord Darnley retaliated for what he termed 'wifely rejection' by spending more time with his drinking cronies. He scarcely spoke a civil word to her, until one night he came to her private supper room where we'd gathered to be quiet, for she was weary and anxious.

Rizzio was softly strumming his lute. I was by the fire. Opposite me the queen had just picked up her embroidery when Darnley entered without ceremony from the private staircase.

'Husband!' Mary contrived to be welcoming, although I knew she'd wanted a peaceful evening. She was exhausted after a long day of council debate on how best to deal with her half-brother, who was hiding somewhere in England. She patted the stool beside her. 'My lord, come sit by me.'

Darnley shook his head in a discontented manner. Rizzio paused in his playing and then continued more quietly.

'You are out of sorts?' Mary observed. 'Can I help you in any way?'

'Yes, you can,' Darnley said shortly. 'You can give me the dukedom of Inverloch.'

This was contentious. The Duke of Inverloch was in prison for sedition and his land and title could not be disposed of until he was tried and found guilty.

Rizzio loudly plucked a single string on his lute. 'Forgive me, your grace,' he said in an innocent voice. 'I believe I played a wrong note.'

Darnley glared at him. '*Majesties*,' he said.

David Rizzio returned his look with a blank stare.

'*Majesties*,' Lord Darnley repeated. 'I am King Henry of Scotland. Therefore there are two majesties in this room.'

'I do beg your pardon, sire. I did not have the wit to catch your meaning.'

'You mountebank!' Darnley leaped at him. 'You have wit enough to parry words with me.' He would have struck Rizzio had not Mary stayed his hand, but he pushed her back into her chair.

Mary gasped in outrage but managed to speak. 'Go now, Davie,' she said quickly. 'You are dismissed.'

'Davie? *Davie!*' Darnley almost screeched. 'You address that man by a familiar first name?'

Mary hesitated as Rizzio scurried from the room. 'He is a good servant and . . . I look upon many of those who serve me with friendship.'

'And does *he* call you by *your* own given name?'

'Of course not.' But her lie was not well enough told to be convincing. Mary tried to appease her husband, but it was as if everything she said heaped kindling upon the fire of Darnley's anger, causing yet more sparks to burst forth. He left in a vile temper and Mary collapsed, weeping, on my shoulder.

From that day their relationship changed for ever.

That Darnley had laid rough hands upon her while she carried his child shocked Mary beyond reason. Now debilitated in the seventh month of her pregnancy, she cried bitter tears, bemoaning to attendants. 'Am I not faithful to him? Do I not do all I can to humour him?'

'Some men do not welcome a baby,' said Jean, Countess of Argyll. 'They fear the child will take the attention they want focused solely on them.'

Mary's friends and ladies tried to protect her as Darnley's behaviour grew increasingly outrageous. Rizzio, grateful to her for saving him a beating, was even more ingratiating. He appeared to have business with everyone at court – the servants of foreign ambassadors sought him out, and now he had access to the household purse, for he said he needed ready money with which to buy information. One day I decided to follow him as he hurried away with gold coin in his hand. He went first to his own room, which didn't surprise me as I thought he probably used only half the money he ever took to pay his informants. Then he went by the servants' stairs to the abbey cloister, where someone was waiting under the arches.

I heard Rizzio speak, and then the man in the shadows

replied. There was something familiar about the inflection of his speech. I crept closer. They were talking in Italian, but where Rizzio was fluent, this man was not. My stomach turned over in fear. The voice was that of the Count of Cluny!

During Darnley's illness Mary had, at my suggestion, appointed more food tasters. After this, the Count had disappeared and I thought he'd returned to France, thwarted in his intentions. He must have been awaiting his next instruction from Catherine de' Medici. Now here he was within the Palace of Holyrood, liaising with Mary's inner circle of trusted attendants! I inched forward, the better to hear their conversation.

'I don't want money for the information I gave you,' the Count of Cluny spoke.

'What *do* you want?' asked Rizzio, immediately putting the coins back inside his tunic.

'A letter came to you . . .'

'There are many letters,' he replied. 'After all, I am secretary to the queen.'

'One specific letter sent not long ago to the Queen of Scots from her family of Guise,' Cluny said irritably. 'I know you have it, even though it was delivered secretly.'

'Then you know more than I do, sir.'

'Have a care, little music man,' Cluny hissed. 'You may find yourself singing a different note.'

'I neither sing nor speak to entertain you but only my queen,' Rizzio replied arrogantly. 'And as I am in favour and you are not, I think you'll find your powers somewhat limited here.'

'My powers may be more than you can begin to guess,'

the Count of Cluny replied nastily. 'And I do know that you hold and withhold information depending on how you reckon your own profit.'

'In your case, sir,' Rizzio said, 'I see no profit at all.'

I wasn't a friend of David Rizzio. He assumed too much and made sly comments to the younger girls when the queen was absent, but as I slipped away I wondered if Rizzio understood the magnitude of his mistake. Most likely he'd judged his informant to be a minor noble of no standing or wealth, not realizing that the Count of Cluny was an agent of the most ruthless and clever ruler in Europe. Although I hadn't much liking for Master David, I was afraid for him.

But my concern for Mary was more pressing than any I might have for Rizzio. If the Count of Cluny wanted the Guise letter, then it must contain important news. I was sure Rizzio had not yet given it to the queen, for she'd not mentioned anything unusual in her recent correspondence, and now I wondered if her secretary was engaged in a double game of holding up or destroying letters. It must still be in his apartments which, when he was not there, he kept locked with a key held about his person. He might be in the middle of decoding it, using one of the complicated ciphers he employed to keep the queen's correspondence private.

That evening I kept my eyes on him, and saw the key dangling from a chain attached to a gilt button on his doublet, impossible to remove without undressing. I spoke to Rhanza, explaining to her that it was for the queen's benefit that I needed the key. As she was one of the girls Rizzio had annoyed with suggestive remarks, she had no liking for him. Keen to help, yet she didn't see how, for when she serviced his room Rizzio insisted on being present. She wasn't allowed to loiter in his bedchamber but only clean his privy room, and he watched her all the while.

The next morning, although it was very cold for the beginning of March, I went out riding through Holyrood Park. I reined my horse in and surveyed the façade of the palace. On the top level I could pick out Rizzio's room, with its mullioned windows and privy chute. Fantastical schemes went through my head – of lowering myself on a rope from an overhanging buttress to the window ledge – perhaps during the night when Rizzio took off his clothes. I shuddered. If I slipped, I'd fall into the lion pit situated below.

When I discussed this with Rhanza, she shook her head. 'Maister Rizzio keeps the windae lockit fast, so feart is he of catching cauld.'

'There must be a way,' I insisted. I went over what she'd told me of his habits. 'He stands within his privy room as you clean it?'

'Mair close than I would wish. He ne'er lets me oot his sicht.'

'Then we need a problem with the privy itself,' I said, thinking aloud. 'If it overflowed with effluence in the early morning, he might summon you to try to clear it!'

'I dinna ken how this helps ye.' Rhanza was perplexed.

'Master Rizzio will stand within the privy room to over-see you, and you will take much longer to clear up the mess. I will wait in the corridor and try to slip into his room. His doublet with the key attached will be in his bedchamber. If you find me a piece of soft moulding, or even soap, I can take an impression! Could you get a locksmith to make a duplicate?'

Rhanza hesitated.

'You do not know a locksmith?'

'I ken a keymakkar,' she replied. 'It's just that Maister Rizzio will be in his nightclothes, and . . .'

'Oh!' I said. 'How stupid I am! I forgot that away from the queen he behaves like a rake.'

'I'll dae it,' said Rhanza, 'for ma queen. If Maister Rizzio tries onything, I'll fend him aff with a shovelful of sh—'

'Very good,' I said quickly. 'Whatever we decide to do, we must do it tonight.'

It was Rhanza who devised the method of blocking the privy. While performing her duties that day she stuffed cloths up the inside of the privy chute in the room below Rizzio's. In the middle of the night we crept into the attics and emptied the pails of sewage and manure Rhanza had collected from the palace middens down into Rizzio's chute. And she contrived to be near his room when, at daybreak, the door opened and he rang a summoning bell in the corridor.

'You, girl!'

Rhanza hurried to him, carrying her bucket and broom.

I waited until they'd gone inside. Silently I approached the door and put my ear to the panel. I could hear nothing. I turned the handle. I had an excuse ready: I would claim that the queen had woken early and wanted her secretary urgently. I'd not thought how to explain it to Mary if I was forced to use this tactic. The door creaked open. There was no one in the bedchamber, and I smelled the stench from the privy.

I heard Rizzio say, 'I should call for the midden men . . .'

'Nay, sir,' Rhanza replied. 'I can manage.'

'Might there be other things you could manage for me?'

Rizzio's voice was muffled. He must have a scarf over his mouth and nose.

The door to the privy room was ajar. I could see half of Rizzio's back. I tiptoed into the bedchamber and carefully lifted the doublet, which was lying over a chair. The key was not there.

My heart failed. Disappointment swept through me. All this for nothing. He must put it around his neck as he slept. I glanced at his bed. On a sudden impulse I lifted the pillow. The key was underneath!

Hands shaking, I lifted it and pressed it into the soft moulding that Rhanza had secured for me. As I did so, I heard Rizzio say, 'I must step into my bedroom to fetch a pomander else I shall faint with the smell.'

'Sir!' Rhanza cried. 'Dinna leave me!'

I knew that she was too tough to be overcome by the work she was doing. She was trying to delay him for my benefit. I ran from the room and did not stop until I reached my own.

An hour later Rhanza came to the royal apartments carrying a jug of wild flowers for the queen. I passed her the mould and some money. By nightfall she had returned with a new key.

Later I was more relaxed as I approached Rizzio's room for the second time. I knew he was with the queen, who was receiving the Earl of Bothwell and the new Lord Huntly in the great hall. As the locksmith had advised, Rhanza had coated the key shaft in goose fat, and on the second attempt it turned. I was inside!

Considering no one tided for him, Rizzio's room was remarkably well ordered. His writing desk was neat, the correspondence meticulously filed. His headings were in Italian, which gave me no problem, but this letter was more recent. I opened his letter case, but I could only see his code book. It was quite bulky, for he was cunning enough to use many different ciphers. As I picked it up, I gazed about the room. Where would Rizzio hide such an important letter?

Then I looked down at the book in my hand, and slowly opened it. Inside was a single sheet bearing the seal of the new young Duke of Guise.

I unfolded the paper. Rizzio had most of it decoded and I needed only to read a few lines to realize that this letter was momentous. The Guises were attempting to marry the queen to Catherine de' Medici's third son, Prince Henri of Anjou!

The letter proposed that the Cardinal of Lorraine petition the pope for an annulment of Mary's marriage to Darnley, and that she should then be betrothed to Prince Henri. Henri of Anjou was ten years younger than Mary and was Catherine de' Medici's favourite child. Her second son, now King Charles, was not healthy, and had as yet no heir, so his younger brother might inherit. But, I reflected, Catherine had barely tolerated Mary as a daughter-in-law when she'd been married to Francis and had made no secret of her lack of support for Scotland. This was not her doing. It was surely a scheme hatched by the Guise family to increase their influence in France through Mary. Ridiculous as it might seem, Henri's name had already been put forward by his mother as a possible suitor for Elizabeth of England. This ploy would both rekindle Catherine de' Medici's enmity for Mary and stoke the wrath of Queen Elizabeth.

I doubted if Mary would agree to this: it might mean that the child she carried would be deemed illegitimate and thus ineligible to succeed to the throne. But even if she rejected the Guise proposal, Mary's enemies would seize upon it as proof that she was embroiled in plots to re-establish France as an ally of Scotland.

As I left Rizzio's room I tried to marshal my thoughts. This was why the Count of Cluny was here in Scotland. Catherine de' Medici must have suspicions of the Guises' intentions, and had sent him to find out . . . and perhaps to eliminate any obstacle that might get in the way of her plans.

I longed to discuss this with someone. Duncan? I'd hardly seen him since he'd taken on the task of watching Lord Darnley. Gavin? There was no news from him since he'd gone north. The queen herself? No, I couldn't alarm Mary, who was already distressed by her pregnancy, but I would speak to her personal cook and food tasters and exhort them to be vigilant.

Today was the ninth of March; parliament was already in session. On the twelfth an order would be laid down against Lord James Stuart and the rest of the rebel lords living in England to confiscate their titles and lands. That would bring a conclusion to one matter, and by then I might know what to do about the secret letter.

Chapter 34

'Oh!' Mary let out a little squeal.

I'd reached the great hall as the reception was ending and Mary's attendants were preparing to escort her to her apartments.

'Majesty?' The Countess Jean was by her side at once, an anxious expression on her face.

'I am well,' Mary reassured her. She indicated her swollen belly. 'The baby kicked me!'

'Pray God it is a lusty boy.'

Mary turned to me, her eyes big with wonder. 'It is an amazing sensation, Jenny – the most wondrous thing – to feel life inside you. God grant that, in time, you too will have that experience.' She looked from me to Sir Duncan Alexander.

My face flamed red, and for once his composure too was disturbed. Mary chuckled when she saw that her teasing had found its mark.

Jean clucked her tongue at this silliness and spoke to Mary. 'Majesty, you should rest. If the baby is kicking, it is because it is hungry. Try to eat some food and retire early this night.'

'I will not sleep,' Mary declared, 'for this baby is too restless for that. However,' she went on as Jean opened her mouth to protest, 'a few of us can take supper together in my private room. Master David Rizzio may strum his lute while we play cards. That will lull me more than tossing and turning in my bed.'

'If I may be excused . . . ?' said Duncan Alexander.

'Won't you wait and play a round or two with us?' Mary asked him.

He glanced to where some of the Scots lords were bunched together. 'I believe I may be needed elsewhere.'

'You must assure me that you're not off to carouse in the streets of Edinburgh,' Mary paused, 'as I am told other young men do.'

She was referring to the stories that had been circulating about the behaviour of her husband. For the last few months Lord Darnley had taken to staying out to all hours visiting drinking dens and inns of low repute.

Duncan looked at the queen very earnestly. 'I assure you that I will not.'

'Then you may take your leave, Sir Duncan.' Mary dismissed him with a gesture and a smile.

Having been given permission to go, I thought he would walk directly to the door, but he didn't. As the queen, with Rizzio and the others, began to exit the hall, he fiddled with his cuffs, then inspected each finger of his gloves before putting them on. Thus it happened that by the time he was ready to quit the room he was almost in step with me. And he didn't move to one side as he should have done to allow me to pass through the door before him. Instead, he turned his head very slightly and, scarcely moving his lips, murmured into my hair, 'Keep the knife I gave you close at hand before you retire this night, and every other night from now on.'

I opened my mouth to ask the meaning of this remark, but he brushed past me.

The queen was making her way towards the royal suite. I hesitated, pondering Duncan's words. Should I fetch the knife now from where I kept it in my rooms? He'd advised me to have it to hand when I retired. I hurried after the queen, resolving to get it as soon as she decided to change into her nightwear, and then stay close beside her with the rest of her attendants.

The small supper room was busy with people. I was reassured when I saw among them Captain Erskine of the palace guard. The queen was already seated, with food on the table in front of her. When I entered, she called out, 'Ah, there you are, Jenny. We could not wait for you to join us before starting to eat.' She patted the bump that was the child growing inside her and said, 'The future King of Scotland is demanding to be fed.'

Along with everyone else I laughed at her remark. The noise must have masked the opening of the door to the turret staircase that connected the queen's rooms to those of her husband.

'And what of the present King of Scotland?' said a voice. 'Is he not also entitled to some food?'

There was a stunned silence. The smile vanished from Mary's face as Lord Darnley advanced into the room. Everyone tensed, expecting a spiteful remark or bad-tempered outburst.

'No matter,' he said. 'I have already eaten,' and he slid onto a stool beside the queen and pinched her cheek in a friendly way.

This was extraordinary.

'My lord, you do us an honour—' she began, when the door opened again, this time with a terrific crash.

A figure clad in full armour stood there. It was Lord Ruthven. He raised his arm and pointed at Rizzio.

'So it please your grace, let the man Davie come from your presence here.'

It was the queen who recovered first. 'For what reason?' she asked.

'He hath given great offence to your person and this realm.'

There was a slight movement as Darnley tried to make a space between himself and the queen. At once Mary cried out to her husband, 'What do you know of this? Why is this man here?'

'Nothing.' The benign look on his face had been replaced by one of trepidation. 'I know nothing.'

'Come, sire,' Lord Ruthven called to him, 'you cannot say you know nothing when it is clear that you know all that will come to pass this night.'

Mary gripped the edge of the table with both hands. 'I command you to leave now. If Master Rizzio has made offence, then I will deal with him in due course according to the law.'

Ruthven ignored her and addressed himself to Darnley. 'Sire, the moment has come for you to take your wife into your care.'

She started to rise from her seat, but Darnley fastened his arms around her. In that moment those of us who had watched this, immobile with shock, leaped to her defence. Apart from Rizzio. He scuttled round behind the queen, trying to hide, cowering in terror.

Lord Ruthven, seeing the men in the room scrambling to arrest him, pulled out a dagger, shouting, 'Stand back! Lay not your hands upon me!'

It was a signal. More men emerged from the turret stair, and others burst in from the main corridor. I recognized Lord Morton and Lord Lindsay before I was crushed behind the door. The table overturned, dishes cascaded to the floor as would have the candelabra, except that Jean snatched it up.

It might have been better had darkness descended upon us.

Rizzio screeched – the piercing high-pitched sound of a terrified animal. He retreated into a window alcove with the queen before him as he clung to her dress.

Ruthven and another pursued him, while his fellow assassins, Morton, Lindsay and the rest, overpowered Captain Erskine and the queen's men.

Rizzio screamed and screamed, 'Save me! I implore you, majesty. I am your loyal servant. Save me!'

Hampered by the wide drapes of her maternity dress Mary tried to defend the little Italian, while he held onto the folds of her skirts. One of the assassins menaced the queen with his pistol as a Douglas kinsman of Morton pulled Darnley's dagger from his belt. Lunging over Mary's shoulder, he stabbed Rizzio.

Rizzio yelled louder, 'Justice! Justice!'

Mary shrieked, 'Leave him! Leave him!'

But they dragged Rizzio, still howling, out from behind her towards the door. There they stabbed him again and again. Darnley, who had been standing, slack-jawed, now saw that it was safe for him to act. He ran forward shouting, 'Throw him downstairs! Throw him down the stairs!'

Blood spurting from every part of his body, Rizzio was hauled across the floor and tossed down into the hall below. Jean and I went to the queen but were shouldered aside as a commotion sounded from the courtyard.

Darnley looked out of the window. 'There is a group of townsfolk with sticks and torches wanting to know if anything is amiss. What can we do?'

'You are the king,' the Douglas murderer said impatiently. 'Command them to leave.'

Mary tried to push her way forward to scream for help, but Darnley held her firm.

'Say a word to bring them near,' Lindsay growled, 'and I'll cut thee in collops. I will open the window and you will call out to them that you are safe and that they should go away.'

Mary looked at me. If the townspeople came to her aid there would be a bloodbath. She and her child would die and the murderers could tell any story they pleased. We both knew this.

She showed herself at the window and waved until the people dispersed.

'Do you understand the situation now?' Darnley asked her.

She exchanged a glance with me. I gave a tiny nod of my head.

'Yes,' she said and, letting out a moan, sank to the floor.

They led Mary's ladies away, leaving only me to attend her while Darnley escorted Lord Ruthven down the turret staircase. As soon as he'd gone Mary bent over clutching her stomach and sobbing, 'They would have killed me and the babe. Dear God, they might yet do it.'

'This is not a time for hysterics or fainting,' I told her. 'When Lord Darnley returns you must speak to him and ask him what he intends to do with you. Make him take responsibility for what has happened.'

The queen sat down upon a stool. I put my arm under her elbow. 'Stand up,' I said. 'So that when he comes into the room you can look into his eyes.'

I helped her to her feet and then said, 'I have to leave for a few moments.'

'Don't go! Jenny, do not leave me.'

'I must,' I said, 'but I will return as quickly as I can.'

Mary grabbed my hand to keep me with her. In an urgent whisper I said, 'I go to Master Rizzio's room where he keeps your correspondence.'

'I have no need of any letter at this moment.'

'I think there is one there that I should destroy before it is seen by others. It was recently sent to you by the Duke of Guise.'

Mary's face turned grey, and I realized that Rizzio must have told her of the contents even as he was deciphering it.

We could hear Darnley's footsteps approaching.

'Yes,' Mary said. 'Go, with all speed.'

I hurried from the room.

From downstairs came shouts and laughter: the rebels, mainly members of the Douglas clan, had control of the palace. Gavin was on Tayside and Duncan had left Holyrood earlier, so I knew that at least they were safe. I wondered what had become of those loyal to the queen. The new Earl of Huntly had been with Bothwell in the palace, but Bothwell was cunning and a fierce fighter and would not have succumbed without a struggle. I peered over the balustrade.

David Rizzio's lifeless body was sprawled over a chest in the hall below. As I watched, Lord Lindsay came stumbling along and plunged his dagger into the corpse. 'Take that, you fop, you popish schemer, you flatterer, you . . .' He slurred his words drunkenly.

My gorge rose as he gloated over the corpse. There was an acrid taste in my mouth as I swallowed my bile. Like Mary, I didn't realise the venom that jealousy could produce. These lords had been deeply envious of Rizzio's charm and talents, but, more importantly, they were excluded from her private matters. They'd used Darnley to gain access to the queen and kidnap her for their own ends.

I moved away lest Lindsay glance up and notice me. The sound of carousing continued, but it wouldn't be long before they thought to break into Rizzio's room and ransack his possessions. I hurried there. The letter case was on his desk. I rifled through it. There it was! The letter with the Guise seal. I took it and the cipher book and thrust them inside my dress. But when I tried to return to the queen's apartments, Douglas clansmen were guarding the door and I was barred from entering.

Chapter 35

None of the queen's friends were to be allowed to see her.

I waited in the corridor, braving the jeers and rude remarks of the men-at-arms whose lords had taken over the palace.

'The queen must have a female attendant!' Countess Jean was loud in her entreaties. She knew the guards and used their individual names as she spoke to them. 'You, Master Yeovil, and thyself, Ruari of Granton, shame on you that you defile the good name of your family! If you do not let us attend to the queen, then you commit not just regicide but murder of an innocent babe. The world will know of your dishonour with the blood of an unborn king upon your hands!'

At last they relented and selected one of the maids to bring what we thought the queen might need.

The person chosen was Rhanza. Everything she carried was thoroughly searched before she went inside. When she came out she was holding a jug of flowers. Ever since that first day, when the queen had given her the ring from her finger, the girl always made sure there were fresh flowers in Mary's bedchamber. The wife of one of the conspirators took the jug, set it upon a table and pulled Rhanza into another room. Despite her squeals of protest, the woman stripped her and searched her again. Rhanza returned, her eyes cast down, while the men made coarse jokes. Head bent, she made to pick up the jug of flowers.

'One moment!' Master Yeovil shouted. He snatched the jug, emptied it and examined the inside and the underside. Then he thrust it at the girl. 'Clear up that mess, then get out of here. And remember, if you speak to anyone I'll slit your throat myself.'

After another day of fruitless waiting I went to my room. In the fireplace I burned the Guise letter and Rizzio's cipher book. With no access to the codes the queen's enemies would have difficulty in understanding her private business. I knelt then to say a prayer for the repose of the soul of Rizzio – for whatever faults he might have had, Master David did not deserve to die in such a manner. I prayed also for our poor chaplain as Jean told me that he too had been murdered. And then I prayed for Duncan and for Gavin, for Mary and myself. It wasn't until I was retiring to catch a few hours' sleep that I noticed on the table beside my bed the jug of wild flowers. My queen was denied even that solace. I looked at it again. The stems were broken. They were the wild flowers that had been in the jug, flung on the floor, and then retrieved by Rhanza.

The same flowers.

I sat up in bed. Why had Rhanza removed them from Mary's room? Had the queen asked her to do this? And why would the maid then place them in my room? Had Mary asked her to do that too?

Taking the flowers from the jug, I inspected it. Had Mary scratched a message inside? There was no mark there, nor on the bottom either. I began to turn it right side up to set it down again when I saw that the inside of the handle was hollow. Curved round as it was, this fact wasn't obvious. I brought it closer to examine it. Inside the handle was a spill of tightly rolled paper.

A message from a captured queen!

On bare feet I padded to my window. Light shone from the room where the queen was being held prisoner. I recalled one of the games we'd played in our youth in the Castle of Blois, where Mary had invented a code for signalling to Francis when the royal children were supposed to be in bed asleep. I took my candle to the window and covered and uncovered it several times. I waited, then tried again, and again. Hour after hour I did this, until finally, at about half past four in the morning there was an answering signal!

Tears of relief ran from my eyes. It was a small comfort for me that Mary now knew I'd received her message. I hoped it was a comfort to her.

Afterwards Mary told me what had passed between her and her husband that evening. When he returned to her room Darnley had expected her to rail against him and to screech and cry, but Mary was composed. 'Husband,' she told him. 'We are in gravest danger.'

'*We?* I think not, madam,' he said loftily. 'By consorting with lower types and spending overlong in the company of that jackanapes, Rizzio, it is you who have brought disrepute to our name and caused this outcome.'

If not brave on her own behalf, Mary was determined that nothing should harm her child. She fixed Darnley with a steely look and he faltered. He might have left her alone once more except that she detained him by placing her hand on the side of his face. 'Do they mean to imprison me and have you rule in my stead? Would they go so far as to murder me? An attack on my person would be monstrous. Also I carry your child, the future King of Scotland, and who knows, perhaps of England too? Sixteen years will pass before the boy gains majority. We must be there to guide him and not let others do it in our stead. Would you hand over your son to these rogues? Having seen how badly they treated an anointed queen, do you trust them with the safety of your own person?'

It was evident to her, she said, that her words caused Darnley some thought.

She had gone on: 'By attacking me thus they attack you, and I verily do believe Ruthven hath bewitched you to make you allow him into my presence to do this.'

Now Darnley saw a way in which he might extricate himself from the situation. 'Bewitched?' he repeated.

'Yes,' Mary replied. 'With lies and half-truths they lured you to do this wickedness. And perhaps now, having no further need of you . . .' She moved away, so that her husband stood isolated in their chamber.

Darnley began to pluck at his sleeve. 'What is to be done, Mary?' he said pathetically. 'My Mary, oh my Mary, what's to be done?'

'We must find a way to summon aid.'

'The Douglas family hold the palace. No one can help us.' Darnley slumped down in a chair, leaving her standing. His self-concern knew no bounds.

'Then, my lord, we must help ourselves. You will send the guards away, saying there is no need of them as I am too ill to even rise from my bed and, in any case, you are in constant attendance.'

That was all Mary told him. She didn't trust Darnley with

the rest of the plan she'd outlined in the note inside the jug. But she'd told me to which tavern to send Rhanza with the message, and I knew what else to prepare and when to be ready.

I thought we'd lost any chance of escape, when, within a day, Lord James Stuart appeared. He claimed to have ridden from England as soon as he'd heard about the murder of Rizzio and the attack upon his half-sister. With cool effrontery he proceeded to tell Mary how to repair the situation. The queen excelled herself in subtlety, listening to him attentively and appearing to agree with his advice to pardon the murderers.

Then she asked for a midwife to be sent for, saying that the baby was coming and already she was suffering the pangs of labour.

In the night she and Darnley came creeping along the corridor to me, and using the route that Rhanza had shown us when we'd gone in disguise into Edinburgh, we slipped out of Holyrood Palace.

There we met Mary's faithful page Anthony Standen, the captain of the guard and a few others. It was not a complete surprise to find that the person who was waiting for us on the other side of the wall with swift horses was Duncan Alexander.

'You are safe,' I said, my heart lifting at the sight of him.

'We have a way to go yet before we can say that,' he replied. His answer forestalled my rising emotions but as I looked into his eyes, I saw that he was struggling to hold his own feelings in check. His jaw was tight and his hands shook as he adjusted his horse's girth. He went to assist the queen mount pillion behind Captain Erskine, but before he did so, he put his hand upon my shoulder. 'I am glad to see you, Jenny.'

Then he offered me his arm to help me up to ride with him. And on our mad dash for freedom that night, I clung onto him, leaning my face against his back and crying wild tears of relief.

It was to Dunbar Castle we rode where James Hepburn, the Earl of Bothwell, greeted the queen by bowing to kiss her extended fingers, saying, 'Majesty, it is good to see you. They say you planned the escape, and I admire you for riding furiously through the night being seven months gone with child.'

'My Lord of Bothwell,' said Mary, 'they tell me that you and Huntly got away by climbing out of a rear window and leaping over the lion pit.'

'Pity the lion had I slipped and fallen in,' he replied.

Mary laughed and sat down to eat breakfast with him. Then, without resting, she dictated letters to summon her supporters. Before the week was up Bothwell had raised two thousand of his Borderers men. Lord Seton and Lord Fleming arrived and soon many more flocked to her standard.

Ten days after Rizzio's assassination Mary was ready. With her at our head we rode back into Edinburgh in front of an army of eight thousand men. Duncan Alexander went to confer with the governor of the castle while I went to the Palace of Holyrood with Mary – to find Lord James Stuart awaiting us there.

'The conspirators are gone into England,' he informed Mary.

'I know this.' She drew off her gloves and handed them

to her page. 'As I also know that England, most likely, is where this plot was hatched.'

This was a direct challenge, for Lord James had been sheltering just across the Border since Mary had defeated his insurrection. They faced each other. Mary, with renewed confidence in her own ability radiating from her, appeared so much taller than her half-brother. I wished and willed with all my strength that she would cast off this duplicitous man who ultimately worked to serve his own ends.

'Then you will also be aware that I did not arrive in Scotland until after the deed had taken place.'

'Are you telling me, James, that the death of Rizzio in no way pleases you?'

'I would lie if I said that,' he replied, 'for I felt he influenced you overmuch, and a monarch needs the advice of wise Scots-born councillors.'

'And you consider yourself such a man?' Mary's voice was heavy with sarcasm.

'Not just myself,' said Lord James, 'but all those you banished when we asked you to reconsider your marriage to Lord Darnley.'

'When you made your request for me to reconsider my wedding plans you were accompanied by armed men!' Mary laughed.

'A misunderstanding,' Lord James said smoothly. 'We may have acted hastily out of concern for you, but we had only your best interests at heart. Is it not true' – he cleared his throat – 'that your husband has indeed become an ... *encumbrance*?'

Mary was silent.

'your grace needs advisers.' Lord James's tone had altered

to silken persuasion. 'The lords who came to England with me have tried to advance the cause of you, and any child you may have, being recognized as heir to the English throne. Our cousin Elizabeth joins me in her concern for your welfare.'

No! I thought. *Please, no!* I looked around. Where was Duncan Alexander? He would quickly see through the false words of this charlatan. Gavin of Strathtay stood to the side. He was listening to Lord James and nodding. Inwardly I groaned. He also was being taken in.

'I have the Earl of Huntly, Lord Bothwell, William Maitland and some others to help me govern,' Mary said.

'Re-instate myself,' Lord James purred, 'and then add the Earl of Argyll to your council, and Scotland will have a wise, prudent and merciful ruler.'

Mary paced the room. Then she inclined her head.

I felt as though the world had fallen away at my feet.

Chapter 36

'Was there nothing you could do?'

The day the names of the new governing council became public, Duncan Alexander sent me a message to meet him privately that night in the cloister walk of Holyrood Abbey.

'Do not chastise me,' I said. 'Lord James has the tongue of a flattering deceiver and there is no proof to link him to the murder of David Rizzio.'

Duncan nodded. 'It will never be clear who was part of the greater conspiracy against the queen.'

'Lord Darnley has begged Mary to believe his innocence,' I said, 'but I was there that night and saw how he behaved. He allowed Ruthven and the rest into his apartments below so that they could more easily enter her room by the private staircase.'

'Did she not pay any heed to the document recently presented to her? It carries her husband's signature agreeing to Rizzio's murder in exchange for his promise to pardon the exiled Protestant lords, including Lord James Stuart.'

'Darnley claims it to be a forgery,' I said. 'When she confronted him with it, he had a fit of temper and went off to sulk. After the baby is born Mary wants to find a means to separate from him.'

'The Lennox Stuarts are aware of Mary's feelings,' said

Duncan. 'I fear for her safety.' Then he added, 'And the safety of those around her.'

Did he mean me? In the darkness I could scarcely make out his face, far less his expression.

'Can you persuade her that she should move to Edinburgh Castle in time for her confinement?' he asked.

'I think so. I'll say it is for the child's sake.'

'Good girl,' said Duncan.

A little thrill of joy went through me. Years ago I'd been jealous of Marie Livingston when he had praised her with those words.

'What?' He'd noticed a change in my manner.

'Oh. I was just thinking of a time in France when we had to seek shelter in Amboise.'

'Let's hope for a different outcome,' Duncan said grimly, saluted and left.

Within weeks the queen's household was in the castle, and there, in the middle of June, Mary went into labour.

To begin with we took turns to walk with her around the cramped birthing chamber, and then, as Mary's labour continued, we sat or knelt beside her while Marie Seton plaited her hair and bathed her forehead with lavender water. I'd never attended a birth before. Fear and excitement swirled in my head. As the hours passed and Mary's distress increased the midwife brought jasper and eagle stone, both reputed to hasten childbirth.

'I put more faith in the relic of St Margaret,' gasped Mary, squirming in her anguish.

I glanced at the reliquary, which had been placed on the table beside the bed, and wondered what Duncan's opinion of that would be. More than once we'd argued over the belief of the saints' intervention in the happenings of this world. And I thought, I'd rather have him around to disagree with than not at all.

'Here is Marie Fleming returned with her sister, who is supposed to have the skills of a spey-wife,' I said to Mary. 'Let's hope she can fulfil her promise to make you more comfortable.'

During a respite between her contractions Mary asked me. 'Do you really think that my discomfort can be transferred to another person?'

I shrugged, unwilling either to tell an outright lie or to make Mary lose hope of her pain easing. Perhaps if she *thought* that Marie Fleming's sister could cause this to happen, then it would indeed give her some relief. Lady Reres, another lady-in-waiting, had already volunteered to bear the queen's labour for her. Marie Fleming and her sister muttered incantations, threw seed pods in the air and, after elaborate preparations, tied a string dipped in the urine of both women to the pinkie of each to form a 'nervous current', as they termed it, between them.

'Ah! Ah! Ah!' Mary clutched herself and shrieked.

'Ah! Ah! Ah!' Lady Reres did the same.

'This has the element of farce,' Countess Jean said in an aside to me.

'We appear to be doubling the pain, not lessening it,' I observed.

'Lady Reres is at least distracting me,' Mary panted, sweat streaming from her body.

All the women were red-faced, foreheads damp with perspiration, for even though it was summer, a fire burned in the grate. My own limbs ached, not because of any magic wrought by the Fleming sisters, but due to my empathy with my friend and boon companion.

After another hour of torment, the midwife announced that we should help the queen to her bed. Each taking an arm to support her, Jean and I assisted Mary into a squatting position, as directed by the midwife.

'This may be my first child, but by my faith it will be my last!' Mary cried out as the pangs increased in intensity. 'I will never lie with a man again.'

'In the throes of childbirth,' said Jean, 'all women say that.'

Mary bellowed and gripped the countess's hands with all her strength. 'I do mean it,' she said. 'Verily I do mean it.'

'Ah yes,' Jean replied wryly. 'We all say that too.' With difficulty she loosened Mary's fingers from her hands. 'Majesty,' she said, looking at the blood oozing from the places where Mary's nails had dug into her, 'I know not what is taking place under your shift, but judging by the marks on my hands, this baby is due to be born very soon.'

The whole length of the queen's body writhed in her efforts to expel the child. Jean and I held her secure as, with grunts and sighs, the women supporting her back bore down upon her shoulders as if they too were in labour. Mary shrieked, then let forth a shuddering groan of what might have been agony or possibly ecstasy. A great moan of utter relief followed as the future King of Scotland slithered out into the world.

'He has arrived!' the midwife shouted.

'Majesty,' Jean declared formally. 'You have a son.'

'A boy?' Mary cried out. 'You tell me it is a boy!'

'I tell ye it is a boy. And a good healthy one at that.' The midwife gave the child to his mother. 'With a fine caul about him.'

'Is it an ill omen?' Mary asked fearfully.

'Luck and long life,' the midwife said firmly. 'That's what a caul over a bairn's head means.'

'I'll name him James for my father.' Mary smiled as she lay upon her pillows and cradled her son in her arms. 'Jamie, my bonny boy,' she whispered. She touched the membrane that covered the child's head. 'He comes with good luck attached.'

'It is well that he does,' said Jean, 'for he'll need it to rule the kingdom he inherits.'

The birth of the prince was greeted with frenzied celebration and an outpouring of joy from the country. Hundreds of bonfires were lit and people danced in the streets. A small separate court was created for Prince James as favours and exquisite presents poured in from all over Europe to welcome him to the world.

Lord Darnley, however, was vexed at the prospect of his son receiving gifts and titles that would outrank his own, and he began to make vague threats against the crown. The queen, overcome with anxiety, moved the baby inland for more security, to Stirling Castle. In the autumn, although not fully recovered, Mary took up the reins of government once again. To enforce her royal presence she decided to make a royal tour of the lands south of Edinburgh, holding courts of justice and dealing with lawbreaking. We said farewell to baby James, who was thriving, and set off south. While in Jedburgh a messenger came to tell us that the Earl of Bothwell lay dying in his Border stronghold.

Escorted by an armed guard and a group of nobles, including Lord James Stuart, Sir Duncan Alexander and Sir Gavin of Strathtay, we made the five-hour journey across craggy terrain to Hermitage Castle.

'I will receive the rough edge of Jean's tongue when she hears of this,' I said to Mary. 'You are not yet fully recovered from the birth of your baby.'

But I could not dissuade her – even though she herself knew how poor her health was.

'Would you have me let the Earl of Bothwell die alone when he has done so much for me, Jenny?'

But far from being dangerously ill, we found Bothwell propped up in bed drinking red wine and playing dice.

'I heard that you were seriously indisposed,' Mary told him in some annoyance. 'That you were suffering from an affliction that made you unable to walk.'

'Indeed I am,' he replied. 'It was an affliction of a sword across my legs.' And, to the consternation of those present, he drew aside the bedsheet to reveal his naked limbs wrapped in bloodstained bandages.

'You shock me, sir,' the queen reprimanded him. 'Please cover yourself.'

Bothwell looked up at her and muttered indistinctly, 'I've a mind to shock you more.' But he pulled over his covers and lay back upon his pillows. 'I fear I have taken too much wine,' he said by way of apology, 'and am fatigued with battling to keep order here among the reivers.'

'Your attacker should be properly charged and brought before the queen's court for judgement,' Lord James Stuart said pompously. 'Where is the man who gave you these injuries?'

Bothwell laughed at him. 'In various places,' he replied. 'His head is impaled upon a pikestaff at the nearest cross-roads. His hands and feet I put in a sack and delivered to his wife.'

'James, you are incorrigible.' The queen waved for a chair to be brought and sat down by the bedside.

James.

Mary was unaware of the reaction she'd caused by her use of Bothwell's first name. Gavin made a sardonic moue, but I saw stunned disbelief on the face of Lord James Stuart. It was gone in an instant, but his manner altered. From then on he watched Mary and Bothwell with the heightened awareness of a cat on a mouse hunt.

We stayed barely an hour, for Duncan was impatient to be on the road to Jedburgh. On the return journey our pace flagged as the queen was weary. In the gloaming of the early evening she discovered she'd lost her timepiece. She reined in her horse.

'It was a gift,' she said. 'I would go back to look for it.'

But Duncan shook his head. 'Majesty, we must go on.'

Seeing the queen's distress, Gavin volunteered to turn round to search for it.

'No,' Duncan said sharply before Mary could reply.

I stared at him. He was fidgeting and peering into the fronds of mist settling over the bog land. We were now separated from the main party. Behind us, faintly, we heard the jingle of a bridle, and what might have been the snort of a horse.

'Ride on,' said Duncan. There was an urgency in his voice. 'Ride on at once.'

We reached Jedburgh very late. The queen, content now

in her mind that her most loyal Scots lord would live, was herself exhausted in body. She took some soup before retiring and soon we were both asleep.

I was awoken in the early hours by Mary coughing and crying out for help.

Chapter 37

At first I thought she had caught cold, but after several days it was obvious that it was something more serious.

Lord James Stuart sent for his own physician, who recommended a diet of barley soup. But Mary's condition worsened, her breathing was laboured and her body racked with coughs. The coughing fits led to bouts of vomiting then to convulsions. Away from Holyrood we had fewer attendants with us and the accommodation was cramped but I hardly left her room. When I went to the kitchen to oversee the making of barley soup I enquired as to the whereabouts of Sir Duncan Alexander. He had ridden off somewhere, I was told. By the end of October, hardly able to lift her head from the pillow and thinking she had not long to live, Mary called for her half-brother.

Lord James appeared deeply moved at the sight of the queen so ravaged by illness, her face gaunt and her once lustrous hair spread out, dull and limp, on her pillow. 'My sister,' he said, 'I would not see you like this under any circumstances.'

'See me as I am, my brother,' said Mary, 'for if you wait any longer I fear you will not see me at all.'

I watched as he approached the bed but noted that he did not come close to her. His manner was strange. It was clear that Mary harboured no infection that he might catch, yet he held back from her. I thought that perhaps he felt guilty, knowing how badly he'd treated her in the past.

'I want you to promise that you will guard and defend my child,' Mary begged him. 'He is to be crowned king, for, though it grieves my heart to say this about the man I once dearly loved, his father must not rule Scotland. If you be in charge of my son, then raise him honestly until he is able to govern this country of ours.'

Lord James agreed to this readily, as well he might, for it indicated that he would have the power of regent for a dozen years or more while Prince James grew up. Then he spoke to his doctor before he left. 'Make sure that my sister doesn't suffer,' he said.

'I understand.' The doctor bowed his head.

On his way out Lord James almost bumped into another man entering the room.

'Ah!' I hurried over. It was Monsieur Arnault, Mary's French doctor, who'd been sent to Stirling at the beginning of the month to tend to one of those guarding the baby prince.

'Why are you here?' Lord James demanded.

The man was surprised. 'The queen is ill. I was sent for.'

'Who sent for you?'

'I, I . . .' Monsieur Arnault stammered. 'I assumed it was the queen herself.' He looked to me for support.

I had no idea what to say. The queen had fallen ill so suddenly and grievously that she'd been unable to summon her trusted French doctor. Had she done so, I would have known.

Lord James turned to me. 'It was you, wasn't it? You are always there, aren't you, Lady Ginette? Listening to everything and dripping words into the queen's ear.'

I was taken aback by his hostility, but before I could respond he spoke again to the French doctor. 'Be careful with any medicine you may give my sister. If the queen dies I will hold you responsible.'

'I will do all I can,' Monsieur Arnault replied with dignity, but Lord James had gone, taking his own physician with him.

A very brief examination let the doctor see that the queen was terribly ill. He went to warm himself by the fire and then suggested I might open a window. I shivered at this, for it was an old superstition that so doing allowed a dying person's soul to fly more quickly through the air and thus ease its transition from this world to the next. Sadness overwhelmed me. I was about to lose the friend of my childhood, the friend of my life, with no one to share my grief. A noise below made me look down. Duncan Alexander was leading two horses towards the farrier's yard. Anger rose in me like before when he'd disappeared in a time of crisis, reappearing afterwards.

Monsieur Arnault and I nursed the queen as her life force ebbed away. In the last week of October she lost the power of speech and lay almost lifeless in her bed.

I thought of happier times in France, of Mary's wedding celebrations, and a sudden image came to me of the prophet Nostradamus and his proclamations predicting the death of three persons of royal blood present in the room that night. King Henri, *the lion in a golden cage*, Dauphin Francis, *the rise of the poison*, and now Mary – all *royal and brave to meet their end*.

Yet, I mused, Nostradamus's third prediction had referred to *the fall of the axe* . . .

'I cannot explain it.' Monsieur Arnault shook his head. 'I

medicate her majesty and she appears to rally. Then she fails again, and each time she slips further out of this world.'

It was evening time, with frost riming the windows. He was sitting by the fire with his medical books and I sat opposite. There was a soft tap on the door and a servant entered bearing a tray with the little nourishment the queen took each day. So reduced was Mary that no solid food passed her lips, just this bowl of broth, prepared in an individual portion by her own cook and sent direct from the kitchen, covered, to keep it warm.

Except that it was not covered. My eyes rested on the pot lid, which was askew. I glanced up. The servant's eyes slid away from mine as she placed the tray upon the table by the door.

The soup pot was not covered.

I leaped to my feet and lifted the lid. 'What is this?' I asked. One or two leaves of green floated on the surface.

'I – I don't know,' the servant girl mumbled.

'A herb of some sort?' I asked quietly, even though my heart was racing.

The girl shrugged.

It was mint. Enough to obscure any other taste and cause no alarm if someone noticed an unfamiliar flavour in barley soup.

Mint to mask a Medici poison.

Mary's food was always prepared by her own cook, tasted in the kitchen and then covered – to be uncovered at her bedside. In the panic and the long hours of my vigil it had not always been possible for me to oversee this. How many times had I missed being there?

'Wait one moment,' I said to the girl, 'and take some of

these things away.' I pointed to the dirty goblets and napkins. As she bent to pick them up, I took from my sleeve the dagger than Duncan had given me and which, after Rizzio's death, I always carried with me. I came up behind the servant girl and placed it at her throat.

'I will plunge this into your neck if you do not answer me at once: has anyone tampered with this food?'

She began to tremble with fright. 'Telling the truth is your only hope,' I said. 'If you do not speak, then you die right now.'

By the fire the doctor was gazing at me, open-mouthed. 'Summon the queen's guard,' I told him, 'and quickly.'

He returned with Gavin of Strathtay and Duncan Alexander, and had obviously told them of my suspicions. The girl was now loudly protesting her innocence of any crime.

Duncan smiled at her pleasantly. 'There is a simple way for you to prove that you know nothing of this matter,' he said. He offered her the bowl of soup. 'Drink it,' he ordered.

She screamed and dashed the bowl from his hands.

Monsieur Arnault gave the queen an emetic which caused her to vomit black blood. Then he forced her to drink a tablespoon of warm wine and I helped him to wrap her cold limbs in strips of blanket. I lay beside her in the bed and held her close to me and whispered in her ear that I would be bereft without her and that I would not let her go. Her lips moved soundlessly and I thought she heard me, so I continued to say words of encouragement and persuasion: 'Your bonny son is pining for you, Mary. He needs you to arrange his Christening Banquet. Prince Jamie wants his mama to sing him a lullaby in French and Scots.'

I began to sing cradle songs as I'd done those years ago in France when she'd become demented upon hearing of the death of her mother.

'There is faint colour on her lips,' Monsieur Arnault whispered to me.

'Praise be!' I murmured in reply.

I got up from Mary's side so that we might reapply the blanket compresses.

'Listen,' he said.

There was silence from the bed, no sign of the rattling cough of the last weeks. I leaned over in alarm, then I heard the sound of quiet breathing. Mary was enjoying the most peaceful sleep she'd had for many weeks.

Chapter 38

In November Mary was fit enough to travel to Edinburgh, but her health was impaired. She was constantly weak and subject to frequent episodes of nervous exhaustion. And her mind was troubled.

Her husband, fearing more than ever that he would be set aside in favour of his son became wilder in his behaviour, publicly hinting that the child might not be his. He threatened to travel abroad to enlist the help of the Catholic monarchs in Europe, claiming that his wife had shamed her religion by conceding to Protestant demands and was no longer mentally fit to govern.

The latest rumour was that the Lennox Stuarts were plotting to be rid of the queen in a more decisive way. I was convinced that someone had already attempted to poison Mary in Jedburgh, but I had no proof. There'd been no opportunity to question the unfortunate servant girl. The next morning she was found dead inside the cellar where Duncan Alexander had locked her – no wound on her body, only a mottled rash upon her neck.

Mary arranged to confer with her lords, including Bothwell and William Maitland, at Craigmillar Castle on the outskirts of the city, to explore the possibility of an annulment or a divorce. Lord James Stuart was not present as his wife was unwell and he wished to remain by her side.

'The problem is that any action along those lines might render your child illegitimate.' Duncan spoke first at the meeting.

'Petition the pope,' Mary ordered. 'Find out what can be done, for I need to be rid of my husband before he does my child and myself permanent harm.'

'You are agreed then,' William Maitland said slowly, 'that in some way kingly power is removed from Lord Darnley?'

'I am,' Mary said.

'Better,' said Bothwell, 'that Lord Darnley be removed from kingly power.'

Mary's eyes flickered towards him and then away. 'Whatever method must be by consent of parliament.'

He gave a sly smile. 'Before or afterwards?'

Maitland tutted.

Mary glanced from one to the other. 'What is the advice of my brother, Lord James Stuart?'

'If he were here, we might ask him,' said Bothwell, 'but he contrives not to be.'

William Maitland kept his gaze fixed upon the queen's face. 'Lord James will look through his fingers at whatever solution is found for this problem.'

'Then I hope the problem can be solved to all our satisfactions,' Mary said wearily.

I came forward to help her rise but was forestalled by Bothwell, who took my place and Mary's arm.

'Lean upon me,' he said in a rough, kindly tone.

'I do.' Mary smiled at him. 'I do.'

'Be wary of James Hepburn, the Lord of Bothwell,' Jean

cautioned the queen, for she had noticed her strolling with him in the garden at Craigmillar.

'He is one of my most loyal lords,' Mary replied. There were pink spots on her cheeks. 'And I do like his way of dealing. He attends to matters directly, without subterfuge.'

'Bothwell attends directly to anyone in a skirt,' Jean responded tartly. 'They say he called upon the wife of the Border reiver whom he beheaded to offer his condolences.'

'I'll wager that was not all he offered her,' said Marie Fleming.

'Do not allow passion to govern your acts,' Jean went on. 'I well know how that can be the downfall of a woman.' Separated from her husband, the Earl of Argyll, she had dallied with several gentlemen of the court.

Mary's face was disapproving, but then she smiled as she replied, 'In future I will not be seduced by the handsome appearance of any noble lord. When I struggled in childbed, did I not cry out that I would never lie with a man again?'

'Yes,' said Jean, 'and didn't I tell you that is what all women say in childbirth?'

The other women laughed.

'We become swayed by their professions of love,' said Marie Fleming.

'Their flattery,' said Marie Seton.

'Their gifts,' I said, thinking of the flowers Duncan had once given me for my birthday.

'Their looks,' said Jean. She closed her eyes and gave a little moan. 'And lips,' she added.

We chuckled in merriment.

'From this day forth it is by his deeds that I will judge a man,' said Mary. 'Their actions to support me will be how I take their measure.'

Which brought our minds back to James Hepburn, Earl of Bothwell.

When Mary mentioned Bothwell's name again to me in private, I was more dismissive of him. We were at Stirling Castle preparing for the baptism of Prince Jamie, and she'd ordered special suits of clothing for three of her lords, Lord James Stuart, the Earl of Argyll and, of course, Bothwell.

'My Lord Bothwell has been a constant strength and support to me throughout my troubles,' she explained, 'and deserves such a reward.'

'It's more than that, isn't it?' I replied. 'You are attracted to him too.'

'In some ways I am,' she admitted, 'but this time I am thinking of what's best for Scotland. Many of my lords, including the Earl of Argyll, have rebelled against me at one time or another. James Hepburn, Earl of Bothwell, never has. His loyalty is absolute.' She looked at me and added, 'Trust is the foundation of a relationship.'

I fingered the rich cloth of the lords' christening outfits, with its fine embroidery worked with jewels. 'In time they will all want more than pretty suits,' I said sourly. 'Yes, they will help you by engineering Darnley into a position where he can do no harm, but then they will jostle each other to see who can fill the vacuum.'

'Why, Jenny, you are not normally so intemperate,' Mary chided me. 'I thought Gavin of Strathtay kept you amused with his wit, and where is Sir Duncan Alexander? When he

was last in our company I saw you give him dour looks, and
yet he still watches you.'

'Does he?' I said in surprise.

Mary nodded. 'Often. When he thinks no one else
notices, I see him gazing at you.'

Should this cause me pleasure or concern? He and I had
not spoken at length since Jedburgh and doubts were lingering in my mind. True, he had effectively discovered the
servant girl's part in what might have been a plot against
the queen, but it was he who had locked the girl in a cellar
where, within hours, she'd died.

For the christening of her son Mary wanted her ladies to
dress in red but I refused. Red was a colour I would not wear
again, and coming across the petticoat that Duncan had
given me in my clothes chest, I handed it to the queen. 'Since
your illness at Jedburgh you feel the cold more than I do,' I
said to her. 'I would like you to have this.'

The Protestant lords and the delegation from England stood
outside the Chapel as the baptismal rite and liturgy were
performed in the Catholic tradition. Lord Darnley did not
appear, but kept to his rooms, drinking wine and ranting
against his wife and her advisers, while his son was christened
Charles James, to be known as James, in memory of his
maternal grandfather, the previous king.

Balls and masques were followed by bonfires and a
spectacular fireworks display. Mary begged him, but Lord
Darnley would not attend the celebrations

'Jenny, by doing this he casts doubt on the legitimacy of
our son.' She was wringing her hands. 'His wickedness is
far-reaching. The ambassadors and foreign dignitaries who

are my guests will carry stories of this home with them.'

There was nothing I could say. Darnley's behaviour was foolhardy and cruel. Lord James Stuart took advantage of Mary's distressed state to push his own agenda, and pressed her on matters he'd been pursuing for the last six months. On the very evening of the christening I heard him say to her, 'At this joyous time perhaps your grace might consider looking kindly on the petition of those of your lords residing in England who wish to come home.'

Lord Ruthven was now dead of natural causes, and two of his accomplices had been executed for their part in imprisoning the queen and murdering her chaplain. Mary had agreed to think about a reconciliation with the Earl of Morton, Lord Lindsay and some of the others who'd plotted to kill Rizzio. Lord James Stuart had worked ceaselessly with William Maitland to persuade her that giving these men the queen's pardon was the best way to achieve unity among the nobles. After consideration Mary saw wisdom in this.

'If they are at home,' she told me, 'I can have them watched. Otherwise they'll stay in England, planning another rebellion. And as John Knox has gone there on extended leave from his ministry at St Giles, perhaps it is better that my truculent lords are away from his influence.'

Anything else was unworkable. She could not survive if she antagonized the whole of the Douglas clan – which meant excusing Morton and Lindsay.

However, before signing the pardon, Mary felt entitled to register her resentment. 'You are aware that you are asking me to forgive the men who murdered my loyal servant David Rizzio?'

Lord James was ready with a diplomatic answer. 'They

were certainly involved, it's true, but their motive was to protect your grace from one they saw as a schemer and a spy who might lead you to unwise deeds.'

When he heard of the pardons Lord Darnley entered the queen's rooms in agitation, and almost ran to catch at her sleeve. At first I thought he was set on having another row, but then I realized that he was trembling with fear, not rage.

'You have made it intolerable for me to live at court!' he cried. 'Perhaps to live at all. The lords who will return, Morton and the rest, bear me ill intent, for they believe I betrayed them.'

'You have always protested your innocence in the murder of Rizzio,' Mary retorted, 'so should have nothing to fear from these people.'

'I am going away to be with my family in the west,' Darnley told her, 'where I will be safer.'

'There is nowhere now that is truly safe for that man,' Gavin commented when I relayed this conversation to him.

We were walking in the castle gardens. Gavin had asked me to spend some time with him as he too had to leave Stirling having been called to Tayside to visit his ailing mother.

'When I am at court again, Jenny,' he took my hand in his, 'may I apply to the queen that we may be betrothed?'

I allowed him to lace his fingers with mine. Sir Gavin was courteous, handsome and of noble standing, and he often made me laugh with his comic observations about life at court. Now he moved towards me and his face was close to mine. 'Think on it,' he said softly, and brushed his lips against my cheek.

I closed my eyes as I felt a small frisson of pleasure. 'I

will,' I promised him. 'I will.' I owed it to him to make an honest reply. But how could I when I did not know the answer? The feelings I had for Gavin did not match, in either intensity or depth, those I bore for Duncan. I reflected on the state of my dearest friend, Mary, who'd been caught in the trap of love. Perhaps it was better to marry a man for companionship rather than passion.

I intended to tell no one of Gavin's proposal but, as was the way within the court, our interlude in the gardens of the castle was soon public knowledge. I refused to discuss it with the Maries or Jean, who hounded me to hear every romantic detail. It had the opposite effect on Duncan Alexander. No longer did he dally in a corridor to exchange views with me, and I became awkward when he was in our company. Mary did not press me, and spoke only to say that she would accede to whatever I wished. I had no idea what my answer would be when Gavin returned.

At about the same time Lord Darnley left to visit his parents, complaining that he was being shown respect by neither his wife nor the nobles.

'Today he is frightened,' Mary said wretchedly as she watched him go, 'but soon he will be plotting another scheme to seize the throne.'

So worried was I about Mary I had no time to think of my own life and loves. The failure of her marriage caused her the deepest heartache. Those closest to her, Marie Seton and Jean, agreed that she needed rest. We persuaded her to take time off and so brought baby James to Holyrood Palace, where Mary was able to enjoy being a mother and playing with her child. Her women vied with each other to carry him from his crib to her arms each morning. My pleasure was tinged with longing that I might be so fortunate as to hold and hug a baby of my own. But then I thought of who might father my child and my mind clouded with indecision.

I was carrying the baby in the palace gardens one day, crooning as I nursed him in my arms, when I sensed that I was not alone. I glanced up. Duncan Alexander was standing on the path watching me. He came to admire the child, whereupon Prince James opened his eyes and smiled.

'He likes you,' I said.

'I'm glad someone here does,' Duncan replied.

'I like you too, my Lord of Knoydart,' I said.

He offered his finger to the baby, who grasped it his chubby fist and took it to his mouth. 'See! He also trusts me.' Duncan lifted his head to look at me intently. 'Do you?' he asked.

I bridled under his scrutiny. 'Did you come here to question me?'

'No.' Duncan shook his head. 'Although at some point there are matters I'd like us to discuss.' He paused. 'I came here to inform the queen that her husband, Lord Darnley, has been taken ill. Quite seriously ill.'

Chapter 39

'I must go to him,' said Mary.

'Enter the den of the Lennox Stuarts and the Douglas family?' exclaimed Jean. 'You know how those parents dote on their son, and they would do you down for causing him upset.'

'Lord Darnley came to visit me when I was ill in Jedburgh,' said Mary.

'After you had recovered,' Jean pointed out.

'He is my husband and has sent me a note to say he thinks he is dying and wants to see me one last time.'

Jean held her head in her hands. 'A woman is at her most vulnerable when a man appeals to the caring side of her nature.'

'I agree,' I said. 'You have such a soft heart, Mary, that you do not see he might ensnare you.'

'I am not so naïve. I will be well guarded. Besides,' Mary said, 'what else can I do with this man? When he's apart from me he becomes a focus of rebellion. I'm told that if I divorce him, the Catholics in England will use him against Elizabeth and support his claim to the Scottish and English thrones because they consider me too indulgent to Protestantism. Yet the Protestants, with Knox's influence, think me a Catholic sympathizer and fed Lord Darnley's envy of Rizzio to make him strike against me. I intend to persuade my husband to rejoin my court, for it's best that I know where he is and who with. It's a lesson I learned from Catherine de' Medici: the more dangerous your enemy, the nearer to one's person you should have him.'

So we went with Mary and escorted Lord Darnley to Edinburgh. He lay on a litter with his face veiled as he wished no one to see the pockmarks on his skin. His doctors had diagnosed smallpox. He was devastated that his good looks might be lost, but grateful that Mary had travelled to be with him and touched that she'd brought him herbal infusions and a lavender pillow to soothe his sleep.

'It does remind me of the time we first met,' she told us. 'He was such a pretty lad, and so poorly that—'

'You mothered him, and then, when you couldn't give him all that he wanted as his real mother was in the habit of doing, he showed himself to be the petulant and spoiled child he truly is.'

Mary flushed at this rebuke from Jean.

'We have no wish to be harsh.' I spoke quickly to cover any offence in Jean's words. 'It's only that we don't want you lulled into a believing a false promise of good behaviour and have you hurt once again.'

For fear of contagion Prince James was sent back to Stirling Castle, but, to Mary's disappointment, Lord Darnley refused to enter Holyrood Palace.

'Do you blame him?' Duncan reasoned with her. 'Bothwell is here at the moment. Would you sleep sound under the same roof as James Hepburn if you'd tried to have him murdered?'

'It is because I am under the same roof as men like your-self and James Hepburn that I *do* sleep sound at night,' Mary said sincerely.

Involuntarily I nodded in agreement. Whereas Mary might be thinking more of Bothwell, I recognized that my own instinct focused on Duncan as our true protector.

A compromise was reached, and on the first of February Darnley was installed in a house at Kirk o' Field at the city wall. Hardly had he arrived when he demanded a change of bed and expensive redecoration of his rooms. He persuaded the queen to sleep in the room below his on a couple of nights as he said he was apprehensive at being in the house with only a few servants to protect him. In the week that followed she visited him every day, bringing courtiers with her to entertain him. Sometimes they played cards, and one night he reminded her of the time he'd paid her gambling debt to save her losing her tourmaline ring. Mary twisted the ring where it sat upon her finger. He smiled at her and she smiled in return.

Bothwell and Lord James Stuart, who were present, frowned at this exchange.

'You also wear the ring I gave you on our wedding day,' Darnley said to Mary.

'Yes,' she replied softly.

A tear oozed from his eye. 'My beloved wife,' he murmured.

'In the will I made before my confinement,' said Mary, 'I left instructions for that ring, my wedding ring, to be returned to you if I died in childbirth.'

'You did?' he asked. 'Even though you thought I had a hand in Rizzio's' – he hesitated – 'in what happened to Rizzio?'

'I had to prepare myself for the worst so I could hold no grudge. I might have died giving birth to your son.'

'My son,' Darnley repeated, as though the concept was strange to him.

'He is very like you,' Mary said swiftly, taking the opportunity to reassure him that the child was his, 'and grows more handsome by the day.' Not adding, as she had on one occasion, 'Let the poor babe not have his father's nature. I pray God to spare him that.'

Darnley stretched out his hand to her and said tentatively, 'Perhaps we might make more?'

Mary did not take her husband's hand, but neither did she move away from him.

He gave a smile of triumph. 'Then we could have a dozen sons who would become lords in their own right. We might make a privy council of our own and relieve some of these men' – he waved his hand at the nobles gathered in the room – 'of their titles and land.'

The queen's smile faded at her husband's crass words. Lord James Stuart quietly departed. Bothwell flung down his hand of cards and strode out.

On Saturday Duncan Alexander came to me in Holyrood Palace. 'I may have to leave suddenly,' he said, 'and I came to advise you to be vigilant. Since Darnley's return to Edinburgh the city vibrates with tension.'

'Is it not the excitement of the preparations for tomorrow's wedding of Bastien Pages?' This man was one of the queen's favourites; he organized entertainments for her, and courtiers were planning to attend the ceremony dressed in elaborate costumes.

'I believe it's more than that.'

I was keen to have him share his information, for I too was aware of a throbbing undercurrent of unrest but unable to find a specific reason. 'What else do you know?' I asked him.

Duncan shook his head in frustration. 'I haven't enough funds to pay for the spies to keep abreast of every plot and conspiracy being hatched around us. I'll keep listening and watching and I urge you to do the same.'

'All I have heard is that Darnley has said he is fit enough to be moved and now wishes to come here to Holyrood Palace to be by the queen . . .' I paused. 'That's good, isn't it?'

'Lord James Stuart will be very put out by that,' said Duncan. 'He doesn't want a reconciliation between the queen and her husband. Nor, I suspect, would Bothwell, now.'

'Not even for the peace of the realm?' I asked.

Duncan grimaced. 'Personal ambition outweighs any concerns Lord James might have for the peace of the realm. And what my Lord of Bothwell wants is—' He did not finish the sentence. 'My mind is spinning,' he went on. 'I cannot fathom what they might do.'

'Probably nothing at the moment,' I said, 'for Lord James's wife is taken ill. He begged leave to quit the court and Edinburgh and go to her tonight.'

'God's truth!' said Duncan. 'This is sinister. That wily fox has slipped away so that he may not be implicated in whatever happens.'

Bastien's wedding took place the next day, and in the evening the queen went to visit Darnley. They rolled dice and chatted, and eventually she said that as luck was not running her way she should go home, whereupon Darnley said, 'Wait here tonight again. I am so comforted when I know you sleep below me.' He opened his eyes wide to show he meant no suggestiveness in the remark.

Mary winked at me and said, 'Come, take my seat in this game, Sir Duncan.'

Duncan shook his head and went out of the room. I crossed to the door. He was pacing the corridor.

'We must get the queen away from here.' He put his finger to his lips as I started to ask why.

I went back just in time to hear the queen say, 'I'll play no more.' She stifled a yawn. 'I feel too tired to ride home to Holyrood tonight.

Bothwell spoke up, 'They expect you for the ceremony of the bedding of the bride.'

'I am sure the newlyweds will manage that very well without me,' she quipped.

Everyone laughed.

Bothwell said tersely, 'It would better that you went for—'

William Maitland interrupted him suavely, 'Is the bridegroom, Bastien Pages, not the man who organized the wonderful masque for the christening ceremony of Prince James?'

'Why yes,' said Mary, 'and I am in his debt, for he made that a most memorable occasion and impressed our foreign ambassadors.'

'And is there not another masque of his devising to be performed before the happy couple retire for the night?'

Mary stood up. 'That is true, and they may be waiting for me before they begin as I said I would attend.'

'Best not let the bridegroom become too impatient,' Bothwell added.

There was more laughter, but when Mary bade her husband farewell, Darnley was not laughing. 'Stay with me this night,' he begged.

'I cannot,' she told him. 'I have a duty to those who serve

me. Tomorrow you will come to Holyrood. We will be together then.'

To ease his pain at their parting and as a token of her goodwill, she drew off the tourmaline ring from her finger and gave it to him.

I awoke in the middle of the night.

My bedroom was thick with silence and shadows. Being the beginning of February it was very cold in Scotland, yet I left the warm nest of my covers to go to the window. The palace slumbered. Darkness enveloped the earth. Only the Duty Watch were visible, warming themselves by a brazier in the courtyard. I heard the muffled sound of hooves. A lone horseman was leading his horse quietly towards the exit gate. He exchanged words with the porter, who opened up and let him through. It was Duncan Alexander. He mounted his horse and rode off in the direction of Kirk o' Field.

What had prompted this midnight excursion? Had he received a message to say that Lord Darnley was unwell? I would have to wait until morning to find out.

In bed once more I lay in a restless, half-dreaming state. Sliding on the edge of oblivion, I woke as the massive bang of an explosion rocked the palace and the city. My bed curtains shook and I sprang up, clutching at the sheets. I thought they must have fired the cannon from the castle wall. Great God, we were under attack! Had the English sent an army to invade us? A fleet to blockade the port of Leith?

I scrambled from bed and, without slippers or dressing gown, ran to the queen's room. The corridors were filling with people, and a hubbub sounded from the streets outside:

cries of fear, and then the sound of the city alarm bells clanging.

Bothwell appeared, still dressed in his finery from the previous evening, but with a sword in his hand. He cleared everyone apart from myself from the queen's apartments, summoned the palace guard and sent messengers out, directing them to go and ensure that Lord Darnley was safe. In the mêlée I looked in vain for Duncan.

We opened a window, and now there was no mistaking where the noise had come from. The smell of gunpowder floated on the wind. Above Kirk o' Field flames lit the sky.

'My husband!' Mary exclaimed. 'I must go to him.'

'You must stay in the palace!' Captain Erskine was adamant.

In shock the queen did not respond.

'Majesty!' he said loudly. 'There may be an attack on your person. Lord Bothwell instructed me to remain close to you until he returned.'

Bothwell ran in, bringing his messenger, who was sweating with exertion.

'No point in the queen going there,' the man said. 'No point in any of us. I have just come from the house at Kirk o' Field. It is completely destroyed. Whoever was caught in that blast has not survived.'

It was then I thought of the man I'd seen ride towards there earlier. He would have been in the house at Kirk o' Field as the explosion occurred.

'Duncan?' I cried out. 'Where is Sir Duncan Alexander!'

Chapter 40

'I am here,' said a quiet voice.

Duncan had entered the room behind me.

'And where were you before?' Bothwell was staring hard at him.

'I might ask you the same question, sir,' he parried.

The two men faced each other, and I realized that whatever friendship had been between them before had ended this night.

'Among my courtiers there are few upon whom I can rely,' Mary spoke out. 'You are two such men. I beg you in this crisis, let there be no conflict between you. I charge you to investigate what has happened and report to me.'

When they'd left, Mary sat down upon her bed, shaking. 'Sir Duncan Alexander, James Hepburn the Earl of Bothwell, and William Maitland were the three men who encouraged me to return to the palace last night. If they had not done so I would be dead. And so might you.'

We held onto each other for comfort. If Mary had decided to sleep at Kirk o' Field, I would, most likely, have also stayed to keep her company.

'They must have had suspicions of a plot,' I reasoned.

'But not necessarily be part of it,' Mary added quickly.

* * *

In the morning we learned of the horrible events at Kirk o' Field.

Lord Darnley's dead body and that of his servant were found lying in the neighbouring garden, untouched by the explosion. Most likely they'd heard the murderers setting the powder fuse and had tried to escape, but were caught and killed. There were no marks upon their corpses. It was believed they'd been smothered.

It was Bothwell who brought the queen this news, and after making the announcement in the presence of her attendants, he asked to speak to her alone. Mary sat immobile in her chair. Despite the intimidating presence of Bothwell and the fact that the armed men at the door were in his pay, I refused to leave.

Mary raised her head. 'You may go, Jenny. I will grant the Earl of Bothwell a private audience.'

She spent more than an hour with him while he convinced her that he had no part in the murder of her husband.

'The Earl of Bothwell was loyal to my mother as he is to me,' she told me. 'He lives by his family motto and is faithful unto death.'

Mary would not be moved on this, becoming utterly convinced of Bothwell's innocence. And to show that she believed in him, and, to let others know this, in the days that followed she gave him gifts, sought his advice, and agreed that it should be his men who guarded her son.

'Can you not speak to the queen?' Duncan Alexander asked me more than once. 'By behaving like this she is on a path to disaster.'

'Mary listens to no one on this matter,' I said. 'Not Marie Seton, nor Jean, nor myself. She insists Bothwell is blameless.'

'We may never know the whole truth,' he said. 'Bothwell is guilty, I'm sure of it, but he is one of many. It is the talk of Edinburgh that his close friend, James Balfour, recently bought a quantity of gunpowder.'

'Bothwell has asked the queen to make James Balfour governor of Edinburgh Castle, while he will be given the Orkney Islands.'

'Then he digs a pit for himself. The lords who must have joined him in this conspiracy – Morton, Lindsay, James Stuart and the rest – will be consumed with rage. They did it in case the Lennox Stuarts managed to gain enough support to remove Mary and have Darnley rule as regent until his son came of age, or perhaps kill the child too and have Darnley proclaimed king. With him gone, they won't now tolerate a more deadly adversary. Bothwell is doomed, and by siding with him, so also is the queen. Already there are salacious posters appearing in the streets, accusing Mary, not only of being intimate with Bothwell, but of having conspired to kill her husband.'

Although Duncan had named Lord James Stuart as a co-conspirator, he wasn't in Edinburgh at the time of Darnley's murder, so no blame could be attached to him. In the midst of the rapidly increasing scandal he asked leave to go to London on family business.

Mary moaned as she read his letter. 'My brother is deserting me when I need strong men around me.'

I was deeply disturbed by this. Was he going to London to rally support against Mary? On previous occasions he'd accepted help from England for his own ends. Bothwell reassured the queen that she would fare better without her half-brother.

Surrounded by enemies, Mary refused to charge anyone with her husband's murder. It was left to Darnley's father, the Earl of Lennox, to demand justice, and he named the Earl of Bothwell as the man he wanted brought to trial.

'You cannot appear at a public trial, James,' Mary said to Bothwell when we heard he'd been summoned to the Tolbooth in Edinburgh at the beginning of April.

'Indeed I will,' was his reply. 'But I'll take some of my Borderers with me, and we'll see who dares appear to accuse me.'

With several thousand men billeted in Edinburgh and no one prepared to press charges of any sort, the Earl of Bothwell was acquitted by the court.

Four days later he carried the sceptre in the royal procession as the queen opened parliament.

After that Bothwell was in constant attendance on Mary.

I watched, helpless, as he wove around her a sticky web of charm and cajolement. Foreign dignitaries and councillors could not have an audience alone with her without incurring his resentment. He came to visit her when we went to stay at Lord Seton's family home, one of the few places where Mary felt safe among friends. Bothwell insisted on numerous private meetings with her.

'He proposes to her continually,' I confided to Jean and Marie Seton.

'What, exactly, does my Lord of Bothwell propose?' Jean asked sarcastically.

I blinked. 'Why, marriage,' I replied.

'With James Hepburn, one cannot always be sure,' she replied. 'He already has a wife.'

'He claims his wife has agreed to divorce him.'

'I hope the queen has refused him.'

'Yes, and she receives letters from France advising her not to marry him, but . . .'

'But what?' Jean asked in alarm.

'She feels they do not understand the situation here.'

'Who does? I, who have lived here my entire life, can scarce follow the tortuous path of Scots politics.'

'Her French relatives still hope to gain in some way if Mary makes a marriage of state. But she has been let down by them before. I suppose that is the great attraction of Bothwell. He has never disappointed her.'

'I have heard that said about him before in connection with women,' Jean quipped.

'Gracious!' Marie Seton shook her head at her.

'Sir Duncan Alexander is in Edinburgh,' I said, 'and has sent me note to say that Bothwell has coerced some of the lords and bishops into agreeing that it might be a good idea.'

'Some of those are people whose opinion carry great weight with the queen,' Marie Seton said in a worried tone. 'William Maitland, for instance.'

William Maitland, one of Mary's first advisers in Scotland, was now married to Marie Fleming, and the queen rated his wisdom highly. Therefore it was significant that he was among the group of courtiers who, shortly after this, went with Mary to Stirling to visit her son, now ten months old. We dallied there for a few days, playing with the prince, who was an alert and happy child. On our return, on the outskirts of Edinburgh, we were stopped on the road by the Earl of Bothwell and his men.

'There is unrest in the streets,' he told us, 'and my spies

have uncovered a plot to assassinate the queen. The rest of you ride on to Holyrood as normal. I will take the queen with some of her attendants to my castle at Dunbar for safety.'

I urged my horse on to draw abreast of Mary's. 'I am unhappy with this,' I said. 'Perhaps we should go on to Edinburgh, for Sir Duncan Alexander is there.'

Mary glanced around helplessly. 'I do not know what to do for the best . . .'

The nobles with her looked ill at ease. Her personal guard began to close about her. Bothwell's men put their hands to their swords.

Mary raised her hand to forestall any violence. 'I will go to Dunbar. If I cannot trust the Earl of Bothwell, whom can I trust?'

'Bothwell had an army with him,' I told Duncan later. 'We protested, but we could not stop him from doing what he wanted.'

And neither could I stop him from doing what he wanted when he took Mary to his own apartments in Dunbar Castle for the night and barred anyone else from entering.

On May the sixth Mary and I travelled separately to Edinburgh, where Mary made an announcement that she was convinced of Bothwell's devotion to herself and to Scotland and would acquiesce with those nobles who thought she should marry him. They were free to wed, as Bothwell's wife had just been granted a divorce.

When we were alone together the night before her wedding, I didn't need to ask Mary the question why. In deep distress, she told me, 'My courses were due. They are late.'

'You may be carrying his child?'

She nodded.

'There are many reasons for a woman's monthlies to be late,' I pointed out. 'Ill health, tension, a cold.'

Mary shook her head.

'But it *can* happen. Mine have been delayed on occasion, and I knew I couldn't be pregnant for I have never . . .' My voice faded away.

'I've had to loosen my clothes.'

'Bloating is quite a common ailment in women,' I babbled on. 'An upset or irregularity of the bowels can cause a swollen stomach.'

'Already I feel life inside me.'

I stopped talking. I'd heard women say this. Especially with a second baby when they have become more familiar with their body and can practically pinpoint the very moment of conception.

'They were due about ten days after he abducted me,' said Mary. 'I know that they will not come. What am I to do? There is no way to conceal it. A woman pregnant with no named father is an outcast. If I appeared in public, I might be stoned in the streets. The best I could look for is to be banished to France. I know he has an affection for me, but his heart and his ambition is bound to Scotland, so he . . . he might not come with me' – she smiled sadly – 'even if I were prepared to follow him to the ends of the earth in a white petticoat. I would lose my son, my kingdom, my country, and my friends. It would kill me, and the child within me. I have to marry him.'

'There must be some redress in law,' I protested. 'If he forced his will upon you . . .?'

'I cannot speak of it,' she said. 'I *will* not speak of it.'

And she never did. Not then, nor later.

And the world was left to wonder about the days Mary had spent in Dunbar Castle with James Hepburn, the Earl of Bothwell. And I wondered too why the lords who'd been forced to accompany us to Dunbar had not raised any objection when we were compelled to go there. And why Mary herself had not argued with her abductor.

No matter the whys and wherefores, I was witnessing Duncan Alexander's premonition of doom unfolding before me and was powerless to halt it. I found myself wishing that the pregnancy would fail or Bothwell might be killed in battle. What was I thinking? Wishing death upon another human being? Had I become like those people who eliminated anyone who stood in their way or proved inconvenient to their plans?

At Holyrood Duncan asked me, 'What's amiss?'

'Nothing,' I said dully. 'Nothing at all.'

He looked hurt that I would not share whatever was troubling me. But I knew that Mary's life depended upon silence.

I was sick in my spirit and he must have noticed and took pity on me, for, in a moderate tone he asked, 'Has the queen indeed gone quite mad, as rumour claims she has?'

'No,' I said, 'but I would not blame her if she had, so ill used and abused has she been.'

Duncan's eyes focused upon my face. 'I understand,' he said slowly. 'At least, I think I understand.'

There was a silence.

'By Bothwell?'

I nodded.

'The brigand! When he can have his choice of many women – and,' he added viciously, 'often does.'

'Even though he is seizing his chance for advancement, I do think perhaps he might love the queen.'

'Perhaps. Yes, perhaps you are right,' Duncan conceded. 'She is a striking woman, and very witty and compassionate.'

My heart jolted. And I wondered that I could feel jealousy when I was considering casting this man off for another.

'Mary has always been attracted by Bothwell's strength and held to him as her most unwavering supporter, and he has proved that at some cost to himself,' I said. 'Therein may love grow, and they may fare well together.'

'If they were a lord and lady with estates to govern, maybe,' said Duncan. 'But Mary is queen. The Lennox Stuarts and the Douglas family have become her implacable enemies. They see Bothwell, and include Mary, as the prime cause of the death of their idolized son, whom they thought would, one day, be sole ruler of Scotland. Already they prepare to swarm around them like hounds at a stag. The lords who bonded with Bothwell to kill Darnley now have him and Mary as useful scapegoats. They did not risk so much to get rid of Darnley only to see him replaced by another tyrant who will take their authority from them. All these factions will unite to tear them down.'

'I won't abandon her,' I said.

'Nor should you.' He smiled at me and said, 'I will try to guard you both.'

Then he did an unexpected thing. He leaned forward and kissed me on the forehead.

Without quite knowing what I was doing, I reacted by

wrapping my arms around his waist and holding onto him. I needed Duncan's strength and resoluteness. For a moment I believed absolutely that he would keep me safe, and I understood why Mary Stuart clung to Bothwell despite sound reason showing it to be an error.

Duncan stood completely still. I detached myself and stood back. Although close to tears, I was strangely unembarrassed by my actions. 'I am happy that we are friends again,' I said.

'Friends,' he repeated. 'Yes indeed, Jenny. I have always wanted to be a friend to you.'

Chapter 41

Mary Stuart, Queen of Scots, and James Hepburn, Earl of Bothwell, were married on the fifteenth of May 1567.

The service was conducted according to the Protestant rite, and within a day Mary was bitterly regretting her perceived betrayal of her own faith.

'I have ransomed my soul and my salvation!' she cried, and her body was racked with sobs. 'I have lost what was most dear to me. I should have died at Jedburgh when I was still worthy of redemption.'

I could find no words to help her. Mary's physical and mental energy was expended. Each day Marie Seton and I had to coax her to eat and dress. She didn't read her correspondence and wouldn't see ambassadors or attend council meetings. When Bothwell presented himself to do the latter a furious row broke out between him and William Maitland, which ended with Maitland resigning his post.

I took a different tone with Mary when I learned of this and bullied her into being more active. 'Whatever God rules in Heaven,' I told her, 'would not wish to see you like this. Think of your mother, who fought to keep your country for you. Your presence is required in matters of state.'

Mary rallied a little, but now Bothwell had tasted power and held sway over her, and all business was conducted with him there.

As Duncan had predicted, the disparate factions joined forces, and at the beginning of June, Morton, Lindsay and the others announced they intended to take Mary away from her husband, declare their marriage invalid, and reinstate her to rule alone until her son came of age.

Mary became hysterical when she heard the names of those against her: 'Some of these men put their names to the document agreeing to my marriage with James Hepburn! How can they now side with rebel lords who oppose it?'

'We can defeat this confederation of rebellious nobles,' Bothwell bragged confidently during a hastily convened council of war. He pointed to one of the Border lords, the Earl of Borthwick, who had come with an offer of support in the face of the rebel proclamation. 'As I am loyal to queen and crown, so are my friends loyal to me.'

'Apart from one who is most crucial.' Duncan Alexander had arrived late and unkempt to the meeting.

Bothwell glared at him. 'Who might that be?'

'He who governs Edinburgh Castle.'

'James Balfour is there by my favour and will not desert me.'

'Morton has offered to overlook any link Balfour might have to the death of Lord Darnley. As our cunning earl holds the receipt Balfour signed for the purchase of the gunpowder, your erstwhile friend has decided to throw in his lot in with the rebels.'

'I'll rip that base traitor's head from his shoulders!' Bothwell jumped up from the table to rush from the room.

Mary shrieked for Duncan to bar his path.

'James Balfour stocked and armed the garrison before revealing his change of heart,' Duncan said, forcing Bothwell back to his chair. 'He'll barricade himself in and withstand any siege we might mount.'

Bothwell sat down, grinding his teeth in fury and promising a thousand painful deaths for Balfour should he ever catch him.

'The queen cannot remain here,' Duncan spoke again. 'If it comes to war we cannot defend Holyrood Palace.'

'Your grace is welcome at my castle,' offered Lord Borthwick.

We packed hurriedly and left that night. Duncan saw us onto the road and then went to alert Lords Seton and Fleming and inform the Hamilton Stuarts that a battle was most likely.

With a detachment of troops, the Earl of Morton followed us to Borthwick and camped before the castle. We stood on the battlements as his representatives approached as if to parley, but instead they hurled such abuse and taunts that Bothwell had to be restrained from running downstairs to throw himself upon them. He fumed at his forced inaction but declared that he'd send a messenger to Huntly to bring reinforcements from the north. The next day the unfortunate messenger was paraded before us, bleeding about the head and face where his nose and ears had been hacked off. Mary swooned against me at the grotesque spectacle and I began again to think of Amboise.

'Give up the Earl of Bothwell!' Morton shouted up at her. 'Allow us to rescue you from his evil influence.'

Mary steadied herself and made to refuse him when a thought came to me: 'Say that you want to deliberate on his offer,' I told her.

'Never.' She was resolute. 'I'm no craven betrayer of those who protect me.'

'Pretend to agree. It will give us time.'

Even hot-headed Bothwell could see the sense in this. 'If they think you are considering their proposal, they'll be off-guard tonight,' he said to Mary.

'Then we can send another messenger,' she agreed.

'No,' said Bothwell. 'I must be the one who goes. Only I can raise the Border families, and it will easier for me to contact Huntly and the rest. And you, my love,' he stroked her hair, 'will be safer here with me gone.'

Despite her protests, Bothwell insisted on carrying out his plan. That evening they took their leave of each other while I stood at the window of the great hall, looking down at the cooking fires of the rebel camp. I was joined by Lord Borthwick, who'd found a man who knew a secret way through the valley forest. We turned at the sound of foot-steps. Bothwell was emerging from the turret staircase that led to Mary's room. I wished him good fortune for although I disliked him I would not have wanted Morton to get his hands on him. Then I went to Mary and we huddled together under a blanket in the window embrasure of her room.

'Do you love him?' I asked.

'He is going out to risk his life for me. How can I not love him?'

We held onto each other until dawn, when we heard the blast of a hunting horn from the distant hills. Then we knew that he'd won free, whereupon we both gave way to a fit of weeping.

When Morton and the others realized that Bothwell had eluded them, their anger intensified and they let us know that they intended to bring up heavy ordnance. Borthwick

Castle was a high, twin-towered building with solid walls more than six feet thick, but nothing can withstand unrelenting cannon fire. Lord Borthwick was too much of a gentleman to voice his concerns to the queen, yet we sensed that he was worried.

'I wish Sir Duncan Alexander were here to release us from this trap we are in,' I said to Mary.

Bothwell sent word to say that if Mary could try to leave the castle while our enemy was busy bringing up their cannon then someone would be there to lead us to safety.

'Being a woman, I have always been made to feel inferior, but I will show that I am as brave as any man,' Mary declared. 'Give me a sword and I will fight my way through!'

'My mind is more on how we went from Blois to Amboise,' I replied. I showed her the knife Duncan had given me that night, which I always kept about me. 'We might try our luck as lads again to make our escape.'

Duncan was in my thoughts as we dressed ourselves in tunic, hose and boots and pinned our tightly rolled hair under caps. I remembered how angrily he'd spoken to me, and I saw now that it might have been anxiety that had caused him to behave thus. I was shaking with nerves as Mary and I went over to one of the smaller windows of the great hall. Lord Borthwick had ordered the windows on the other side to be opened wide and his musicians to play merry tunes as loudly as possible.

'The sound of sound of singing and dancing should distract them from what is taking place elsewhere,' Mary whispered to me.

I looked at her. Her spirits were rising, as if the call to action had stirred her courage. The stable groom had made a rope harness for us to sit in, and amidst the racket of bag-pipes, viola and trumpet we were lowered from the window. Our guide took us to the postern gate and we flitted like shadows across the sward below. We passed so close to the enemy camp that we could hear them speaking. Their talk was of how easily the castle would fall once the cannon arrived and the walls were brought down.

In the forest Bothwell himself awaited us, and we went by a circuitous route to Dunbar Castle on the coast. We rode in to see Duncan Alexander standing in the courtyard, sending off envoys to muster men, money and arms. He broke off from his work for long enough to inspect us and comment, 'I'd not trust those two rough lads with a dagger, far less a sword or a musket.'

Mary laughed, and I did too. I knew that he'd done it to release the tension, for we were in a sorry state, but I didn't know whether to slap him or kiss him. There was no time for anything other than to eat, change into whatever women's clothing was available, then ride out from Dunbar to join up with the rest of Mary's supporters before we were cut off from them again.

On the fifteenth of June, when we'd assembled all the forces we could, we met with the opposing army south of Edinburgh at Carberry Hill. Morton united with Lindsay, Argyll and Kircaldy of Grange, a man of formidable military experience. Lord Fleming's men were away in the west, hold-ing Dumbarton Castle, and neither Huntly's troops nor the main body of the Hamilton Stuarts had arrived to help us.

We waited under the banner of the lion rampant while the hot June day passed with delegations going to and fro between both sides.

The rebel lords promised safe conduct and their renewed obedience if the queen abandoned the Earl of Bothwell and gave herself over to them. Mary stated that if they put down their arms and returned to their homes she would convene a special parliament to investigate the death of Lord Darnley and abide by its findings.

Hour upon hour the parley went on. At one point Mary had to dissuade Bothwell from responding to an insulting challenge for single combat made by Lord Lindsay. And all the time the unregulated Border men, frustrated by the lack of action, thirsty and hungry, drifted away in groups to forage and skirmish. Many did not return. By evening Mary saw her forces in disarray and was increasingly fearful that Bothwell would gallop forward to do something rash and vainglorious and be killed. So when Kirkcaldy of Grange, a man she held to be honourable, came and gave her his word that she would be well treated if she went with him, she believed him. But Mary, who prized loyalty above all other virtues, would not betray her husband. She refused to surrender the Earl of Bothwell. She commanded her husband to leave, and with tearful farewells and promises to be soon reunited, he departed and she prepared to meet with the rebel lords.

As soon as he was aware of Mary's intention, Duncan put his hand on the bridle of my horse and pulled it beside his own.

'Leave me be!' I cried.

'We can best help the queen by staying free,' he said, and ignoring my wishes, he tried to make off, taking me with him.

I struck out at him with my whip and, spurring my horse, rode after Mary.

She was already within the enemy camp, where the common men had begun to shout vile words at her. Her face registered shock. Kirkcaldy of Grange was outraged, and unsheathing his sword, he beat at their shoulders with the flat of the blade. We came to where the rebel lords were gathered, and Kirkcaldy of Grange shouted to them, 'Call your men to order. This was not the agreed terms of surrender!'

The Earl of Morton, standing with the odious Lindsay and the new Lord Ruthven, whose father had led the assassination of Rizzio, shook his head and laughed. 'The woman, Mary Stuart, is our prisoner now, and we will conduct her to the city jail.'

I felt sick to my stomach. I realized that they had tricked us and we could expect no mercy.

By the time we got to Edinburgh Mary's hair was unpinned, her clothes spattered with mud, and her face streaked with tears. At the city gate she was greeted with howls of derision from bands of vagrants organized by the rebels.

'Drown the witch!'

'Flog her!'

Mary stretched out her hand to me for aid, but as I reached for her I was struck on the arm. The soldiers closed in on her and we were separated. Rough hands seized my reins. My horse reared, and I was tumbling down to meet the hard cobblestones.

A cool cloth on my head. A blurred shape near me. I tried to sit up.

'Wheesht, wheesht. Ye maun rest.'

It was Rhanza.

Seeing a familiar friendly face, I began to cry.

'Dinna greet,' she said. 'Dinna greet.'

'The queen?' I said. 'Where is she?'

Rhanza's own eyes filled with tears as she told me they'd locked Mary in a room in the provost's house and no one was permitted to see her.

'What will they do to her?' I asked.

'Naebody kens,' Rhanza replied. 'But they'll nae let her gang free again.'

I went upstairs and met Marie Seton and Jean. They'd heard that the queen had demanded that parliament hold an official enquiry into the death of Lord Darnley; if Bothwell was found guilty, she would divorce and imprison him.

'Morton will not grant her that, nor any of the rest,' I said, 'for their own guilt would be revealed. Bothwell claims to have proof, a bond he can produce signed by them.'

We sat there throughout the night and all the next day, sending Rhanza out into Edinburgh at intervals to garner any news. Her trips were bringing us nothing, but then she returned at nine in the evening saying that the queen was coming to Holyrood!

We ran to the palace windows. A hostile group, armed with sticks and cudgels, was milling around the Canongate.

A great unease took hold of me. 'How will they get the queen here safely?'

And then, in the distance, the sound of a banging drum. The crowd yelled in anticipation. More people ran to join in. Some paused to rip up cobblestones from the street and hold them high above their heads.

'They'll tear her apart as soon as she appears, for the soldiers will not fire upon the townsfolk,' whispered Jean.

The drumbeat sounded louder. The mob began to stamp their feet and bay for blood.

'Blessed Mother in Heaven protect her,' Marie Seton prayed as we held onto each other in fright.

Suddenly a silence descended and, amid mutterings of discontent, an avenue cleared among the people.

'Look!' I cried. 'They have brought out the Blue Blanket!'

Spread below us was the huge Scottish Crafts banner of Edinburgh, gifted to the city by the crown nearly a hundred years ago for loyalty in defending the Scottish king. The rebel lords were using this, with its emblems of crown, thistle and saltire, as a canopy to hold over the queen. Under its traditional protection Mary was bravely trying to walk upright towards the royal palace.

It was the Earl of Morton, scion of the Douglas clan, and a man I considered even more callous and brutal than Lord James Stuart, who escorted Mary to the royal apartments.

The servants rushed to prepare food and fresh clothing, and we cried out in joy when we saw the queen. Marie Seton brushed her hair while Jean and I helped her change her clothes. Mary was weeping and trembling and laughing and crying – and, although she tried not to display it to her captors, very, very afraid.

'I saw William Maitland in the High Street,' she told us. 'I called to him but he looked the other way. He was always the steadying influence among my fractious advisers, and he agreed, as some of the others did, that I should marry Bothwell. I don't understand. Why has he turned against me?'

I signalled Marie Seton with a tiny shake of my head. At the moment everybody who was close to Mary feared for their lives. There were no armed men here to protect us if the Douglas family decided to kill us all this very night. But we dare not voice these fears to Mary. We had to keep her strong.

'Come and eat,' Marie Seton said gently.

We led her to the table. 'I must have some food,' she agreed. 'I've eaten nothing from fear of being poisoned and I'll need my strength to travel, for they've said they'll take me to be with Prince James tonight.'

But she had only swallowed a few spoonfuls when Morton suddenly announced that the queen must leave.

'I am going to visit my son?' Mary questioned him. 'You did give me to believe that you would allow me that.'

'Stand up!' he ordered.

We all got ready to go with her, but he pointed at me and said, 'You!'

And so we set off in the half-darkness of the Scottish midsummer. But we were not riding to Stirling to see the baby prince. The Earl of Morton had lied about that, as he had done about many other things. We were bound for Kinross, for Loch Leven Castle, and captivity.

Chapter 42

We arrived at the castle on the island late in the night, to be greeted by Sir William Douglas, with his wife and mother in close attendance. It was obvious they had been expecting us.

Mary clung to me. 'Morton and the rest never intended to keep their promise to reinstate me if I abandoned Bothwell,' she said.

'Liars and traitors,' I agreed. I held my head high and stared at the people who were to become our jailors. 'Liars and traitors,' I repeated, 'as are all the Douglas family.'

'No! We are not!'

The outburst had come from someone standing in the background. By the light of the torches I saw that the speaker was a young lad.

'Be quiet, Willie!' snapped Sir William Douglas.

I took this boy to be Sir William and Lady Douglas's son, but it transpired that Willie was an orphaned cousin who lived with them as a servant and boat keeper.

First we were searched by old Lady Douglas, who was both Sir William's mother and also the mother of Lord James Stuart, and therefore did us no favours. She took away my dagger, but failed to find the rings and jewelled hairclips that I'd hidden in the toes of my stockings in the hope that they might prove useful as bribes. Then we were hustled to a dank tower room and left there without food or water or a candle for the dark. We sat huddled together with our backs against the door until daybreak, too afraid to close our eyes lest an assassin creep in to murder us as we slept. In the early dawn, a scratching sounded outside. Cautiously I opened the door a crack. There stood the young lad who, the evening before, had shouted out that he was not a traitor.

'I brought you some bread.' He thrust a warm loaf into my hands. 'Do not tell anyone I gave it to you.'

'Who is it, Jenny?' the queen asked, her voice quavering in fear.

'The boy who spoke up last night, to deny he was a traitor,' I answered.

'The one called Willie?' the queen said. 'Willie Douglas?'

'She remembers my name!' The boy's face beamed in amazement and delight. 'The Queen of Scots knows who I am!'

Eating little food for fear of being poisoned, and debilitated by her ordeal, Mary miscarried her pregnancy within weeks of her imprisonment.

It was brutal and bloody. One night she woke, crying and holding her stomach. When I went to her, the bedsheets were soaked red. I'd no idea what to do, and in panic ran for old Lady Douglas, who came at once. Between us we birthed not one but two dead babies. Mary had been carrying twins.

'Boys.' With her thumb Lady Douglas made a small sign of the cross on each of their foreheads.

I raised my eyebrows at this but said nothing.

'Best not to look upon them,' she advised Mary. She sighed. 'That's what they told me when I lost my own.'

Mary nodded, and Lady Douglas put the two scraps of humanity in an empty pillowcase and took them away. Only then did Mary give vent to her feelings and weep uncontrollably. And I did too, holding her and rocking her in my arms.

Lady Douglas, returning with a basin of beef tea, gave us harsh comfort by saying, 'Better they are gone now with their eyes shut. Accept what has come to pass. As brood of Bothwell, they would have been taken from you and murdered within a twelvemonth.'

'There is truth in what Lady Douglas says,' I told Mary when the older woman departed. 'Take strength from her example. She's gone through your experience and remains a formidable woman.'

Mary curled in upon herself and I cuddled her until finally she fell asleep.

She never again spoke of that pain-filled night – except once, many weeks later, when she commented wryly, 'Allow Lord Bothwell that he would seed not one but two babes in me with single effort.'

Loss of blood and our living conditions caused Mary's health to decline. In empathy, old Lady Douglas, who'd also suffered child loss, provided better food and an increase in our supply of candles. She sometimes stopped by to chat, and was with us one day when the Earl of Morton and Lord Lindsay arrived to see the queen. Mary was very low in body and spirit and so I refused them entry to her bedchamber.

Morton stood back and nodded at Lindsay, who came forward, put his two hands around my throat, lifted me bodily from the doorway and flung me into the room. Mary scarcely had the strength to scream as I crashed to the floor.

'There is something here that requires the signature of Mary Stuart.' Morton produced a document as he approached the queen's bed.

'This is outrageous!' For once the severe Lady Douglas spoke in sympathy for Mary. 'You must leave and return later.'

'Hear me well, madam,' Morton snarled. 'If I leave with this unsigned, I will return later with an execution warrant for all within this castle. Though you be a Douglas, you will still be damned.'

Lady Douglas knocked over her stool as she fled.

'Bring the girl here,' Morton told Lindsay, 'to help her mistress sit up in her bed.'

I was still struggling to get my breath, but I staggered to my feet as Lindsay approached. I'd no wish to have his hands upon me again. The pair remained in the room and did not turn their backs in deference as I gently put my arms around Mary's shoulders and bolstered the pillows behind her back. For that lack of respect alone I hated them.

'I must know what you want me to sign,' Mary asked in a querulous voice.

'Your abdication in favour of your son.'

'I cannot give up my throne until I attend a meeting of my privy council.'

'You will, else Lindsay here will cut your throat.' Morton thrust a pen into Mary's hand.

'I need to think on this. I should consult with my privy councillors.'

Oh, how I loved my queen in that moment! Desperately ill and faced with two murderous ruffians, yet still she tried to resist.

Snatching a dirk from his belt, Lord Lindsay pushed Morton aside and placed the blade along the queen's neck. 'You are one second from death.'

Mary signed the papers. Then she slid down the bed and turned her face to the wall.

At the end of July Mary's son was crowned King James VI at Stirling, where John Knox, having returned from England, preached the sermon.

'It is almost amusing, is it not, Jenny,' Mary said when she heard this, 'that this self-acclaimed man of virtue absents himself while others do evil deeds on his behalf.'

We were in the gardens, where we were now allowed free access and sat for an hour on the summer afternoons. Since the signing of the abdication papers, when our jailors had been threatened with death, our conditions within Loch Leven Castle had improved.

'Lord James Stuart is also expected to return to Scotland soon,' I said. This piece of news was conveyed to me in a whisper by Willie Douglas.

'Ah, my brother, James,' Mary sighed, 'so desperate to be king and prevented by an accident of birth.'

Her mood was generally low, but she received some solace from an unexpected source in a letter that was smuggled to her.

'It's from Throckmorton, the former English ambassador to France!' she exclaimed.

Mary was not overly pleased with the advice her old

friend offered – which was to divorce Bothwell at once and save herself – but she was heartened to learn that Queen Elizabeth was horrified that the Scots lords should treat a reigning monarch in such a way.

'That's what Elizabeth says in public,' I commented. 'In private she may say something else.'

'You are jaded in your opinions,' Mary reprimanded me. 'I believe it is because you are missing the company of Sir Gavin – or could it be Sir Duncan Alexander?'

I *was* missing Gavin and his light-hearted manner, and also Duncan's company, erratic though it had always been. I was also concerned for Duncan's safety, but reckoned had he been captured after our surrender at Carberry I would have heard. But that wasn't the reason for my comment about Queen Elizabeth. I too was receiving smuggled notes, mainly from the loyal Marie Seton, who was collecting every piece of information on our behalf. Thus I knew that Lord James Stuart had taken possession of Mary's personal jewels, and even now both Elizabeth of England and Catherine de' Medici were vying with each other as to who could bid highest to possess Mary's famous black pearls. If something cheerful was communicated to me, then I shared it with Mary; the news of the fate of her beloved jewels I kept to myself.

Having the abdication papers signed and Prince James crowned, there was need of a regent to be appointed to rule until Mary's son came to his majority. In August our jailor, Lord Douglas, tapped on the door to announce a visitor.

'His grace, Lord James Stuart.'

With a sharp intake of breath Mary broke off our conversation. I stood up. This mode of address denoted a person of the highest rank. Mary's half-brother entered her presence as if he were indeed of equal standing to the queen.

Mary regarded him through narrowed eyes.

'You' – Lord James addressed me – 'may leave us.'

'The Lady Ginette will remain,' Mary said deliberately. As he began to protest, she went on, 'There are such wicked lies and ill rumour circulating that it would serve us both well if there were someone present to testify to our conversation.'

'So as not to shame you, we must discuss your conduct in private.' Lord James took me by the elbow and steered me to the door.

His effrontery was appalling but there was nothing I could do – except go swiftly to the adjoining chamber, open the window and lean out to listen as best I could.

For the rest of the afternoon and evening and most of the following day, he subjected Mary to a self-righteous sermon, listing each of her personal faults and all the errors of her life to demonstrate how unfit she was to rule. By the end of the second night he so reduced her, with threats against her own life and suggestions that without his protection her baby son would not survive, that she felt her sanity slipping from her.

By the time he left Loch Leven Mary was forced to accept that Lord James Stuart would become regent of Scotland, with the Earl of Morton as his deputy. It was a blow, for it seemed as if another lock had been put on our prison door.

One advantage to the situation was that the rebel lords, feeling more secure in their position, were prepared to grant Mary some privileges. We were moved to better rooms, clothes were sent from Holyrood, and we could have entertainments. It meant that we had more contact with the servants in the castle. These included young Willie Douglas.

Christmas came and Mary, who had asked for and received her needlework boxes from Holyrood Palace, made gifts for those who'd shown her kindness. I knew that Willie Douglas kept the square of cloth she'd embroidered for him inside his tunic next to his heart.

By the spring of the next year her health had improved and our spirits also. The beating wings and cackling of migrating birds on the loch brought back a memory of Duncan and our ferry ride to Wemyss Castle. Part of me hoped he was out of harm's way in his Knoydart home, yet I also hoped he was working to try to free us from our prison.

Mary had written letters to all those whom she thought might support her, but we had no way of knowing whether these had reached their destination – until one day we had the most welcome surprise. Marie Seton was allowed to join us in Loch Leven.

We hugged and kissed and cried tears of joy, and then asked for cake to celebrate. This was served and as we ate it, Marie brought us up to date on the happenings of the outside world. She prepared us by saying that her first piece of information was gloomy. The Earl of Bothwell was captured and imprisoned in Denmark, with small hope of release.

'I fear Bothwell is doomed.' Marie Seton had the good sense to know that, in circumstances like these, cold truth was best. 'Private papers and bribe monies are being sent from Scotland to Denmark to ensure that he never goes free.'

'Poor James,' Mary said and then fell silent. After a minute she roused herself. 'I will pray. It's all I can do for him now. Perhaps later, if I gain my freedom . . .'

I exchanged a worried look with Marie Seton. Mary's relationship with Bothwell was the most disastrous of her life. And yet, without him she'd surely be dead by now.

'Praying is indeed all we can do,' Marie Seton said firmly, trying to close the subject.

'God knows,' I murmured, 'he'll need it. And now,' I went on, 'you have other more cheering news for us?'

'Old Lady Douglas searched me and my clothes thoroughly and even had the heels knocked off my shoes.' Marie Seton gave us a conspiratorial smile. 'But she did not find the letters I brought you.'

'You have letters!' Mary exclaimed, clapping her hands in excitement.

'Majesty!' I put my finger to my lips and nodded towards the door.

'*Real* letters?' She lowered her voice.

My own heart was racing as I asked, 'Uncensored ones from true friends?'

In answer Marie Seton began to unwind her hair. 'Am I not the most skilled hairdresser in Europe that I can use crushed paper as padding for my coiffure?'

We fell upon her, laughing and giggling, and declared her to be the best hairdresser, not only of Europe, but of the New World and any other world yet to be discovered.

There were scribbled messages, notes of support and pledges of loyalty from, among others, Lord Fleming, the Hamilton Stuarts, Sir David of Cairncross, Lord Herries, and of course Lord Seton. And in addition, a letter of apology and recommitment to her cause from the Earl of Argyll, who had sided with the rebels at Carberry Hill. There was also one for me from Gavin, urging me to remain cheerful and to let him know if he could help in any way.

'Sir Duncan Alexander sends no word?' I asked Marie Seton in as neutral a tone as I could muster.

'Sir Duncan is planning your liberation,' she replied. 'He intends to smuggle you and the queen across the loch.'

'What about you?' Mary asked her.

'When the time comes, I am to dress myself as your grace and sit with my embroidery at the window, where I may be seen by all as you both secretly leave the island in servant guise.' She held up her hand as we began to protest. 'I have brought two travelling cloaks for this purpose. There is to be no argument on this, else it cannot take place.'

Despite our entreaties, Marie refused to change the plan, and again there was wisdom in her words. She had the skill to arrange her headdress so that from a distance she looked like our queen. I was the better horsewoman to accompany the queen in her flight, and had no link to Scots nobility, as a Seton had, to protect me from the Douglas wrath if I remained behind.

The prospect of escape changed everything. Once again Mary's hair was shining auburn and she no longer stooped over in sickness and despair. She walked proudly about the castle and grounds. On festive occasions and holy days we put on our most elaborate clothes, and as we sat down to eat, we pretended that we were at Holyrood Palace or Stirling Castle or one of the royal châteaux in France. Then one of us would strum a lute or mandolin while the others danced with imaginary ambassadors and kings. As the weather improved, we went outside to enjoy some playacting:

'Your grace, the King of Spain requests that you might accompany him in a galliard,' Mary said to me in her role of one of my ladies-in-waiting.

'Pray convey my deepest regrets to the King of Spain,' I replied haughtily, 'but I am already engaged to dance the morelia with the Emperor.'

On this day we were alone, because the wife of our jailor was in confinement, with her mother-in-law, old Lady Douglas, attending her. As Willie Douglas came through the gardens from the jetty on the loch, the queen intercepted him, saying, 'Master Willie Douglas, I do believe the Queen of Scots wishes to offer you a knighthood for your loyal services.'

The lad's face went white and then red. 'Majesty,' he stuttered, and then halted, probably remembering that he was not supposed to address Mary in this way.

Mary laughed gaily and indicated me. 'It is Jenny who wears my crown today.' Then, heaving a great sigh, she brushed a tear from her eye and said, 'I fear I will never be Queen of Scots again. However,' she removed one of her pearl-drop earrings and gave it to him, 'I'd like you to accept this as a token of my intent.'

The lad fell on his knees before her.

'Rise quickly,' I told him, 'lest you are seen by the guards.'

He went off in a daze.

It was by such gestures that Mary engendered loyalty. I was sure that there was nothing calculated in these actions: the gift of the silver ring to Rhanza, the pearl earring to Willie. They were born of her generosity of spirit.

At the end of April Willie Douglas brought me a loaf of bread. 'I thank you, Willie,' I said, 'but the queen and I have already eaten.'

'You may want to eat some more,' he replied, holding the bread out for me to take.

PART TWO: MARY, QUEEN OF SCOTS

I crumbled it in my fingers, thinking I might as well feed the birds as let it go hard. There was crackle of paper. A note, handwritten:

Be ready. Await the signal

Chapter 43

'It may be a trap.' The constant betrayals we'd suffered had made me suspicious. 'I do not recognize the writing.'

Marie Seton examined it. 'It is from my brother!'

Mary was ecstatic. 'Our loyal friends must have a plan, else they would not send that message.' She was rummaging in our clothes chest and pulled to the top the red petticoat I'd given her in Stirling. 'I'll wear this,' she said. 'Now we must find other garb that no one will remark upon.'

A few days later we had a Maying feast where the Douglas family joined us at noon to eat at tables set out upon the grass. May was held to be Mary's month, and so the queen was happy to take part in the singing and dancing. This helped distract us from our nervousness and our jailors from their vigilance. After the meal I walked with Mary and old Lady Douglas by the water's edge. Lady Douglas enquired after Mary's health and Mary replied, thanking her for her kindness when she'd miscarried.

'I could not but help you. As you lay there, your features reminded me so much of—' Lady Douglas stopped.

Mary stopped as she caught the sense what the older woman was saying. 'You mean my father?' she said. 'You have a memory of my father by whom you bore my half-brother, Lord James?'

'I have no wish to bring you grief,' the older woman said sincerely.

'You do not offend me,' Mary replied. 'As my mother forgave my father his transgressions, so do I. Please do tell me more. I am eager to know anything about him.'

'He was kind and handsome,' said Lady Douglas. 'You are like him in many ways.'

I gazed out across the loch as they walked on, and suddenly, to my consternation, I saw a party of horsemen on the other shore. There were no visitors expected at the castle. It might be our rescue party!

I glanced around. We were approaching the far side of the small island. The riders must have taken their route to avoid being spied from the castle battlements, and we had inadvertently led Lady Douglas in this direction! I looked ahead. Mary and Lady Douglas were beginning to ascend to a viewpoint. If Lady Douglas spotted the horsemen, our rescue would be discovered. I ran to catch up with them, breaking rudely into their conversation.

'My Lady Douglas, I hear you speak well of our former king. It is a pity that we cannot speak so well of the son you bore him, for Lord James Stuart has caused my mistress a great deal of upset.'

'Jenny!' Mary was aghast. She turned to Lady Douglas. 'Please excuse the Lady Ginette. I—' She did not finish her sentence, for Lady Douglas had turned abruptly and was marching back to the castle.

'Jenny?' Mary stared at me.

I took her by the arm and hurried her after Lady Douglas, explaining as I did so the reason for my outburst. From then on we were in apprehension, wondering when and how a rescue attempt might take place.

Lord Douglas attended Mary for an evening drink before going to sup in his own apartments. He wandered over to where I was standing by the window and, looking down, remarked, 'I must find proper employment for the orphan boy, Willie. It isn't right that he whiles away his time messing about in the boats.'

I glanced down. Willie Douglas was tying up the boats with heavy chains. My breath choked in my lungs and my throat constricted. It might mean nothing at all, but in tandem with the riders I'd seen earlier, Willie's actions might have great significance. I took a deep breath and flicked a glance to Mary.

'If you would assist me, my Lord Douglas,' Mary held out her arm, 'I think I might retire and leave you to attend to your wife and mother.'

As he went to escort Mary from the room, I risked another glance from the window. The boats were all securely fastened.

All bar one.

In a state of suppressed excitement, we waited in the queen's bedchamber. We decided to get ready in case this really was the night. Hands shaking, we dressed Marie Seton in the queen's clothes, and Mary and I put on homespun aprons and shabby cloaks. We waited by the window, but nothing stirred in the yard below. After an hour we saw Willie Douglas carrying a tray of food covered in a large napkin towards Lord Douglas's rooms in the opposite tower.

'I thought Willie would be part of it.' Mary's voice was

trembling. 'If he is serving Lord Douglas supper, then we have wasted our time in preparation.'

'Perhaps not,' I said. 'He might slip away as his master eats. I think you should lie down and let Marie Seton and myself keep watch.'

I went to the bed and opened the bedcurtains.

There on Mary's pillow lay a pearl earring.

'It is the signal!' I said.

Mary picked it up. She clasped it to her breast. 'Can it be? Will it really happen?'

We waited in silence. None of us wanted to talk of what might happen should we fail to escape. Willie Douglas would be executed, I thought. Perhaps they would kill Mary and me too – tell everyone that we'd drowned in the loch while trying to flee the island. There would be an outcry, but what could anyone do? Elizabeth of England would express her deepest regret. Catherine de' Medici would feign grief for the loss of her former daughter-in-law. Both would want Mary's black pearls to adorn their mourning dress.

It was not until later that we found out how it was done. When clearing the supper table, Willie Douglas dropped a napkin over the castle keys where Sir William had laid them down. Then he had gathered them up with the dirty dishes and walked out of the room.

Marie Seton beckoned us to the window when she saw him coming into the courtyard. He stopped and looked up.

'Go!' Marie lifted her embroidery and took her place in the window seat, forbidding us to come near her for a farewell hug.

Drawing the cloaks about us, Mary and I tiptoed downstairs and joined Willie, who was now unlocking the castle gates. Once outside, we pressed ourselves against the curtain wall while he relocked them. For several seconds he stood there thinking what to do, and then threw the keys into the mouth of a nearby cannon. My heart was crashing in my chest. I expected a shout or gunfire above our heads. We went to where the boats were tied up. Just as Willie was helping Mary climb into the unchained one, I glanced to the side and noticed some washerwomen by the rocks. We stared at them, as they did us. One of them raised her hand. My stomach cramped in a spasm of terror.

'God speed your grace,' the woman whispered across the water.

Then we were in the boat, Mary lying on the floor, with me crouched beside her. Willie took the oars and, with a grinding and a creaking, we pulled away.

'If they should pursue us—' Mary began.

'I have chained the rest of the boats,' Willie said. 'They cannot follow us.'

Horses on the other side. As the boat came gliding in to shore, their champing and blowing seemed unnaturally and frighteningly loud. I raised my head. Figures moved in the dusk. One I'd have known anywhere, even in the gloaming of the spring night.

Chapter 44

They were cheering Mary on the road before we got to Lord Seton's castle at Niddry.

With the news racing ahead of us, even though it was past midnight as we drew near Winchburgh, folks had come out with lanterns and torches to call to their queen and wish her well. In high euphoria Mary greeted her friends and supporters, clasping their hands and insisting each one embrace Willie Douglas as the queen's saviour.

'Your name will be remembered in history for all time,' she promised, and praised him so that I thought he might burst with pride.

Within hours we were at Lord Hamilton's Palace in the west, with that branch of the Stuarts who were avowed enemies of the Lennox side of the family. There, Mary officially renounced her abdication. Nine earls and bishops and twice that amount of lords pledged their support, including the Earl of Argyll, who had been with Morton at Carberry Hill. Men and money, arms and horses began to assemble under the queen's standard.

So quickly did our numbers grow that I was as hopeful as Mary that we could easily rout the rebels if they attacked us.

Duncan was of a different opinion. 'Hamilton is too difficult to defend,' he said. 'Lord Herries is still mustering his horse and we don't have enough cannon or war-weathered soldiers to engage the enemy army.'

'Sir Gavin has sent word to say that he is on his way from Strathtay,' I said, 'and Huntly will surely come too.'

'The clans are gathering for their Queen,' Mary said proudly.

'We cannot wait for them,' said Duncan. 'For as they come, so also will others to help the rebels. Lord James Stuart was not idle during the year of your captivity.' His face was drawn with strain and lack of sleep. 'Your half-brother used your precious jewels, the privy purse and his power as regent to disburse lands and titles to anyone he chose. He generously rewarded his cronies who brought you down at Carberry Hill, and has attracted many more sycophants who are now rushing to his aid.'

'There are some who do not consider it right to imprison and usurp an anointed queen.' Mary smiled at the Earl of Argyll. She'd made him commander of the main body of our foot soldiers as he'd expressed his disgust at Morton breaking his promise of the queen's safe conduct at Carberry Hill, and had now joined her cause.

I recalled what Bothwell had said about Argyll facing both ways on his horse. His estranged wife, Jean, had an honest, forthright character. There must be good reason why she would not live as a wife with this man.

In the face of Duncan's pessimism Mary offered to negotiate with the rebel lords. Lord James Stuart refused.

With Bothwell in captivity we'd no seasoned military leader, nor any hope of bringing his wild Borderers north to help us.

'We could go to parliament,' suggested Lord Hamilton.

'Would parliament listen to me?' asked Mary. 'Is there any hope that I'd even arrive there alive?'

Duncan shook his head. 'John Knox has been preaching vehemently against you, demanding your death. I could not vouch for your safety in the capital.'

'That is sufficient warning for me,' Mary said. 'If Sir Duncan Alexander cannot ensure my life, then no one can.'

It was at this point that I began to think that we might lose. Every instinct I had screamed agreement with Mary. *If Sir Duncan Alexander cannot ensure my life, then no one can.*

'What is the alternative?' she asked.

'We head for Dumbarton Castle and make that our base. Under Lord Fleming the garrison there has remained loyal to you throughout your imprisonment.'

'And if my half-brother's army intercepts us on the way?'

Our infantry commander, the Earl of Argyll, hesitated, and then said, 'I suppose we might face them in battle.'

'So be it,' said Mary. 'If battle comes, then let us try it!'

She was less confident that night as I lay beside her in her bed, unsleeping.

'I fear for the life of my son,' she whispered in the darkness.

'It's not in their interests to kill him,' I reassured her. 'They will hold him safe as ransom.'

'I also fear for our lives.'

I turned to face her. 'In truth, I too am very frightened,' I told her. 'But I would rather be free and face my enemy, no matter what the outcome.'

The sun was rising before Mary fell asleep. Outside, in the forecourt of the palace, I heard the sound of horses and men. I went to the window and slipped between the curtain and the glass. Below me, officers were organizing groups of archers and pikemen and giving instruction. Duncan Alexander was going up and down among them, consulting, and issuing notes of information. As I watched, he stopped for a moment and glanced up at my window.

My heart gave such a leap that I put my hand to my breast.

He raised his own and lifted his blue bonnet in a salute.

I placed my palm against the windowpane.

'May God protect you this day, Duncan Alexander,' I whispered. 'May God protect all of us.'

We marched towards Dumbarton.

It seemed an appropriate place to make our stand, for it was from that fortress on its rock that French ships had plucked Mary to safety when she was a child. There were men there who could sally forth to help us if we managed to draw Lord James Stuart so far west before his reinforcements arrived.

But our enemy had veteran commanders on his side who knew how to fight and, more importantly in this case, where to stage a confrontation.

It was the thirteenth of May when they met with us outside Glasgow, just beyond the village of Langside, where they'd secured a position from which to block our route. I found a vantage place with Mary while our commanders deployed the troops. As our advance parties with Lord Hamilton thrust forward through the narrow streets they came under withering fire from Lord James Stuart's hagbutters, who lay concealed behind hedgerows, walls and bushes.

I saw the puffs of powder smoke and heard the report of the guns, and the shouts and screams of the wounded and dying. The musket shots raked through our men. Trapped in the wynds and alleys between the houses, they were easy prey, and we could see them running and hunkering down to avoid being killed. I covered my face with my hands. Many of them were boys, some as young as thirteen or fourteen.

The pounding of horses' hooves caused me to raise my head. With flags flying and swords unsheathed Lord Herries' cavalry charged to their aid, trampling down the shrubbery and the hagbutters with it. A rousing cheer sounded out as they surged through. Now it was up to Argyll to move the main force into the breach. With Highland battle cries and swinging claymores, his front lines began to run down into the village in ragged formation.

'Stay by the queen,' Duncan said to me. 'At all times, do not leave her side.'

'Where are you going?' I asked him.

'To check on our illustrious infantry commander,' he retorted.

I saw him gallop up to the Earl of Argyll. As Jean's husband, Argyll was also kin to Lord James. But while Jean was true to Mary, in the past this man had switched sides depending on his own advantage. As I watched, the earl espied Duncan approaching him. Immediately he ceased talking to the officers with him and gazed out towards the enemy. Swivelling in his saddle, he glanced at the queen, standing beside me on the hill. Then he put both hands on his chest and fell forward on his horse.

'*Jesu!*' Mary cried out. 'What's amiss?'

The earl's lieutenants clustered around to help him from

his horse. Duncan appeared to be urging them to lead their men in the assault. He waved his hands and arms in the air, motioning towards the opposing side. I looked in that direction.

A full phalanx of Lord James Stuart's pikemen was advancing towards us. We heard a trumpet sound, and immediately they thrust out their fourteen-foot-long weapons in serried ranks to form a schiltron. Bristling spear tips glinted as they closed together, impregnable in their tightly locked formation. Upon seeing this, many of Argyll's men flung down their weapons and fled from the field.

'Help him!' I shouted, as Duncan and his horse were swept along in the mêlée. 'To Alexander! To Duncan Alexander!'

Mary had rushed to her own horse and was already mounted. I hastened to follow her, as did some of her braver lords – David of Cairncross being one. We galloped towards our men below. Just as we arrived there, so did Duncan, dishevelled, but still on his horse.

'For the queen and for Scotland!' he yelled. 'To me! To me!' He drew his sword and held it aloft. 'We fight for Mary, Queen of Scots!'

But these so-called soldiers were arguing amongst themselves. Some were related to the men of Argyll who had run away, and they too wanted to give up. Others berated and mocked them for their cowardice and stupidity in thinking to flee when it was clear that we had superior numbers.

Mary rode among them, exhorting them to fight. When they did not rally, she galloped to the front and prepared to lead a charge herself.

Duncan was beside her and tried to grab at her reins, but

she pulled her horse away, screaming, 'I will win, or I will die! Never, never, will I suffer the indignity and torture of prison again!'

I had managed to reach her side. 'Another day!' I shouted to her. 'Your victory will be another day!'

She struggled to escape us, but between us, using our own mounts, we turned hers back.

'Look!' said Duncan. 'Your army is disarray. If you go forward, you may be captured, not killed!'

Lord Herries came up to us. 'Let's to Dumfries and Terregles House,' he said. 'I can shelter you there.'

At last Mary conceded. And so we left, with the queen crying out, again and again, the same three words:

'I am lost! I am lost!'

Chapter 45

We whipped our horses and rode as though a thousand demons pursued us.

At the first river crossing Duncan leaped from his horse, burst into the nearest cottage, snatched an axe from the woodpile and ran back to chop at the supports of the bridge. He was yelling like a madman: 'Find hatchets! Saws! Anything you can lay your hands on to bring this bridge down. Already James Stuart will have a price on the queen's head and be sending out scouting parties.'

Some of the cavalrymen who'd fled with us dismounted, ran to surrounding barns and farmhouses and grabbed what they could to hack at the ropes and trestles.

'Take Lady Ginette and the queen and ride on!' Duncan shouted to Lord Herries and David of Cairncross.

'No!' I cried.

Sir David wrested the axe from Duncan's hand and pushed him towards his horse. 'You go with Lord Herries and the rest to escort the queen to safety,' he said. 'I and my men will finish this work and catch up with you on the road.'

Thereafter we travelled southwards like fugitives through mountains and thick forests to Terregles.

By day we hid. There were those who, at great risk to themselves, helped us – loyal men and women in the fortified houses and villages we passed. People who waited in the shadows under trees with fresh horses and baskets of provisions. During the daylight hours Mary slept a sleep of exhaustion. The men took turns on watch or to go and seek news and food. On the second evening after the battle at Langside I awoke to find our camp empty apart from Duncan Alexander. Beside me, Mary still slumbered. I stole away so as not to disturb her and went to where Duncan sat propped against a tree.

'Eat,' he said, offering me a piece of cheese.

I took it from him, saying, 'Why did the Earl of Argyll not give the order to attack?'

'I doubt he ever had any intention of giving the order,' Duncan said cynically. 'I suspect he has been playing a double game all the while.'

'You knew Mary's cause was lost before we joined battle?'

'Jenny, from first I met the Queen of Scots I knew her cause was hopeless.'

I gazed at him in surprise.

'Fate was unkind to her,' he explained. 'Born a woman when a male heir was wanted, with a destiny to rule a country riven by the greed of certain selfish lords, where clan loyalties override obedience to the crown. Despite her intelligence and considerable charm, the queen's own naivety and her early training in France didn't prepare her for the situations she was eventually forced to confront.'

'She did as well as she was able,' I said. 'But there are matters that arise in life where, if you compromise, then you lose your self-respect.' I was not just referring to Mary here, but to my own circumstances with regard to my relationship with Duncan: I'd decided that, no matter how much I desired him, I would not give myself to a man about whom I harboured doubts.

He nodded. 'Yes, pardoning rebels when harsh punishment might have been more appropriate, and remaining a Catholic when it would have served her better to become Protestant . . . These decisions were not politic, but I can admire her for trying to remain true to herself.'

'If you knew Mary's cause was doomed, then why have you supported her?'

'The estates I inherited were awarded to my family in exchange for a lifelong oath of fealty to the Scottish crown. Mary's mother sent me to France and charged me with guarding her daughter until she came to Scotland to claim her throne.'

'You discharged that duty,' I said, 'yet have remained by her side all this time.'

'I have,' he replied. He stared at me, an unreadable expression on his face.

'I know the reason,' I said.

'You do?'

'Like many others,' I said with a sigh, 'you are half in love with the Queen of Scots.'

'It wasn't for love of *her*, you ninny,' Duncan said in exasperation. 'It was for love of *you*, Jenny.'

'*Me?*'

'You,' he repeated. 'Jenny, I am in love with you.'

Scarcely breathing, I stared at him. Everything around me faded. I saw only his face. Nothing else existed in this moment of time.

Leaning across, he cupped my face in his hands. 'From

the beginning.' He rested his forehead on mine. 'Always and for ever. It was you, Jenny.'

A flare of happiness ignited within me. 'Wh-when . . .?' I stammered.

'When we first met, I thought you liked me. But then you scratched my face, so I was forced to admit I might have been wrong in that assessment.' He put his hand to his cheek. 'I think I still bear the mark.'

'I reacted that way because of something I witnessed,' I said quickly. My senses tumbled over each other as I spoke. *He loves me. Duncan actually does love me.*

'I realized that later. But at the time my pride was hurt and I thought you—' He broke off.

'A silly fickle girl, as many in that court were, with no thought in her head but to lead a man on and then play with his affections,' I finished for him.

'Quite.' He smiled. 'But then, as I watched you and your feeble attempts at spying to protect the queen, I saw that you must have integrity to act that way.'

'Feeble attempts!' I said indignantly.

'Oh, don't be offended. It is a compliment to say that you are not devious. And anyway' – he moved closer – 'we cannot afford the luxury of a quarrel now, however tempting the prospect of making up might be.'

'I was very adept at seeking out information,' I told him, 'and alert for any danger to the queen.'

'You were incredibly brave in trying to eat a piece of every pastry that you thought might have been poisoned. Although there might have been a more straightforward way to deal with that threat.' He laughed. 'By tipping the contents of the sideboard down the privy chute, perhaps?'

'I thought if I bit into them all, then I'd find out if there was a plot to kill her.'

'And did you not think that you put yourself in danger by tasting them?'

'I intended to spit out any where the flavour was unusual.'

'Or be sick?' he asked wryly.

I recalled the vomiting episode and my shame and embarrassment. 'I've heard that causing oneself to retch helps negate the effects of poison,' I said huffily.

'I wasn't sure if you were inordinately greedy or just crazy,' he replied.

'Also,' I added defensively, 'I didn't want the person I suspected to know that I was aware he was a poisoner.'

Duncan looked at me with interest. 'Who was that?'

'The Count of Cluny,' I said, and I told him of the conversation I'd overheard between Catherine de' Medici and the count and why I'd scratched his face.

Duncan sat up straighter. 'The Count of Cluny *was* here in Scotland. He came via England in the party accompanying Darnley when he first met Mary in Fife.'

'I know,' I said. 'I thought he might still be around, working secretly, for I'm sure it was his poison that was used in the attempt on Mary's life at Jedburgh.'

'No, Cluny is in France, and has been for some time,' Duncan said, 'but it may be that there is an agent here to whom he gave some of his poisons.'

Mary was stirring, and seeing this, he stood up. I spoke hurriedly: 'There is one person I know he spoke to, for I saw them myself.'

Duncan paused in the act of helping me to rise. 'Who?' he asked tersely.

'Rizzio. One night at Holyrood I followed him and watched them chatting secretly together.'

'You have played dangerous games, Jenny.' Duncan's face showed concern. 'Remember what happened to Rizzio.'

'I well remember,' I replied, cross at what I took to be his patronizing tone. 'I was there. Master David Rizzio did not deserve such a brutal end.'

'Indeed, no.' He held me for a second as he drew me to my feet. 'Let's hope the little Italian is playing his lute in Heaven.'

'We must find out who else the Count of Cluny spoke to privately,' I said.

And then a chill came over me. The only other person I absolutely knew that the Count had spoken to in private was Duncan Alexander himself. Gavin had told me he had seen them together in the garden at Wemyss Castle. Immediately after that Darnley had been taken unwell, and I'd seen Duncan wiping the dinner plates. He had also been at Jedburgh when there had been an attempt to poison the queen.

Mary was calling for me, and we prepared for another gruelling ride when darkness came. I busied myself with sorting her clothes and my own, but all the while thoughts churned in my head.

Duncan.

Duncan?

I'd suspected an attempt had been made to poison Darnley and Duncan had removed the evidence from the dinner dishes – Duncan, who had absented himself from Holyrood on the night of Rizzio's murder when he might have remained to defend us. It was Duncan I'd seen riding off in haste to Kirk o' Field just before the explosion occurred and then returning unharmed. Duncan in the tower with Catherine de' Medici. Duncan who had locked up the maid-servant at Jedburgh, who then died that night. At Carberry Hill he had urged me to leave Mary and ride away. It was Duncan who had been with the Earl of Argyll before he'd mysteriously collapsed, and who then gave instructions to his officers. Perhaps he'd overcome the earl by some noxious gas kept in a bottle about his person and then encouraged his soldiers to flee. And now, with clever words, he blamed the earl for the disastrous outcome.

As we saddled up, I leaned my head against the pommel for a moment. My bones and muscles ached with riding almost non-stop for two nights and my mind was awash with confusing thoughts. My elation was now being swept aside by suspicion.

Could it be that Duncan *had* been sent from Scotland to watch over Mary – but not by her mother? Perhaps he was in the employ of Lord James Stuart, to keep his half-sister under surveillance and undermine her in whatever way he could.

Chapter 46

At Terregles a council was held, where Mary decided she would go to England to seek help from Elizabeth.

Her announcement was met with protests and groans of disbelief.

Duncan spoke up, 'Majesty, you would be safer in France.'

'It's better that I'm nearer Scotland,' Mary replied, 'so that I can keep contact with my supporters.'

'Do not go to England then,' advised Lord Herries. 'Stay here and we can keep you hidden.'

'I agree,' said Sir David of Cairncross, who had arrived intact with his men barely an hour previously. 'In England Elizabeth is surrounded by ruthless advisers. Like her father and his father before him, she does not hesitate to eliminate potential enemies.'

'My loyal friends,' said Mary, 'I thank you, but I am a crowned queen. Elizabeth will respect the office even if she holds no love for me. I trust that she'll not refuse me succour. After my betrayal and capture at Carberry she expressed her outrage that nobles would do such a thing to an anointed queen. She has little sympathy with John Knox, who has been an instigator of many rebellious incidents against me. When I was imprisoned in Loch Leven, she sent Throckmorton, her best ambassador, who smuggled notes to me with words of encouragement and advice.'

Mary resisted the torrent of counter argument from her advisers. They listed examples of Elizabeth's duplicity: she'd sheltered the rebel Scots lords, colluded with Lord James Stuart; she was committed to Protestantism, and had consistently refused to name Mary or Mary's heirs as her own successors.

'Elizabeth is my cousin, almost a sister to me,' Mary declared. 'In past times we planned to meet, but circumstances prevented it. This is an opportunity that she cannot overlook, and when I see her and explain my predicament in person, I am sure she will help me with arms and wise advice.'

'Queen Elizabeth's greatest fear,' said Duncan Alexander, 'surely must be for Scotland to be used as a base by a European power, such as Spain or France, to attack England. Matters of religion and personal loyalties will come second to such an overriding concern. I would hazard Lord James Stuart has given her an undertaking that under his rule it will not happen. So for that reason, if for no other, Elizabeth will never support you.'

Despite these logical arguments, Mary still refused to change her mind.

'Try to persuade her otherwise,' Duncan said to me as I made to follow the queen from the council chamber.

In the privacy of her bedroom Mary broke down. 'My son,' she cried. 'My beloved son.'

And then I understood. She, who had been forced to separate from her adored mother and had suffered the lack all her life, could not bear the same happening to her own child.

'If I go to France, I doubt if Catherine de' Medici would

furnish me with soldiers to return to fight for my throne. And even if she did, then Morton and Lindsay and perhaps even Lord James Stuart would threaten to torture or kill my bonny prince.' Mary wiped away her tears. 'The only hope for his life, the only hope I have of ever seeing him again, is to appeal to the mercy of the English queen. Elizabeth has the guile I don't possess to achieve some kind of reconciliation.'

I helped Mary to bed and lay down beside her. Around three in the morning she fell into a deep sleep. Feeling weak through tiredness and thirst, I thought I might go and find something to drink. Duncan was sitting in a chair in the corridor outside the queen's room. As I came out, he stood up and looked into my face. I shook my head. A great weariness came over me and I felt myself at breaking point, but I resisted the temptation to fall into his arms. He went with me to the kitchens and I sat upon a stool while he found a couple of goblets, set one on front of me and opened a bottle of wine.

'We should talk,' he said. 'I have voiced my love for you, yet you hold back from speaking to me of what is in your heart.'

I looked up at him, tall and handsome, his eyes greygreen in the muted lamplight. My heart ached with love for him . . . Had witnessing the duplicity and falseness surrounding Mary over the years made me unable to trust?

'There are things we must discuss.' I looked directly at him. 'You are a spy.'

'Yes,' he admitted. 'I am a spy.'

'Who pays you?' I asked. 'To whom do you report?'

As Duncan hesitated to answer, someone spoke from the

kitchen doorway: 'Why do you not tell the Lady Ginette that you are in the pay of Catherine de' Medici?'

Duncan spun round, reaching for his sword as he did. Gavin of Strathtay walked slowly into the room, raising his hands high to show that he wasn't armed.

'What are you doing here?' Duncan demanded.

'Although detained on Tayside by my mother's illness, when I heard of the escape from Loch Leven, I came as fast as I could to be with Jenny,' said Gavin. 'I have a deep concern for her, and for the queen also, and have made it my business to keep a watchful eye upon them both.'

'*Are* you paid by Catherine de' Medici?' I could hardly ask Duncan the question for fear of his answer.

He extended his hands to me. 'Jenny, you must understand—'

'He has passed on to her things you told him in conversation,' said Gavin. 'What you thought was casual chat was him seeking information because you were close to Mary Stuart. When he arrived in France, an emissary of Catherine de' Medici offered to pay him to do this.'

I stared at Duncan. 'Is this true?'

'Jenny—' he began again.

'Is it true?' I cried out. 'Did Catherine de' Medici pay you for information that I gave you?'

Duncan spoke quickly. 'I had to do it. It meant that I was better placed to know her intentions and those of her chief poisoner, the Count of Cluny.'

'That's why you came into the pantry!' I exclaimed. 'You were there to ensure that the food was poisoned.'

'I was there to check that it wasn't!' he shouted in reply. 'I'd seen the Count of Cluny in the corridor and knew his reputation. Mary's mother sent me to France for the sole purpose of guarding Mary. I had a duty to watch over her personally, so to begin with I approached you as a way of being closer to the queen. And yes, I accepted bribes from Catherine de' Medici, but it was because I thought it would give me insight into her plans. But then something happened that changed everything. I fell in love with you.'

'This is quite nonsensical.' Gavin had come to the table. Lifting the bottle of wine, he poured some into each of the two goblets Duncan had set out. 'To declare affection for someone whom you admit shamelessly using to obtain information beggars belief.'

I looked from one to the other. Duncan was agitated while Gavin was quite calm.

From his tunic Duncan pulled a slip of paper. 'I have your note, Jenny.'

'What note?'

'The note you wrote to thank me for the flowers I gave you on your sixteenth birthday when we were at the French court. Would I keep that next my heart throughout these years if I did not care for you?'

I shook my head.

Gavin pointed at Duncan. 'He is a traitor and always has been.'

At this Duncan drew his sword. But Gavin had been waiting for that very move. As Duncan's sword cleared its scabbard, he had a kitchen stool in his hand and struck him full in the face with it. Duncan fell, cracking his head on the fireplace.

I leaped up and ran to where he lay sprawled on the hearth.

'Listen to me . . .' he whispered as I bent over him. 'Do not drink from the wine glass he offers you.'

Gavin came up behind me. 'What is he saying?'

'He says he loves me,' I sobbed, tears coursing down my face.

'Then let him say it no more!' Leaning down, Gavin dealt Duncan another blow upon the head to render him unconscious. He then stooped to pick up his sword.

As he did so, I turned and swiftly moved the wine goblets so that their positions were reversed. My hands were trembling, my thoughts racing. *Why had I done that?*

'You are shaking.' Gavin put his arm around my shoulders. 'Let me help you sit down.'

He settled me on my seat once more and laid Duncan's sword on the table next to his hand. 'Drink some wine,' he said, lifting the other goblet. 'It will help steady your nerves.'

I took hold of the wine goblet in front of me and brought it to my lips, then paused. There was a flicker in Gavin's eyes. Disappointment?

'We need a drink after the hard work of killing traitors,' he said.

'Yes,' I agreed, but with every fibre of my being I wanted to scream, *It is you who are the traitor that you would betray the queen and kill the noblest man in Scotland.* Seeing Duncan hurt and facing death, yet thinking only to gasp out a warning to save me, had convinced me of his honesty.

Gavin replaced his own glass upon the table. 'You are in shock?' he asked. He looked concerned, but there was an edge to his voice.

I nodded to give myself time to think. I had to stay clear-headed. I had no means of protecting myself. The dagger that

Duncan had given me at Amboise had been taken from me at Loch Leven. Gavin was nearest the kitchen door. If I made a dash to reach it then he would cut me down and both Duncan and I would die. And the queen too, most likely, for Gavin would immediately rush upstairs to do this, and if unable to escape, he'd concoct a suitable story to explain our deaths. If I alone drank the wine and nothing happened, then Gavin would know I'd swapped the goblets round. He must drink at the same time I did.

'I am in shock,' I agreed, 'but relieved as well. Let's drink – not just to the end of a traitor, but to our future too.' I raised my goblet in a toast.

Gavin merely touched his own.

'I thought you would join me,' I said lightly, and sipped some of the wine.

As he saw me swallow a mouthful, Gavin lifted his goblet and drank long and deeply. 'All of it, Jenny,' he encouraged me. 'It is for the best.'

I finished and turned my goblet upside down to show him that no drop remained.

Gavin laughed. 'Good obedient child.' He drained his and then said, 'Do you feel faint?'

'Yes,' I answered truthfully. A horrible suspicion came into my mind. Had he suspected that I knew he was the traitor and rearranged the glasses? Had he reset them so that I would take the one with the poison?

'Your face is pale,' Gavin continued. 'Are you perspiring?'

'I do feel giddy,' I said. And I did.

He wiped his brow. As he did so, the lamplight glinted on a gemstone he was wearing. I stared at his hand. On his finger was a tourmaline ring. The queen's ring.

'Ah . . .' Gavin followed my gaze and looked down at his hand.

'You took that from the body of Lord Darnley,' I whispered.

'Yes.' He spread his fingers and studied the ring. 'I'd barely time to get away after the explosion when your insufferable Duncan Alexander arrived to try to rescue the queen's husband. I don't know how he got wind of the plot – probably the boasting of his one-time friend Bothwell, who was always too loud-mouthed.'

Duncan had gone out that night to Kirk o' Field to try to rescue Darnley! That was why Bothwell was glaring at him in the queen's apartments, and why they'd fallen out afterwards.

'Were you ever on Tayside to visit your relatives?' I asked.

'Not for many months, but it was a convenient excuse for being absent from court when I had other tasks to perform.'

'But you held Holyrood Palace for the queen when Lord James first rebelled against her!'

'No.' Gavin shook his head. 'I was holding it for Lord James Stuart. When he saw that the populace was not with him, he decided that I could be of most use by remaining and pretending to be Mary's loyal supporter. And what better way to do that than to woo the Lady Ginette?' He looked at me and I read regret in his eyes. 'But I did have a strong liking for you, Jenny.'

'The night the queen first met Lord Darnley you told me that Duncan had been speaking to the Count of Cluny in the garden of Wemyss Castle, but it was really you, wasn't it?'

Gavin nodded. 'Cluny had been sent to bring me some of his poisons and to let me know that his mistress, the Medici woman, would weep no tears over Mary's death. He did mention your name as one who was extremely loyal to Mary but inquisitive and possibly dangerous. So I thought it wise to send you off on a false trail. And I was right to do so, for it was you who thwarted my attempt to poison Darnley. I know you had the queen appoint more food tasters. Although I am sure Sir Duncan also suspected something similar.'

Which was why Duncan was wiping the dinner plates – to examine the leftovers for traces of poison.

'And, of course, at Jedburgh . . .' Gavin wiped his face again, quite happy to talk while he waited for the poison to work on me. 'The kitchen maid was easily seduced. I'd delay her on the stairs and murmur flatteries in her ear while taking the opportunity to slip poison into the soup she carried. When she was caught, I passed her some food through the cellar window. She ate it without question, thinking I cared for her.'

'But why?' I asked. 'Who pays you to destroy the queen?'

'Those who desire to rule Scotland.' Gavin smirked. 'I am in the pay of more than one master who would like to achieve that end.'

My stomach heaved at the wickedness of this man to take innocent lives so easily. And a despair came over me, thinking how I'd laughed and joked with him, unaware of his evil intent. I stood up and swayed. 'I fear I will faint.'

'Yes, you will,' he said nastily, 'and very soon. I have given you an especially large dose of poison, for I have to reach the queen and despatch her before dawn.'

I put my fingers into my mouth.

Gavin shook his head. 'No retching will dislodge it. By now it will have already have entered the stomach destroying the gullet. And,' he coughed, 'within a minute or so—' He coughed again and looked surprised. Then he put his hand to his lips. When it came away, it had blood on it. 'What . . .?' he said. His hands scrabbled to where Duncan's sword lay.

I grabbed the table edge and, with a supreme effort, upended it. Gavin got to his feet as goblets, sword and wine bottle cascaded and crashed upon the floor.

'You tricked me!'

A terrible sound rent the air as he clutched at his chest, his face convulsing wildly. His eyes bulged from his head. 'Blood!' He spluttered violently, and red gore sprayed forth from his nose and mouth. 'Ah. I am dead by my own hand!' He staggered and fell down, his body in spasm, fingers clawing at his throat.

Screaming loud enough to wake the house, I stepped over Gavin and rushed to where Duncan lay. I knelt beside him and took his head into my lap. Covering his face with kisses, I repeated over and over again,

'I trusted you, my love. I trusted you, my love. My love, my love, my love.'

Chapter 47

Our last night in Scotland was spent at Dundrennan Abbey.

The next afternoon we went to find the boat that was to take Mary Stuart across the River Solway into England. Duncan and I begged to go with her but she refused, saying, 'Marie Seton and Rhanza will come to me. You must go to France, Jenny. Take the letters I have written to Catherine de' Medici and plead my case for me. And you' – she addressed herself to Duncan – 'will go with Jenny.'

'I swore an oath to protect the Queen of Scots,' he said stubbornly. 'I cannot abandon you.'

'I have my faithful Willie Douglas, who has vowed not to leave my side,' said Mary. 'And,' she went on, deliberately brutal, gazing at his battered face and head, 'wounded as you are, Sir Duncan, you are of no use to me.'

She gave me a token, a curl of her beautiful auburn hair. I put it in my father's silver locket, which I wore around my neck.

'I have nothing to give you in return,' I protested.

'I will have your red petticoat to keep.' Mary laughed. 'For although England may be warmer than Scotland, I'll warrant it's not as hot as France.'

A sudden stark fear overcame me. 'No, don't take that,' I said. 'I believe the colour red is unlucky.'

'I know you do,' she said sweetly. 'That's why I choose to

take the petticoat, for you'll never put it on.' She turned to Duncan. 'Do you mind so much if I own the underskirt you gifted to Jenny?'

'If it please your grace,' he said gallantly. 'It would be an honour for us if you accept it.'

'Let me have it, Jenny,' she cajoled me. 'If things do not go well for me, then I'll wear it and take comfort in thinking of you, my loyal friend.'

She graciously thanked those who had been true to her, and as the boat sailed, she stood erect in the prow, looking back as if loath to take her eyes away from Scotland.

Mary Stuart was regal then, that last time I saw her. And later, even though poor health and age had taken their toll, they said that she was regal at the end. That she walked to face her death with all the dignity and bearing of a crowned queen.

Chapter 48

As one of her ladies fetched the red petticoat from the clothes chest, Mary Stuart's composure faltered and she gave a small sob. 'I wish Jenny were here,' she said. 'If only Ginette, my sweet loyal Jenny, were here, it would be so much easier to bear.'

Gathering the petticoat in her hands, she crushed it against her breast. 'Red!' she cried. 'Red for the blood that has been spilled, and red for the blood that will soon flow from my severed head.'

Wearing a dress of figured black satin trimmed with jet, with beads at her belt and a crucifix in her hand, Mary was led to her execution.

She readily forgave her executioners, saying that her death would be an end to all her suffering, and exhorted those members of her household who were present not to lament for her, but instead, to relate to others that she died a true woman to her religion and a true woman of Scotland and France. Then she bade them farewell and, having been disrobed, stood there in her red petticoat. For a moment her hands were lost as her fingers gripped the folds of crimson cloth.

A lace handkerchief was placed over her face and fastened

behind her head. Whereupon she knelt down and laid her head upon the block.

'*In the end is my beginning.*'

Epilogue

I did not attend the service in Notre Dame Cathedral in Paris, where Catherine de' Medici made a false show of mourning the woman she refused to help – the woman who had been wife to her eldest son and a queen of France. Duncan and I remained on my father's lands in the south, where we live in happiness, as far away as possible from the intrigues, corruption and hypocrisy of the court. On the morning I received the dreadful news of Mary's execution we took our daughter to pray in the little chapel on our estate and to light a candle for the repose of the soul of the woman whom we had both loved.

Afterwards, when we came out into the sunshine and I saw the blossom beginning to show bud on the trees, I thought of the many occasions when, as a child, I'd played with Mary Stuart in the gardens of the royal châteaux.

I felt tears falling on my cheeks.

Our daughter looked anxiously at my face and then turned to Duncan and said, 'Why is Mama crying?'

He drew her close to him and said, 'Your mother grieves on the death of a close friend.'

'Who was she?'

'A great lady; generous of nature and good in spirit. She was both Queen of France and Queen of Scots.'

'What was her name?' our daughter asked him.

'Her name was Mary,' Duncan told her. 'In French we say it as "Marie".'

'Oh!' she exclaimed. 'Why, that is my name!'

I held out my arms to both of them. And my husband and daughter came to me and we embraced in a tight circle of love.

Postscript

After hiding in England for many years, Captain Montgomery of the Scots Guard, who had accidentally caused the death of King Henri, returned to France to lead a revolt against the crown. He was defeated and captured. In accordance with yet another Nostradamus prophecy, Catherine de' Medici sent six noblemen to bring him to Paris, where she finally had her revenge by having him executed.

Lord James Stuart lasted less than three years as regent of Scotland before being assassinated by one of the Hamilton Stuarts.

The Earl of Morton was also regent for a time, his rule being noted for its cruel atrocities. He was eventually convicted and executed for complicity in the murder of Lord Darnley.

When Mary, Queen of Scots agreed to go with the rebel lords at Carberry Hill, the Earl of Bothwell managed to escape from Scotland to try to raise support for her cause. However, he was seized, and imprisoned in Denmark. Here he was held in terrible conditions and, his health damaged, he died there eleven years later. While in captivity, both Mary and Bothwell wrote accounts of the major events of their lives.

Upon reaching his majority, Mary's son ruled as King

James VI of Scotland. When Elizabeth I died the reign of the Tudors in England ended and the crowns of Scotland and England were united. Thus Mary Stuart's son was crowned King James I of both countries.

In time, King James arranged for his mother, Mary, to be buried with full honours beneath a splendid monument in Westminster Abbey, where Mary, Queen of Scots, lies to this day.

Notes

Apart from researching Leonardo da Vinci for *The Medici Seal*, I have never encountered a more fascinating historical character than Mary, Queen of Scots.

Intelligent, extremely well-educated, sweet-natured, witty, talented, beautiful, and . . . elusive. It is unfortunate, to say the least, that she is often dismissed in history books as 'rash and foolish', receiving little credit for what she managed to do, despite living among venality and brutality. As soon as she gave birth to a healthy boy her life was forfeit – instead of battling to control her, those desperate for power in Scotland moved focus to seize the child in order to manipulate him, indoctrinate him against his mother, hold him in thrall and bend him to their will. Ill-served by her father, who contributed greatly to her problems by siring so many illegitimate offspring, she inherited a kingdom beset by financial, religious and legal strife. It is a tribute to Mary that she survived so long and engendered loyalty in so many who knew her.

More historical notes on this book at:
www.theresabreslin.com

Information on Mary, Queen of Scots at:
http://www.marie-stuart.co.uk

http://www.bbc.co.uk/scotland/education/int/hist/mary/
www.historic-scotland.gov.uk/mary-queen-of-scots.pdf

Acknowledgements

As always I am grateful for the huge amount of help I receive from:

  My family
  Annie, Lauren, Sue, Sophie, Clare, Lisa *et al* at Random
    House
  Laura Cecil
  Penni Killick
  Georgia Lawe
  Borders Council
  Borthwick Castle Hotel
  Blairs Museum
  Glasgow City Libraries
  Naomi Tarrant
  Visit Scotland, especially the Jedburgh Office
  Mary, Queen of Scots, House, Jedburgh
  The Marie Stuart Society
  Staff of Moray District Library
  Ian Leith
  Dunfermline Abbey guides
  Margot Aked
  The National Library of Scotland
  Hugh Rae
  SCRAN
  HISTORY GIRLS
  Bibliothèque Carnegie, Reims